Innocent

Innocent

Marie Corelli

MINT EDITIONS

Innocent was first published in 1914

This edition published by Mint Editions 2021.

ISBN 9781513281568 | E-ISBN 9781513286587

Published by Mint Editions®

 MINT
EDITIONS

minteditionbooks.com

Publishing Director: Jennifer Newens
Design & Production: Rachel Lopez Metzger
Project Manager: Micaela Clark
Typesetting: Westchester Publishing Services

CONTENTS

BOOK I

HER FANCY

I

The old by-road went rambling down into a dell of deep green shadow. It was a reprobate of a road,—a vagrant of the land,—having long ago wandered out of straight and even courses and taken to meandering aimlessly into many ruts and furrows under arching trees, which in wet weather poured their weight of dripping rain upon it and made it little more than a mud pool. Between straggling bushes of elder and hazel, blackberry and thorn, it made its solitary shambling way, so sunken into itself with long disuse that neither to the right nor to the left of it could anything be seen of the surrounding country. Hidden behind the intervening foliage on either hand were rich pastures and ploughed fields, but with these the old road had nothing in common. There were many things better suited to its nature, such as the melodious notes of the birds which made their homes year after year amid its bordering thickets, or the gathering together in springtime of thousands of primroses, whose pale, small, elfin faces peeped out from every mossy corner,—or the scent of secret violets in the grass, filling the air with the delicate sweetness of a breathing made warm by the April sun. Or when the thrill of summer drew the wild roses running quickly from the earth skyward, twining their stems together in fantastic arches and tufts of deep pink and flush-white blossom, and the briony wreaths with their small bright green stars swung pendent from over-shadowing boughs like garlands for a sylvan festival. Or the thousands of tiny unassuming herbs which grew up with the growing speargrass, bringing with them pungent odours from the soil as from some deep-laid storehouse of precious spices. These choice delights were the old by-road's peculiar possession, and through a wild maze of beauty and fragrance it strayed on with a careless awkwardness, getting more and more involved in tangles of green,—till at last, recoiling abruptly as it were upon its own steps, it stopped short at the entrance to a cleared space in front of a farmyard. With this the old by-road had evidently no sort of business whatever, and ended altogether, as it were, with a rough shock of surprise at finding itself in such open quarters. No arching trees or twining brambles were here,—it was a wide, clean brick-paved place chiefly possessed by a goodly company of promising fowls, and a huge cart-horse. The horse was tied to his manger in an open shed, and munched and munched with all the steadiness and goodwill of the sailor's wife who offended Macbeth's first witch. Beyond the farmyard was the farmhouse itself,—a long, low, timbered building with a broad tiled roof supported by huge oaken rafters and crowned with many gables,—a building proudly declaring itself as of the days of Elizabeth's yeomen, and bearing about it the honourable marks of age and long stress of weather. No such farmhouses are built nowadays, for life has become with us less than a temporary thing,—a coin to be spent rapidly as soon as gained, too valueless for any interest upon it to be sought or desired. In olden times it was apparently not considered such cheap currency. Men built their homes to last not only for their own lifetime, but for the lifetime of their children and their children's children; and the idea that their children's children might possibly fail to appreciate the strenuousness and worth of their labours never entered their simple brains.

The farmyard was terminated at its other end by a broad stone archway, which showed as in a semi-circular frame the glint of scarlet geraniums in the distance, and in the shadow cast by this embrasure was the small unobtrusive figure of a girl. She stood idly watching the hens pecking at their food and driving away their offspring from every chance of sharing bit or sup with them,—and as she noted the greedy triumph of the strong over the weak, the great over the small, her brows drew together in a slight frown of something like scorn. Yet hers was not a face that naturally expressed any of the unkind or harsh emotions. It was soft and delicately featured, and its rose-white tints were illumined by grave, deeply-set grey eyes that were full of wistful and questioning pathos. In stature she was below the middle height and slight of build, so that she seemed a mere child at first sight, with nothing particularly attractive about her except, perhaps, her hands. These were daintily shaped and characteristic of inbred refinement, and as they hung listlessly at her sides looked scarcely less white than the white cotton frock she wore. She turned presently with a movement of impatience away from the sight of the fussy and quarrelsome fowls, and looking up at the quaint gables of the farmhouse uttered a low, caressing call. A white dove flew down to her instantly, followed by another and yet another. She smiled and extended her arms, and a whole flock of the birds came fluttering about her in a whirl of wings, perching on her shoulders and alighting at her feet. One that seemed to enjoy a position of special favouritism, flew straight against her breast,—she caught it and held it there. It remained with her quite contentedly, while she stroked its velvety neck.

MARIE CORELLI

"Poor Cupid!" she murmured. "You love me, don't you? Oh yes, ever so much! Only you can't tell me so! I'm glad! You wouldn't be half so sweet if you could!"

She kissed the bird's soft head, and still stroking it scattered all the others around her by a slight gesture, and went, followed by a snowy cloud of them, through the archway into the garden beyond. Here there were flower-beds formally cut and arranged in the old-fashioned Dutch manner, full of sweet-smelling old-fashioned things, such as stocks and lupins, verbena and mignonette,—there were box-borders and clumps of saxifrage, fuchsias, and geraniums,—and roses that grew in every possible way that roses have ever grown, or can ever grow. The farmhouse fronted fully on this garden, and a magnificent "Glory" rose covered it from its deep black oaken porch to its highest gable, wreathing it with hundreds of pale golden balls of perfume. A real "old" rose it was, without any doubt of its own intrinsic worth and sweetness,—a rose before which the most highly trained hybrids might hang their heads for shame or wither away with envy, for the air around it was wholly perfumed with its honey-scented nectar, distilled from peaceful years upon years of sunbeams and stainless dew. The girl, still carrying her pet dove, walked slowly along the narrow gravelled paths that encircled the flower-beds and box-borders, till, reaching a low green door at the further end of the garden, she opened it and passed through into a newly mown field, where several lads and men were about busily employed in raking together the last swaths of a full crop of hay and adding them to the last waggon which stood in the centre of the ground, horseless, and piled to an almost toppling height. One young fellow, with a crimson silk tie knotted about his open shirt-collar, stood on top of the lofty fragrant load, fork in hand, tossing the additional heaps together as they were thrown up to him. The afternoon sun blazed burningly down on his uncovered head and bare brown arms, and as he shook and turned the hay with untiring energy, his movements were full of the easy grace and picturesqueness which are often the unconscious endowment of those whose labour keeps them daily in the fresh air. Occasional bursts of laughter and scraps of rough song came from the others at work, and there was only one absolutely quiet figure among them, that of an old man sitting on an upturned barrel which had been but recently emptied of its home-brewed beer, meditatively smoking a long clay pipe. He wore a smock frock and straw hat, and under the brim of the straw hat, which was well pulled down over his forehead, his filmy eyes gleamed with an alert watchfulness. He seemed to be counting every morsel of hay that was being added to the load and pricing it in his mind, but there was no actual expression of either pleasure or interest on his features. As the girl entered the field, and her gown made a gleam of white on the grass, he turned his head and looked at her, puffing hard at his pipe and watching her approach only a little less narrowly than he watched the piling up of the hay. When she drew sufficiently near him he spoke.

"Coming to ride home on last load?"

She hesitated.

"I don't know. I'm not sure," she answered.

"It'll please Robin if you do," he said.

A little smile trembled on her lips. She bent her head over the dove she held against her bosom.

"Why should I please Robin?" she asked.

His dull eyes sparkled with a gleam of anger.

"Please Robin, please ME," he said, sharply—"Please yourself, please nobody."

"I do my best to please YOU, Dad!" she said, gently, yet with emphasis.

He was silent, sucking at his pipe-stem. Just then a whistle struck the air like the near note of a thrush. It came from the man on top of the haywaggon. He had paused in his labour, and his face was turned towards the old man and the girl. It was a handsome face, lighted by a smile which seemed to have caught a reflex of the sun.

"All ready, Uncle!" he shouted—"Ready and waiting!"

The old man drew his pipe from his mouth.

"There you are!" he said, addressing the girl in a softer tone,—"He's wanting you."

She moved away at once. As she went, the men who were raking in the last sweepings of the hay stood aside for her to pass. One of them put a ladder against the wheel of the waggon.

"Going up, miss?" he asked, with a cheerful grin.

She smiled a response, but said nothing.

The young fellow on top of the load looked down. His blue eyes sparkled merrily as he saw her.

"Are you coming?" he called.

She glanced up.

"If you like," she answered.

"If I like!" he echoed, half-mockingly, half-tenderly; "You know I like! Why, you've got that wretched bird with you!"

"He's not a wretched bird," she said,—"He's a darling!"

"Well, you can't climb up here hugging him like that! Let him go,—and then I'll help you."

For all answer she ascended the ladder lightly without assistance, still holding the dove, and in another minute was seated beside him.

"There!" she said, as she settled herself comfortably down in the soft, sweet-smelling hay. "Now you've got your wish, and I hope Dad is happy."

"Did he tell you to come, or did you come of your own accord?" asked the young man, with a touch of curiosity.

"He told me, of course," she answered; "I should never have come of my own accord."

He bit his lip vexedly. Turning away from her he called to the haymakers:

"That'll do, boys! Fetch Roger, and haul in!"

The sun was nearing the western horizon and a deep apricot glow warmed the mown field and the undulating foliage in the far distance. The men began to scatter here and there, putting aside their long wooden rakes, and two of them went off to bring Roger, the cart-horse, from his shed.

"Uncle Hugo!"

The old man, who still sat impassively on the beer-barrel, looked up. "Ay! What is it?"

"Are you coming along with us?"

Uncle Hugo shook his head despondently.

"Why not? It's the last load this year!"

"Ay!" He lifted his straw hat and waved it in a kind of farewell salute towards the waggon, repeating mechanically: "The last load! The very last!"

Then there came a cessation of movement everywhere for the moment. It was a kind of breathing pause in Nature's everlasting chorus,—a sudden rest, as it seemed, in the very spaces of the air. The young man threw himself down on the hay-load so that he faced the girl, who sat quiet, caressing the dove she held. He was undeniably good-looking, with an open nobility of feature which is uncommon enough among well-born and carefully-nurtured specimens of the human race, and is perhaps still more rarely to be found among those whose lot in life is one of continuous hard manual labour. Just now he looked singularly attractive, the more so, perhaps, because he was unconscious of it. He stretched out one hand towards the girl and touched the hem of her white frock.

"Are you feeling kind?"

Her eyes lightened with a gleam of merriment.

"I am always kind."

"Not to me! Not as kind as you are to that bird."

"Oh, poor Cupid! You're jealous of him!"

He moved a little nearer to her.

"Perhaps I am!" And he spoke in a lower tone. "Perhaps I am, Innocent! I grudge him the privilege of lying there on your dear little white breast! I am envious when you kiss him! I want you to kiss ME!"

His voice was tremulous,—he turned up his face audaciously.

She looked at him with a smile.

"I will if you like!" she said. "I should think no more of kissing you than of kissing Cupid!"

He drew back with a gesture of annoyance.

"I wouldn't be kissed at all that way," he said, hotly.

"Why not?"

"Because it's not the right way. A bird is not a man!"

She laughed merrily.

"Nor a man a bird, though he may have a bird's name!" she said. "Oh, Robin, how clever you are!"

He leaned closer.

"Let Cupid go!" he pleaded,—"I want to ride home on the last load with you alone."

Another little peal of laughter escaped her.

"I declare you think Cupid an actual person!" she said. "If he'll go, he shall. But I think he'll stay."

She loosened her hold of the dove, which, released, gravely hopped up to her shoulder and sat there pruning its wing. She glanced round at it.

"I told you so!" she said,—"He's a fixture."

"I don't mind him so much up there," said Robin, and he ventured to take one of her hands in his own,—"but he always has so much of you; he nestles under your chin and is caressed by your sweet lips,—he has all, and I have,—nothing!"

"You have one hand," said Innocent, with demure gravity.

"But no heart with it!" he said, wistfully. "Innocent, can you never love me?"

She was silent, looking at him critically,—then she gave a little sigh.

"I'm afraid not! But I have often thought about it."

"You have?"—and his eyes grew very tender.

"Oh yes, often! You see, it isn't your fault at all. You are—well!"—here she surveyed him with a whimsical air of admiration,—"you are quite a beautiful man! You have a splendid figure and a good face, and kind eyes and well-shaped feet and hands,—and I like the look of you just now with that open collar and that gleam of sunlight in your curly hair—and your throat is almost white, except for a touch of sunburn, which is RATHER becoming!—especially with that crimson silk tie! I suppose you put that tie on for effect, didn't you?"

He flushed, and laughed lightly.

"Naturally! To please You!"

"Really? How thoughtful of you! Well, you are charming,—and I shouldn't mind kissing you at all. But it wouldn't be for love."

"Wouldn't it? What would it be for, then?"

Her face lightened up with the illumination of an inward mirth and mischief.

"Only because you look pretty!" she answered.

He threw aside her hand with an angry gesture of impatience.

"You want to make a fool of me!" he said, petulantly.

"I'm sure I don't! You are just lovely, and I tell you so. That is not making a fool of you!"

"Yes, it is! A man is never lovely. A woman may be."

"Well, I'm not," said Innocent, placidly. "That's why I admire the loveliness of others."

"You are lovely to me," he declared, passionately.

She smiled. There was a touch of compassion in the smile.

"Poor Robin!" she said.

At that moment the hidden goddess in her soul arose and asserted her claim to beauty. A rare indefinable charm of exquisite tenderness and fascination seemed to environ her small and delicate personality with an atmosphere of resistless attraction. The man beside her felt it, and his heart beat quickly with a thrilling hope of conquest.

"So you pity me!" he said,—"Pity is akin to love."

"But kinsfolk seldom agree," she replied. "I only pity you because you are foolish. No one but a very foolish fellow would think ME lovely."

He raised himself a little and peered over the edge of the hay-load to see if there was any sign of the men returning with Roger, but there was no one in the field now except the venerable personage he called Uncle Hugo, who was still smoking away his thoughts, as it were, in a dream of tobacco. And he once more caught the hand he had just let go and covered it with kisses.

"There!" he said, lifting his head and showing an eager face lit by amorous eyes. "Now you know how lovely you are to me! I should like to kiss your mouth like that,—for you have the sweetest mouth in the world! And you have the prettiest hair,—not raw gold which I hate,—but soft brown, with delicious little sunbeams lost in it,—and such a lot of it! I've seen it all down, remember! And your eyes would draw the heart out of any man and send him anywhere,—yes, Innocent!—anywhere,—to Heaven or to Hell!"

She coloured a little.

"That's beautiful talk!" she said,—"It's like poetry, but it isn't true!"

"It is true!" he said, with fond insistence. "And I'll MAKE you love me!"

"Ah, no!" A look of the coldest scorn suddenly passed over her features—"that's not possible. You could never MAKE me do anything! And—it's rude of you to speak in such a way. Please let go my hand!"

He dropped it instantly, and sprang erect.

"All right! I'll leave you to yourself,—and Cupid!" Here he laughed rather bitterly. "What made you give that bird such a name?"

"I found it in a book," she answered,—"It's a name that was given to the god of Love when he was a little boy."

"I know that! Please don't teach me my A.B.C.," said Robin, half-sulkily.

She leaned back laughing, and singing softly:

> *"Love was once a little boy,*
> *Heigh-ho, Heigh-ho!*
> *Then 'twas sweet with him to toy,*
> *Heigh-ho, Heigh-ho!"*

Her eyes sparkled in the sun,—a tress of her hair, ruffled by the hay, escaped and flew like a little web of sunbeams against her cheek. He looked at her moodily.

"You might go on with the song," he said,—"'Love is now a little man—'"

"'And a very naughty one!'" she hummed, with a mischievous upward glance.

Despite his inward vexation, he smiled.

"Say what you like, Cupid is a ridiculous name for a dove," he said.

"It rhymes to stupid," she replied, demurely,—"And the rhyme expresses the nature of the bird and—the god!"

"Pooh! You think that clever!"

"I don't! I never said a clever thing in my life. I shouldn't know how. Everything clever has been written over and over again by people in books."

"Hang books!" he exclaimed. "It's always books with you! I wish we had never found that old chest of musty volumes in the panelled room."

"Do you? Then you are sillier than I thought you were. The books taught me all I know,—about love!"

"About love! You don't know what love means!" he declared, trampling the hay he stood upon with impatience. "You read and read, and you get the queerest ideas into your head, and all the time the world goes on in ways that are quite different from what You are thinking about,—and lovers walk through the fields and lanes everywhere near us every year, and you never appear to see them or to envy them—"

"Envy them!" The girl opened her eyes wide. "Envy them! Oh, Cupid, hear! Envy them! Why should I envy them? Who could envy Mr. and Mrs. Pettigrew?"

"What nonsense you talk!" he exclaimed,—"Mr. and Mrs. Pettigrew are married folk, not lovers!"

"But they were lovers once," she said,—"and only three years ago. I remember them, walking through the lanes and fields as you say, with arms round each other,—and Mrs. Pettigrew's hands were always dreadfully red, and Mr. Pettigrew's fingers were always dirty,—and they married very quickly,—and now they've got two dreadful babies that scream all day and all night, and Mrs. Pettigrew's hair is never tidy and Pettigrew himself—well, you know what he does!—"

"Gets drunk every night," interrupted Robin, crossly,—"I know! And I suppose you think I'm another Pettigrew?"

"Oh dear, no!" And she laughed with the heartiest merriment. "You never could, you never would be a Pettigrew! But it all comes to the same thing—love ends in marriage, doesn't it?"

"It ought to," said Robin, sententiously.

"And marriage ends—in Pettigrews!"

"Innocent!"

"Don't say 'Innocent' in that reproachful way! It makes me feel quite guilty! Now,—if you talk of names,—THERE's a name to give a poor girl,—Innocent! Nobody ever heard of such a name—"

"You're wrong. There were thirteen Popes named Innocent between the years 402 and 1724," said Robin, promptly,—"and one of them, Innocent the Eleventh, is a character in Browning's 'Ring and the Book.'"

"Dear me!" And her eyes flashed provocatively. "You astound me with your wisdom, Robin! But all the same, I don't believe any girl ever had such a name as Innocent, in spite of thirteen Popes. And perhaps the Thirteen had other names?"

"They had other baptismal names," he explained, with a learned air. "For instance, Pope Innocent the Third was Cardinal Lothario before he became Pope, and he wrote a book called 'De Contemptu Mundi sive de Miseria Humanae Conditionis!'"

She looked at him as he uttered the sonorous sounding Latin, with a comically respectful air of attention, and then laughed like a child,— laughed till the tears came into her eyes.

"Oh Robin, Robin!" she cried—"You are simply delicious! The most enchanting boy! That crimson tie and that Latin! No wonder the village girls adore you! 'De,'—what is it? 'Contemptu Mundi,' and Misery Human Conditions! Poor Pope! He never sat on top of a hay-load in his life I'm sure! But you see his name was Lothario,—not Innocent."

"His baptismal name was Lothario," said Robin, severely.

She was suddenly silent.

"Well! I suppose *I* was baptised?" she queried, after a pause.

"I suppose so."

"I wonder if I have any other name? I must ask Dad."

Robin looked at her curiously;—then his thoughts were diverted by the sight of a squat stout woman in a brown spotted print gown and white sunbonnet, who just then trotted briskly into the hay-field, calling at the top of her voice:

"Mister Jocelyn! Mister Jocelyn! You're wanted!"

"There's Priscilla calling Uncle in," he said, and making a hollow of his hands he shouted:

"Hullo, Priscilla! What is it?"

The sunbonnet gave an upward jerk in his direction and the wearer shrilled out:

"Doctor's come! Wantin' yer Uncle!"

The old man, who had been so long quietly seated on the upturned barrel, now rose stiffly, and knocking out the ashes of his pipe turned towards the farmhouse. But before he went he raised his straw hat again and stood for a moment bareheaded in the roseate glory of the sinking sun. Innocent sprang upright on the load of hay, and standing almost at the very edge of it, shaded her eyes with one hand from the strong light, and looked at him.

"Dad!" she called—"Dad, shall I come?"

He turned his head towards her.

"No, lass, no! Stay where you are, with Robin."

He walked slowly, and with evident feebleness, across the length of the field which divided him from the farmhouse garden, and opening the green gate leading thereto, disappeared. The sun-bonneted individual called Priscilla walked or rather waddled towards the hay-waggon, and setting her arms akimbo on her broad hips, looked up with a grin at the young people on top.

"Well! Ye're a fine couple up there! What are ye a-doin' of?"

"Never mind what we're doing," said Robin, impatiently. "I say, Priscilla, do you think Uncle Hugo is really ill?"

Priscilla's face, which was the colour of an ancient nutmeg, and almost as deeply marked with contrasting lines of brown and yellow, showed no emotion.

"He ain't hisself," she said, bluntly.

"No," said Innocent, seriously,—"I'm sure he isn't." Priscilla jerked her sunbonnet a little further back, showing some tags of dusty grey hair.

"He ain't been hisself for this past year," she went on—"Mr. Slowton, bein' only a kind of village physic-bottle, don't know much, an' yer uncle ain't bin satisfied. Now there's another doctor from London staying up 'ere for 'is own poor 'elth, and yer Uncle said he'd like to 'ave 'is opinion,—so Mr. Slowton, bein' obligin' though ignorant, 'as got 'im in to see yer Uncle, and there they both is, in the best parlour, with special wine an' seedies on the table."

"Oh, it'll be all right!" said Robin, cheerfully,—"Uncle Hugo is getting old, of course, and he's a bit fanciful."

Priscilla sniffed the air.

"Mebbe—and mebbe not! What are you two waitin' for now?"

"For the men to come back with Roger. Then we'll haul home."

"You'll 'ave to wait a bit longer, I'm thinkin'," said Priscilla—"They's all drinkin' beer in the yard now an' tappin' another barrel to drink at when the waggon comes in. There's no animals on earth as ever thirsty as men! Well, good luck t'ye! I must go, or there'll be a smell of burnin' supper-cakes."

She settled her sunbonnet anew and trotted away,—looking rather like a large spotted mushroom mysteriously set in motion and rolling, rather than walking, off the field.

When she was gone, Innocent sat down again upon the hay, this time without Cupid. He had flown off to join his mates on the farmhouse gables.

"Dad is really not well," she said, thoughtfully; "I feel anxious about him. If he were to die,—" At the mere thought her eyes filled with tears. "He must die some day," answered Robin, gently,—"and he's old,—nigh on eighty."

"Oh, I don't want to remember that," she murmured. "It's the cruellest part of life—that people should grow old, and die, and pass away from us. What should I do without Dad? I should be all alone, with no one in the world to care what becomes of me."

"*I* care!" he said, softly.

"Yes, you care—just now"—she answered, with a sigh; "and it's very kind of you. I wish I could care—in the way you want me to—but—"

"Will you try?" he pleaded.

"I do try—really I do try hard," she said, with quite a piteous earnestness,—"but I can't feel what isn't HERE,"—and she pressed both hands on her breast—"I care more for Roger the horse, and Cupid the dove, than I do for you! It's quite awful of me—but there it is! I love—I simply adore"—and she threw out her arms with an embracing gesture—"all the trees and plants and birds!—and everything about the farm and the farmhouse itself—it's just the sweetest home in the world! There's not a brick or a stone in it that I would not want to kiss if I had to leave it—but I never felt that way for you! And yet I like you very, very much, Robin!—I wish I could see you married to some nice girl, only I don't know one really nice enough."

"Nor do I!" he answered, with a laugh, "except yourself! But never mind, dear!—we won't talk of it any more, just now at any rate. I'm a patient sort of chap. I can wait!"

"How long?" she queried, with a wondering glance.

"All my life!" he answered, simply.

MARIE CORELLI

A silence fell between them. Some inward touch of embarrassment troubled the girl, for the colour came and went flatteringly in her soft cheeks and her eyes drooped under his fervent gaze. The glowing light of the sky deepened, and the sun began to sink in a mist of bright orange, which was reflected over all the visible landscape with a warm and vivid glory. That strange sense of beauty and mystery which thrills the air with the approach of evening, made all the simple pastoral scene a dream of incommunicable loveliness,—and the two youthful figures, throned on their high dais of golden-green hay, might have passed for the rustic Adam and Eve of some newly created Eden. They were both very quiet,—with the tense quietness of hearts that are too full for speech. A joy in the present was shadowed with a dim unconscious fear of the future in both their thoughts,—though neither of them would have expressed their feelings in this regard one to the other. A thrush warbled in a hedge close by, and the doves on the farmhouse gables spread their white wings to the late sunlight, cooing amorously. And again the man spoke, with a gentle firmness:

"All my life I shall love you, Innocent! Whatever happens, remember that! All my life!"

II

The swinging open of a great gate at the further end of the field disturbed the momentary silence which followed his words. The returning haymakers appeared on the scene, leading Roger at their head, and Innocent jumped up eagerly, glad of the interruption.

"Here comes old Roger!" she cried,—"bless his heart! Now, Robin, you must try to look very stately! Are you going to ride home standing or sitting?"

He was visibly annoyed at her light indifference.

"Unless I may sit beside you with my arm round your waist, in the Pettigrew fashion, I'd rather stand!" he retorted. "You said Pettigrew's hands were always dirty—so are mine. I'd better keep my distance from you. One can't make hay and remain altogether as clean as a new pin!"

She gave an impatient gesture.

"You always take things up in the wrong way," she said—"I never thought you a bit like Pettigrew! Your hands are not really dirty!"

"They are!" he answered, obstinately. "Besides, you don't want my arm round your waist, do you?"

"Certainly not!" she replied, quickly.

"Then I'll stand," he said;—"You shall be enthroned like a queen and I'll be your bodyguard. Here, wait a minute!"

He piled up the hay in the middle of the load till it made a high cushion where, in obedience to his gesture, Innocent seated herself. The men leading the horse were now close about the waggon, and one of them, grinning sheepishly at the girl, offered her a daintily-made wreath of wild roses, from which all the thorns had been carefully removed.

"Looks prutty, don't it?" he said.

She accepted it with a smile.

"Is it for me? Oh, Larry, how nice of you! Am I to wear it?"

"If ye loike!" This with another grin.

She set it on her uncovered head and became at once a model for a Romney; the wild roses with their delicate pink and white against her brown hair suited the hues of her complexion and the tender grey of her eyes;—and when, thus adorned, she looked up at her companion, he was fain to turn away quickly lest his admiration should be too plainly made manifest before profane witnesses.

Roger, meanwhile, was being harnessed to the waggon. He was a handsome creature of his kind, and he knew it. As he turned his bright soft glance from side to side with a conscious pride in himself and his surroundings, he seemed to be perfectly aware that the knots of bright red ribbon tied in his long and heavy mane meant some sort of festival. When all was done the haymakers gathered round.

"Good luck to the last load, Mr. Clifford!" they shouted.

"Good luck to you all!" answered Robin, cheerily.

"Good luck t'ye, Miss!" and they raised their sun-browned faces to the girl as she looked down upon them. "As fine a crop and as fair a load next year!"

"Good luck to you!" she responded—then suddenly bending a little forward she said almost breathlessly: "Please wish luck to Dad! He's not well—and he isn't here! Oh, please don't forget him!"

They all stared at her for a moment, as if startled or surprised, then they all joined in a stentorian shout.

"That's right, Miss! Good luck to the master! Many good years of life to him, and better crops every year!"

She drew back, smiling her thanks, but there were tears in her eyes. And then they all started in a pretty procession—the men leading Roger, who paced along the meadow with equine dignity, shaking his ribbons now and again as if he were fully conscious of carrying something more valuable than mere hay,—and above them all smiled the girl's young face, framed in its soft brown hair and crowned with the wild roses, while at her side stood the very type of a model Englishman, with all the promise of splendid life and vigour in the build of his form, the set of his shoulders and the poise of his handsome head. It was a picture of youth and beauty and lovely nature set against the warm evening tint of the sky,—one of those pictures which, though drawn for the moment only on the minds of those who see it, is yet never forgotten.

Arriving presently at a vast enclosure, in which already two loads of hay were being stacked, they were hailed with a cheery shout by several other labourers at work, and very soon a strong smell of beer began to mingle with the odour of the hay and the dewy scent of the elder flowers and sweet briar in the hedges close by.

"Have a drop, Mr. Clifford!" said one tall, powerful-looking man who seemed to be a leader among the others, holding out a pewter tankard full and frothing over.

Robin Clifford smiled and put his lips to it.

"Just to your health, Landon!" he said—"I'm not a drinking man."

"Haymaking's thirsty work," commented the other. "Will Miss Jocelyn do us the honour?"

The girl made a wry little face.

"I don't like beer, Mr. Landon," she said—"It's horrid stuff, even when it's home-brewed! I help to make it, you see!"

She laughed gaily—they all laughed with her, and then there was a little altercation which ended in her putting her lips to the tankard just offered to Robin and sipping the merest fleck of its foam. Landon watched her,—and as she returned the cup, put his own mouth to the place hers had touched and drank the whole draught off greedily. Robin did not see his action, but the girl did, and a deep blush of offence suffused her cheeks. She rose, a little nervously.

"I'll go in now," she said—"Dad must be alone by this time."

"All right!" And Robin jumped lightly from the top of the load to the ground and put the ladder up for her to descend. She came down daintily, turning her back to him so that the hem of her neat white skirt fell like a little snowflake over each rung of the ladder, veiling not only her slim ankles but the very heels of her shoes. When she was nearly at the bottom, he caught her up and set her lightly on the ground.

"There you are!" he said, with a laugh—"When you get into the house you can tell Uncle that you are a Rose Queen, a Hay Queen, and Queen of everything and everyone on Briar Farm, including your very humble servant, Robin Clifford!"

"And your humblest of slaves, Ned Landon!" added Landon, with a quick glance, doffing his cap. "Mr. Clifford mustn't expect to have it all his own way!"

"What the devil are you talking about?" demanded Robin, turning upon him with a sudden fierceness.

Innocent gave him an appealing look.

"Don't!—Oh, don't quarrel!" she whispered,—and with a parting nod to the whole party of workers she hurried away.

With her disappearance came a brief pause among the men. Then Robin, turning away from Landon, proceeded to give various orders. He was a person in authority, and as everyone knew, was likely to be the owner of the farm when his uncle was dead. Landon went close up to him.

"Mr. Clifford," he said, somewhat thickly, "you heard what I said just now? You mustn't expect to have it all your own way! There's other men after the girl as well as you!"

Clifford glanced him up and down.

"Yourself, I suppose?" he retorted.

"And why not?" sneered Landon.

"Only because there are two sides to every question," said Clifford, carelessly, with a laugh. "And no decision can be arrived at till both are heard!"

He climbed up among the other men and set to work, stacking steadily, and singing in a fine soft baritone the old fifteenth-century song:

> *"Yonder comes a courteous knight,*
> *Lustily raking over the hay,*
> *He was well aware of a bonny lass,*
> *As she came wandering over the way.*
> *Then she sang Downe a downe, hey downe derry!*

> *"Jove you speed, fair ladye, he said,*
> *Among the leaves that be so greene,*
> *If I were a king and wore a crown,*
> *Full soon faire Ladye shouldst thou be queene.*
> *Then she sang Downe a downe, hey downe derry!"*

Landon looked up at him with a dark smile.

"Those laugh best who laugh last!" he muttered, "And a whistling throstle has had its neck wrung before now!"

Meanwhile Innocent had entered the farmhouse. Passing through the hall, which,—unaltered since the days of its original building,—was vaulted high and heavily timbered, she went first into the kitchen to see Priscilla, who, assisted by a couple of strong rosy-cheeked girls, did all the housework and cooking of the farm. She found that personage rolling out pastry and talking volubly as she rolled:

"Ah! You'll never come to much good, Jenny Spinner," she cried. "What with a muck of dirty dishes in one corner and a muddle of ragged clouts in another, you're the very model of a wife for a farm hand! Can't sew a gown for yerself neither, but bound to send it into town to be made for ye, and couldn't put a button on a pair of breeches for fear of 'urtin' yer delicate fingers! Well! God 'elp ye when the man comes as ye're lookin' for! He'll be a fool anyhow, for all men are that,—but he'll be twice a fool if he takes you for a life-satchel on his shoulders!"

Jenny Spinner endured this tirade patiently, and went on with the washing-up in which she was engaged, only turning her head to look at Innocent as she appeared suddenly in the kitchen doorway, with her hair slightly dishevelled and the wreath of wild roses crowning her brows.

"Priscilla, where's Dad?" she asked.

"Lord save us, lovey! You gave me a real scare coming in like that with them roses on yer head like a pixie out of the woods! The master? He's just where the doctors left 'im, sittin' in his easy-chair and looking out o' window."

"Was it—was it all right, do you think?" asked the girl, hesitatingly.

"Now, lovey, don't ask me about doctors, 'cos I don't know nothin' and wants to know nothin', for they be close-tongued folk who never sez what they thinks lest they get their blessed selves into hot water. And whether it's all right or all wrong, I couldn't tell ye, for the two o' them went out together, and Mr. Slowton sez 'Good-arternoon, Miss Friday!' quite perlite like, and the other gentleman he lifts 'is 'at quite civil, so I should say 'twas all wrong. For if you mark me, lovey, men's allus extra perlite when they thinks there's goin' to be trouble, hopin' they'll get somethin' for theirselves out of it."

Innocent hardly waited to hear her last words.

"I'm going to Dad," she said, quickly, and disappeared.

Priscilla Friday stopped for a minute in the rolling-cut of her pastry. Some great stress of thought appeared to be working behind her wrinkled brow, for she shook her head, pursed her lips and rolled up her eyes a great many times. Then she gave a short sigh and went on with her work.

The farmhouse was a rambling old place, full of quaint corners, arches and odd little steps up and down leading to cupboards, mysterious recesses and devious winding ways which turned into dark narrow passages, branching right and left through the whole breadth of the house. It was along one of these that Innocent ran swiftly on leaving the kitchen, till she reached a closed door, where pausing, she listened a moment-then, hearing no sound, opened it and went softly in. The room she entered was filled with soft shadows of the gradually falling dusk, yet partially lit by a golden flame of the after-glow which shone through the open latticed window from the western sky. Close to the waning light sat the master of the farm, still clad in his smock frock, with his straw hat on the table beside him and his stick leaning against the arm of his chair. He was very quiet,—so quiet, that a late beam of the sun, touching the rough silver white of his hair, seemed almost obtrusive, as suggesting an interruption to the moveless peace of his attitude. Innocent stopped short, with a tremor of nervous fear.

"Dad!" she said, softly.

He turned towards her.

"Ay, lass! What is it?"

She did not answer, but came up and knelt down beside him, taking one of his brown wrinkled hands in her own and caressing it. The silence between them was unbroken for quite two or three minutes; then he said:

"Last load in all safe?"

"Yes, Dad!"

"Not a drop of rain to wet it, and no hard words to toughen it, eh?"

"No, Dad."

She gave the answer a little hesitatingly. She was thinking of Ned Landon. He caught the slight falter in her voice and looked at her suspiciously.

"Been quarrelling with Robin?"

"Dear Dad, no! We're the best of friends."

He loosened his hand from her clasp and patted her head with it.

"That's right! That's as it should be! Be friends with Robin, child! Be friends!—be lovers!"

She was silent. The after-glow warmed the tints of her hair to russet-gold and turned to a deeper pink the petals of the roses in the wreath she wore. He touched the blossoms and spoke with great gentleness.

"Did Robin crown thee?"

She looked up, smiling.

"No, it's Larry's wreath."

"Larry! Ay, poor Larry! A good lad—but he can eat for two and only work for one. 'Tis the way of men nowadays!"

Another pause ensued, and the western gold of the sky began to fade into misty grey.

"Dad," said the girl then, in a low tone—"Do tell me—what did the London doctor say?"

He lifted his head quickly, and his old eyes for a moment flashed as though suddenly illumined by a flame from within.

"Say! What should he say, lass, but that I am old and must expect to die? It's natural enough—only I haven't thought about it. It's just that—I haven't thought about it!"

"Why should you think about it?" she asked, with quick tenderness—"You will not die yet—not for many years. You are not so very old. And you are strong."

He patted her head again.

"Poor little wilding!" he said—"If you had your way I should live for ever, no doubt! But an' you were wise with modern wisdom, you would say I had already lived too long!"

For answer, she drew down his hand and kissed it.

"I do not want any modern wisdom," she said—"I am your little girl and I love you!"

A shadow flitted across his face and he moved uneasily. She looked up at him.

"You will not tell me?"

"Tell you what?"

"All that the London doctor said."

He was silent for a minute's space—then he answered.

"Yes, I will tell you, but not now. To-night after supper will be time enough. And then—"

"Yes—then?" she repeated, anxiously.

"Then you shall know—you will have to know—" Here he broke off abruptly. "Innocent!"

"Yes, Dad?"

"How old are you now?"

"Eighteen."

"Ay, so you are!" And he looked at her searchingly. "Quite a woman! Time flies! You're old enough to learn—"

"I have always tried to learn," she said—"and I like studying things out of books—"

"Ay! But there are worse things in life than ever were written in books," he answered, wearily—"things that people hide away and are ashamed to speak of! Ay, poor wilding! Things that I've tried to keep from you as long as possible—but—time presses, and, I shall have to speak—"

She looked at him earnestly. Her face paled and her eyes grew dark and wondering.

"Have I done anything wrong?" she asked.

"You? No! Not you! You are not to blame, child! But you've heard the law set out in church on Sundays that 'The sins of the fathers shall be visited on the children even unto the third and fourth generation.' You've heard that?"

"Yes, Dad!"

"Ay!—and who dare say the fourth generation are to blame! Yet, though they are guiltless, they suffer most! No just God ever made such a law, though they say 'tis God speaking. *I* say 'tis the devil!"

His voice grew harsh and loud, and finding his stick near his chair, he took hold of it and struck it against the ground to emphasise his words.

"I say 'tis the devil!"

The girl rose from her kneeling attitude and put her arms gently round his shoulders.

"There, Dad!" she said soothingly,—"Don't worry! Church and church things seem to rub you up all the wrong way! Don't think about them! Supper will be ready in a little while and after supper we'll have a long talk. And then you'll tell me what the doctor said."

His angry excitement subsided suddenly and his head sank on his breast.

"Ay! After supper. Then—then I'll tell you what the doctor said."

His speech faltered. He turned and looked out on the garden, full of luxuriant blossom, the colours of which were gradually merging into indistinguishable masses under the darkening grey of the dusk.

She moved softly about the room, setting things straight, and lighting two candles in a pair of tall brass candlesticks which stood one on either side of a carved oak press. The room thus illumined showed itself to be a roughly-timbered apartment in the style of the earliest Tudor times, and all the furniture in it was of the same period. The thick gate-legged table—the curious chairs, picturesque, but uncomfortable—the two old dower chests—the quaint three-legged stools and upright settles, were a collection that would have been precious to the art dealer and curio hunter, as would the massive eight-day clock with its grotesquely painted face, delineating not only the hours and days but the lunar months, and possessing a sonorous chime which just now struck eight with a boom as deep as that of a cathedral bell. The sound appeared to startle the old farmer with a kind of shock, for he rose from his chair and grasped his stick, looking about him as though for the moment uncertain of his bearings.

"How fast the hours go by!" he muttered, dreamily. "When we're young they don't count—but when we're old we know that every hour brings us nearer to the end-the end, the end of all! Another night closing in—and the last load cleared from the field—Innocent!"

The name broke from his lips like a cry of suffering, and she ran to him trembling.

"Dad, dear, what is it?"

He caught her outstretched hands and held them close.

"Nothing—nothing!" he answered, drawing his breath quick and hard—"Nothing, lass! No pain—no—not that! I'm only frightened! Frightened!—think of it!—me frightened who never knew fear! And I—I wouldn't tell it to anyone but you—I'm afraid of what's coming—of what's bound to come! 'Twould always have come, I know—but I never thought about it—it never seemed real! It never seemed real—"

Here the door opened, admitting a flood of cheerful light from the outside passage, and Robin Clifford entered.

"Hullo, Uncle! Supper's ready!"

The old man's face changed instantly. Its worn and scared expression smoothed into a smile, and, loosening his hold of Innocent, he straightened himself and stood erect.

"All right, my lad! You've worked pretty late!"

"Yes, and we've not done yet. But we shall finish stacking tomorrow," answered Clifford—"Just now we're all tired and hungry."

"Don't say you're thirsty!" said the old farmer, his smile broadening. "How many barrels have been tapped to-day?"

"Oh, well! You'd better ask Landon,"—and Clifford's light laugh had a touch of scorn in it,—"he's the man for the beer! I hardly ever touch it—Innocent knows that."

"More work's done on water after all," said Jocelyn. "The horses that draw for us and the cattle that make food for us prove that. But we think we're a bit higher than the beasts, and some of us get drunk to prove it! That's one of our strange ways as men! Come along, lad! And you, child,"—here he turned to Innocent—"run and tell Priscilla we're waiting in the Great Hall."

He seemed to have suddenly lost all feebleness, and walked with a firm step into what he called the Great Hall, which was distinguished by this name from the lesser or entrance hall of the house. It was a nobly proportioned, very lofty apartment, richly timbered, the roof being supported by huge arched beams curiously and intricately carved. Long narrow boards on stout old trestles occupied the centre, and these were spread with cloths of coarse but spotlessly clean linen and furnished with antique plates, tankards and other vessels of pewter which would have sold for a far larger sum in the market than solid silver. A tall carved chair was set at the head of the largest table, and in this Farmer Jocelyn seated himself. The men now began to come in from the fields in their work-a-day clothes, escorted by Ned Landon, their only attempt at a toilet having been a wash and brush up in the outhouses; and soon the hall presented a scene of lively bustle and activity. Priscilla, entering it from the kitchen with her two assistants, brought in three huge smoking joints on enormous pewter dishes,—then followed other good things of all sorts,—vegetables, puddings, pasties, cakes and fruit, which Innocent helped to set out all along the boards in tempting array. It was a generous supper fit for a "Harvest Home"—yet it was only Farmer Jocelyn's ordinary way of celebrating the end of the haymaking,—the real harvest home was another and bigger festival yet to come. Robin Clifford began to carve a sirloin of beef,—Ned Landon, who was nearly opposite him, actively apportioned slices of roast pork, the delicacy most favoured by the majority, and when all the knives and forks were going and voices began to be loud and tongues discursive, Innocent slipped into a chair by Farmer Jocelyn and sat between him and Priscilla. For not only the farm hands but all the servants on the place were at table, this haymaking supper being the annual order of the household. The girl's small delicate head, with its coronal of wild roses, looked strange and incongruous among the rough specimens of manhood about her, and sometimes as the laughter became boisterous, or some bucolic witticism caught her ear, a faint flush coloured the paleness of her cheeks and a little nervous tremor ran through her frame. She drew as closely as she could to the old farmer, who sat rigidly upright and quiet, eating nothing but a morsel of bread with a bowl of hot salted milk Priscilla had put before him. Beer was served freely, and was passed from man to man in leather "blackjacks" such as were commonly used in olden times, but which are now considered mere curiosities. They were, however, ordinary wear at Briar Farm, and had been so since very early days. The Great Hall was lighted by tall windows reaching almost to the roof and traversed with shafts of solid stonework; the one immediately opposite Farmer Jocelyn's chair showed the very last parting glow of the sunset like a dull red gleam on a dark sea. For the rest, thick home-made candles of a torch shape fixed into iron sconces round the walls illumined the room, and burned with unsteady flare, giving rise to curious lights and shadows as though ghostly figures were passing to and fro, ruffling the air with their unseen presences. Priscilla Priday, her wizened yellow face just now reddened to the tint of a winter apple by her recent exertions in the kitchen, was not so much engaged in eating her supper as in watching her master. Her beady brown eyes roved from him to the slight delicate girl beside him with inquisitive alertness. She felt and saw that the old man's thoughts were far away, and that something of an unusual nature was troubling his mind. Priscilla was an odd-looking creature but faithful;—her attachments were strong, and her dislikes only a shade more violent,—and just now she entertained very uncomplimentary sentiments towards "them doctors" who had, as she surmised, put her master out of sorts with himself, and caused anxiety to the "darling child," as she invariably called Innocent when recommending her to the guidance of the Almighty in her daily and nightly prayers. Meanwhile the noise at the supper table grew louder and more incessant, and sundry deep potations of home-brewed ale began to do their work. One man, seated near Ned Landon, was holding forth in very slow thick accents on the subject of education:

"Be eddicated!" he said, articulating his words with difficulty,—"That's what I says, boys! Be eddicated! Then everything's right for us! We can kick all the rich out into the mud and take their goods and enjoy 'em for ourselves. Eddication does it! Makes us all we wants to be,—members o' Parli'ment and what not! I've only one boy,—but he'll be eddicated as his father never was—"

"And learn to despise his father!" said Robin, suddenly, his clear voice ringing out above the other's husky loquacity. "You're right! That's the best way to train a boy in the way he should go!"

There was a brief silence. Then came a fresh murmur of voices and Ned Landon's voice rose above them.

"I don't agree with you, Mr. Clifford," he said—"There's no reason why a well-educated lad should despise his father."

"But he often does," said Robin—"reason or no reason."

"Well, you're educated yourself," retorted Landon, with a touch of envy,—"You won a scholarship at your grammar school, and you've been to a University."

"What's that done for me?" demanded Robin, carelessly,—"Where has it put me? Just nowhere, but exactly where I might have stood all the time. I didn't learn farming at Oxford!"

"But you didn't learn to despise your father either, did you, sir?" queried one of the farm hands, respectfully.

"My father's dead," answered Robin, curtly,—"and I honour his memory."

"So your own argument goes to the wall!" said Landon. "Education has not made you think less of him."

"In my case, no," said Robin,—"but in dozens of other cases it works out differently. Besides, you've got to decide what education Is. The man who knows how to plough a field rightly is as usefully educated as the man who knows how to read a book, in my opinion."

"Education," interposed a strong voice, "is first to learn one's place in the world and then know how to keep it!"

All eyes turned towards the head of the table. It was Farmer Jocelyn who spoke, and he went on speaking:

"What's called education nowadays," he said, "is a mere smattering and does no good. The children are taught, especially in small villages like ours, by men and women who often know less than the children themselves. What do you make of Danvers, for example, boys?"

A roar of laughter went round the table.

"Danvers!" exclaimed a huge red-faced fellow at the other end of the board,—"Why he talks yer 'ead off about what he's picked up here and there like, and when I asked him to tell me where my son is as went to Mexico, blowed if he didn't say it was a town somewheres near New York!"

Another roar went round the table. Farmer Jocelyn smiled and held up his hand to enjoin silence.

"Mr. Danvers is a teacher selected by the Government," he then observed, with mock gravity. "And if he teaches us that Mexico is a town near New York, we poor ignorant farm-folk are bound to believe him!"

They all laughed again, and he continued:

"I'm old enough, boys, to have seen many changes, and I tell you, all things considered, that the worst change is the education business, so far as the strength and the health of the country goes. That, and machine work. When I was a youngster, nearly every field-hand knew how to mow,—now we've trouble enough to find an extra man who can use a scythe. And you may put a machine on the grass as much as you like, you'll never get the quality that you'll get with a well-curved blade and a man's arm and hand wielding it. Longer work maybe, and risk of rain—but, taking the odds for and against, men are better than machines. Forty years we've scythed the grass on Briar Farm, and haven't we had the finest crops of hay in the county?"

A chorus of gruff voices answered him:

"Ay, Mister Jocelyn!"

"That's right!"

"I never 'member more'n two wet seasons and then we got last load in 'tween showers," observed one man, thoughtfully.

"There ain't never been nothin' wrong with Briar Farm hay crops anyway—all the buyers knows that for thirty mile round," said another.

"And the wheat and the corn and the barley and the oats the same," struck in the old farmer again—"all the seed sown by hand and the harvest reaped by hand, and every man and boy in the village or near it has found work enough to keep him in his native place, spring, summer, autumn and winter, isn't that so?"

"Ay, ay!"

"Never a day out o' work!"

"Talk of unemployed trouble," went on Jocelyn, "if the old ways were kept up and work done in the old fashion, there'd be plenty for all England's men to do, and to feed fair and hearty! But the idea nowadays is to rush everything just to get finished with it, and then to play cards or football, and get drunk till the legs don't know whether it's land or water they're standing on! It's the wrong way about, boys! It's the wrong way about! You may hurry and scurry along as fast as you please, but you miss most good things by the way; and there's only one end to your racing—the grave! There's no such haste to drop into THAT, boys! It'll wait! It's always waiting! And the quicker you go the quicker you'll get to it! Take time while you're young! That time for me is past!"

He lifted his head and looked round upon them all. There was a strange wild look in his old eyes,—and a sudden sense of awe fell on the rest of the company. Farmer Jocelyn seemed all at once removed from them to a height of dignity above his ordinary bearing. Innocent's rose-crowned head drooped, and tears sprang involuntarily to her eyes. She tried to hide them, not so well, however, but that Priscilla Priday saw them.

"Now, lovey child!" she whispered,—"Don't take on! It's only the doctors that's made him low like and feelin' blue, and he ain't takin' sup or morsel, but we'll make him have a bite in his own room afterwards. Don't you swell your pretty eyes and make 'em red, for that won't suit me nor Mr. Robin neither, come, come!—that it won't!"

Innocent put one of her little hands furtively under the board and pressed Priscilla's rough knuckles tenderly, but she said nothing. The silence was broken by one of the oldest men present, who rose, tankard in hand.

"The time for good farming is never past!" he said, in a hearty voice—"And no one will ever beat Farmer Jocelyn at that! Full cups, boys! And the master's health! Long life to him!"

The response was immediate, every man rising to his feet. None of them were particularly unsteady except Ned Landon, who nearly fell over the table as he got up, though he managed to straighten himself in time.

"Farmer Jocelyn!"

"To Briar Farm and the master!"

"Health and good luck!"

These salutations were roared loudly round the table, and then the whole company gave vent to a hearty 'Hip-hip-hurrah!' that roused echoes from the vaulted roof and made its flaring lights tremble.

"One more!" shouted Landon, suddenly, turning his flushed face from side to side upon those immediately near him—"Miss Jocelyn!"

There followed a deafening volley of cheering,—tankards clinked together and shone in the flickering light and every eye looked towards the girl, who, colouring deeply, shrank from the tumult around her like a leaf shivering in a storm-wind. Robin glanced at her with a half-jealous, half-anxious look, but her face was turned away from him. He lifted his tankard and, bowing towards her, drank the contents. When the toast was fully pledged, Farmer Jocelyn got up, amid much clapping of hands, stamping of feet and thumping on the boards. He waited till quiet was restored, and then, speaking in strong resonant accents, said:

"Boys, I thank you! You're all boys to me, young and old, for you've worked on the farm so long that I seem to know your faces as well as I know the shape of the land and the trees on the ridges. You've wished me health and long life—and I take it that your wishes are honest—but I've had a long life already and mustn't expect much more of it. However, the farm will go on just the same whether I'm here or elsewhere,—and no man that works well on it will be turned away from it,—that I can promise you! And the advice I've always given to you I give to you again,—stick to the land and the work of the land! There's nothing finer in the world than the fresh air and the scent of the good brown earth that gives you the reward of your labour, always providing it is labour and not 'scamp' service. When I'm gone you'll perhaps remember what I say,—and think it not so badly said either. I thank you for your good wishes and"—here he hesitated—"my little girl here thanks you too. Next time you make the hay—if I'm not with you—I ask you to be as merry as you are to-night and to drink to my memory! For whenever one master of Briar Farm has gone there's always been another in his place!—and there always will be!" He paused,—then lifting a full tankard which had been put beside him, he drank a few drops of its contents—"God bless you all! May you long have the will to work and the health to enjoy the fruits of honest labour!"

There was another outburst of noisy cheering, followed by a new kind of clamour,

"A song!"

"A song!"

"Who'll begin?"

"Where's Steevy?"

"Little Steevy!"

"Steevy! Wheer be ye got to?" roared one old fellow with very white hair and a very red face—"ye're not so small as ye can hide in yer mother's thimble!"

A young giant of a man stood up in response to this adjuration, blushing and smiling bashfully.

"Here I be!"

"Sing away, lad, sing away!"

"Wet yer pipe, and whistle!"

"Tune up, my blackbird!"

Steevy, thus adjured, straightened himself to his full stature of over six feet and drank off a cupful of ale. Then he began in a remarkably fine and mellow tenor:

"Would you choose a wife
For a happy life,
Leave the town and the country take;
Where Susan and Doll,
And Jenny and Moll,
Follow Harry and John,
While harvest goes on,
And merrily, merrily rake!"

"The lass give me here,
As brown as my beer,

That knows how to govern a farm;
That can milk a cow,
Or farrow a sow,
Make butter and cheese,
And gather green peas,
And guard the poultry from harm."

"This, this is the girl,
Worth rubies and pearl,
The wife that a home will make!
We farmers need
No quality breed,
But a woman that's won
While harvest goes on,
*And we merrily, merrily rake!"**

A dozen or more stentorian voices joined in the refrain:

"A woman that's won
While harvest goes on,
And we merrily, merrily rake."

"Bravo!"
"Good for you, Steevy!"
"First-class!"
"Here's to you, my lad!"
The shouting, laughter and applause continued for many minutes, then came more singing of songs from various rivals to the tuneful Steevy. And presently all joined together in a boisterous chorus which ran thus:

"A glass is good and a lass is good,
And a pipe is good in cold weather,
The world is good and the people are good,
And we're all good fellows together!"

In the middle of this performance Farmer Jocelyn rose from his place and left the hall, Innocent accompanying him. Once he looked

---

* Old Song 1740.

back on the gay scene presented to him—the disordered supper-table, the easy lounging attitudes of the well-fed men, the flare of the lights which cast a ruddy glow on old and young faces and sparkled over the burnished pewter,—then with a strange yearning pain in his eyes he turned slowly away, leaning on the arm of the girl beside him, and went,—leaving the merry-makers to themselves.

III

Returning to the room where he had sat alone before supper, he sank heavily into the armchair he had previously occupied. The window was still open, and the scent of roses stole in with every breath of air,—a few stars sparkled in the sky, and a faint line of silver in the east showed where the moon would shortly rise. He looked out in dreamy silence, and for some minutes seemed too much absorbed in thought to notice the presence of Innocent, who had seated herself at a small table near him, on which she had set a lit candle, and was quietly sewing. She had forgotten that she still wore the wreath of wild roses,—the fragile flowers were drooping and dying in her hair, and as she bent over her work and the candlelight illumined her delicate profile, there was something almost sculptural in the shape of the leaves as they encircled her brow, making her look like a young Greek nymph or goddess brought to life out of the poetic dreams of the elder world. She was troubled and anxious, but she tried not to let this seem apparent. She knew from her life's experience of his ways and whims that it was best to wait till the old man chose to speak, rather than urge him into talk before he was ready or willing. She glanced up from her sewing now and again and saw that he looked very pale and worn, and she felt that he suffered. Her tender young heart ached with longing to comfort him, yet she knew not what she should say. So she sat quiet, as full of loving thoughts as a Madonna lily may be full of the dew of Heaven, yet mute as the angelic blossom itself. Presently he moved restlessly, and turning in his chair looked at her intently. The fixity of his gaze drew her like a magnet from her work and she put down her sewing.

"Do you want anything, Dad?"

He rose, and began to fumble with the buttons of his smock.

"Ay—just help me to get this off. The working day is over,—the working clothes can go!"

She was at his side instantly and with her light deft fingers soon disembarrassed him of the homely garment. When it was taken off a noticeable transformation was effected in his appearance. Clad in plain dark homespun, which was fashioned into a suit somewhat resembling the doublet and hose of olden times, his tall thin figure had a distinctly aristocratic look and bearing which was lacking when clothed in the labourer's garb. Old as he was, there were traces of intellect and even beauty in his features,—his head, on which the thin white hair shone like spun silver, was proudly set on his shoulders in that unmistakable line which indicates the power and the will to command; and as he unconsciously drew himself upright he looked more like some old hero of a hundred battles than a farmer whose chief pride was the excellence of his crops and the prosperity of his farm managed by hand work only. For despite the jeers of his neighbours, who were never tired of remonstrating with him for not "going with the times," Jocelyn had one fixed rule of farming, and this was that no modern machinery should be used on his lands. He was the best employer of labour for many and many a mile round, and the most generous as well as the most exact paymaster, and though people asserted that there was no reasonable explanation for it, nevertheless it annually happened that the hand-sown, hand-reaped crops of Briar Farm were finer and richer in grain and quality, and of much better value than the machine-sown, machine-reaped crops of any other farm in the county or for that matter in the three counties adjoining. He stood now for a minute or two watching Innocent as she looked carefully over his smock frock to see if there were any buttons missing or anything to be done requiring the services of her quick needle and thread,—then as she folded it and put it aside on a chair he said with a thrill of compassion in his voice:

"Poor little child, thou hast eaten no supper! I saw thee playing with the bread and touching no morsel. Art not well?"

She looked up at him and tried to smile, but tears came into her eyes despite her efforts to keep them back.

"Dear Dad, I am only anxious," she murmured, tremulously. "You, too, have had nothing. Shall I fetch you a glass of the old wine? It will do you good."

He still bent his brows thoughtfully upon her.

"Presently—presently—not now," he answered. "Come and sit by me at the window and I'll tell you—I'll tell you what you must know. But see you, child, if you are going to cry or fret, you will be no help to me and I'll just hold my peace!"

She drew a quick breath, and her face paled.

"I will not cry," she said,—"I will not fret. I promise you, Dad!"

She came close up to him as she spoke. He took her gently in his arms and kissed her.

"That's a brave girl!" And holding her by the hand he drew her towards the open window—"Look out there! See how the stars shine! Always the same, no matter what happens to us poor folk down here,—

they twinkle as merrily over our graves as over our gardens,—and yet if we're to believe what we're taught nowadays, they're all worlds more or less like our own, full of living creatures that suffer and die like ourselves. It's a queer plan of the Almighty, to keep on making wonderful and beautiful things just to destroy them! There seems no sense in it!"

He sat down again in his chair, and she, obeying his gesture, brought a low stool to his feet and settled herself upon it, leaning against his knee. Her face was upturned to his and the flickering light of the tall candles quivering over it showed the wistful tender watchfulness of its expression—a look which seemed to trouble him, for he avoided her eyes.

"You want to know what the London doctor said," he began. "Well, child, you'll not be any the better for knowing, but it's as I thought. I've got my death-warrant. Slowton was not sure about me,—but this man, ill as he is himself, has had too much experience to make mistakes. There's no cure for me. I may last out another twelve months—perhaps not so long—certainly not longer."

He saw her cheeks grow white with the ashy whiteness of a sudden shock. Her eyes dilated with pain and fear, and a quick sigh escaped her, then she set her lips hard.

"I don't believe it," she said, adding with stronger emphasis—"I Won't believe it!"

He patted the small hand that rested on his knee.

"You won't? Poor little girl, you must believe it!—and more than that, you must be prepared for it. Even a year's none too much for all that has to be done,—'twill almost take me that time to look the thing square in the face and give up the farm for good."—Here he paused with a kind of horror at his own words—"Give up the farm!—My God! And for ever! How strange it seems!"

The tumult in her mind found sudden speech.

"Dad, dear! Dad! It isn't true! Don't think it! Don't mind what the doctor says. He's wrong—I'm sure he's wrong! You'll live for many and many a happy year yet—oh yes, Dad, you will! I'm sure of it! You won't die, darling Dad! Why should you?"

She broke off with a half-smothered sob.

"Why should I?" he said, with a perplexed frown; "Ah!—that's more than I can tell you! There's neither rhyme nor reason in it that I can see. But it's the rule of life that it should end in death. For some the end is swift—for some it's slow—some know when it's coming—some don't,—the last are the happiest. I've been told, you see,—and it's no use my fighting against the fact,—a year at the most, perhaps less, is the longest term I have of Briar Farm. Your eyes are wet—you promised you wouldn't cry."

She furtively dashed away the drops that were shining on her lashes. Then she forced a faint quivering smile.

"I'm not crying, Dad," she said. "There's nothing to cry for," and she fondled his hand in her own—"The doctors are wrong. You're only a little weak and run down—you'll be all right with rest and care—and—and you shan't die! You shan't die! I won't let you."

He drew a long breath and passed his hand across his forehead as though he were puzzled or in pain.

"That's foolish talk," he said, with some harshness; "You've got trouble to meet, and you must meet it. I'm bound to show you trouble—but I can show you a way out of it as well."

He paused a moment,—a light wind outside the lattice swayed a branch of roses to and fro, shaking out their perfume as from a swung censer.

"The first thing I must tell you," he went on, "is about yourself. It's time you should know who you are."

She looked up at him startled.

"Who I am?" she repeated,—then as she saw the stern expression on his face a sudden sense of fear ran through her nerves like the chill of an icy wind and she waited dumbly for his next word. He gripped her hand hard in his own.

"Now hear me out, child!" he said—"Let me speak on without interruption, or I shall never get through the tale. Perhaps I ought to have told you before, but I've put it off and put it off, thinking 'twould be time enough when you and Robin were wed. You and Robin—you and Robin!—your marriage bells have rung through my brain many and many a night for the past two years and never a bit nearer are you to the end of your wooing, such fanciful children as you both are! And you're so long about it and I've so short a time before me that I've made up my mind it's best to let you have all the truth about yourself before anything happens to me. All the truth about yourself—as far as I know it."

He paused again. She was perfectly silent. She trembled a little—wondering what she was going to hear. It must be something dreadful, she thought,—something for which she was unprepared,—something that might, perhaps, like a sudden change in the currents of the air, create darkness where there had been sunshine, storm instead of calm. His grip on her hand was strong enough to hurt her, but she was not conscious of it. She only wished he would tell her the worst at once and quickly. The worst,—for she instinctively felt there was no best.

"It was eighteen years ago this very haymaking time," he went on, with a dreamy retrospective air as though he were talking to himself,— "The last load had been taken in. Supper was over. The men had gone home,—Priscilla was clearing the great hall, when there came on a sudden storm—just a flash of lightning—I can see it now, striking a blue fork across the windows—a clap of thunder—and then a regular downpour of rain. Heavy rain, too,—buckets-full—for it washed the yard out and almost swamped the garden. I didn't think much about it,— the hay was hauled in dry, and that was all my concern. I stood under a shed in the yard and watched the rain falling in straight sheets out of a sky black as pitch—I could scarcely see my own hand if I stretched it out before me, the night was so dark. All at once I heard the quick gallop of a horse's hoofs some way off,—then the sound seemed to die away,—but presently I heard the hoofs coming at a slow steady pace down our muddy old by-road—no one can gallop THAT, in any weather. And almost before I knew how it came there, the horse was standing at the farmyard gate, with a man in the saddle carrying a bundle in front of him. He was the handsomest fellow I ever saw, and when he dismounted and came towards me, and took off his cap in the pouring rain and smiled at me, I was fairly taken with his looks. I thought he must be something of a king or other great personage by his very manner. 'Will you do me a kindness?' he said, as gently as you please. 'This is a farm, I believe. I want to leave my little child here in safe keeping for a night. She is such a baby,—I cannot carry her any further through this storm.' And he put aside the wrappings of the bundle he carried and showed me a small pale infant asleep. 'She's motherless,' he added, 'and I'm taking her to my relatives. But I have to ride some distance from here on very urgent business, and if you will look after her for to-night I'll call for her to-morrow. Poor little innocent! She's hungry and fretful. I haven't anything to give her and the storm looks like continuing. Will you let her stay with you?' 'Certainly!' said I, without thinking a bit further about it. 'Leave her here by all means. We'll see she gets all she wants.' He gave me the child at once and said in a very soft voice: 'You are most generous!—"verily I have not found so great a faith, no not in

Israel!" You're sure you don't mind?' 'Not at all!' I answered him,—'You'll come back for her to-morrow, of course.' He smiled and said—'Oh yes, of course! To-morrow! I'm really very much obliged to you!' Then he seemed to think for a moment and put his hand in his pocket, but I stopped him—'No, sir,' I said, 'excuse me, but I don't want any pay for giving a babe a night's shelter.' He looked at me very straight with his big clear hazel eyes, and then shook hands with me. 'You're an honest fellow,' he said,—and he stooped and kissed the child he had put into my arms. 'I'm extremely sorry to trouble you, but the storm is too much for this helpless little creature.' 'You yourself are wet through,' I interrupted. 'That doesn't matter,' he answered,—'for me nothing matters. Thank you a thousand times! Good-night!' The rain was coming down faster than ever and I stepped back into the shed, covering the child up so that the drifting wet should not beat upon it. He came after me and kissed it again, saying 'Good-night, poor little innocent, good-night!' three or four times. Then he went off quickly and sprang into his saddle and in the blur of rain I saw horse and man turn away. He waved his hand once and his handsome pale face gleamed upon me like that of a ghost in the storm. 'Till to-morrow!' he called, and was gone. I took the child into the house and called Priscilla. She was always a rough one as you know, even in her younger days, and she at once laid her tongue to with a will and as far as she dared called me a fool for my pains. And so I was, for when I came to think of it the man was a stranger to me, and I had never asked him his name. It was just his handsome face and the way he had with him that had thrown me off my guard as it were; so I stood and looked silly enough, I suppose, while Priscilla fussed about with the baby, for it had wakened and was crying. Well!"—and Jocelyn heaved a short sigh—"That's about all! We never saw the man again, and the child was never claimed; but every six months I received a couple of bank-notes in an envelope bearing a different postmark each time, with the words: 'For Innocent' written inside—"

She uttered a quick, almost terrified exclamation, and drew her hand away from his.

"Every six months for a steady twelve years on end," he went on,— "then the money suddenly stopped. Now you understand, don't you? You were the babe that was left with me that stormy night; and you've been with me ever since. But you're not My child. I don't know whose child you are!"

He stopped, looking at her.

She had risen from her seat beside him and was standing up. She was trembling violently, and her face seemed changed from the round and mobile softness of youth to the worn pallor and thinness of age. Her eyes were luminous with a hard and feverish brilliancy.

"You—you don't know whose child I am!" she repeated,—"I am not yours—and you don't know—you don't know who I belong to! Oh, it hurts me!—it hurts me, Dad! I can't realise it! I thought you were my own dear father!—and I loved you!—oh, how much I loved you!—yet you have deceived me all along!"

"I haven't deceived you," he answered, impatiently. "I've done all for the best—I meant to tell you when you married Robin—"

A flush of indignation flew over her cheeks.

"Marry Robin!" she exclaimed—"How could I marry Robin? I'm nothing! I'm nobody! I have not even a name!"

She covered her face with her hands and an uncontrollable sob broke from her.

"Not even a name!" she murmured—"Not even a name!"

With a sudden impulsive movement she knelt down in front of him like a child about to say its prayers.

"Oh, help me, Dad!" she said, piteously—"Comfort me! Say something—anything! I feel so lost—so astray! All my life seems gone!—I can't realise it! Yes, I know! You have been very kind,—all kindness, just as if I had been your own little girl. Oh, why did you tell me I was your own?—I was so proud to be your daughter—and now—it's so hard—so hard! Only a few moments ago I was a happy girl with a loving father as I thought—now I know I'm only a poor nameless creature,—deserted by my parents and left on your hands. Oh, Dad dear! I've given you years of trouble!—I hope I've been good to you! It's not my fault that I am what I am!"

He laid his wrinkled hand on her bowed head.

"Dear child, of course it's not your fault! That's what I've said all along. You're innocent, like your name,—and you've been a blessing to me all your days,—the farm has been brighter for your living on it,—so you've no cause to worry me or yourself about what's past long ago and can't be helped. No one knows your story but Priscilla,—no one need ever know."

She sprang up from her kneeling attitude.

"Priscilla!" she echoed—"She knew, and she never said a word!"

"If she had, she'd have got the sack," answered Jocelyn, bluntly. "You were brought up always as MY child."

He broke off, startled by the tragic intensity of her look.

"I want to know how that was," she said, slowly. "You told me my mother died when I was born."

He avoided her eyes.

"Well, that was true, or so I suppose," he said. "The man who brought you said you were motherless. But I—I have never married."

"Then how could you tell Robin—and everyone else about here that I was your daughter?"

He grew suddenly angry.

"Child, don't stare at me like that!" he exclaimed, with all an old man's petulance. "It doesn't matter what I said—I had to let the neighbours think you were mine—"

A light flashed in upon her, and she gave vent to a shuddering cry.

"Dad! Oh, Dad!"

Gripping both arms of his chair he raised himself into an upright posture.

"What now?" he demanded, almost fiercely—"What trouble are you going to make of it?"

"Oh, if it were only trouble," she exclaimed, forlornly. "It's far worse! You've branded me with shame! Oh, I understand now! I understand at last why the girls about here never make friends with me! I understand why Robin seems to pity me so much! Oh, how shall I ever look people in the face again!"

His fuzzy brows met in a heavy frown.

"Little fool!" he said, roughly,—"What shame are you talking of? I see no shame in laying claim to a child of my own, even though the claim has no reality. Look at the thing squarely! Here comes a strange man with a baby and leaves it on my hands. You know what a scandalous, gossiping little place this is,—and it was better to say at once the baby was mine than leave it to the neighbours to say the same thing and that I wouldn't acknowledge it. Not a soul about here would have believed the true story if I had told it to them. I've done everything for the best—I know I have. And there'll never be a word said if you marry Robin."

Her face had grown very white. She put up her hand to her head and her fingers touched the faded wreath of wild roses. She drew it off and let it drop to the ground.

"I shall never marry Robin!" she said, with quiet firmness—"And I will not be considered your illegitimate child any longer. It's cruel of you to have made me live on a lie!—yes, cruel!—though you've been so kind in other things. You don't know who my parents were—you've no right to think they were not honest!"

He stared at her amazed. For the first time in eighteen years he began to see the folly of what he had thought his own special wisdom. This girl, with her pale sad face and steadfast eyes, confronted him with the calm reproachful air of an accusing angel.

"What right have you?" she went on. "The man who brought me to you,—poor wretched me!—if he was my father, may have been good and true. He said I was motherless; and he, or someone else, sent you money for me till I was twelve. That did not look as if I was forgotten. Now you say the money has stopped—well!—my father may be dead." Her lips quivered and a few tears rolled down her cheeks. "But there is nothing in all this that should make you think me basely born,—nothing that should have persuaded you to put shame upon me!"

He was taken aback for a minute by her words and attitude—then he burst out angrily:

"It's the old story, I see! Do a good action and it turns out a curse! Basely born! Of course you are basely born, if that's the way you put it! What man alive would leave his own lawful child at a strange farm off the high-road and never claim it again? You're a fool, I tell you! This man who brought you to me was by his look and bearing some fine gentleman or other who had just the one idea in his head—to get rid of an encumbrance. And so he got rid of you—"

"Don't go over the whole thing again!" she interrupted, with weary patience-"-I was an encumbrance to him—I've been an encumbrance to you. I'm sorry! But in no case had you the right to set a stigma on me which perhaps does not exist. That was wrong!"

She paused a moment, then went on slowly:

"I've been a burden on you for six years now,—it's six years, you say, since the money stopped. I wish I could do something in return for what I've cost you all those six years,—I've tried to be useful."

The pathos in her voice touched him to the quick.

"Innocent!" he exclaimed, and held out his arms.

She looked at him with a very pitiful smile and shook her head.

"No! I can't do that! Not just yet! You see, it's all so unexpected—things have changed altogether in a moment. I can't feel quite the same—my heart seems so sore and cold."

He leaned back in his chair again.

"Ah, well, it is as I thought!" he said, irritably. "You're more concerned about yourself than about me. A few minutes ago you only cared to know what the doctors thought of my illness, but now it's nothing to you that I shall be dead in a year. Your mind is set on your own trouble, or what you choose to consider a trouble."

She heard him like one in a dream. It seemed very strange to her that he should have dealt her a blow and yet reproach her for feeling the force of it.

"I am sorry!" she said, patiently. "But this is the first time I have known real trouble—you forget that!—and you must forgive me if I am stupid about it. And if the doctors really believe you are to die in a year I wish I could take your place, Dad!—I would rather be dead than live shamed. And there's nothing left for me now,—not even a name—"

Here she paused and seemed to reflect.

"Why am I called Innocent?"

"Why? Because that's the name that was written on every slip of paper that came with each six months' money," he answered, testily. "That's the only reason I know."

"Was I baptised by that name?" she asked.

He moved uneasily.

"You were never baptised."

"Never baptised!" She echoed the words despairingly,—and then was silent for a minute's space. "Could you not have done that much for me?" she asked, plaintively, at last—"Would it have been impossible?"

He was vaguely ashamed. Her eyes, pure as a young child's, were fixed upon him in appealing sorrow. He began to feel that he had done her a grievous wrong, though he had never entirely realised it till now. He answered her with some hesitation and an effort at excuse.

"Not impossible—no,—maybe I could have baptised you myself if I had thought about it. 'Tis but a sprinkle of water and 'In the Name of the Father, Son, and Holy Ghost.' But somehow I never worried my head—for as long as you were a baby I looked for the man who brought you day after day, and in my own mind left all that sort of business for him to attend to—and when he didn't come and you grew older, it fairly slipped my remembrance altogether. I'm not fond of the Church or its ways,—and you've done as well without baptism as with it, surely. Innocent is a good name for you, and fits your case. For you're innocent of the faults of your parents whatever they were, and you're innocent of my blunders. You're free to make your own life pleasant if you'll only put a bright face on it and make the best of an awkward business."

She was silent, standing before him like a little statuesque figure of desolation.

"As for the tale I told the neighbours," he went on—"it was the best thing I could think of. If I had said you were a child I had taken in to adopt, not one of them would have believed me; 'twas a case of telling one lie or t'other, the real truth being so queer and out of the common, so I chose the easiest. And it's been all right with you, my girl, whichever way you put it. There may be a few stuck-up young huzzies in the village that aren't friendly to you, but you may take it that it's more out of jealousy of Robin's liking for you than anything else. Robin loves you—you know he does; and all you've got to do is to make him happy. Marry him, for the farm will be his when I'm dead, and it'll give me a bit of comfort to feel that you're settled down with him in the old home. For then I know it'll go on just the same—just the same—"

His words trailed off brokenly. His head sank on his chest, and some slow tears made their difficult way out of his eyes and dropped on his silver beard.

She watched him with a certain grave compassion, but she did not at once go, as she would usually have done, to put her arms round his neck and console him. She seemed to herself removed miles away from him and from everything she had ever known. Just then there was a noise of rough but cheery voices outside shouting "good-night" to each other, and she said in a quiet tone:

"The men are away now. Is there anything you want before I go to bed?"

With a sudden access of energy, which contrasted strangely with his former feebleness, he rose and confronted her.

"No, there's nothing I want!" he said, in vehement tones—"Nothing but peace and quietness! I've told you your story, and you take it ill. But recollect, girl, that if you consider any shame has been put on you, I've put equal shame on myself for your sake—I, Hugo Jocelyn,—against whom never a word has been said but this,—which is a lie—that my child, mine!—was born out of wedlock! I suffered this against myself solely for your sake—I, who never wronged a woman in my life!—I, who never loved but one woman, who died before I had the chance to marry her!—and I say and I swear I have sacrificed something of my name and reputation to you! So that you need not make trouble because you also share in the sacrifice. Robin thinks you're my child, and therefore his cousin,—and he counts nothing against you, for he knows that what the world would count against you must be my fault and would be my fault, if the lie I started against myself was true. Marry Robin, I tell you!—and if you care to make me happy, marry him before I die. Then you're safe out of all harm's way. If you Don't marry him—"

Her breath came and went quickly—she folded her hands across her bosom, trying to still the loud and rapid beating of her heart, but her eyes were very bright and steadfast.

"Yes? What then?" she asked, calmly.

"Then you must take the consequences," he said. "The farm and all I have is left to Robin,—he's my dead sister's son and my nearest living kin—"

"I know that," she said, simply, "and I'm glad he has everything. It's right that it should be so. I shall not be in his way. You may be quite sure of that. But I shall not marry him."

"You'll not marry him?" he repeated, and seemed about to give vent to a torrent of invective when she extended her hands clasped together appealingly.

"Dad, don't be angry!—it only hurts you and it does no good! Just before supper you reminded me of what they say in Church that 'the sins of the fathers should be visited on the children, even unto the third and fourth generation.' I will not visit the sin of my father and mother on anyone. If you will give me a little time I shall be able to understand everything more clearly, and perhaps bear it better. I want to be quite by myself. I must try to see myself as I am,—unbaptised, nameless, forsaken! And if there is anything to be done with this wretched little self of mine, it is I that must do it. With God's help!" She sighed, and her lips moved softly again in the last words, "With God's help!"

He said nothing, and she waited a moment as if expecting him to speak. Then she moved to the table where she had been sitting and folded up her needlework.

"Shall I get you some wine, Dad?" she asked presently in a quiet voice.

"No!" he replied, curtly—"Priscilla can get it."

"Then good-night!"

Still standing erect he turned his head and looked at her.

"Are you going?" he said. "Without your usual kiss?—your usual tenderness? Why should you change to me? Your own father—if he was your father—deserted you,—and I have been, a father to you in his place, wronging my own honourable name for your sake; am I to blame for this? Be reasonable! The laws of man are one thing and the laws of God are another,—and we have to make the best we can of ourselves between the two. There's many a piece of wicked injustice in the world, but nothing more wicked than to set shame or blame on a child that's born without permit of law or blessing of priest. For it's not the child's fault,—it's brought into the world without its own consent,—and yet the world fastens a slur upon it! That's downright brutal and senseless!—for if there is any blame attached to the matter it should be fastened on the parents, and not on the child. And that's what I thought when you were left on my hands—I took the blame of you on myself, and I was careful that you should be treated with every kindness and respect—mind you that! Respect! There's not a man on the place that doesn't doff his cap to you; and you've been as my own daughter always. You can't deny it! And more than that"—here his strong voice faltered—"I've loved you!—yes-I've loved you, little Innocent—"

She looked up in his face and saw it quivering with suppressed emotion, and the strange cold sense of aloofness that had numbed her senses suddenly gave way like snow melting in the spring. In a moment she was in his arms, weeping out her pent-up tears on his breast, and he, stroking her soft hair, soothed her with every tender and gentle word he could think of.

"There, there!" he murmured, fondly. "Thou must look at it in this way, dear child! That if God deprived thee of one father he gave thee another in his place! Make the best of that gift before it be taken from thee!"

IV

There are still a few old houses left in rural England which are as yet happily unmolested by the destroying ravages of modern improvement, and Briar Farm was one of these. History and romance alike had their share in its annals, and its title-deeds went back to the autumnal days of 1581, when the Duke of Anjou came over from France to England with a royal train of noblemen and gentlemen in the hope to espouse the greatest monarch of all time, "the most renowned and victorious" Queen Elizabeth, whose reign has clearly demonstrated to the world how much more ably a clever woman can rule a country than a clever man, if she is left to her own instinctive wisdom and prescience. No king has ever been wiser or more diplomatic than Elizabeth, and no king has left a more brilliant renown. As the coldest of male historians is bound to admit, "her singular powers of government were founded equally on her temper and on her capacity. Endowed with a great command over herself, she soon obtained an uncontrolled ascendant over her people. Few sovereigns of England succeeded to the throne under more difficult circumstances, and none ever conducted the government with such uniform success and felicity." Had Elizabeth been weak, the Duke of Anjou might have realised his ambitious dream, with the unhappiest results for England; and that he fortunately failed was entirely due to her sagacity and her quick perception of his irresolute and feeble character. In the sumptuous train attendant upon this "Petit Grenouille," as he styled himself in one of his babyish epistles to England's sovereign majesty, there was a certain knight more inclined to the study of letters than to the breaking of lances,—the Sieur Amadis de Jocelin, who being much about the court in the wake of his somewhat capricious and hot-tempered master, came, unfortunately for his own peace of mind, into occasional personal contact with one of the most bewitching young women of her time, the Lady Penelope Devereux, afterwards Lady Rich, she in whom, according to a contemporary writer, "lodged all attractive graces and beauty, wit and sweetness of behaviour which might render her the mistress of all eyes and hearts." Surrounded as she was by many suitors, his passion was hopeless from the first, and that he found it so was evident from the fact that he suddenly disappeared from the court and from his master's retinue, and was never heard of by the great world again. Yet he was not far away. He had not the resolution to leave England, the land which enshrined the lady of his love,—and he had lost all inclination to return to France. He therefore retired into the depths of the sweet English country, among the then unspoilt forests and woodlands, and there happening to find a small manor-house for immediate sale, surrounded by a considerable quantity of land, he purchased it for the ready cash he had about him and settled down in it for the remainder of his life. Little by little, such social ambitions as he had ever possessed left him, and with every passing year he grew more and more attached to the simplicity and seclusion of his surroundings. He had leisure for the indulgence of his delight in books, and he was able to give the rein to his passion for poetry, though it is nowhere recorded that he ever published the numerous essays, sonnets and rhymed pieces which, written in the picturesque caligraphy of the period, and roughly bound by himself in sheepskin, occupied a couple of shelves in his library. He entered with animation and interest into the pleasures of farming and other agricultural pursuits, and by-and-bye as time went on and the former idol of his dreams descended from her fair estate of virtue and scandalised the world by her liaison with Lord Mountjoy, he appears to have gradually resigned the illusions of his first love, for he married a simple village girl, remarkable, so it was said, for her beauty, but more so for her skill in making butter and cheese. She could neither read nor write, however, and the traditions concerning the Sieur Amadis relate that he took a singular pleasure in teaching her these accomplishments, as well as in training her to sing and to accompany herself upon the lute in a very pretty manner. She made him an excellent wife, and gave him no less than six children, three boys and three girls, all of whom were brought up at home under the supervision of their father and mother, and encouraged to excel in country pursuits and to understand the art of profitable farming. It was in their days that Briar Farm entered upon its long career of prosperity, which still continued. The Sieur Amadis died in his seventieth year, and by his own wish, expressed in his "Last Will and Testament," was buried in a sequestered spot on his own lands, under a stone slab which he had himself fashioned, carving upon it his recumbent figure in the costume of a knight, a cross upon his breast and a broken sword at his side. His wife, though several years younger than himself, only lived a twelve-month after him and was interred by his side. Their resting-place was now walled off, planted thickly with flowers, and held sacred by every succeeding heir to the farm as the burial-place of the first Jocelyns. Steadily and in order, the families springing from the parent tree of the French knight Amadis had occupied Briar Farm in unbroken succession, and through three centuries the property had been kept intact, none of its possessions being dispersed and none of its land being sold. The house was practically in the same sound condition as when the Sieur Amadis fitted and furnished it for his own occupation,—there was the same pewter, the same solid furniture, the same fine tapestry, preserved by the careful mending of many hundreds of needles worked by hands long ago mingled with the dust of the grave, and, strange as it may seem to those who are only acquainted with the flimsy manufactures of to-day, the same stout hand-wrought linen, which, mended and replenished each year, lasted so long because never washed by modern methods, but always by hand in clear cold running water. There were presses full of this linen, deliriously scented with lavender, and there were also the spinning-wheels that had spun the flax and the hand-looms on which the threads had been woven. These were witnesses to the days when women, instead of gadding abroad, were happy to be at home—when the winter evenings seemed short and bright because as they sat spinning by the blazing log fire they were cheerful in their occupation, singing songs and telling stories and having so much to do that there was no time to indulge in the morbid analysis of life and the things of life which in our present shiftless day perplex and confuse idle and unhealthy brains.

And now after more than three centuries, the direct male line of Amadis de Jocelin had culminated in Hugo, commonly called Farmer Jocelyn, who, on account of some secret love disappointment, the details of which he had never told to anyone, had remained unmarried. Till the appearance on the scene of the child, Innocent, who was by the village folk accepted and believed to be the illegitimate offspring of this ill-starred love, it was tacitly understood that Robin Clifford, his nephew, and the only son of his twin sister, would be the heir to Briar Farm; but when it was seen how much the old man seemed to cling to Innocent, and to rely upon her ever tender care of him, the question arose as to whether there might not be an heiress after all, instead of an heir. And the rustic wiseacres gossiped, as is their wont, watching with no small degree of interest the turn of events which had lately taken place in the frank and open admiration and affection displayed by Robin for his illegitimate cousin, as it was thought she was, and as Farmer Jocelyn had tacitly allowed it to be understood. If the two young people married, everybody agreed it would be the right thing, and the best possible outlook for the continued prosperity of Briar Farm. For after all, it was the farm that had to be chiefly considered, so they opined,—the farm was an historic and valuable property as well as an excellent paying concern. The great point to be attained was that it should go on as it had always gone on from the days of the Sieur Amadis,—and that it should be kept in the possession of the same family. This at any rate was known to be the cherished wish of old Hugo Jocelyn, though he was not given to any very free expression of his feelings. He knew that his neighbours envied him, watched him and commented on his actions,—he knew also that the tale he had told them concerning Innocent had to a great extent whispered away his own good name and fastened a social slur upon the girl,—yet he could not, according to his own views, have seen any other way out of the difficulty. The human world is always wicked-tongued; and it is common knowledge that any man or woman introducing an "adopted" child into a family is at once accused, whether he or she be conscious of the accusation or not, of passing off his own bastard under the "adoption" pretext. Hugo Jocelyn was fairly certain that none of his neighbours would credit the romantic episode of the man on horseback arriving in a storm and leaving a nameless child on his hands. The story was quite true,—but truth is always precisely what people refuse to believe.

The night on which Innocent had learned her own history for the first time was a night of consummate beauty in the natural world. When all the gates and doors of the farm and its outbuildings had been bolted and barred for the night, the moon, almost full, rose in a cloudless heaven and shed pearl-white showers of radiance all over the newly-mown and clean-swept fields, outlining the points of the old house gables and touching with luminous silver the roses that clambered up the walls. One wide latticed window was open to the full inflowing of the scented air, and within its embrasure sat a lonely little figure in a loose white garment with hair tumbling carelessly over its shoulders and eyes that were wet with tears. The clanging chime of the old clock below stairs had struck eleven some ten minutes since, and after the echo of its bell had died away there had followed a heavy and intense silence. The window looked not upon the garden, but out upon the fields and a suggestive line of dark foliage edging them softly in the distance,—away down there, under a huge myriad-branched oak, slept the old knight

Sieur Amadis de Jocelin and his English rustic wife, the founders of the Briar Farm family. The little figure in the dark embrasure of the window clasped its white hands and turned its weeping eyes towards that ancient burial-place, and the moon-rays shone upon its fair face with a silvery glimmer, giving it an almost spectral pallor. "Why was I ever born?" sighed a trembling voice—"Oh, dear God! Why did you let it be?"

The vacant air, the vacant fields looked blankly irresponsive. They had no sympathy to give,—they never have. To great Mother Nature it is not important how or why a child is born, though she occasionally decides that it shall be of the greatest importance how and why the child shall live. What does it matter to the forces of creative life whether it is brought into the world "basely," as the phrase goes, or honourably? The child exists,—it is a human entity—a being full of potential good or evil,—and after a certain period of growth it stands alone, and its parents have less to do with it than they imagine. It makes its own circumstances and shapes its own career, and in many cases the less it is interfered with the better. But Innocent could not reason out her position in any cold-blooded or logical way. She was too young and too unhappy. Everything that she had taken pride in was swept from her at once. Only that very morning she had made one of her many pilgrimages down to the venerable oak beneath whose trailing branches the Sieur Amadis de Jocelin lay, covered by the broad stone slab on which he had carved his own likeness, and she had put a little knot of the "Glory" roses between his mailed hands which were folded over the cross on his breast, and she had said to the silent effigy:

"It is the last day of the haymaking, Sieur Amadis! You would be glad to see the big crop going in if you were here!"

She was accustomed to talk to the old stone knight in this fanciful way,—she had done so all her life ever since she could remember. She had taken an intense pride in thinking of him as her ancestor; she had been glad to trace her lineage back over three centuries to the love-lorn French noble who had come to England in the train of the Duc d'Anjou—and now—now she knew she had no connection at all with him,—that she was an unnamed, unbaptised nobody—an unclaimed waif of humanity whom no one wanted! No one in all the world—except Robin! He wanted her;—but perhaps when he knew her true history his love would grow cold. She wondered whether it would be so. If it were she would not mind very much. Indeed it would be best, for she felt she could never marry him.

MARIE CORELLI

"No, not if I loved him with all my heart!" she said, passionately—"Not without a name!—not till I have made a name for myself, if only that were possible!"

She left the window and walked restlessly about her room, a room that she loved very greatly because it had been the study of the Sieur Amadis. It was a wonderful room, oak-panelled from floor to ceiling, and there was no doubt about its history,—the Sieur Amadis himself had taken care of that. For on every panel he had carved with his own hand a verse, a prayer, or an aphorism, so that the walls were a kind of open notebook inscribed with his own personal memoranda. Over the wide chimney his coat-of-arms was painted, the colours having faded into tender hues like those of autumn leaves, and the motto underneath was "Mon coeur me soutien." Then followed the inscription:

"Amadis de Jocelin,
Knight of France,
Who here seekynge Forgetfulness did here fynde Peace."

Every night of her life since she could read Innocent had stood in front of these armorial bearings in her little white night-gown and had conned over these words. She had taken the memory and tradition of Amadis to her heart and soul. He was HER ancestor,—hers, she had always said;—she had almost learned her letters from the inscriptions he had carved, and through these she could read old English and a considerable amount of old French besides. When she was about twelve years old she and Robin Clifford, playing about together in this room, happened to knock against one panel that gave forth a hollow reverberant sound, and moved by curiosity they tried whether they could open it. After some abortive efforts Robin's fingers closed by chance on a hidden spring, which being thus pressed caused the panel to fly open, disclosing a narrow secret stair. Full of burning excitement the two children ran up it, and to their delight found themselves in a small square musty chamber in which were two enormous old dower-chests, locked. Their locks were no bar to the agility of Robin, who, fetching a hammer, forced the old hasps asunder and threw back the lids. The coffers were full of books and manuscripts written on vellum, a veritable sixteenth-century treasure-trove. They hastened to report the find to Farmer Jocelyn, who, though never greatly taken with books or anything concerning them, was sufficiently interested to go with the eager children and look at the discovery they had made. But as he could make nothing of either books or manuscripts himself, he gave over the whole collection to Innocent, saying that as they were found in her part of the house she might keep them. No one—not even Robin—knew how much she had loved and studied these old books, or how patiently she had spelt out the manuscripts; and no one could have guessed what a wide knowledge of literature she had gained or what fine taste she had developed from her silent communications with the parted spirit of the Sieur Amadis and his poetical remains. She had even arranged her room as she thought he might have liked it, in severe yet perfect taste. It was now her study as it had been his,—the heavy oak table had a great pewter inkstand upon it and a few loose sheets of paper with two or three quill pens ready to hand,—some quaint old vellum-bound volumes and a brown earthenware bowl full of "Glory" roses were set just where they could catch the morning sunshine through the lattice window. One side of the room was lined with loaded bookshelves, and at its furthest end a wide arch of roughly hewn oak disclosed a smaller apartment where she slept. Here there was a quaint little four-poster bedstead, hung with quite priceless Jacobean tapestry, and a still more rare and beautiful work of art—an early Italian mirror, full length and framed in silver, a curio worth many hundreds of pounds. In this mirror Innocent had surveyed herself with more or less disfavour since her infancy. It was a mirror that had always been there—a mirror in which the wife of the Sieur Amadis must have often gazed upon her own reflection, and in which, after her, all the wives and daughters of the succeeding Jocelyns had seen their charms presented to their own admiration. The two old dower-chests which had been found in the upper chamber were placed on either side of the mirror, and held all the simple home-made garments which were Innocent's only wear. A special joy of hers lay in the fact that she knew the management of the secret sliding panel, and that she could at her own pleasure slip up the mysterious stairway with a book and be thus removed from all the household in a solitude which to her was ideal. To-night as she wandered up and down her room like a little distraught ghost, all the happy and romantic associations of the home she had loved and cherished for so many years seemed cut down like a sheaf of fair blossoms by a careless reaper,—a sordid and miserable taint was on her life, and she shuddered with mingled fear and grief as she realised that she had not even the simple privilege of ordinary baptism. She was a nameless waif, dependent on the charity of Farmer Jocelyn. True, the

MARIE CORELLI

old man had grown to love her and she had loved him—ah!—let the many tender prayers offered up for him in this very room bear witness before the throne of God to her devotion to her "father" as she had thought him! And now—if what the doctors said was true—if he was soon to die—what would become of her? She wrung her little hands in unconscious agony.

"What shall I do?" she murmured, sobbingly—"I have no claim on him, or on anyone in the world! Dear God, what shall I do?"

Her restless walk up and down took her into her sleeping-chamber, and there she lit a candle and looked at herself in the old Italian mirror. A little woe-begone creature gazed sorrowfully back at her from its shining surface, with brimming eyes and quivering lips, and hair all tossed loosely away from a small sad face as pale as a watery moon, and she drew back from her own reflection with a gesture of repugnance.

"I am no use to anybody in any way," she said, despairingly—"I am not even good-looking. And Robin—poor foolish Robin!—called me 'lovely' this afternoon! He has no eyes!"

Then a sudden thought flew across her brain of Ned Landon. The tall powerful-looking brute loved her, she knew. Every look of his told her that his very soul pursued her with a reckless and relentless passion. She hated him,—she trembled even now as she pictured his dark face and burning eyes;—he had annoyed and worried her in a thousand ways—ways that were not sufficiently open in their offence to be openly complained of, though had Farmer Jocelyn's state of health given her less cause for anxiety she might have said something to him which would perhaps have opened his eyes to the situation. But not now,—not now could she appeal to anyone for protection from amorous insult. For who was she—what was she that she should resent it? She was nothing!—a mere stray child whose parents nobody knew,—without any lawful guardian to uphold her rights or assert her position. No wonder old Jocelyn had called her "wilding"—she was indeed a "wilding" or weed,—growing up unwanted in the garden of the world, destined to be pulled out of the soil where she had nourished and thrown contemptuously aside. A wretched sense of utter helplessness stole over her,—of incapacity, weakness and loneliness. She tried to think,—to see her way through the strange fog of untoward circumstance that had so suddenly enshrouded her. What would happen when Farmer Jocelyn died? For one thing she would have to quit Briar Farm. She could not stay in it when Robin Clifford was its master. He would marry, of course; he would be sure to marry; and there would be no place for her in his home. She would have to earn her bread; and the only way to do that would be to go out to service. She had a good store of useful domestic knowledge,—she could bake and brew, and wash and scour; she knew how to rear poultry and keep bees; she could spin and knit and embroider; indeed her list of household accomplishments would have startled any girl fresh out of a modern Government school, where things that are useful in life are frequently forgotten, and things that are not by any means necessary are taught as though they were imperative. One other accomplishment she had,—one that she hardly whispered to herself—she could write,—write what she herself called "nonsense." Scores of little poems and essays and stories were locked away in a small old bureau in a corner of the room,—confessions and expressions of pent-up feeling which, but for this outlet, would have troubled her brain and hindered her rest. They were mostly, as she frankly admitted to her own conscience, in the "style" of the Sieur Amadis, and were inspired by his poetic suggestions. She had no fond or exaggerated idea of their merit,—they were the result of solitary hours and long silences in which she had felt she must speak to someone,—exchange thoughts with someone,—or suffer an almost intolerable restraint. That "someone" was for her the long dead knight who had come to England in the train of the Duc d'Anjou. To him she spoke,—to him she told all her troubles—but to no one else did she ever breathe her thoughts, or disclose a line of what she had written. She had often wondered whether, if she sent these struggling literary efforts to a magazine or newspaper, they would be accepted and printed. But she never made the trial, for the reason that such newspaper literature as found its way into Briar Farm filled her with amazement, repulsion and disgust. There was nothing in any modern magazine that at all resembled the delicate, pointed and picturesque phraseology of the Sieur Amadis! Strange, coarse slang-words were used,—and the news of the day was slung together in loose ungrammatical sentences and chopped-up paragraphs of clumsy construction, lacking all pith and eloquence. So, repelled by the horror of twentieth-century "style," she had hidden her manuscripts deeper than ever in the old bureau, under little silk sachets of dried rose-leaves and lavender, as though they were love-letters or old lace. And when sometimes she shut herself up and read them over she felt like one of Hamlet's "guilty creatures sitting at a play." Her literary attempts seemed to reproach her for their inadequacy, and when she made some fresh addition to her store of written thoughts, her crimes seemed to herself doubled and weighted. She would often sit musing, with a little frown puckering her brow, wondering why she should be moved to write at all, yet wholly unable to resist the impulse.

To-night, however, she scarcely remembered these outbreaks of her dreaming fancy,—the sordid, hard, matter-of-fact side of life alone presented itself to her depressed imagination. She pictured herself going into service—as what? Kitchen-maid, probably,—she was not tall enough for a house-parlourmaid. House-parlourmaids were bound to be effective,—even dignified,—in height and appearance. She had seen one of these superior beings in church on Sundays—a slim, stately young woman with waved hair and a hat as fashionable as that worn by her mistress, the Squire's lady. With a deepening sense of humiliation, Innocent felt that her very limitation of inches was against her. Could she be a nursery-governess? Hardly; for though she liked good-tempered, well-behaved children, she could not even pretend to endure them when they were otherwise. Screaming, spiteful, quarrelsome children were to her less interesting than barking puppies or squealing pigs;—besides, she knew she could not be an efficient teacher of so much as one accomplishment. Music, for instance; what had she learned of music? She could play on an ancient spinet which was one of the chief treasures of the "best parlour" of Briar Farm, and she could sing old ballads very sweetly and plaintively,—but of "technique" and "style" and all the latter-day methods of musical acquirement and proficiency she was absolutely ignorant. Foreign languages were a dead letter to her—except old French. She could understand that; and Villon's famous verses, "Ou sont les neiges d'antan?" were as familiar to her as Herrick's "Come, my Corinna, let us go a-maying." But, on the whole, she was strangely and poorly equipped for the battle of life. Her knowledge of baking, brewing, and general housewifery would have stood her in good stead on some Colonial settlement,—but she had scarcely heard of these far-away refuges for the destitute, as she so seldom read the newspapers. Old Hugo Jocelyn looked upon the cheap daily press as "the curse of the country," and never willingly allowed a newspaper to come into the living-rooms of Briar Farm. They were relegated entirely to the kitchen and outhouses, where the farm labourers smoked over them and discussed them to their hearts' content, seldom venturing, however, to bring any item of so-called "news" to their master's consideration. If they ever chanced to do so, he would generally turn round upon them with a few cutting observations, such as,—

"How do you know it's true? Who gives the news? Where's the authority? And what do I care if some human brute has murdered his wife and blown out his own brains? Am I going to be any the better for reading such a tale? And if one Government is in or t'other out, what does it matter to me, or to any of you, so long as you can work and pay your way? The newspapers are always trying to persuade us to meddle in other folks's business;—I say, take care of your own affairs!—serve God and obey the laws of the country, and there won't be much going wrong with you! If you must read, read a decent book—something that will last—not a printed sheet full of advertisements that's fresh one day and torn up for waste paper the next!"

Under the sway of these prejudiced and arbitrary opinions, it was not possible for Innocent to have much knowledge of the world that lay outside Briar Farm. Sometimes she found Priscilla reading an old magazine or looking at a picture-paper, and she would borrow these and take them up to her own room surreptitiously for an hour or so, but she was always more or less pained and puzzled by their contents. It seemed to her that there were an extraordinary number of pictures of women with scarcely any clothes on, and she could not understand how they managed to be pictured at all in such scanty attire.

"Who are they?" she asked of Priscilla on one occasion—"And how is it that they are photographed like this? It must be so shameful for them!"

Priscilla explained as best she could that they were "dancers and the like."

"They lives by their legs, lovey!" she said soothingly—"It's only their legs that gits them their bread and butter, and I s'pose they're bound to show 'em off. Don't you worry 'ow they gits done! You'll never come across any of 'em!"

Innocent shut her sensitive mouth in a firm, proud line.

"I hope not!" she said.

And she felt as if she had almost wronged the sanctity of the little study which had formerly belonged to the Sieur Amadis by allowing such pictures to enter it. Of course she knew that dancers and actors, both male and female, existed,—a whole troupe of them came every year to the small theatre of the country town which, by breaking out into an eruption of new slate-roofed houses among the few remaining picturesque gables and tiles of an earlier period, boasted of its "advancement" some eight or ten miles away; but her "father," as she had thought him, had an insurmountable objection to what he termed "gadding abroad," and would not allow her to be seen even at the annual fair in the town, much less at the theatre. Moreover, it happened once that a girl in the village had run away with a strolling player and had gone on the stage,—an incident which had caused a great sensation in the tiny wood-encircled hamlet, and had brought all the old women of the place out to their doorsteps to croak and chatter, and prognosticate terrible things in the future for the eloping damsel. Innocent alone had ventured to defend her.

"If she loved the man she was right to go with him," she said.

"Oh, don't talk to me about love!" retorted Priscilla, shaking her head—"That's fancy rubbish! You know naught about it, dearie! On the stage indeed! Poor little hussy! She'll be on the street in a year or two, God help her!"

"What is that?" asked Innocent. "Is it to be a beggar?"

Priscilla made no reply beyond her usual sniff, which expressed volumes.

"If she has found someone who really cares for her, she will never want," Innocent went on, gently. "No man could be so cruel as to take away a girl from her home for his own pleasure and then leave her alone in the world. It would be impossible! You must not think such hard things, Priscilla!"

And, smiling, she had gone her way,—while Priscilla, shaking her head again, had looked after her, dimly wondering how long she would keep her faith in men.

On this still moonlight night, when the sadness of her soul seemed heavier than she could bear, her mind suddenly reverted to this episode. She thought of the girl who had run away; and remembered that no one in the village had ever seen or heard of her again, not even her patient hard-working parents to whom she had been a pride and joy.

"Now she had a real father and mother!" she mused, wistfully— "They loved her and would have done anything for her—yet she ran away from them with a stranger! I could never have done that! But I have no father and no mother—no one but Dad!—ah!—how I have loved Dad!—and yet I don't belong to him—and when he is dead—"

Here an overpowering sense of calamity swept over her, and dropping on her knees by the open window she laid her head on her folded arms and wept bitterly.

A voice called her in subdued accents once or twice, "Innocent! Innocent!"—but she did not hear.

Presently a rose flung through the window fell on her bent head. She started up, alarmed.

"Innocent!"

Timidly she leaned out over the window-sill, looking down into the dusky green of clambering foliage, and saw a familiar face smiling up at her. She uttered a soft cry.

"Robin!"

"Yes—it's Robin!" he replied. "Innocent, what's the matter? I heard you crying!"

"No—no!" she answered, whisperingly—"It's nothing! Oh, Robin!— why are you here at this time of night? Do go away!"

"Not I!" and Robin placed one foot firmly on the tough and gnarled branch of a giant wistaria that was trained thickly all over that side of the house—"I'm coming up!"

"Oh, Robin!" And straightway Innocent ran back into her room, there to throw on a dark cloak which enveloped her so completely that only her small fair head showed above its enshrouding folds,—then returning slowly she watched with mingled interest and trepidation the gradual ascent of her lover, as, like another Romeo, he ascended the natural ladder formed by the thick rope-like twisted stems of the ancient creeper, grown sturdy with years and capable of bearing a much greater weight than that of the light and agile young man, who, with a smile of amused triumph, at last brought himself on a level with the window-sill and seated himself on its projecting ledge.

"I won't come in," he said, mischievously—"though I might!—if I dared! But I mustn't break into my lady's bower without her sovereign permission! I say, Innocent, how pretty you look! Don't be frightened!— dear, dear little girl,—you know I wouldn't touch so much as a hair of your sweet little head! I'm not a brute—and though I'm longing to kiss you I promise I won't even try!"

She moved away from him into the deeper shadow, but a ray of the moon showed him her face, very pale, with a deep sadness upon it which was strange and new to him.

"Tell me what's wrong?" he asked. "I've been too wide-awake and restless to go to bed,—so I came out in the garden just to breathe the air and look up at your window—and I heard a sound of sobbing like that of a little child who was badly hurt—Innocent!"

For she had suddenly stretched out her hands to him in impulsive appeal.

MARIE CORELLI

"Oh yes—that's true!—I am badly hurt, Robin!" she said, in low trembling accents—"So badly hurt that I think I shall never get over it!"

Surprised, he took her hands in his own with a gentle reverence, though to be able to draw her nearer to him thus, set his heart beating quickly.

"What is it?" he questioned her, anxiously, as all unconsciously she leaned closer towards him and he saw her soft eyes, wet with tears, shining upon him like stars in the gloom. "Is it bad news of Uncle Hugo?"

"Bad news of him, but worse of me!" she answered, sighingly. "Oh, Robin, shall I tell you?"

He looked at her tenderly. The dark cloak about her had fallen a little aside, and showed a gleam of white neck emerging from snowy drapery underneath—it was, to his fancy, as though a white rose-petal had been suddenly and delicately unfurled. He longed to kiss that virginal whiteness, and trembled at the audacity of his own desire.

"Yes, dear, tell me!" he murmured, abstractedly, scarcely thinking of what he was saying, and only conscious of the thrill and ecstasy of love which seemed to him the one thing necessary for existence in earth or heaven.

And so, with her hands still warmly held in his, she told him all. In a sad voice, with lowered eyes and quivering lips, she related her plaintive little history, disclosing her unbaptised shame,—her unowned parentage,—her desperately forlorn and lonely condition. And Robin listened—amazed and perplexed.

"It seems to be all my fault," concluded Innocent, sorrowfully—"and yet it is not really so! Of course I ought never to have been born—but I couldn't help it, could I? And now it seems quite wrong for me to even live!—I am not wanted—and ever since I was twelve years old your Uncle has only kept me out of charity—"

But at this Robin started as though some one had struck him.

"Innocent!" he exclaimed—"Do not say such a thing!—do not think it! Uncle Hugo has LOVED you!—and you—you have loved him!"

She drew her hands away from his and covered her face.

"I know!—I know!" and her tears fell fast again—"But I am not his, and he is not mine!"

Robin was silent. The position was so unexpected and bewildering that he hardly knew what to say. But chiefly he felt that he must try and comfort this little weeping angel, who, so far as he was concerned, held his life subservient to her charm. He began talking softly and cheerily:

"Why should it matter so much?" he said. "If you do not know who you are—if none of us know—it may be more fortunate for you than you can imagine! We cannot tell! Your own father may claim you—your own mother—such things are quite possible! You may be like the princess of a fairy-tale—rich people may come and take you away from Briar Farm and from me—and you will be too grand to think of us any more, and I shall only be the poor farmer in your eyes—you will wonder how you could ever have spoken to me—"

"Robin!" Her hands dropped from her face and she looked at him in reproachful sadness. "Why do you say this? You know it could never be true!—never! If I had a father who cared for me, he would not have forgotten—and my mother, if she were a true mother, would have tried to find me long ago! No, Robin!—I ought to have died when I was a baby. No one wants me—I am a deserted child—'base-born,' as your Uncle Hugo says,—and of course he is right—but the sin of it is not mine!"

She had such a pitiful, fragile and fair appearance, standing half in shadow and half in the mystic radiance of the moon, that Robin Clifford's heart ached with love and longing for her.

"Sin!" he echoed—"Sin and you have never met each other! You are like your name, innocent of all evil! Oh, Innocent! If you could only care for me as I care for you!"

She gave a shivering sigh.

"Do you—can you care?—Now?" she asked.

"Of course! What is there in all this story that can change my love for you? That you are not my cousin?—that my uncle is not your own father? What does that matter to me? You are someone else's child, and if we never know who that someone is, why should we vex ourselves about it? You are you!—you are Innocent!—the sweetest, dearest little girl that ever lived, and I adore you! What difference does it make that you are not Uncle Hugo's daughter?"

"It makes a great difference to me," she answered, sadly—"I do not belong any more to the Sieur Amadis de Jocelin!"

Robin stared, amazed—then smiled.

"Why, Innocent!" he exclaimed—"Surely you're not worrying your mind over that old knight, dead and gone more than three hundred years ago! Dear little goose! How on earth does he come into this trouble of yours?"

"He comes in everywhere!" she replied, clasping and unclasping her hands nervously as she spoke. "You don't know, Robin!—you would never understand! But I have loved the Sieur Amadis ever since I can remember;—I have talked to him and studied with him!—I have read his old books, and all the poems he wrote—and he seemed to be my friend! I thought I was born of his kindred—and I was proud of it— and I felt it would be my duty to live at Briar Farm always because he would wish his line quite unbroken—and I think—perhaps—yes, I think I might have married you and been a good wife to you just for his sake!—and now it is all spoiled!—because though you will be the master of Briar Farm, you will not be the lineal descendant of the Sieur Amadis! No,—it is finished!—all finished with your Uncle Hugo!— and the doctors say he can only live a year!"

Her grief was so touching and pathetic that Robin could not find it in his heart to make a jest of the romance she had woven round the old French knight whose history had almost passed into a legend. After all, what she said was true—the line of the Jocelyn family had been kept intact through three centuries till now—and a direct heir had always inherited Briar Farm. He himself had taken a certain pride in thinking that Uncle Hugo's "love-child," as he had believed her to be, was at any rate, love-child or no, born of the Jocelyn blood—and that when he married her, as he hoped and fully purposed to do, he would discard his own name of Clifford and take that of Jocelyn, in order to keep the continuity of associations unbroken as far as possible. All these ideas were put to flight by Innocent's story, and, as the position became more evident to him, the smiling expression on his face changed to one of gravity.

"Dear Innocent," he said, at last—"Don't cry! It cuts me to the heart! I would give my very life to save you from a sorrow—you know I would! If you ever thought, as you say, that you could or would marry me for the sake of the Sieur Amadis, you might just as well marry me now, even though the Sieur Amadis is out of it. I would make you so happy! I would indeed! And no one need ever know that you are not really the lineal descendant of the Knight—"

She interrupted him.

"Priscilla knows," she said—"and, no matter how you look at it, I am 'base-born.' Your Uncle Hugo has let all the village folk think I am his illegitimate child—and that is 'base-born' of itself. Oh, it is cruel! Even you thought so, didn't you?"

Robin hesitated.

"I did not know, dear," he answered, gently—"I fancied—"

"Do not deny it, Robin!" she said, mournfully. "You did think so! Well, it's true enough, I suppose!—I am 'base-born'—but your uncle is not my father. He is a good, upright man—you can always be proud of him! He has not sinned,—though he has burdened me with the shame of sin! I think that is unfair,—but I must bear it somehow, and I will try to be brave. I'm glad I've told you all about it,—and you are very kind to have taken it so well—and to care for me still—but I shall never marry you, Robin!—never! I shall never bring my 'base-born' blood into the family of Jocelyn!"

His heart sank as he heard her—and involuntarily he stretched out his arms in appeal.

"Innocent!" he murmured—"Don't be hard upon me! Think a little longer before you leave me without any hope! It means so much to my life! Surely you cannot be cruel? Do you care for me less than you care for that old knight buried under his own effigy in the garden? Will you not think kindly of a living man?—a man who loves you beyond all things? Oh, Innocent!—be gentle, be merciful!"

She came to him and took his hands in her own.

"It is just because I am kind and gentle and merciful," she said, in her sweet, grave accents, "that I will not marry you, dear! I know I am right,—and you will think so too, in time. For the moment you imagine me to be much better and prettier than I am—and that there is no one like me!—poor Robin!—you are blind!—there are so many sweet and lovely girls, well born, with fathers and mothers to care for them—and you, with your good looks and kind ways, could marry any one of them—and you will, some day! Good-night, dear! You have stayed here a long time talking to me!—just suppose you were seen sitting on this window-ledge so late!—it is past midnight!—what would be said of me!"

"What could be said?" demanded Robin, defiantly. "I came up here of my own accord,—the blame would be mine!"

She shook her head sadly, smiling a little.

"Ah, Robin! The man is never blamed! It's always the woman's fault!"

"Where's your fault to-night?" he asked.

"Oh, most plain!" she answered. "When I saw you coming, I ought to have shut the window, drawn the curtains, and left you to clamber down the wall again as fast as you clambered up! But I wanted to tell you what had happened—and how everything had changed for me—and now—now that you know all—good-night!"

He looked at her longingly. If she would only show some little sign of tenderness!—if he might just kiss her hand, he thought! But she withdrew into the shadow, and he had no excuse for lingering.

"Good-night!" he said, softly. "Good-night, my angel Innocent! Good-night, my little love!"

She made no response and moved slowly backward into the room. But as he reluctantly left his point of vantage and began to descend, stepping lightly from branch to branch of the accommodating wistaria, he saw the shadowy outline of her figure once more as she stretched out a hand and closed the lattice window, drawing a curtain across it. With the drawing of that curtain the beauty of the summer night was over for him, and poising himself lightly on a tough stem which was twisted strongly enough to give him adequate support and which projected some four feet above the smooth grass below, he sprang down. Scarcely had he touched the ground when a man, leaping suddenly out of a thick clump of bushes near that side of the house, caught him in a savage grip and shook him with all the fury of an enraged mastiff shaking a rat. Taken thus unawares, and rendered almost breathless by the swiftness of the attack, Clifford struggled in the grasp of his assailant and fought with him desperately for a moment without any idea of his identity,—then as by a dexterous twist of body he managed to partially extricate himself, he looked up and saw the face of Ned Landon, livid and convulsed with passion.

"Landon!" he gasped—"What's the matter with you? Are you mad?"

"Yes!" answered Landon, hoarsely—"And enough to make me so! You devil! You've ruined the girl!"

With a rapid movement, unexpected by his antagonist, Clifford disengaged himself and stood free.

"You lie!" he said—"And you shall pay for it! Come away from the house and fight like a man! Come into the grass meadow yonder, where no one can see or hear us. Come!"

Landon paused, drawing his breath thickly, and looking like a snarling beast baulked of its prey.

"That's a trick!" he said, scornfully—"You'll run away!"

"Come!" repeated Clifford, vehemently—"You're more likely to run away than I am! Come!"

Landon glanced him over from head to foot—the moonbeams fell brightly on his athletic figure and handsome face—then turned on his heel.

"No, I won't!" he said, curtly—"I've done all I want to do for to-night. I've shaken you like the puppy you are! To-morrow we'll settle our differences."

For all answer Clifford sprang at him and struck him smartly across the face. In another moment both men were engaged in a fierce tussle, none the less deadly because so silent. A practised boxer and wrestler, Clifford grappled more and more closely with the bigger but clumsier man, dragging him steadily inch by inch further away from the house as they fought. More desperate, more determined became the struggle, till by two or three adroit manoeuvres Clifford got his opponent under him and bore him gradually to the ground, where, kneeling on his chest, he pinned him down.

"Let me go!" muttered Landon—"You're killing me!"

"Serve you right!" answered Clifford—"You scoundrel! My uncle shall know of this!"

"Tell him what you like!" retorted Landon, faintly—"I don't care! Get off my chest!—you're suffocating me!"

Clifford slightly relaxed the pressure of his hands and knees.

"Will you apologise?" he demanded.

"Apologise?—for what?"

"For your insolence to me and my cousin."

"Cousin be hanged!" snarled Landon—"She's no more your cousin than I am—she's only a nameless bastard! I heard her tell you so! And fine airs she gives herself on nothing!"

"You miserable spy!" and Clifford again held him down as in a vise—"Whatever you heard is none of your business! Will you apologise?"

"Oh, I'll apologise, if you like!—anything to get your weight off me!"—and Landon made an abortive effort to rise. "But I keep my own opinion all the same!"

Slowly Robin released him, and watched him as he picked himself up, with an air of mingled scorn and pity. Landon laughed forcedly, passing one hand across his forehead and staring in a dazed fashion at the shadows cast on the ground by the moon.

"Yes—I keep my own opinion!" he repeated, stupidly. "You've got the better of me just now—but you won't always, my pert Cock Robin! You won't always. Don't you think it! Briar Farm and I may part company—

but there's a bigger place than Briar Farm—there's the world!—that's a wide field and plenty of crops growing on it! And the men that sow those kind of crops and reap them and bring them in, are better farmers than you'll ever be! As for your girl!"—here his face darkened and he shook his fist towards the lattice window behind which slept the unconscious cause of the quarrel—"You can keep her! A nice 'Innocent' She is!—talking with a man in her bedroom after midnight!—why, I wouldn't have her as a gift—not now!"

Choking with rage, Clifford sprang towards him again—Landon stepped back.

"Hands off!" he said—"Don't touch me! I'm in a killing mood! I've a knife on me—you haven't. You're the master—I'm the man—and I'll play fair! I've my future to think of, and I don't want to start with a murder!"

With this, he turned his back and strode off, walking somewhat unsteadily like a blind man feeling his way.

Clifford stood for a moment, inert. The angry blood burned in his face,—his hands were involuntarily clenched,—he was impatient with himself for having, as he thought, let Landon off too easily. He saw at once the possibility of mischief brewing, and hastily considered how it could best be circumvented.

"The simplest way out of it is to make a clean breast of everything," he decided, at last. "Tomorrow I'll see Uncle Hugo early in the morning and tell him just what has happened."

Under the influence of this resolve, he gradually calmed down and re-entered the house. And the moonlight, widening and then waning over the smooth and peaceful meadows of Briar Farm, had it all its own way for the rest of the night, and as it filtered through the leafy branches of the elms and beeches which embowered the old tomb of the Sieur Amadis de Jocelin it touched with a pale glitter the stone hands of his sculptured effigy,—hands that were folded prayerfully above the motto,—"Mon coeur me soutien!"

V

As early as six o'clock the next morning Innocent was up and dressed, and, hastening down to the kitchen, busied herself, as was her usual daily custom, in assisting Priscilla with the housework and the preparation for breakfast. There was always plenty to do, and as she moved quickly to and fro, fulfilling the various duties she had taken upon herself and which she performed with unobtrusive care and exactitude, the melancholy forebodings of the past night partially cleared away from her mind. Yet there was a new expression on her face—one of sadness and seriousness unfamiliar to its almost child-like features, and it was not easy for her to smile in her ordinary bright way at the round of scolding which Priscilla administered every morning to the maids who swept and scrubbed and dusted and scoured the kitchen till no speck of dirt was anywhere visible, till the copper shone like mirrors, and the tables were nearly as smooth as polished silver or ivory. Going into the dairy where pans of new milk stood ready for skimming, and looking out for a moment through the lattice window, she saw old Hugo Jocelyn and Robin Clifford walking together across the garden, engaged in close and earnest conversation. A little sigh escaped her as she thought: "They are talking about me!"—then, on a sudden impulse, she went back into the kitchen where Priscilla was for the moment alone, the other servants having dispersed into various quarters of the house, and going straight up to her said, simply—

"Priscilla dear, why did you never tell me that I wasn't Dad's own daughter?"

Priscilla started violently, and her always red face turned redder,—then, with an effort to recover herself, she answered—

"Lord, lovey! How you frightened me! Why didn't I tell you? Well, in the first place, 'twasn't none of my business, and in the second, 'twouldn't have done any good if I had."

Innocent was silent, looking at her with a piteous intensity.

"And who is it that's told you now?" went on Priscilla, nervously—"some meddlin' old fool—"

Innocent raised her hand, warningly.

"Hush, Priscilla! Dad himself told me—"

"Well, he might just as well have kept a still tongue in his head," retorted Priscilla, sharply. "He's kept it for eighteen years, an' why he

MARIE CORELLI

should let it go wagging loose now, the Lord only knows! There's no making out the ways of men,—they first plays the wise and silent game like barn-door owls,—then all on a suddint-like they starts cawing gossip for all they're worth, like crows. And what's the good of tellin' ye, anyway?"

"No good, perhaps," answered Innocent, sorrowfully—"but it's right I should know. You see, I'm not a child any more—I'm eighteen—that's a woman—and a woman ought to know what she must expect more or less in her life—"

Priscilla leaned on the newly scrubbed kitchen table and looked across at the girl with a compassionate expression.

"What a woman must expect in life is good 'ard knocks and blows," she said—"unless she can get a man to look arter her what's not of the general kicking spirit. Take my advice, dearie! You marry Mr. Robin!— as good a boy as ever breathed—he'll be a kind fond 'usband to ye, and arter all that's what a woman thrives best on—kindness—an' you've 'ad it all your life up to now—"

"Priscilla," interrupted Innocent, decidedly—"I cannot marry Robin! You know I cannot! A poor nameless girl like me!—why, it would be a shame to him in after-years. Besides, I don't love him—and it's wicked to marry a man you don't love."

Priscilla smothered a sound between a grunt and a sigh.

"You talks a lot about love, child," she said—"but I'm thinkin' you don't know much about it. Them old books an' papers you found up in the secret room are full of nonsense, I'm pretty sure—an' if you believes that men are always sighin' an' dyin' for a woman, you're mistaken—yes, you are, lovey! They goes where they can be made most comfortable— an' it don't matter what sort o' woman gives the comfort so long as they gits it."

Innocent smiled, faintly.

"You don't know anything about it, Priscilla," she answered—"You were never married."

"Thank the Lord and His goodness, no!" said Priscilla, with an emphatic sniff—"I've never been troubled with the whimsies of a man, which is worse than all the megrims of a woman any day. I've looked arter Mr. Jocelyn in a way—but he's no sort of a man to worry about— he just goes reglar to the farmin'—an' that's all—a decent creature always, an' steady as his own oxen what pulls the plough. An' when he's gone, if go he must, I'll look arter you an' Mr. Robin, an' please God, I'll dance your babies on my old knees—" Here she broke off and turned her head away. Innocent ran to her, surprised.

"Why, Priscilla, you're crying!" she exclaimed—"Don't do that! Why should you cry?"

"Why indeed!" blubbered Priscilla—"Except that I'm a doiterin' fool! I can't abear the thoughts of you turnin' yer back on the good that God gives ye, an' floutin' Mr. Robin, who's the best sort o' man that ever could fall to the lot of a little tender maid like you—why, lovey, you don't know the wickedness o' this world, nor the ways of it—an' you talks about love as if it was somethin' wonderful an' far away, when here it is at yer very feet for the pickin' up! What's the good of all they books ye've bin readin' if they don't teach ye that the old knight you're fond of got so weary of the world that arter tryin' everythin' in turn he found nothin' better than to marry a plain, straight country wench and settle down in Briar Farm for all his days? Ain't that the lesson he's taught ye?"

She paused, looking hopefully at the girl through her tears—but Innocent's small fair face was pale and calm, though her eyes shone with a brilliancy as of suppressed excitement.

"No," she said—"He has not taught me that at all. He came here to 'seek forgetfulness'—so it is said in the words he carved on the panel in his study,—but we do not know that he ever really forgot. He only 'found peace,' and peace is not happiness—except for the very old."

"Peace is not happiness!" re-echoed Priscilla, staring—"That's a queer thing to say, lovey! What do you call being happy?"

"It is difficult to explain"—and a swift warm colour flew over the girl's cheeks, expressing some wave of hidden feeling—"Your idea of happiness and mine must be so different!" She smiled—"Dear, good Priscilla! You are so much more easily contented than I am!"

Priscilla looked at her with a great tenderness in her dim old grey eyes.

"See here, lovey!" she said—"You're just like a young bird on the edge of a nest ready to fly. You don't know the world nor the ways of it. Oh, my dear, it ain't all gold harvests and apples ripening rosy in the sun! You've lived all your life in the open country, and so you've always had the good God near you,—but there's places where the houses stand so close together that the sky can hardly make a patch of blue between the smoking chimneys—like London, for instance—ah!—that's where you'd find what the world's like, lovey!—where you feels so lonesome that you wonders why you ever were born—"

"I wonder that already," interrupted the girl, quickly. "Don't worry me, dear! I have so much to think about—my life seems so altered and strange—I hardly understand myself—and I don't know what I shall do with my future—but I cannot—I will not marry Robin!"

She turned away quickly then, to avoid further discussion.

A little later she went into the quaint oak-panelled room where the fateful disclosures of the past night had been revealed to her. Here breakfast was laid, and the latticed window was set wide open, admitting the sweet scent of stocks and mignonette with every breath of the morning air. She stood awhile looking out on the gay beauty of the garden, and her eyes unconsciously filled with tears.

"Dear home!" she murmured—"Home that is not mine—that never will be mine! How I have loved you!—how I shall always love you!"

A slow step behind her interrupted her meditations—and she looked around with a smile as timid as it was tender. There was her "Dad"—the same as ever,—yet now to her mind so far removed from her that she hesitated a moment before giving him her customary good-morning greeting. A pained contraction of his brow showed her that he felt this little difference, and she hastened to make instant amends.

"Dear Dad!" she said, softly,—and she put her soft arms about him and kissed his cheek—"How are you this morning? Did you sleep well?"

He took her arms from his shoulders, and held her for a moment, looking at her scrutinisingly from under his shaggy brows.

"I did not sleep at all," he answered her—"I lay broad awake, thinking of you. Thinking of you, my little innocent, fatherless, motherless lamb! And you, child!—you did not sleep so well as you should have done, talking with Robin half the night out of window!"

She coloured deeply. He smiled and pinched her crimsoning cheek, apparently well pleased.

"No harm, no harm!" he said—"Just two young doves cooing among the leaves at mating time! Robin has told me all about it. Now listen, child!—I'm away to-day to the market town—there's seed to buy and crops to sell—I'll take Ned Landon with me—" he paused, and an odd expression of sternness and resolve clouded his features—"Yes!—I'll take Ned Landon with me—he's shrewd enough when he's sober—and he's cunning enough, too, for that matter!—yes, I'll take him with me. We'll be off in the dog-cart as soon as breakfast's done. My time's getting short, but I'll attend to my own business as long as I can—I'll look after Briar Farm till I die—and I'll die in harness. There's plenty of work to do yet—plenty of work; and while I'm away you can settle up things—"

Here he broke off, and his eyes grew fixed in a sudden vacant stare. Innocent, frightened at his unnatural look, laid her hand caressingly on his arm.

"Yes, dear Dad!" she said, soothingly—"What is it you wish me to do?"

The stare faded from his eyeballs, and his face softened.

"Settle up things," he repeated, slowly, and with emphasis—"Settle up things with Robin. No more beating about the bush! You talked to him long enough out of window last night, and mind you!—somebody was listening! That means mischief! *I* don't blame you, poor wilding!—but remember, SOMEBODY WAS LISTENING! Now think of that and of your good name, child!—settle with Robin and we'll have the banns put up next Sunday."

While he thus spoke the warm rose of her cheeks faded to an extreme pallor,—her very lips grew white and set. Her hurrying thoughts clamoured for utterance,—she could have expressed in passionate terms her own bitter sense of wrong and unmerited shame, but pity for the old man's worn and haggard look of pain held her silent. She saw and felt that he was not strong enough to bear any argument or opposition in his present mood, so she made no sort of reply, not even by a look or a smile. Quietly she went to the breakfast table, and busied herself in preparing his morning meal. He followed her and sat heavily down in his usual chair, watching her furtively as she poured out the tea.

"Such little white hands, aren't they?" he said, coaxingly, touching her small fingers when she gave him his cup—"Eh, wilding? The prettiest lily flowers I ever saw! And one of them will look all the prettier for a gold wedding-ring upon it! Ay, ay! We'll have the banns put up on Sunday."

Still she did not speak; once she turned away her head to hide the tears that involuntarily rose to her eyes. Old Hugo, meanwhile, began to eat his breakfast with the nervous haste of a man who takes his food more out of custom than necessity. Presently he became irritated at her continued silence.

"You heard what I said, didn't you?" he demanded—"And you understood?"

She looked full at him with sorrowful, earnest eyes.

"Yes, Dad. I heard. And I understood."

MARIE CORELLI

He nodded and smiled, and appeared to take it for granted that she had received an order which it was her bounden duty to obey. The sun shone brilliantly in upon the beautiful old room, and through the open window came a pleasant murmuring of bees among the mignonette, and the whistle of a thrush in an elm-tree sounded with clear and cheerful persistence. Hugo Jocelyn looked at the fair view of the flowering garden and drew his breath hard in a quick sigh.

"It's a fine day," he said—"and it's a fine world! Ay, that it is! I'm not sure there's a better anywhere! And it's a bit difficult to think of going down for ever into the dark and the cold, away from the sunshine and the sky—but it's got to be done!"—here he clenched his fist and brought it down on the table with a defiant blow—"It's got to be done, and I've got to do it! But not yet—not quite yet!—I've plenty of time and chance to stop mischief!"

He rose, and drawing himself up to his full height looked for the moment strong and resolute. Taking one or two slow turns up and down the room, he suddenly stopped in front of Innocent.

"We shall be away all day," he said—"I and Ned Landon. Do you hear?"

There was something not quite natural in the tone of his voice, and she glanced up at him in a little surprise.

"Well, what are you wondering at?" he demanded, a trifle testily—"You need not open your eyes at me like that!"

She smiled faintly.

"Did I open my eyes, Dad?" she said—"I did not mean to be curious. I only thought—"

"You only thought what?" he asked, with sudden heat—"What did you think?"

"Oh, just about your being away all day in the town—you will be so tired—"

"Tired? Not I!—not when there's work to do and business to settle!" He rubbed his hands together with a kind of energetic expectancy. "Work to do and business to settle!" he repeated—"Yes, little girl! There's not much time before me, and I must leave everything in good order for you and Robin."

She dropped her head, and the expression of her face was hidden from him.

"You and Robin!" he said, again. "Ay, ay! Briar Farm will be in the best of care when I'm dead, and it'll thrive well with young love and hope to keep it going!" He came up to her and took one of her little hands in his own. "There, there!" he went on, patting it gently—"We'll think no more of trouble and folly and mistakes in life; it'll be all joy and peace for you, child! Take God's good blessing of an honest lad's love and be happy with it! And when I come home to-night,"—he paused and appeared to think for a moment—"yes!—when I come home, let me hear that it's all clear and straight between you—and we'll have the banns put up on Sunday!"

She said not a word in answer. Her hand slid passively from his hold,—and she never looked up. He hesitated for a moment—then walked towards the door.

"You'll have all the day to yourself with Robin," he added, glancing back at her—"There'll be no spies about the place, and no one listening, as there was last night!"

She sprang up from her chair, moved at last by an impulse of indignation.

"Who was it?" she asked—"I said nothing wrong—and I do not care!—but who was it?"

A curious strained look came into old Hugo's eyes as he answered— "Ned Landon."

She looked amazed,—then scared.

"Ned Landon?"

"Ay! Ned Landon. He hasn't the sweetest of tempers and he isn't always sober. He's a bit in the way sometimes,—ay, ay!—a bit in the way! But he's a good farm hand for all that,—and his word stands for something! I'd rather he hadn't heard you and Robin talking last night—but what's done is done, and it's a mischief easy mended—"

"Why, what mischief can there be?" the girl demanded, her colour coming and going quickly—"And why should he have listened? It's a mean trick to spy upon others!"

He smiled indulgently.

"Of course it's a mean trick, child!—but there's a good many men— and women too—who are just made up of mean tricks and nothing more. They spend their lives in spying upon their neighbours and interfering in everybody's business. You'd soon find that out, my girl, if you lived in the big world that lies outside Briar Farm! Ay!—and that reminds me—" Here he came from the door back into the room again, and going to a quaint old upright oaken press that stood in one corner, he unlocked it and took out a roll of bank-notes. These he counted

MARIE CORELLI

carefully over to himself, and folding them up put them away in his breast pocket. "Now I'm ready!" he said—"Ready for all I've got to do! Good-bye, my wilding!" He approached her, and lifting her small face between his hands, kissed it tenderly. "Bless thee! No child of my own could be dearer than thou art! All I want now is to leave thee in safe and gentle keeping when I die. Think of this and be good to Robin!"

She trembled under his caress, and her heart was full of speechless sorrow. She longed to yield to his wishes,—she knew that if she did so she would give him happiness and greater resignation to the death which confronted him; and she also knew that if she could make up her mind to marry Robin Clifford she would have the best and the tenderest of husbands. And Briar Farm,—the beloved old home—would be hers!—her very own! Her children would inherit it and play about the fair and fruitful fields as she had done—they, too, could be taught to love the memory of the old knight, the Sieur Amadis de Jocelin—ah!—but surely it was the spirit of the Sieur Amadis himself that held her back and prevented her from doing his name and memory grievous wrong! She was not of his blood or race—she was nameless and illegitimate,— no good could come of her engrafting herself like a weed upon a branch of the old noble stock—the farm would cease to prosper.

So she thought and so she felt, in her dreamy imaginative way, and though she allowed old Hugo to leave her without vexing him by any decided opposition to his plans, she was more than ever firmly resolved to abide by her own interior sense of what was right and fitting. She heard the wheels of the dog-cart grating the gravel outside the garden gate, and an affectionate impulse moved her to go and see her "Dad" off. As she made her appearance under the rose-covered porch of the farm-house door, she perceived Landon, who at once pulled off his cap with an elaborate and exaggerated show of respect.

"Good-morning, Miss Jocelyn!"

He emphasized the surname with a touch of malice. She coloured, but replied "Good-morning" with a sweet composure. He eyed her askance, but had no opportunity for more words, as old Hugo just then clambered up into the dog-cart, and took the reins of the rather skittish young mare which was harnessed to it.

"Come on, Landon!" he shouted, impatiently—"No time for farewells!" Then, as Landon jumped up beside him, he smiled, seeing the soft, wistful face of the girl watching him from beneath a canopy of roses.

"Take care of the house while I'm gone!" he called to her;—"You'll find Robin in the orchard."

He laid the lightest flick of the whip on the mare's ears, and she trotted rapidly away.

Innocent stood a moment gazing after the retreating vehicle till it disappeared,—then she went slowly into the house. Robin was in the orchard, was he? Well!—he had plenty of work to do there, and she would not disturb him. She turned away from the sunshine and flowers and made her way upstairs to her own room. How quiet and reposeful it looked! It was a beloved shrine, full of sweet memories and dreams,— there would never be any room like it in the world for her, she well knew. Listlessly she sat down at the table, and turned over the pages of an old book she had been reading, but her eyes were not upon it.

"I wonder!" she said, half aloud—then paused.

The thought in her mind was too daring for utterance. She was picturing the possibility of going quietly away from Briar Farm all alone, and trying to make a name and career for herself through the one natural gift she fancied she might possess, a gift which nowadays is considered almost as common as it was once admired and rare. To be a poet and romancist,—a weaver of wonderful thoughts into musical language,— this seemed to her the highest of all attainment; the proudest emperor of the most powerful nation on earth was, to her mind, far less than Shakespeare,—and inferior to the simplest French lyrist of old time that ever wrote a "chanson d'amour." But the doubt in her mind was whether she, personally, had any thoughts worth expressing,—any ideas which the world might be the happier or the better for knowing and sharing? She drew a long breath,—the warm colour flushed her cheeks and then faded, leaving her very pale,—the whole outlook of her life was so barren of hope or promise that she dared not indulge in any dream of brighter days. On the face of it, there seemed no possible chance of leaving Briar Farm without some outside assistance—she had no money, and no means of obtaining any. Then,—even supposing she could get to London, she knew no one there,—she had no friends. Sighing wearily, she opened a deep drawer in the table at which she sat, and took out a manuscript—every page of it so neatly written as to be almost like copper-plate—and set herself to reading it steadily. There were enough written sheets to make a good-sized printed volume—and she read on for more than an hour. When she lifted her eyes at last they were eager and luminous.

"Perhaps," she half whispered—"perhaps there is something in it after all!—something just a little new and out of the ordinary—but—how shall I ever know!"

Putting the manuscript by with a lingering care, she went to the window and looked out. The peaceful scene was dear and familiar—and she already felt a premonition of the pain she would have to endure in leaving so sweet and safe a home. Her thoughts gradually recurred to the old trouble—Robin, and Robin's love for her,—Robin, who, if she married him, would spend his life gladly in the effort to make her happy,—where in the wide world would she find a better, truer-hearted man? And yet—a curious reluctance had held her back from him, even when she had believed herself to be the actual daughter of Hugo Jocelyn,—and now—now, when she knew she was nothing but a stray foundling, deserted by her own parents and left to the care of strangers, she considered it would be nothing short of shame and disgrace to him, were she to become his wife.

"I can always be his friend," she said to herself—"And if I once make him understand clearly how much better it is for us to be like brother and sister, he will see things in the right way. And when he marries I am sure to be fond of his wife and children—and—and—it will be ever so much happier for us all! I'll go and talk to him now."

She ran downstairs and out across the garden, and presently made a sudden appearance in the orchard—a little vision of white among the russet-coloured trees with their burden of reddening apples. Robin was there alone—he was busied in putting up a sturdy prop under one of the longer branches of a tree heavily laden with fruit. He saw her and smiled—but went on with his work.

"Are you very busy?" she asked, approaching him almost timidly.

"Just now, yes! In a moment, no! We shall lose this big bough in the next high wind if I don't take care."

She waited—watching the strength and dexterity of his hands and arms, and the movements of his light muscular figure. In a little while he had finished all he had to do—and turning to her said, laughingly—

"Now I am at your service! You look very serious!—grave as a little judge, and quite reproachful! What have I done?—or what has anybody done that you should almost frown at me on this bright sun-shiny morning?"

She smiled in response to his gay, questioning look.

"I'm sorry I have such a depressing aspect," she said—"I don't feel very happy, and I suppose my face shows it."

He was silent for a minute or two, watching her with a grave tenderness in his eyes.

By and by he spoke, gently—

"Come and stroll about a bit with me through the orchard,—it will cheer you to see the apples hanging in such rosy clusters among the grey-green leaves. Nothing prettier in all the world, I think!—and they are just ripening enough to be fragrant. Come, dear! Let us talk our troubles out!"

She walked by his side, mutely—and they moved slowly together under the warm scented boughs, through which the sunlight fell in broad streams of gold, making the interlacing shadows darker by contrast. There was a painful throbbing in her throat,—the tension of struggling tears which strove for an outlet,—but gradually the sweet influences of the air and sunshine did good work in calming her nerves, and she was quite composed when Robin spoke again.

"You see, dear, I know quite well what is worrying you. I'm worried myself—and I'd better tell you all about it. Last night—" he paused.

She looked up at him, quickly.

"Last night?—Well?"

"Well—Ned Landon was in hiding in the bushes under your window—and he must have been there all the time we were talking together. How or why he came there I cannot imagine. But he heard a good deal—and when you shut your window he was waiting for me. Directly I got down he pounced on me like a tramp-thief, and—now there!—don't look so frightened!—he said something that I couldn't stand, so we had a jolly good fight. He got the worst of it, I can tell you! He's stiff and unfit to work to-day—that's why Uncle Hugo has taken him to the town. I told the whole story to Uncle Hugo this morning—and he says I did quite right. But it's a bore to have to go on 'bossing' Landon—he bears me a grudge, of course—and I foresee it will be difficult to manage him. He can hardly be dismissed—the other hands would want to know why; no man has ever been dismissed from Briar Farm without good and fully explained reasons. This time no reasons could be given, because your name might come in, and I won't have that—"

"Oh, Robin, it's all my fault!" she exclaimed. "If you would only let me go away! Help me—do help me to go away!"

He stared at her, amazed.

"Go away!" he echoed—"You! Why, Innocent, how can you think of such a thing! You are the very life and soul of the place—how can you talk of going away! No, no!—not unless"—here he drew nearer and looked at her steadily and tenderly in the eyes—"not unless you will let me take you away!—just for a little while!—as a bridegroom takes a bride—on a honeymoon of love and sunshine and roses—"

He stopped, deterred by her look of sadness.

"Dear Robin," she said, very gently—"would you marry a girl who cannot love you as a wife should love? Won't you understand that if I could and did love you I should be happier than I am?—though now, even if I loved you with all my heart, I would not marry you. How could I? I am nothing—I have no name—no family—and can you think that I would bring shame upon you? No, Robin!—never! I know what your Uncle Hugo wishes—and oh!—if I could only make him happy I would do it!—but I cannot—it would be wrong of me—and you would regret it—"

"I should never regret it," he interrupted her, quickly. "If you would be my wife, Innocent, I should be the proudest, gladdest man alive! Ah, dear!—do put all your fancies aside and try to realise what good you would be doing to the old man if he felt quite certain that you would be the little mistress of the old farm he loves so much—I will not speak of myself—you do not care for me!—but for him—"

She looked up at him with a sudden light in her eyes.

"Could we not pretend?" she asked.

"What do you mean?"

"Why, pretend that we're engaged—just to satisfy him. Couldn't you make things easy for me that way?"

"I don't quite understand," he said, with a puzzled air—"How would it make things easy?"

"Why, don't you see?" and she spoke with hurried eagerness—"When he comes home to-night let him think it's all right—and then—then I'll run away by myself—and it will be my fault—"

"Innocent! What are you talking about?"—and he flushed with vexation. "My dear girl, if you dislike me so much that you would rather run away than marry me, I won't say another word about it. I'll manage to smooth things over with my uncle for the present—just to prevent his fretting himself—and you shall not be worried—"

"You must not be worried either," she said. "You will not understand, and you do not think!—but just suppose it possible that, after all, my own parents did remember me at last and came to look after me—and that they were perhaps dreadful wicked people—"

Robin smiled.

"The man who brought you here was a gentleman," he said—"Uncle Hugo told me so this morning, and said he was the finest-looking man he had ever seen."

Innocent was silent a moment.

"You think he was a 'gentleman' to desert his own child?" she asked.

Robin hesitated.

"Dear, you don't know the world," he said—"There may have been all sorts of dangers and difficulties—anyhow, *I* don't bear him any grudge! He gave you to Briar Farm!"

She sighed, and made no response. Inadvertently they had walked beyond the orchard and were now on the very edge of the little thicket where the tomb of the Sieur Amadis de Jocelin glimmered pallidly through the shadow of the leaves. Innocent quickened her steps.

"Come!" she said.

He followed her reluctantly. Almost he hated the old stone knight which served her as a subject for so many fancies and feelings, and when she beckoned him to the spot where she stood beside the recumbent effigy, he showed a certain irritation of manner which did not escape her.

"You are cross with him!" she said, reproachfully. "You must not be so. He is the founder of your family—"

"And the finish of it, I suppose!" he answered, abruptly. "He stands between us two, Innocent!—a cold stone creature with no heart—and you prefer him to me! Oh, the folly of it all! How can you be so cruel!"

She looked at him wistfully—almost her resolution failed her. He saw her momentary hesitation and came close up to her.

"You do not know what love is!" he said, catching her hand in his own—"Innocent, you do not know! If you did!—if I might teach you—!"

She drew her hand away very quickly and decidedly.

"Love does not want teaching," she said—"it comes—when it will, and where it will! It has not come to me, and you cannot force it, Robin! If I were your wife—your wife without any wife's love for you—I should grow to hate Briar Farm!—yes, I should!—I should pine and die in the very place where I have been so happy!—and I should feel that HE"— here she pointed to the sculptured Sieur Amadis—"would almost rise from this tomb and curse me!"

She spoke with sudden, almost dramatic vehemence, and he gazed at her in mute amazement. Her eyes flashed, and her face was lit up by a glow of inspiration and resolve.

"You take me just for the ordinary sort of girl," she went on—"A girl to caress and fondle and marry and make the mother of your children,—now for that you might choose among the girls about here, any of whom would be glad to have you for a husband. But, Robin, do you think I am really fit for that sort of life always?—can't you believe in anything else but marriage for a woman?"

As she thus spoke, she unconsciously created a new impression on his mind,—a veil seemed to be suddenly lifted, and he saw her as he had never before seen her—a creature removed, isolated and unattainable through the force of some inceptive intellectual quality which he had not previously suspected. He answered her, very gently—

"Dear, I cannot believe in anything else but love for a woman," he said—"She was created and intended for love, and without love she must surely be unhappy."

"Love!—ah yes!" she responded, quickly—"But marriage is not love!"

His brows contracted.

"You must not speak in that way, Innocent," he said, seriously—"It is wrong—people would misunderstand you—"

Her eyes lightened, and she smiled.

"Yes!—I'm sure 'people' would!" she answered—"But 'people' don't matter—to ME. It is truth that matters,—truth,—and love!"

He looked at her, perplexed.

"Why should you think marriage is not love?" he asked—"It is the one thing all lovers wish for—to be married and to live together always—"

"Oh, they wish for it, yes, poor things!" she said, with a little uplifting of her brows—"And when their wishes are gratified, they often wish they had not wished!" She laughed. "Robin, this talk of ours is making me feel quite merry! I am amused!"

"I am not!" he replied, irritably—"You are much too young a girl to think these things—"

She nodded, gravely.

"I know! And I ought to get married while young, before I learn too many of 'these things,'" she said—"Isn't that so? Don't frown, Robin! Look at the Sieur Amadis! How peacefully he sleeps! He knew all about love!"

"Of course he did!" retorted Robin—"He was a perfectly sensible man—he married and had six children."

Innocent nodded again, and a little smile made two fascinating dimples in her soft cheeks.

"Yes! But he said good-bye to love first!"

He looked at her in visible annoyance.

"How can you tell?—what do you know about it?" he demanded.

She lifted her eyes to the glimpses of blue sky that showed in deep clear purity between the over-arching boughs,—a shaft of sunlight struck on her fair hair and illumined its pale brown to gold, so that for a moment she looked like the picture of a young rapt saint, lost in heavenly musing.

Then a smile, wonderfully sweet and provocative, parted her lips, and she beckoned him to a grassy slope beneath one of the oldest trees, where little tufts of wild thyme grew thickly, filling the air with fragrance.

"Come and sit beside me here," she said—"We have the day to ourselves—Dad said so,—and we can talk as long as we like. You ask me what I know?—not much indeed! But I'll tell you what the Sieur Amadis has told me!—if you care to hear it!"

"I'm not sure that I do," he answered, dubiously.

She laughed.

"Oh, Robin!—how ungrateful you are! You ought to be so pleased! If you really loved me as much as you say, the mere sound of my voice ought to fill you with ecstasy! Yes, really! Come, be good!" And she sat down on the grass, glancing up at him invitingly. He flung himself beside her, and she extended her little white hand to him with a pretty condescension.

"There!—you may hold it!" she said, as he eagerly clasped it—"Yes, you may! Now, if the Sieur Amadis had been allowed to hold the hand of the lady he loved he would have gone mad with joy!"

"Much good he'd have done by going mad!" growled Robin, with an affectation of ill-humour—"I'd rather be sane,—sane and normal."

She bent her smiling eyes upon him.

"Would you? Poor Robin! Well, you will be—when you settle down—"

"Settle down?" he echoed—"How? What do you mean?"

"Why, when you settle down with a wife, and—shall we say six children?" she queried, merrily—"Yes, I think it must be six! Like the

Sieur Amadis! And when you forget that you ever sat with me under the trees, holding my hand—so!"

The lovely, half-laughing compassion of her look nearly upset his self-possession. He drew closer to her side.

"Innocent!" he exclaimed, passionately—"if you would only listen to reason—"

She shook her head.

"I never could!" she declared, with an odd little air of penitent self-depreciation—"People who ask you to listen to reason are always so desperately dull! Even Priscilla!—when she asks you to 'listen to reason,' she's in the worst of tempers! Besides, Robin, dear, we shall have plenty of chances to 'listen to reason' when we grow older,—we're both young just now, and a little folly won't hurt us. Have patience with me!—I want to tell you some quite unreasonable—quite abnormal things about love! May I?"

"Yes—if I may too!" he answered, kissing the hand he held, with lingering tenderness.

The soft colour flew over her cheeks,—she smiled.

"Poor Robin!" she said—"You deserve to be happy and you will be!—not with me, but with some one much better, and ever so much prettier! I can see you as the master of Briar Farm—such a sweet home for you and your wife, and all your little children running about in the fields among the buttercups and daisies—a pretty sight, Robin!—I shall think of it often when—when I am far away!"

He was about to utter a protest,—she stopped him by a gesture.

"Hush!" she said.

And there was a moment's silence.

VI

"When I think about love," she began presently, in a soft dreamy voice—"I'm quite sure that very few people ever really feel it or understand it. It must be the rarest thing in all the world! This poor Sieur Amadis, asleep so long in his grave, was a true lover,—and I will tell you how I know he had said good-bye to love when he married. All those books we found in the old dower-chest, that day when we were playing about together as children, belonged to him—some are his own compositions, written by his own hand,—the others, as you know, are printed books which must have been difficult to get in his day, and are now, I suppose, quite out of date and almost unknown. I have read them all!—my head is a little library full of odd volumes! But there is one—a manuscript book—which I never tire of reading,—it is a sort of journal in which the Sieur Amadis wrote down many of his own feelings—sometimes in prose, sometimes in verse—and by following them carefully and piecing them together, it is quite easy to find out his sadness and secret—how he loved once and never loved again—"

"You can't tell that," interrupted Robin—"men often say they can only love once—but they love ever so many times—"

She smiled—and her eyes showed him what a stupid blunder he had made.

"Do they?" she queried, softly—"I am so glad, Robin! For you will find it easy then to love somebody else instead of me!"

He flushed, vexedly.

"I didn't mean that—" he began.

"No? I think you did!—but of course if you had thought twice you wouldn't have said it! It was uttered quite truly and naturally, Robin!—don't regret it! Only I want to explain to you that the Sieur Amadis was not like that—he loved just once—and the lady he loved must have been a very beautiful woman who had plenty of admirers and did not care for him at all. All he writes proves that. He is always grieved to the heart about it. Still he loved her—and he seems glad to have loved her, though it was all no use. And he kept a little chronicle of his dreams and fancies—all that he felt and thought about,—it is beautifully and tenderly written all in quaint old French. I had some trouble to make it out—but I did at last—every word—and when he made up his mind to marry, he finished the little book and never wrote another word in it. Shall I tell you what were the last lines he wrote?"

"It wouldn't be any use," he answered, kissing again the hand he held—"I don't understand French. I've never even tried to learn it."

She laughed.

"I know you haven't! But you've missed a great deal, Robin!—you have really! When I made up my mind to find out all the Sieur Amadis had written, I got Priscilla to buy me a French dictionary and grammar and some other French lesson-books besides—then I spelt all the words carefully and looked them all up in the dictionary, and learned the pronunciation from one of the lesson-books—and by-and-bye it got quite easy. For two years at least it was dreadfully hard work—but now—well!—I think I could almost speak French if I had the chance!"

"I'm sure you could!" said Robin, looking at her, admiringly—"You're a clever little girl and could do anything you wanted to."

Her brows contracted a little,—the easy lightness of his compliment had that air of masculine indifference which is more provoking to an intelligent woman than downright contradiction. The smile lingered in her eyes, however,—a smile of mingled amusement and compassion.

"Well, I wanted to understand the writing of the Sieur Amadis," she went on, quietly—"and when I could understand them I translated them. So I can tell you the last words he wrote in his journal—just before he married,—in fact on the very eve of his marriage-day—" She paused abruptly, and looked for a moment at the worn and battered tomb of the old knight, green with moss and made picturesque by a trailing branch of wild roses that had thrown itself across the stone effigy in an attempt to reach some of its neighbours on the opposite side. Robin followed her gaze with his own, and for a moment was more than usually impressed by the calm, almost stern dignity of the recumbent figure.

"Go on," he said—"What were the words?"

"These"—and Innocent spoke them in a hushed voice, with sweet reverence and feeling—"'Tonight I pull down and put away for ever the golden banner of my life's ideal. It has been held aloft too long in the sunshine of a dream, and the lily broidered on its web is but a withered flower. My life is no longer of use to myself, but as a man and faithful knight I will make it serve another's pleasure and another's good. And because this good and simple girl doth truly love me, though her love was none of my seeking, I will give her her heart's desire, though mine own heart's desire shall never be accomplished,—I will make her my wife, and will be to her a true and loyal husband, so that she may receive from me all she craves of happiness and peace. For though I fain would die rather than wed, I know that life is not given to a man to live selfishly, nor is God satisfied to have it wasted by any one who hath sworn to be His knight and servant. Therefore even so let it be!—I give all my unvalued existence to her who doth consider it valuable, and with all my soul I pray that I may make so gentle and trustful a creature happy. But to Love—oh, to Love a long farewell!—farewell my dreams!—farewell ambition!—farewell the glory of the vision unattainable!—farewell bright splendour of an earthly Paradise!—for now I enter that prison which shall hold me fast till death release me! Close, doors!—fasten, locks!—be patient in thy silent solitude, my Soul!'"

Innocent's voice faltered here—then she said—"That is the end. He signed it 'Amadis.'"

Robin was very quiet for a minute or two.

"It's pretty—very pretty and touching—and all that sort of thing," he said at last—"but it's like some old sonnet or mediaeval bit of romance. No one would go on like that nowadays."

Innocent lifted her eyebrows, quizzically.

"Go on like what?"

He moved impatiently.

"Oh, about being patient in solitude with one's soul, and saying farewell to love." He gave a short laugh. "Innocent dear, I wish you would see the world as it really is!—not through the old-style spectacles of the Sieur Amadis! In his day people were altogether different from what they are now."

"I'm sure they were!" she answered, quietly—"But love is the same to-day as it was then."

He considered a moment, then smiled.

"No, dear, I'm not sure that it is," he said. "Those knights and poets and curious people of that kind lived in a sort of imaginary ecstasy— they exaggerated their emotions and lived at the top-height of their fancies. We in our time are much more sane and level-headed. And it's much better for us in the long run."

She made no reply. Only very gently she withdrew her hand from his.

"I'm not a knight of old," he went on, turning his handsome, sun-browned face towards her,—"but I'm sure I love you as much as ever the Sieur Amadis could have loved his unknown lady. So much indeed do I love you that I couldn't write about it to save my life!—though I did write verses at Oxford once—very bad ones!" He laughed. "But I can do one thing the Sieur Amadis didn't do—I can keep faithful to my Vision of the glory unattainable'—and if I don't marry you I'll marry no-body—so there!"

She looked at him curiously and wistfully.

"You will not be so foolish," she said—"You will not put me into the position of the Sieur Amadis, who married some one who loved him, merely out of pity!"

He sprang up from the grass beside her.

"No, no! I won't do that, Innocent! I'm not a coward! If you can't love me, you shall not marry me, just because you are sorry for me! That would be intolerable! I wouldn't have you for a wife at all under such circumstances. I shall be perfectly happy as a bachelor—perhaps happier than if I married."

"And what about Briar Farm?" she asked.

"Briar Farm can get on as best it may!" he replied, cheerily—"I'll work on it as long as I live and hand it down to some one worthy of it, never fear! So there, Innocent!—be happy, and don't worry yourself! Keep to your old knight and your strange fancies about him—you may be right in your ideas of love, or you may be wrong; but the great point with me is that you should be happy—and if you cannot be happy in my way, why you must just be happy in your own!"

She looked at him with a new interest, as he stood upright, facing her in all the vigour and beauty of his young manhood. A little smile crept round the corners of her mouth.

"You are really a very handsome boy!" she said—"Quite a picture in your way! Some girl will be very proud of you!"

He gave a movement of impatience.

"I must go back to the orchard," he said—"There's plenty to do. And after all, work's the finest thing in the world—quite as fine as love—perhaps finer!"

A faint sense of compunction moved her at his words—she was conscious of a lurking admiration for his cool, strong, healthy attitude towards life and the things of life. And yet she was resentful that he should be capable of considering anything in the world "finer" than love. Work? What work? Pruning trees and gathering apples? Surely there were greater ambitions than these? She watched him thoughtfully under the fringe of her long eyelashes, as he moved off.

"Going to the orchard?" she asked.

"Yes."

She smiled a little.

"That's right!"

He glanced back at her. Had she known how bravely he restrained himself she might have made as much a hero of him as of the knight Amadis. For he was wounded to the heart—his brightest hopes were frustrated, and at the very instant he walked away from her he would have given his life to have held her for a moment in his arms,—to have kissed her lips, and whispered to her the pretty, caressing love-nonsense which to warm and tender hearts is the sweetest language in the world. And with all his restrained passion he was irritated with what, from a man's point of view, he considered folly on her part,—he felt that she despised his love and himself for no other reason than a mere romantic idea, bred of loneliness and too much reading of a literature alien to the customs and manners of the immediate time, and an uncomfortable premonition of fear for her future troubled his mind.

"Poor little girl!" he thought—"She does not know the world!—and when she Does come to know it—ah, my poor Innocent!—I would rather she never knew!"

Meanwhile she, left to herself, was not without a certain feeling of regret. She was not sure of her own mind—and she had no control over her own fancies. Every now and then a wave of conviction came over her that after all tender-hearted old Priscilla might be right—that it would be best to marry Robin and help him to hold and keep Briar Farm as it had ever been kept and held since the days of the Sieur Amadis. Perhaps, had she never heard the story of her actual condition, as told her by Farmer Jocelyn on the previous night, she might have consented to what seemed so easy and pleasant a lot in life; but now it seemed to her more than impossible. She no longer had any link with the far-away ancestor who had served her so long as a sort of ideal—she was a mere foundling without any name save the unbaptised appellation of Innocent. And she regarded herself as a sort of castaway.

She went into the house soon after Robin had left her, and busied herself with sorting the linen and looking over what had to be mended. "For when I go," she said to herself, "they must find everything in order." She dined alone with Priscilla—Robin sent word that he was too busy to come in. She was a little piqued at this—and almost cross when he sent the same message at tea-time,—but she was proud in her way and would not go out to see if she could persuade him to leave his work for half-an-hour. The sun was slowly declining when she suddenly put down her sewing, struck by a thought which had not previously occurred to her—and ran fleetly across the garden to the orchard, where she found Robin lying on his back under the trees with closed eyes. He opened them, hearing the light movement of her feet and the soft flutter of her gown—but he did not rise. She stopped—looking at him.

"Were you asleep?"

He stretched his arms above his head, lazily.

"I believe I was!" he answered, smiling.

"And you wouldn't come in to tea!" This with a touch of annoyance.

"Oh yes, I would, if I had wanted tea," he replied—"but I didn't want it."

"Nor my company, I suppose," she added, with a little shrug of her shoulders. His eyes flashed mischievously.

"Oh, I daresay that had something to do with it!" he agreed.

A curious vexation fretted her. She wished he would not look so handsome—and—yes!—so indifferent. An impression of loneliness and desertion came over her—he, Robin, was not the same to her now—so she fancied—no doubt he had been thinking hard all the day while doing his work, and at last had come to the conclusion that it was wisest after all to let her go and cease to care for her as he had done. A little throbbing pulse struggled in her throat—a threat of rising tears,—but she conquered the emotion and spoke in a voice which, though it trembled, was sweet and gentle.

"Robin," she said—"don't you think—wouldn't it be better—perhaps—"

He looked up at her wonderingly—she seemed nervous or frightened.

"What is it?" he asked—"Anything you want me to do?"

"Yes"—and her eyes drooped—"but I hardly like to say it. You see, Dad made up his mind this morning that we were to settle things together—and he'll be angry and disappointed—"

Robin half-raised himself on one arm.

"He'll be angry and disappointed if we don't settle it, you mean," he said—"and we certainly haven't settled it. Well?"

A faint colour flushed her face.

"Couldn't we pretend it's all right for the moment?" she suggested—"Just to give him a little peace of mind?"

He looked at her steadily.

"You mean, couldn't we deceive him?"

"Yes!—for his good! He has deceived ME all my life,—I suppose for MY good—though it has turned out badly—"

"Has it? Why?"

"It has left me nameless," she answered,—"and friendless."

A sudden rush of tears blinded her eyes—she put her hands over them. He sprang up and, taking hold of her slender wrists, tried to draw those hands down. He succeeded at last, and looked wistfully into her face, quivering with restrained grief.

"Dear, I will do what you like!" he said. "Tell me—what is your wish?"

She waited a moment, till she had controlled herself a little.

"I thought"—she said, then—"that we might tell Dad just for to-night that we are engaged—it would make him happy—and perhaps in a week or two we might get up a quarrel together and break it off—"

Robin smiled.

"Dear little girl!—I'm afraid the plan wouldn't work! He wants the banns put up on Sunday—and this is Wednesday."

Her brows knitted perplexedly.

"Something can be managed before then," she said. "Robin, I cannot bear to disappoint him! He's old—and he's so ill too!—it wouldn't hurt us for one night to say we are engaged!"

"All right!"—and Robin threw back his head and laughed joyously—"I don't mind! The sensation of even imagining I'm engaged to you is quite agreeable! For one evening, at least, I can assume a sort of proprietorship over you! Innocent! I—I—"

He looked so mirthful and mischievous that she smiled, though the teardrops still sparkled on her lashes.

"Well? What are you thinking of now?" she asked.

"I think—I really think—under the circumstances I ought to kiss you!" he said—"Don't you feel it would be right and proper? Even on the stage the hero and heroine ACT a kiss when they're engaged!"

She met his laughing glance with quiet steadfastness.

"I cannot act a kiss," she said—"You can, if you like! I don't mind."

"You don't mind?"

"No."

He looked from right to left—the apple-boughs, loaded with rosy fruit, were intertwined above them like a canopy—the sinking sun made mellow gold of all the air, and touched the girl's small figure with a delicate luminance—his heart beat, and for a second his senses swam in a giddy whirl of longing and ecstasy—then he suddenly pulled himself together.

"Dear Innocent, I wouldn't kiss you for the world!" he said, gently—"It would be taking a mean advantage of you. I only spoke in fun. There!—dry your pretty eyes!—you sweet, strange, romantic little soul! You shall have it all your own way!"

She drew a long breath of evident relief.

"Then you'll tell your uncle—"

"Anything you like!" he answered. "By-the-bye, oughtn't he to be home by this time?"

"He may have been kept by some business," she said—"He won't be long now. You'll say we're engaged?"

"Yes."

"And perhaps"—went on Innocent—"you might ask him not to have the banns put up yet as we don't want it known quite so soon—"

"I'll do all I can," he replied, cheerily—"all I can to keep him quiet, and to make you happy! There! I can't say more!"

Her eyes shone upon him with a grateful tenderness.

"You are very good, Robin!"

He laughed.

"Good! Not I! But I can't bear to see you fret—if I had my way you should never know a moment's trouble that I could keep from you. But I know I'm not a patch on your old stone knight who wrote such a lot about his 'ideal'—and yet went and married a country wench and had six children. Don't frown, dear! Nothing will make me say he was romantic! Not a bit of it! He wrote a lot of romantic things, of course—but he didn't mean half of them!—I'm sure he didn't!"

She coloured indignantly.

"You say that because you know nothing about it," she said—"You have not read his writings."

"No—and I'm not sure that I want to," he answered, gaily. "Dear Innocent, you must remember that I was at Oxford—my dear old father and mother scraped and screwed every penny they could get to send me there—and I believe I acquitted myself pretty well—but one of the best things I learned was the general uselessness and vanity of the fellows that called themselves 'literary.' They chiefly went in for disparaging and despising everyone who did not agree with them and think just as they did. Mulish prigs, most of them!" and Robin laughed his gay and buoyant laugh once more—"They didn't know that I was all the time comparing them with the honest type of farmer—the man who lives an outdoor life with God's air blowing upon him, and the soil turned freshly beneath him!—I love books, too, in my way, but I love Nature better."

"And do not poets help you to understand Nature?" asked Innocent.

"The best of them do—such as Shakespeare and Keats and Tennyson,—but they were of the past. The modern men make you almost despise Nature,—more's the pity! They are always studying THEMSELVES, and analysing THEMSELVES, and pitying THEMSELVES—now *I* always say, the less of one's self the better, in order to understand other people."

Innocent's eyes regarded him with quiet admiration.

"Yes, you are a thoroughly good boy," she said—"I have told you so often. But—I'm not sure that I should always get on with anyone as good as you are!"

She turned away then, and moved towards the house. As she went, she suddenly stopped and clapped her hands, calling:

"Cupid! Cupid! Cu-Coo-pid!"

A flash of white wings glimmered in the sunset-light, and her pet dove flew to her, circling round and round till it dropped on her outstretched arm. She caught it to her bosom, kissing its soft head tenderly, and murmuring playful words to it. Robin watched her, as with this favourite bird-playmate she disappeared across the garden and into the house. Then he gave a gesture half of despair, half of resignation—and left the orchard.

The sun sank, and the evening shadows began to steal slowly in their long darkening lines over the quiet fields, and yet Farmer Jocelyn had not yet returned. The women of the household grew anxious—Priscilla went to the door many times, looking up the tortuous by-road for the first glimpse of the expected returning vehicle—and Innocent stood in the garden near the porch, as watchful as a sentinel and as silent. At last the sound of trotting hoofs was heard in the far distance, and Robin, suddenly making his appearance from the stable-yard where he too had been waiting, called cheerily,—

"Uncle at last! Here he comes!"

Another few minutes and the mare's head turned the corner—then the whole dog-cart came into view with Farmer Jocelyn driving it. But he was quite alone.

Robin and Innocent exchanged surprised glances, but had no time to make any comment as old Hugo just then drove up and, throwing the reins to his nephew, alighted.

"Aren't you very late, Dad?" said Innocent then, going to meet him—
"I was beginning to be quite anxious!"

"Were you? Poor little one! I'm all right! I had business—I was
kept longer than I expected—" Here he turned quickly to Robin—
"Unharness, boy!—unharness!—and come in to supper!"

"Where's Landon?" asked Robin.

"Landon? Oh, I've left him in the town."

He pulled off his driving-gloves, and unbuttoned his overcoat—
then strode into the house. Innocent followed him—she was puzzled
by his look and manner, and her heart beat with a vague sense of fear.
There was something about the old man that was new and strange
to her. She could not define it, but it filled her mind with a curious
and inexplicable uneasiness. Priscilla, who was setting the dishes on
the table in the room where the cloth was laid for supper, had the
same uncomfortable impression when she saw him enter. His face was
unusually pale and drawn, and the slight stoop of age in his otherwise
upright figure seemed more pronounced than usual. He drew up his
chair to the table and sat down,—then ruffling his fine white hair over
his brow with one hand, looked round him with an evidently forced
smile.

"Anxious about me, were you, child?" he said, as Innocent took her
place beside him. "Well, well! you need not have given me a thought!
I—I was all right—all right! I made a bit of a bargain in the town—but
the prices were high—and Landon—"

He broke off suddenly and stared in front of him with strange fixed
eyeballs.

Innocent and Priscilla looked at one another in alarm. There was
a moment's tense stillness,—then Innocent said in rather a trembling
voice—

"Yes, Dad? You were saying something about Landon—"

The stony glare faded from his eyes and he looked at her with a more
natural expression.

"Landon? Did I speak of him? Oh yes!—Landon met with some
fellows he knew and decided to spend the evening with them—he
asked me for a night off—and I gave it to him. Yes—I—I gave it to
him."

Just then Robin entered.

"Hullo!" he exclaimed, gaily—"At supper? Don't begin without me!
I say, Uncle, is Landon coming back to-night?"

Jocelyn turned upon him sharply.

"No!" he answered, in so fierce a tone that Robin stood amazed—"Why do you all keep on asking me about Landon? He loves drink more than life, and he's having all he wants to-night. I've let him off work to-morrow."

Robin was silent for a moment out of sheer surprise.

"Oh well, that's all right, if you don't mind," he said, at last—"We're pretty busy—but I daresay we can manage without him."

"I should think so!" and Hugo gave a short laugh of scorn—"Briar Farm would have come to a pretty pass if it could not get on without a man like Landon!"

There was another silent pause.

Priscilla gave an anxious side-glance at Innocent's troubled face, and decided to relieve the tension by useful commonplace talk.

"Well, Landon or no Landon, supper's ready!" she said, briskly—"and it's been waiting an hour at least. Say grace, Mister Jocelyn, and I'll carve!"

Jocelyn looked at her bewilderedly.

"Say grace?" he queried—"what for?"

Priscilla laughed loudly to cover the surprise she felt.

"What for? Lor, Mister Jocelyn, if you don't know I'm sure I don't! For the beef and potatoes, I suppose, an' all the stuff we eats—'for what we are going to receive—'"

"Ah, yes! I remember—'May the Lord make us truly thankful!'" responded Jocelyn, closing his eyes for a second and then opening them again—"And I'll tell you what, Priscilla!—there's a deal more to be thankful for to-night than beef and potatoes!—a great deal more!"

VII

The supper was a very silent meal. Old Hugo was evidently not inclined to converse,—he ate his food quickly, almost ravenously, without seeming to be conscious that he was eating. Robin Clifford glanced at him now and again watchfully, and with some anxiety,— an uncomfortable idea that there was something wrong somewhere worried him,—moreover he was troubled by the latent feeling that presently his uncle would be sure to ask if all was "settled" between himself and Innocent. Strangely enough, however, the old man made no allusion to the subject. He seemed to have forgotten it, though it had been the chief matter on which he had laid so much stress that morning. Each minute Innocent expected him to turn upon her with the dreaded question—to which she would have had to reply untruly, according to the plan made between herself and Robin. But to her great surprise and relief he said nothing that conveyed the least hint of the wish he had so long cherished. He was irritable and drowsy,—now and again his head fell a little forward on his chest and his eyes closed as though in utter weariness. Seeing this, the practical Priscilla made haste to get the supper finished and cleared away.

"You be off to bed, Mister Jocelyn," she said,—"The sooner the better, for you look as tired as a lame dog that 'as limped 'ome twenty miles. You ain't fit to be racketing about markets an' drivin' bargains."

"Who says I'm not?" he interrupted, sitting bolt upright and glaring fiercely at her—"I tell you I am! I can do business as well as any man— and drive a bargain-ah! I should think so indeed!—a hard-and-fast bargain!—not easy to get out of, I can tell you!—not easy to get out of! And it has cost me a pretty penny, too!"

Robin Clifford glanced at him enquiringly.

"How's that?" he asked—"You generally make rather than spend!"

Jocelyn gave a sudden loud laugh.

"So I do, boy, so I do! But sometimes one has to spend to make! I've done both to-day—I've made and I've spent. And what I've spent is better than keeping it—and what I've made—ay!—what I've made— well!—it's a bargain, and no one can say it isn't a fair one!"

He got up from the supper table and pushed away his chair.

"I'll go," he said—"Priscilla's right—I'm dog-tired and bed's the best place for me." He passed his hand over his forehead. "There's a sort of buzzing in my brain like the noise of a cart-wheel—I want rest." As he spoke Innocent came softly beside him and took his arm caressingly. He looked down upon her with a smile. "Yes, wilding, I want rest! We'll have a long talk out tomorrow—you and I and Robin. Bless thee, child! Good-night!"

He kissed her tenderly and held out one hand to Clifford, who cordially grasped it.

"Good boy!" he said-"Be up early, for there's much to do—and Landon won't be home till late—no—not till late! Get on with the field work— for if the clouds mean anything we shall have rain." He paused a moment and seemed to reflect, then repeated slowly—"Yes, lad! We shall have rain!—and wind, and storm! Be ready!—the fine weather's breaking!"

With that he went, walking slowly, and they heard him stumble once or twice as he went up the broad oak staircase to his bedroom. Priscilla put her head on one side, like a meditative crow, and listened. Then she heaved a sigh, smoothed down her apron and rolled up her eyes.

"Well, if Mister Jocelyn worn't as sober a man as any judge an' jury," she observed—"I should say 'e'd bin drinkin'! But that ain't it. Mr. Robin, there's somethin' gone wrong with 'im—an' I don't like it."

"Nor I," said Innocent, in a trembling voice, suggestive of tears. "Oh, Robin, you surely noticed how strange he looked! I'm so afraid! I feel as if something dreadful was going to happen—"

"Nonsense!" and Robin assumed an air of indifference which he was far from feeling—"Uncle Hugo is tired—I think he has been put out— you know he's quick-tempered and easily irritated—he may have had some annoyance in the town—"

"Ah! And where's Landon?" put in Priscilla, with a dark nod—"That do beat me! Why ever the master should 'ave let a man like that go on the loose for a night an' a day is more than I can make out! It's sort of tempting Providence—that it is!"

Clifford flushed and turned aside. His fight with Landon was fresh in his mind—and he began to wonder whether he had done rightly in telling his uncle how it came about. But meeting Innocent's anxious eyes, which mutely asked him for comfort, he answered—

"Oh, well, there's nothing very much in that, Priscilla! I daresay Landon wanted a holiday—he doesn't ask for one often, and he's kept fairly sober lately. Hadn't we better be off to bed? Things will straighten out with the morning."

MARIE CORELLI

"Do you really think so?" Innocent sighed as she put the question.

"Of course I think so!" answered Robin, cheerily. "We're all tired, and can't look on the bright side! Sound sleep is the best cure for the blues! Good-night, Innocent!"

"Good-night!" she said, gently.

"Good-night, Priscilla!"

"Good-night, Mr. Robin. God bless ye!"

He smiled, nodded kindly to them both, and left the room.

"There's a man for ye!" murmured Priscilla, admiringly, as he disappeared—"A tower of strength for a 'usband, which the Lord knows is rare! Lovey, you'll never do better!"

But Innocent seemed not to hear. Her face was very pale, and her eyes had a strained wistful expression.

"Dad looks very ill," she said, slowly—"Priscilla, surely you noticed—"

"Now, child, don't you worry—'tain't no use"—and Priscilla lit two bedroom candles, giving Innocent one—"You just go up to bed and think of nothing till the morning. Mister Jocelyn is dead beat and put out about something—precious 'ungry too, for he ate his food as though he hadn't 'ad any all day. You couldn't expect him to be pleasant if he was wore out."

Innocent said nothing more. She gave a parting glance round the room to assure herself that everything was tidy, windows bolted and all safe for the night, and for a fleeting moment the impression came over her that she would never see it look quite the same again. A faint cold tremor ran through her delicate little body—she felt lonely and afraid. Silently she followed Priscilla up the beautiful Tudor staircase to the first landing, where, moved by a tender, clinging impulse, she kissed her.

"Good-night, you dear, kind Priscilla!" she said—"You've always been good to me!"

"Bless you, my lovey!" answered Priscilla, with emotion—"Go and sleep with the angels, like the little angel you are yourself! And mind you think twice, and more than twice, before you say 'No' to Mr. Robin!"

With a deprecatory shake of her head, and a faint smile, Innocent turned away, and passed through the curious tortuous little corridor that led to her own room. Once safely inside that quiet sanctum where the Sieur Amadis of long ago had "found peace," she set her candle down on the oak table and remained standing by it for some moments, lost in thought. The pale glimmer of the single light was scarcely sufficient to disperse the shadows around her, but the lattice window was open and admitted a shaft of moonlight which shed a pearly radiance on her little figure, clothed in its simple white gown. Had any artist seen her thus, alone and absorbed in sorrowful musing, he might have taken her as a model of Psyche after her god had flown. She was weary and anxious—life had suddenly assumed for her a tragic aspect. Old Jocelyn's manner had puzzled her—he was unlike himself, and she instinctively felt that he had some secret trouble on his mind. What could it be? she wondered. Not about herself and Robin—for were he as keen on "putting up the banns" as he had been in the morning he would not have allowed the matter to rest. He would have asked straight questions, and he would have expected plain answers,—and they would, in accordance with the secret understanding they had made with each other, have deceived him. Now there was no deception necessary—he seemed to have forgotten—at least for the present—his own dearest desire. With a sigh, half of pain, half of relief, she seated herself at the table, and opening its one deep drawer with a little key which she always wore round her neck, she began to turn over her beloved pile of manuscript, and this occupied her for several minutes. Presently she looked up, her eyes growing brilliant with thought, and a smile on her lips.

"I really think it might do!" she said, aloud—"I should not be afraid to try! Who knows what might happen? I can but fail—or succeed. If I fail, I shall have had my lesson—if I succeed—"

She leaned her head on her two hands, ruffling up her pretty hair into soft golden-brown rings.

"If I succeed!—ah!—if I do! Then I'll pay back everything I owe to Dad and Briar Farm!—oh, no! I can never pay back my debt to Briar Farm!—that would be impossible! Why, the very fields and trees and flowers and birds have made me happy!—happier than I shall ever be after I have said good-bye to them all!—good-bye even to the Sieur Amadis!"

Quick tears sprang to her eyes—and the tapering light of the candle looked blurred and dim.

"Yes, after all," she went on, still talking to the air, "it's better and braver to try to do something in the world, rather than throw myself upon Robin, and be cowardly enough to take him for a husband when I don't love him. Just for comfort and shelter and Briar Farm! It would be shameful. And I could not marry a man unless I loved him quite desperately!—I could not! I'm not sure that I like the idea of marriage at all,—it fastens a man and woman together for life, and the time

MARIE CORELLI

might come when they would grow tired of each other. How cruel and wicked it would be to force them to endure each other's company when they perhaps wished the width of the world between them! No—I don't think I should care to be married—certainly not to Robin."

She put her manuscript by, and shut and locked the drawer containing it. Then she went to the open lattice window and looked out—and thought of the previous night, when Robin had swung himself up on the sill to talk to her, and they had been all unaware that Ned Landon was listening down below. A flush of anger heated her cheeks as she recalled this and all that Robin had told her of the unprepared attack Landon had made upon him and the ensuing fight between them. But now? Was it not very strange that Landon should apparently be in such high favour with Hugo Jocelyn that he had actually been allowed to stay in the market-town and enjoy a holiday, which for him only meant a bout of drunkenness? She could not understand it, and her perplexity increased the more she thought of it. Leaning far out over the window-sill, she gazed long and lovingly across the quiet stretches of meadowland, shining white in the showered splendour of the moon— the tall trees—the infinite and harmonious peace of the whole scene,— then, shutting the lattice, she pulled the curtains across it, and taking her lit candle, went to her secluded inner sleeping-chamber, where, in the small, quaintly carved four-poster bed, furnished with ancient tapestry and lavendered linen, and covered up under a quilt embroidered three centuries back by the useful fingers of the wife of Sieur Amadis de Jocelin, she soon fell into a sound and dreamless slumber.

The hours moved on, bearing with them different destinies to millions of different human lives, and the tall old clock in the great hall of Briar Farm told them off with a sonorous chime and clangour worthy of Westminster itself. It was a quiet night; there was not a breath of wind to whistle through crack or key-hole, or swing open an unbolted door,—and Hero, the huge mastiff that always slept "on guard" just within the hall entrance, had surely no cause to sit up suddenly on his great haunches and listen with uplifted ears to sounds which were to any other creature inaudible. Yet listen he did—sharply and intently. Raising his massive head he snuffed the air—then suddenly began to tremble as with cold, and gave vent to a long, low, dismal moan. It was a weird noise—worse than positive howling, and the dog himself seemed distressfully conscious that he was expressing something strange and unnatural. Two or three times he repeated this eerie muffled cry—then, lying down again, he put his nose between his great paws, and, with a deep shivering sigh, appeared to resign himself to the inevitable. There followed several moments of tense silence. Then came a sudden dull thud overhead, as of a heavy load falling or being thrown down, and a curious inexplicable murmur like smothered choking or groaning. Instantly the great dog sprang erect and raced up the staircase like a mad creature, barking furiously. The house was aroused—doors were flung open—Priscilla rushed from her room half dressed—and Innocent ran along the corridor in her little white nightgown, her feet bare, and her hair falling dishevelled over her shoulders.

"What is it?" she cried piteously—"Oh, do tell me! What is it?"

Robin Clifford, hearing the dog's persistent barking, had hastily donned coat and trousers and now appeared on the scene.

"Hero, Hero!" he called—"Quiet, Hero!"

But Hero had bounded to his master Jocelyn's door and was pounding against it with all the force of his big muscular body, apparently seeking to push or break it open. Robin laid one hand on the animal's collar and pulled him back—then tried the door himself—it was locked.

"Uncle Hugo!"

There was no answer.

He turned to one of the frightened servants who were standing near. His face was very pale.

"Fetch me a hammer," he said—"Something—anything that will force the lock. Innocent!"—and with deep tenderness he took her little cold hands in his own—"I wish you would go away!"

"Why?" and she looked at him with eyes full of terror. "Oh no, no! Let me be with you—let me call him!"—and she knelt outside the closed door—"Dad! Dear Dad! I want to speak to you! Mayn't I come in? I'm so frightened—do let me come in. Dad!"

But the silence remained unbroken.

"Priscilla!"—and Robin beckoned to her—"keep Innocent beside you—I'm afraid—"

Priscilla nodded, turning her head aside a moment to wipe away the tears that were gathering in her eyes,—then she put an arm round Innocent's waist.

"Don't kneel there, lovey," she whispered—"It's no good and you're in the way when they open the door. Come with me!—there's a dear!"—and she drew the trembling little figure tenderly into her arms. "There!—that'll be a bit warmer!" and she signed to one of the farm maids near her to fetch a cloak which she carefully wrapped round the girl's shoulders. Just then the hammer was brought with other tools, and Robin, to save any needless clamour, took a chisel and inserted it in such a manner as should most easily force the catch of the door—but the lock was an ancient and a strong one, and would not yield for some time. At last, with an extra powerful and dexterous movement of his hand, it suddenly gave way—and he saw what he would have given worlds that Innocent should not have seen—old Hugo lying face forward on the floor, motionless. There was a rush and a wild cry—

"Dad! Dad!"

She was beside him in a moment, trying with all her slight strength to lift his head and turn his face.

"Help me—oh, help me!" she wailed. "He has fainted—we must lift him—get some one to lift him on the bed. It is only a faint—he will recover—get some brandy and send for the doctor. Don't lose time!—for Heaven's sake be quick! Robin, make them hurry!"

Robin had already whispered his orders,—and two of the farm lads, roused from sleep and hastily summoned, were ready to do what he told them. With awed, hushed movements they lifted the heavy fallen body of their master between them and laid it gently down on the bed. As the helpless head dropped back on the pillow they saw that all was over,—the pinched ashen grey of the features and the fast glazing eyes told their own fatal story—there was no hope. But Innocent held the cold hand of the dead man to her warm young bosom, endeavouring to take from it its cureless chill.

"He will be better soon," she said,—"Priscilla, bring me that brandy—just a little will revive him, I'm sure. Why do you stand there crying? You surely don't think he's dead?—No, no, that isn't possible! It isn't possible, is it, Robin? He'll come to himself in a few minutes—a fainting fit may last quite a long time. I wish he had not locked his door—we could have been with him sooner."

So she spoke, tremblingly nursing the dead hand in her bosom. No one present had the heart to contradict her—and Priscilla, with the tears running down her face, brought the brandy she asked for and held it while she tenderly moistened the lips of the corpse and tried to force a few drops between the clenched teeth—in vain. This futile attempt frightened her, and she looked at Robin Clifford with a wild air.

"I cannot make him swallow it," she said—"Can you, Robin? He looks so grey and cold!—but his lips are quite warm."

Robin, restraining the emotion that half choked him and threatened to overflow in womanish weeping, went up to her and tried to coax her away from the bedside.

"Dear, if you could leave him for a little it would perhaps be better," he said. "He might—he might recover sooner. We have sent for the doctor—he will be here directly—"

"I will stay here till he comes," replied the girl, quietly. "How can you think I would leave Dad when he's ill? If we could only rouse him a little—"

Ah, that "if"! If we could only rouse our beloved ones who fall into that eternal sleep, would not all the riches and glories of the world seem tame in comparison with such joy! Innocent had never seen death—she could not realise that this calm irresponsiveness, this cold and stiffening rigidity, meant an end to the love and care she had known all her life— love and care which would never be replaced in quite the same way!

The first peep of a silver dawn began to peer through the lattice window, and as she saw this suggestion of wakening life, a sudden dread clutched at her heart and made it cold.

"It will be morning soon," she said—"Priscilla, when will the doctor come?"

Scarcely had she said the words when the doctor entered. He took a comprehensive glance round the room,—at the still form on the bed— at the little crouching girl—figure beside it—at Priscilla, trembling and tearful—at Robin, deadly pale and self-restrained—at the farm-lads and servants.

"When did this happen?" he said.

Robin told him.

"I see!" he said. "He must have fallen forward on getting out of bed. I rather expected a sudden seizure of this kind." He made his brief examination. The eyes of the dead man were open and glassily staring upward—he gently closed the lids over them and pressed them down.

"Nothing to be done," he went on, gently—"His end was painless."

Innocent had risen—she had laid the cold hand of the corpse back on its breast—and she stood gazing vacantly before her in utter misery.

"Nothing to be done?" she faltered—"Do you mean that you cannot rouse him? Will he never speak to me again?"

The doctor looked at her gravely and kindly.

"Not in this world, my dear," he said—"in the next—perhaps! Let us hope so!"

MARIE CORELLI

She put her hand up to her forehead with a bewildered gesture.

"He is dead!" she cried—"Dead! Oh, Robin, Robin! I can't believe it!—it isn't true! Dad, dear Dad! My only friend! Good-bye—good-bye, Dad!—good-bye, Briar Farm—good-bye to everything—oh, Dad!"

Her voice quavered and broke in a passion of tears.

"I loved him as if he were my own father," she sobbed. "And he loved me as if I were his own child! Oh, Dad, darling Dad! We can never love each other again!"

VIII

The news of Farmer Jocelyn's sudden death was as though a cloud-burst had broken over the village, dealing utter and hopeless destruction. To the little community of simple workaday folk living round Briar Farm it was a greater catastrophe than the death of any king. Nothing else was talked of. Nothing was done. Men stood idly about, looking at each other in a kind of stupefied consternation,—women chattered and whispered at their cottage doors, shaking their heads with all that melancholy profundity of wisdom which is not wise till after the event,—the children were less noisy in their play, checked by the grave faces of their parents—the very dogs seemed to know that something had occurred which altered the aspect of ordinary daily things. The last of the famous Jocelyns was no more! It seemed incredible. And Briar Farm? What would become of Briar Farm?

"There ain't none o' th' owd folk left now" said one man, lighting his pipe slowly—"It's all over an' done wi'. Mister Clifford, he's good enow—but he ain't a Jocelyn, though a Jocelyn were his mother. 'Tis the male side as tells. An' he's young, an' he'll want change an' rovin' about like all young men nowadays, an' the place'll be broke up, an' the timber felled, an' th' owd oak'll be sold to a dealer, an' Merrikans'll come an' buy the pewter an' the glass an' the linen, an' by-an'-bye we won't know there ever was such a farm at all—"

"That's your style o' thinkin', is it?" put in another man standing by, with a round straw hat set back upon his head in a fashion which gave him the appearance of a village idiot—"Well, it's not mine! No, by no means! There'll be a Will,—an' Mister Robin he'll find a Way! Briar Farm'll allus be Briar Farm accordin' to MY mind!"

"YOUR mind ain't much," growled the first speaker—"so don't ye go settin' store by it. Lord, Lord! to think o' Farmer Jocelyn bein' gone! Seems as if a right 'and 'ad bin cut off! Onny yesterday I met 'im drivin' along the road at a tearin' pace, with Ned Landon sittin' beside 'im—an' drivin' fine too, for the mare's a tricky one with a mouth as 'ard as iron—but 'e held 'er firm—that 'e did!—no weakness about 'im—an' 'e was talkin' away to Landon while 'e drove, 'ardly lookin' right or left, 'e was that sure of hisself. An' now 'e's cold as stone—who would a' thort it!"

"Where's Landon?" asked the other man.

"I dunno. He's nowhere about this mornin' that I've seen."

At that moment a figure came into view, turning the corner of a lane at the end of the scattered thatched cottages called "the village,"—a portly, consequential-looking figure, which both men recognised as that of the parson of the parish, and they touched their caps accordingly. The Reverend William Medwin, M.A., was a great personage,—and his "cure of souls" extended to three other villages outlying the one of which Briar Farm was the acknowledged centre.

"Good-morning!" he said, with affable condescension—"I hear that Farmer Jocelyn died suddenly last night. Is it true?"

Both men nodded gravely.

"Yes, sir, it's true—more's the pity! It's took us all aback."

"Ay, ay!" and Mr. Medwin nodded blandly—"No doubt-no doubt! But I suppose the farm will go on just the same?—there will be no lack of employment?"

The man who was smoking looked doubtful.

"Nobuddy can tell—m'appen the place will be sold—m'appen it won't. The hands may be kept, or they may be given the sack. There's only Mr. Clifford left now, an' 'e ain't a Jocelyn."

"Does that matter?" and the reverend gentleman smiled with the superior air of one far above all things of mere traditional sentiment. "There is the girl—"

"Ah, yes! There's the girl!"

The speakers looked at one another.

"Her position," continued Mr. Medwin, meditatively tracing a pattern on the ground with the end of his walking-stick, "seems to me to be a little unfortunate. But I presume she is really the daughter of our deceased friend?"

The man who was smoking took the pipe from his mouth and stared for a moment.

"Daughter she may be," he said, "but born out o' wedlock anyhow—an' she ain't got no right to Briar Farm unless th' owd man 'as made 'er legal. An' if 'e's done that it don't alter the muddle, 'cept in the eyes o' the law which can twist ye any way—for she was born bastard, an' there's never been a bastard Jocelyn on Briar Farm all the hundreds o' years it's been standin'!"

Mr. Medwin again interested himself in a dust pattern.

"Ah, dear, dear!" he sighed—"Very sad, very sad! Our follies always find us out, if not while we live, then when we die! I'm sorry! Farmer Jocelyn was not a Churchman—no!—a regrettable circumstance!—still,

I'm sorry! He was a useful person in the parish—quite honest, I believe, and a very fair and good master—"

"None better!" chorussed his listeners.

"True! None better. Well, well! I'll just go up to the house and see if I can be of any service, or—or comfort—"

One of the men smiled darkly.

"Sartin sure Farmer Jocelyn's as dead as door-nails. If so be you are a-goin' to Briar Farm, Mr. Medwin!" he said—"Why, you never set foot in the place while 'e was a livin' man!"

"Quite correct!" and Mr. Medwin nodded pleasantly—"I make it a rule never to go where I'm not wanted." He paused, impressively,—conscious that he had "scored." "But now that trouble has visited the house I consider it my duty to approach the fatherless and the afflicted. Good-day!"

He walked off then, treading ponderously and wearing a composed and serious demeanour. The men who had spoken with him were quickly joined by two or three others.

"Parson goin' to the Farm?" they enquired.

"Ay!"

"We'll 'ave gooseberries growin' on hayricks next!" declared a young, rough-featured fellow in a smock—"anythin' can 'appen now we've lost the last o' the Jocelyns!"

And such was the general impression throughout the district. Men met in the small public-houses and over their mugs of beer discussed the possibilities of emigrating to Canada or New Zealand, for—"there'll be no more farm work worth doin' round 'ere"—they all declared—"Mister Jocelyn wanted MEN, an' paid 'em well for workin' LIKE men!—but it'll all be machines now."

Meanwhile, the Reverend Mr. Medwin, M.A., had arrived at Briar Farm. Everything was curiously silent. All the blinds were down—the stable-doors were closed, and the stable-yard was empty. The sunlight swept in broad slanting rays over the brilliant flower-beds which were now at their gayest and best,—the doves lay sleeping on the roofs of sheds and barns as though mesmerised and forbidden to fly. A marked loneliness clouded the peaceful beauty of the place—a loneliness that made itself seen and felt by even the most casual visitor.

With a somewhat hesitating hand Mr. Medwin pulled the door-bell. In a minute or two a maid answered the summons—her eyes were red with weeping. At sight of the clergyman she looked surprised and a little frightened.

"How is Miss—Miss Jocelyn?" he enquired, softly—"I have only just heard the sad news—"

"She's not able to see anyone, sir," replied the maid, tremulously—"at least I don't think so—I'll ask. She's very upset—"

"Of course, of course!" said Mr. Medwin, soothingly—"I quite understand! Please say I called! Mr. Clifford—"

A figure stepped out from the interior darkness of the shadowed hall towards him.

"I am here," said Robin, gently—"Did you wish to speak to me? This is a house of heavy mourning to-day!"

The young man's voice shook,—he was deadly pale, and there was a strained look in his eyes of unshed tears. Mr. Medwin was conscious of nervous embarrassment.

"Indeed, indeed I know it is!" he murmured—"I feel for you most profoundly! So sudden a shock too!—I—I thought that perhaps Miss Jocelyn—a young girl struck by her first great loss and sorrow, might like to see me—"

Robin Clifford looked at him in silence for a moment. The consolations of the Church! Would they mean anything to Innocent? He wondered.

"I will ask her," he said at last, abruptly—"Will you step inside?"

Mr. Medwin accepted the suggestion, taking off his hat as he crossed the threshold, and soon found himself in the quaint sitting-room where, but two days since, Hugo Jocelyn had told Innocent all her true history. He could not help being impressed by its old-world peace and beauty, furnished as it was in perfect taste, with its window-outlook on a paradise of happy flowers rejoicing in the sunlight. The fragrance of sweet lavender scented the air, and a big china bowl of roses in the centre of the table gave a touch of tender brightness to the old oak panelling on the walls.

"There are things in this room that are priceless!" soliloquised the clergyman, who was something of a collector—"If the place comes under the hammer I shall try to pick up a few pieces."

He smiled, with the pleased air of one who feels that all things must have an end—either by the "hammer" or otherwise,—even a fine old house, the pride and joy of a long line of its owners during three hundred years. And then he started, as the door opened slowly and softly and a girl stood before him, looking more like a spirit than a mortal, clad in a plain white gown, with a black ribbon threaded through her waving fair hair. She was pale to the very lips, and her eyes were swollen and heavy with weeping. Timidly she held out her hand.

"It is kind of you to come," she said,—and paused.

He, having taken her hand and let it go again, stood awkwardly mute. It was the first time he had seen Innocent in her home surroundings, and he had hardly noticed her at all when he had by chance met her in her rare walks through the village and neighbourhood, so that he was altogether unprepared for the refined delicacy and grace of her appearance.

"I am very sorry to hear of your sad bereavement," he began, at last, in a conventional tone—"very sorry indeed—"

She looked at him curiously.

"Are you? I don't think you can be sorry, because you did not know him—if you had known him, you would have been really grieved—yes, I am sure you would. He was such a good man!—one of the best in all the world! I'm glad you have come to see me, because I have often wanted to speak to you—and perhaps now is the right time. Won't you sit down?"

He obeyed her gesture, surprised more or less by her quiet air of sad self-possession. He had expected to offer the usual forms of religious consolation to a sort of uneducated child or farm-girl, nervous, trembling and tearful,—instead of this he found a woman whose grief was too deep and sincere to be relieved by mere talk, and whose pathetic composure and patience were the evident result of a highly sensitive mental organisation.

"I have never seen death before," she said, in hushed tones—"except in birds and flowers and animals—and I have cried over the poor things for sorrow that they should be taken away out of this beautiful world. But with Dad it is different. He was afraid—afraid of suffering and weakness—and he was taken so quickly that he could hardly have felt anything—so that his fears were all useless. And I can hardly believe he is dead—actually dead—can you? But of course you do not believe in death at all—the religion you teach is one of eternal life—eternal life and happiness."

Mr. Medwin's lips moved—he murmured something about "living again in the Lord."

Innocent did not hear,—she was absorbed in her own mental problem and anxious to put it before him.

"Listen!" she said—"When Priscilla told me Dad was really dead—that he would never get off the bed where he lay so cold and white and peaceful,—that he would never speak to me again, I said she was wrong—that it could not be. I told her he would wake presently and laugh at us all for being so foolish as to think him dead. Even Hero, our mastiff, does not believe it, for he has stayed all morning by the bedside and no one dare touch him to take him away. And just now Priscilla has been with me, crying very much—and she says I must not grieve,—because Dad is gone to a better world. Then surely he must be alive if he is able to go anywhere, must he not? I asked her what she knew about this better world, and she cried again and said indeed she knew nothing except what she had been taught in her Catechism. I have read the Catechism and it seems to me very stupid and unnatural—perhaps because I do not understand it. Can you tell me about this better world?"

Mr. Medwin's lips moved again. He cleared his throat.

"I'm afraid," he observed—"I'm very much afraid, my poor child, that you have been brought up in a sad state of ignorance."

Innocent did not like being called a "poor child"—and she gave a little gesture of annoyance.

"Please do not pity me," she said, with a touch of hauteur—"I do not wish that! I know it is difficult for me to explain things to you as I see them, because I have never been taught religion from a Church. I have read about the Virgin and Christ and the Saints and all those pretty legends in the books that belonged to the Sieur Amadis—but he lived three hundred years ago and he was a Roman Catholic, as all those French noblemen were at that time."

Mr. Medwin stared at her in blank bewilderment. Who was the Sieur Amadis? She went on, heedless of his perplexity.

"Dad believed in a God who governed all things rightly,—I have heard him say that God managed the farm and made it what it is. But he never spoke much about it—and he hated the Church—"

The reverend gentleman interrupted her with a grave uplifted hand.

"I know!" he sighed—"Ah yes, I know! A dreadful thing!—a shocking attitude of mind!' I fear he was not saved!"

She looked straightly at him.

"I don't see what you mean," she said—"He was quite a good man—"

"Are you sure of that?" and Mr. Medwin fixed his shallow brown eyes searchingly upon her. "Our affections are often very deceptive—"

A flush of colour overspread her pale cheeks.

"Indeed I am very sure!" she answered, steadily—"He was a good man. There was never a stain on his character—though he allowed people to think wrong things of him for my sake. That was his only fault."

He was silent, waiting for her next word.

"I think perhaps I ought to tell you," she continued—"because then you will be able to judge him better and spare his memory from foolish and wicked scandal. He was not my father—I was only his adopted daughter."

Mr. Medwin gave a slight cough—a cough of incredulity. "Adopted" is a phrase often used to cover the brand of illegitimacy.

"I never knew my own history till the other day," she said, slowly and sadly. "The doctor came to see Dad, with a London specialist, a friend of his—and they told him he had not long to live. After that Dad made up his mind that I must learn all the truth of myself—oh!— what a terrible truth it was!—I thought my heart would break! It was so strange—so cruel! I had grown up believing myself to be Dad's own, very own daughter!—and I had been deceived all my life!—for he told me I was nothing but a nameless child, left on his hands by a stranger!"

Mr. Medwin opened his small eyes in amazement,—he was completely taken aback. He tried to grasp the bearings of this new aspect of the situation thus presented to him, but could not realise anything save what in his own mind was he pleased to call a "cock-and-bull" story.

"Most extraordinary!" he exclaimed, at last—"Did he give you no clue at all as to your actual parentage?"

Innocent shook her head.

"How could he? A man on horseback arrived here suddenly one very stormy night, carrying me in his arms—I was just a little baby—and asked shelter for me, promising to come and fetch me in the morning— but he never came—and Dad never knew who he was. I was kept here out of pity at first—then Dad began to love me—"

The suppressed tears rose to her eyes and began to fall.

"Priscilla can tell you all about it," she continued, tremulously—"if you wish to know more. I am only explaining things a little because I do want you to understand that Dad was really a good man though he did not go to Church—and he must have been 'saved,' as you put it, for he never did anything unworthy of the name of Jocelyn!"

The clergyman thought a moment.

"You are not Miss Jocelyn, then?" he said.

She met his gaze with a sorrowful calmness.

MARIE CORELLI

"No. I am nobody. I have not even been baptised."

He sprang up from his chair, horrified.

"Not baptised!" he exclaimed—"Not baptised! Do you mean to tell me that Farmer Jocelyn never attended to this imperative and sacred duty on your behalf?—that he allowed you to grow up as a heathen?"

She remained unmoved by his outburst.

"I am not a heathen," she said, gently—"I believe in God—as Dad believed. I'm sorry I have not been baptised—but it has made no difference to me that I know of—"

"No difference!" and the clergyman rolled up his eyes and shook his head ponderously—"You poor unfortunate girl, it has made all the difference in the world! You are unregenerate—your soul is not washed clean—all your sins are upon you, and you are not redeemed!"

She looked at him tranquilly.

"That is all very sad for me if it is true," she said—"but it is not my fault. I could not help it. Dad couldn't help it either—he did not know what to do. He expected that I might be claimed and taken away any day—and he had no idea what name to give me—except Innocent—which is a name I suppose no girl ever had before. He used to get money from time to time in registered envelopes, bearing different foreign postmarks—and there was always a slip of paper inside with the words 'For Innocent' written on it. So that name has been my only name. You see, it was very difficult for him—poor Dad!—besides, he did not believe in baptism—"

"Then he was an infidel!" declared Mr. Medwin, hotly.

Her serious blue eyes regarded him reproachfully.

"I don't think you should say that—it isn't quite kind on your part," she replied—"He always thanked God for prosperity, and never complained when things went wrong—that is not being an infidel! Even when he knew he was hopelessly ill, he never worried anyone about it—he was only just a little afraid-and that was perfectly natural. We're all a little afraid, you know—though we pretend we're not—none of us like the idea of leaving this lovely world and the sunshine for ever. Even Hamlet was afraid,—Shakespeare makes him say so. And when one has lived all one's life on Briar Farm—such a sweet peaceful home!—one can hardly fancy anything better, even in a next world! No—Dad was not an infidel—please do not think such a thing!—he only died last night—and I feel as if it would hurt him."

Mr. Medwin was exceedingly embarrassed and annoyed—there was something in the girl's quiet demeanour that suggested a certain intellectual superiority to himself. He hummed and hawed, lurking various unpleasant throaty noises.

"Well—to me, of course, it is a very shocking state of affairs," he said, irritably—"I hardly think I can be of any use—or consolation to you in the matters you have spoken of, which are quite outside my scope altogether. If you have anything to say about the funeral arrangements—but I presume Mr. Clifford—"

"Mr. Clifford is master here now," she answered—"He will give his own orders, and will do all that is best and wisest. As I have told you, I am a name-less nobody, and have no right in this house at all. I'm sorry if I have vexed or troubled you—but as you called I thought it was right to tell you how I am situated. You see, when poor Dad is buried I shall be going away at once—and I had an idea you might perhaps help me—you are God's minister."

He wrinkled up his brows and looked frowningly at her.

"You are leaving Briar Farm?" he asked.

"I must. I have no right to stay."

"Is Mr. Clifford turning you out?"

A faint, sad smile crept round the girl's pretty, sensitive mouth.

"Ah, no! No, indeed! He would not turn a dog out that had once taken food from his hand," she said. "It is my own wish entirely. When Dad was alive there was something for me to do in taking care of him—but now!—there is no need for me—I should feel in the way—besides, I must try to earn my own living."

"What do you propose to do?" asked Mr. Medwin, whose manner to her had completely changed from the politely patronising to the sharply aggressive—"Do you want a situation?"

She lifted her eyes to his fat, unpromising face.

"Yes—I should like one very much—I could be a lady's maid, I think, I can sew very well. But—perhaps you would baptise me first?"

He gave a sound between a cough and a grunt.

"Eh? Baptise you?"

"Yes,—because if I am unregenerate, and my soul is not clean, as you say, no one would take me—not even as a lady's maid."

Her quaint, perfectly simple way of putting the case made him angry.

"I'm afraid you are not sufficiently aware of the importance of the sacred rite,"—he said, severely—"At your age you would need to be instructed for some weeks before you could be considered fit and worthy. Then,—you tell me you have no name!—Innocent is not a name at all for a woman—I do not know who you are—you are ignorant of your parentage—you may have been born out of wedlock—"

She coloured deeply.

"I am not sure of that," she said, in a low tone.

"No—of course you are not sure,—but I should say the probability is that you are illegitimate"—and the reverend gentleman took up his hat to go. "The whole business is very perplexing and difficult. However, I will see what can be done for you—but you are in a very awkward corner!—very awkward indeed! Life will not be very easy for you, I fear!"

"I do not expect ease," she replied—"I have been very happy till now—and I am grateful for the past. I must make my own future."

Her eyes filled with tears as she looked out through the open window at the fair garden which she herself had tended for so long—and she saw the clergyman's portly form through a mist of sorrow as in half-hearted fashion he bade her good-day.

"I hope—I fervently trust—that God will support you in your bereavement," he said, unctuously—"I had intended before leaving to offer up a prayer with you for the soul of the departed and for your own soul—but the sad fact of your being unbaptised places me in a difficulty. But I shall not fail personally to ask our Lord to prepare you for the unfortunate change in your lot!"

"Thank you!" she replied, quietly—and without further salute he left her.

She stood for a moment considering—then sat down by the window, looking at the radiant flowerbeds, with all their profusion of blossom. She wondered dreamily how they could show such brave, gay colouring when death was in the house, and the aching sense of loss and sorrow weighted the air as with darkness. A glitter of white wings flashed before her eyes, and her dove alighted on the window-sill,—she stretched out her hand and the petted bird stepped on her little rosy palm with all its accustomed familiarity and confidence. She caressed it tenderly.

"Poor Cupid!" she murmured—"You are like me—you are unregenerate!—you have never been baptised!—your soul has not been washed clean!—and all your sins are on your head! Yes, Cupid!—we are very much alike!—for I don't suppose you know your own father and mother any more than I know mine! And yet God made you—and He has taken care of you—so far!"

She stroked the dove's satiny plumage gently—and then drew back a little into shadow as she saw Robin Clifford step out from the porch into the garden and hurriedly interrupt the advance of a woman who just then pushed open the outer gate—a slatternly-looking creature with dark dishevelled hair and a face which might have been handsome, but for its unmistakable impress of drink and dissipation.

"Eh, Mr. Clifford—it's you, is it?" she exclaimed, in shrill tones. "An' Farmer Jocelyn's dead!—who'd a' thought it! But I'd 'ave 'ad a bone to pick with 'im this mornin', if he'd been livin'—that I would!—givin' sack to Ned Landon without a warning to me!"

Innocent leaned forward, listening eagerly, with an uncomfortably beating heart. Through all the miserable, slow, and aching hours that had elapsed since Hugo Jocelyn's death, there had been a secret anxiety in her mind concerning Ned Landon and the various possibilities involved in his return to the farm, when he should learn that his employer was no more, and that Robin was sole master.

"I've come up to speak with ye," continued the woman,—"It's pretty 'ard on me to be left in the ditch, with a man tumbling ye off his horse an' ridin' away where ye can't get at 'im!" She laughed harshly. "Ned's gone to 'Merriker!"

"Gone to America!"—Robin's voice rang out in sharp accents of surprise—"Ned Landon? Why, when did you hear that?"

"Just now—his own letter came with the carrier's cart—he left the town last night and takes ship from Southampton to-day. And why? Because Farmer Jocelyn gave him five hundred pounds to do it! So there's some real news for ye!"

"Five hundred pounds!" echoed Clifford—"My Uncle Hugo gave him five hundred pounds!"

"Ay, ye may stare!"—and the woman laughed again—"And the devil has taken it all,—except a five-pun' note which he sends to me to 'keep me goin',' he says. Like his cheek! I'm not his wife, that's true!—but I'm as much as any wife—an' there's the kid—"

Robin glanced round apprehensively at the open window.

"Hush!" he said—"don't talk so loud—"

"The dead can't hear," she said, scornfully—"an' Ned says in his letter that he's been sent off all on account of you an' your light o' love— Innocent, she's called—a precious 'innocent' SHE is!—an' that the old man has paid 'im to go away an' 'old his tongue! So it's all YOUR fault, after all, that I'm left with the kid to rub along anyhow;—he might ave married me in a while, if he'd stayed. I'm only Jenny o' Mill-Dykes now—just as I've always been—the toss an' catch of every man!—but I 'ad a grip on Ned with the kid, an' he'd a' done me right in the end if you an' your precious 'innocent' 'adn't been in the way—"

Robin made a quick stride towards her.

"Go out of this place!" he said, fiercely—"How dare you come here with such lies!"

He stopped, half choked with rage.

Jenny looked at him and laughed—then snapped her fingers in his face.

"Lies, is it?" she said—"Well, lies make good crops, an' Farmer Jocelyn's money'll 'elp them to grow! Lies, indeed! An' how dare I come here? Why, because your old uncle is stiff an' cold an' can't speak no more—an' no one would know what 'ad become o' Ned Landon if I wasn't here to tell them an' show his own letter! I'll tell them all, right enough!—you bet your life I will!"

She turned her back on him and began to walk, or rather slouch, out of the garden. He went up close to her, his face white with passion.

"If you say one word about Miss Jocelyn—" he began.

"Miss Jocelyn!" she exclaimed, shrilly—"That's good!—we ARE grand!"—and she dropped him a mock curtsey—"Miss Jocelyn! There ain't no 'Miss Jocelyn,' an' you know it as well as I do! So don't try to fool ME! Look here, Mr. Robin Clifford"—and she confronted him, with arms akimbo—"you're not a Jocelyn neither!—there's not a Jocelyn left o' the old stock—they're all finished with the one lyin' dead upstairs yonder—and I'll tell ye what!—you an' your 'innocent' are too 'igh an' mighty altogether for the likes o' we poor villagers—seein' ye ain't got nothin' to boast of, neither of ye! You've lost me my man—an' I'll let everyone know how an' why!"

With that she went, banging the gate after her—and Clifford stood inert, furious within himself, yet powerless to do anything save silently endure the taunts she had flung at him. He could have cursed himself for the folly he had been guilty of in telling his uncle about the fight between him and Landon—for he saw now that the old man had secretly worried over the possible harm that might be done to Innocent through Landon's knowledge of her real story, which he had learned through his spying and listening. Whatever that harm could be, was now intensified—and scandal, beginning as a mere whispered suggestion, would increase to loud and positive assertion ere long.

"Poor Uncle Hugo!" and the young man looked up sorrowfully at the darkened windows of the room where lay in still and stern repose all that was mortal of the last of the Jocelyns—"What a mistake you have made! You meant so well!—you thought you were doing a wise thing in sending Landon away—and at such a cost!—but you did not know what he had left behind him—Jenny of the Mill-Dykes, whose wicked tongue would blacken an angel's reputation!"

A hand touched him lightly on the arm from behind. He turned swiftly round and confronted Innocent—she stood like a little figure of white porcelain, holding her dove against her breast.

"Poor Robin!" she said, softly—"Don't worry! I heard everything."

He stared down upon her.

"You heard—?"

"Yes. I was at the open window there—I couldn't help hearing. It was Jenny of the Mill-Dykes—I know her by sight, but not to speak to—Priscilla told me something about her. She isn't a nice woman, is she?"

"Nice?" Robin gasped—"No, indeed! She is—Well!—I must not tell you what she is!"

"No!—you must not—I don't want to hear. But she ought to be Ned Landon's wife—I understood that!—and she has a little child. I understood that too. And she knows everything about me—and about that night when you climbed up on my window-sill and sat there so long. It was a pity you did that, wasn't it?"

"Yes!—when there was a dirty spy in hiding!" said Robin, hotly.

"Ah!—we never imagined such a thing could be on Briar Farm!"—and she sighed—"but it can't be helped now. Poor darling Dad! He parted with all that money to get rid of the man he thought would do me wrong. Oh Robin, he loved me!"

The tears gathered in her eyes and fell slowly like bright raindrops on the downy feathers of the dove she held.

"He loved you, and I love you!" murmured Robin, tenderly. "Dear little girl, come indoors and don't cry any more! Your sweet eyes will be spoilt, and Uncle Hugo could never bear to see you weeping. All the tears in the world won't bring him back to us here,—but we can do our best to please him still, so that if his spirit has ever been troubled, it can be at peace. Come in and let us talk quietly together—we must look at things squarely and straightly, and we must try to do all the things he would have wished—"

"All except one thing," she said, as they went together side by side into the house—"the one thing that can never be!"

"The one thing—the chief thing that shall be!" answered Robin, fiercely—"Innocent, you must be my wife!"

She lifted her tear-wet eyes to his with a grave and piteous appeal which smote him to the heart by its intense helplessness and sorrow.

"Robin,—dear Robin!" she said—"Don't make it harder for me than it is! Think for a moment! I am nameless—a poor, unbaptised, deserted creature who was flung on your uncle's charity eighteen years ago—I am a stranger and intruder in this old historic place—I have no right to be here at all—only through your uncle's kindness and yours. And now things have happened so cruelly for me that I am supposed to be to you—what I am not,"—and the deep colour flushed her cheeks and brow. "I have somehow—through no fault of my own—lost my name!—though I had no name to lose—except Innocent!—which, as the clergyman told me, is no name for a woman. Do you not see that if I married you, people would say it was because you were compelled to marry me?—that you had gone too far to escape from me?—that, in fact, we were a sort of copy of Ned Landon and Jenny of the Mill-Dykes?"

"Innocent!"

He uttered the name in a tone of indignant and despairing protest. They were in the oak parlour together, and she went slowly to the window and let her pet dove fly.

"Ah, yes! Innocent!" she repeated, sadly—"But you must let me go, Robin!—just as I have let my dove fly, so you must let me fly also—far, far away!"

IX

No more impressive scene was ever witnessed in a country village than the funeral of "the last of the Jocelyns,"—impressive in its solemnity, simplicity and lack of needless ceremonial. The coffin, containing all that was mortal of the sturdy, straightforward farmer, whose "old-world" ways of work and upright dealing with his men had for so long been the wonder and envy of the district, was placed in a low waggon and covered with a curiously wrought, handwoven purple cloth embroidered with the arms of the French knight "Amadis de Jocelin," tradition asserting that this cloth had served as a pall for every male Jocelyn since his time. The waggon was drawn by four glossy dark brown cart-horses, each animal having known its master as a friend whose call it was accustomed to obey, following him wherever he went. On the coffin itself was laid a simple wreath of the "Glory" roses gathered from the porch and walls of Briar Farm, and offered, as pencilled faintly on a little scroll—"With a life's love and sorrow from Innocent." A long train of mourners, including labourers, farm-lads, shepherds, cowherds, stable-men and villagers generally, followed the corpse to the grave,—Robin Clifford, as chief mourner and next-of-kin to the dead man, walking behind the waggon with head down-bent and a face on which intense grief had stamped such an impress as to make it look far older than his years warranted. Groups of women stood about, watching the procession with hard eager eyes, and tongues held in check for a while, only to wag more vigorously than ever when the ceremony should be over. Innocent, dressed in deep black for the first time in her life, went by herself to the churchyard, avoiding the crowd—and, hidden away among concealing shadows, she heard the service and watched all the proceedings dry-eyed and heart-stricken. She could not weep any more—there seemed no tears left to relieve the weight of her burning brain. Robin had tenderly urged her to walk with him in the funeral procession, but she refused.

"How can I!—how dare I!" she said—"I am not his daughter—I am nothing! The cruel people here know it!—and they would only say my presence was an insult to the dead. Yes!—they would—Now! He loved me!—and I loved him!—but nobody outside ourselves thinks about that, or cares. You would hardly believe it, but I have already been told how wicked it was of me to be dressed in white when the clergyman called to see me the morning after Dad's death—well, I had no other colour to wear till Priscilla got me this sad black gown—it made me shudder to put it on—it is like the darkness itself!—you know Dad always made me wear white—and I feel as if I were vexing him somehow by wearing black. Oh, Robin, be kind!—you always are!—let me go by myself and watch Dad put to rest where nobody can see me. For after they have laid him down and left him, they will be talking!"

She was right enough in this surmise. Not one who saw Farmer Jocelyn's coffin lowered into the grave failed to notice the wreath of "Glory" roses that went with it—"from Innocent;"—and her name was whispered from mouth to mouth with meaning looks and suggestive nods. And when Robin, with tears thick in his eyes, flung the first handfuls of earth rattling down on the coffin lid, his heart ached to see the lovely fragrant blossoms crushed under the heavy scattered mould, for it seemed to his foreboding mind that they were like the delicate thoughts and fancies of the girl he loved being covered by the soiling mud of the world's cruelty and slander, and killed in the cold and darkness of a sunless solitude.

All was over at last,—the final prayer was said—the final benediction was spoken, and the mourners gradually dispersed. The Reverend Mr. Medwin, assisted by his young curate, had performed the ceremony, and before retiring to the vestry to take off his surplice, he paused by the newly-made grave to offer his hand and utter suitable condolences to Robin Clifford.

"It is a great and trying change for you," he said. "I suppose"—this tentatively—"I suppose you will go on with the farm?"

"As long as I live," answered Clifford, looking him steadily in the face, "Briar Farm will be what it has always been."

Mr. Medwin gave him a little appreciative bow.

"We are very glad of that—very glad indeed!" he said—"Briar Farm is a great feature—a very great feature!—indeed, one may say it is an historical possession. Something would be lacking in the neighbourhood if it were not kept up to its old tradition and—er—reputation. I think we feel that—I think we feel it, do we not, Mr. Forwood?" here turning to his curate with affable condescension.

Mark Forwood, a clever-looking young man with kind eyes and intelligent features, looked at Robin sympathetically.

"I am quite sure," he said, "that Mr. Clifford will take as much pride in the fine old place as his uncle did—but is there not Miss Jocelyn?—the daughter will probably inherit the farm, will she not, as nearest of kin?"

Mr. Medwin coughed obtrusively—and Clifford felt the warm blood rushing to his brows. Yet he resolved that the truth should be told, for the honour of the dead man's name.

"She is not my uncle's daughter," he said, quietly—"My uncle never married. He adopted her when she was an infant—and she was as dear to him as if she had been his own child. Of course she will be amply provided for—there can be no doubt of that."

Mr. Forwood raised his eyes and eyebrows together.

"You surprise me!" he murmured. "Then—there is no Miss Jocelyn?"

Again Robin coloured. But he answered, composedly—

"There is no Miss Jocelyn."

Mr. Medwin's cough here troubled him considerably, and though it was a fine day, he expressed a mild fear that he was standing too long by the open grave in his surplice—he, therefore, retired, his curate following him,—whereupon the sexton, a well-known character in the village, approached to finish the sad task of committing "ashes to ashes, dust to dust."

"Eh, Mr. Clifford," remarked this worthy, as he stuck his spade down in the heaped-up earth and leaned upon it,—"it's a black day, forbye the summer sun! I never thort I'd a' thrown the mouls on the last Jocelyn. For last he is, an' there'll never be another like 'im!"

"You're right there, Wixton," said Robin, sadly—"I know the place can never be the same without him. I shall do my best—but—"

"Ay, ye'll do your best," agreed Wixton, with a foreboding shake of his grizzled head—"but you're not a Jocelyn, an' your best'll be but a bad crutch, though there's Jocelyn blood in ye by ye'r mother's side. Howsomever it's not the same as the male line, do what we will an' say what we like! It's not your fault, no, lad!"—this with a pitying look—"an' no one's blamin' ye for what can't be 'elped—but it's not a thing to be gotten over."

Robin's grave nod of acquiescence was more eloquent than speech.

Wixton dug his spade a little deeper into the pile of earth.

"If Farmer Jocelyn 'ad been a marryin' man, why, that would a' been the right thing," he went on—"He might a' had a fine strappin' son to come arter 'im, a real born-an'-bred Jocelyn—"

Robin listened with acute interest. Why did not Wixton mention Innocent? Did he know she was not a Jocelyn? He waited, and Wixton went on—

"But, ye see, 'e wouldn't have none o' that. An' he took the little gel as was left with 'im the night o' the great storm nigh eighteen years ago that blew down three of our biggest elms in the church-yard—"

"Did you know?" exclaimed Clifford, eagerly—"Did you see—?"

"I saw a man on 'orseback ride up to Briar Farm, 'oldin' a baby in front o' him with one hand, and the reins in t'other—an' he came out from the farm without the baby. Then one mornin' when Farmer Jocelyn was a-walkin' with the baby in the fields I said to 'im, secret-like—'That ain't your child!' an' he sez—'Ow do you know it ain't?' An' I sez—' Because I saw it come with a stranger'—an' he laughed an' said—'It may be mine for all that!' But I knew it worn't! A nice little girl she is too,—Miss Innocent—poor soul! I'm downright sorry for 'er, for she ain't got many friends in this village."

"Why?" Robin asked, half mechanically.

"Why? Well, she's a bit too dainty—like in 'er ways for one thing— then there's gels who are arter You, Mister Clifford!—ay, ay, ye know they are!—sharp 'ussies, all of 'em!—an' they can't abide 'Er, for they thinks you're a-goin' to marry 'er!—Lord forgive me that I should be chitterin' 'ere about marryin' over a buryin'!—but that's the trouble—an' it's the trouble all the world over, wimmin wantin' a man, an' mad for their lives when they thinks another woman's arter 'im! Eh, eh! We should all get along better if there worn't no wimmin jealousies, but bein' men we've got to put up with 'em. Are ye goin' now, Mister?—Well, the Lord love ye an' comfort ye!—ye'll never meet a finer man this side the next world than the one I'm puttin' a cold quilt on!"

Silently Clifford turned away, heavy-hearted and lost in perplexed thought. What was best to be done for Innocent? This was the chief question that presented itself to his mind. He could no longer deny the fact that her position was difficult—almost untenable. Nameless, and seemingly deserted by her kindred, if any such kindred still existed, she was absolutely alone in life, now that Hugo Jocelyn was no more. As he realised this to its fullest intensity, the deeper and more passionate grew his love for her.

"If she would only marry me!" he said under his breath, as he walked home slowly from the church-yard—"It was Uncle Hugo's last wish!"

Then across his brain flashed the memory of Ned Landon and his malignant intention—born of baffled desire and fierce jealousy—to tarnish the fair name of the girl he coveted,—then, his uncle's quixotic and costly way of ridding himself of such an enemy at any price. He understood now old Jocelyn's talk of his "bargain" on the last night of his life,-and what a futile bargain it was, after all!—for was not Jenny of the Mill-Dykes fully informed of the reason why the bargain was made?—and she, the vilest-tongued woman in the whole neighbourhood, would take delight in spreading the story far and wide. Five Hundred Pounds paid down as "hush-money!"—so she would report it—thus, even if he married Innocent it would be under the shadow of a slur and slander. What was wisest to do under the circumstances he could not decide—and he entered the smiling garden of Briar Farm with the saddest expression on his face that anyone had ever seen there. Priscilla met him as he came towards the house.

"I thought ye'd never git here, Mister Robin," she said, anxiously—"Ye haven't forgot there's folks in the hall 'avin' their 'wake' feed an' they'll be wantin' to speak wi' ye presently. Mister Bayliss, which is ye'r uncle's lawyer, 'e wants to see ye mighty partikler, an' there ain't no one to say nothin' to 'em, for the dear little Innocent, she's come back from the cold churchyard like a little image o' marble, an' she's gone an' shut 'erself up in 'er own room, sayin' 'Ask Mister Robin to excuse me'—poor child!—she's fair wore out, that she is! An' you come into the big 'all where there's the meat and the wine laid out, for funeral folk eats more than weddin' folk, bein' longer about it an' a bit solemner in gettin' of it down."

Robin looked at her with strained, haggard eyes.

"Priscilla," he said, huskily—"Death is a horrible thing!"

"Ay, that it is!" and Priscilla wiped the teardrops off her cheeks with a corner of her apron—"An' I've often thought it seems a silly kind o' business to bring us into the world at all for no special reason 'cept to take us out of it again just as folks 'ave learned to know us a bit and find us useful. Howsomever, there's no arguin' wi' the Almighty, an' p'raps it's us as makes the worst o' death instead o' the best of it. Now you go into the great hall, Mr. Robin—you're wanted there."

He went, as desired,—and was received with a murmur of sympathy by those assembled—a gathering made up of the head men about the farm, and a few other personages less familiar to the village, but fairly well known to him, such as corn and cattle dealers from the neighbouring town who had for many years done business with Jocelyn in preference to any other farmer. These came forward and cordially shook hands with Robin, entering at once into conversation with him concerning his future intentions.

"We should like things to go on the same as if th' old man were alive," said one, a miller,—"We don't like changes after all these years. But whether you're up to it, my lad, or not, we don't know—and time'll prove—"

"Time WILL prove," answered Clifford, steadily. "You may rely upon it that Briar Farm will be worked on the same methods which my uncle practised and approved—and there will be no changes, except—the inevitable one"—and he sighed,—"the want of the true master's brain and hand."

"Eh well! You'll do your best, lad!—I'm sure of that!" and the miller grasped his hand warmly—"And we'll all stick by you! There's no farm like Briar Farm in the whole country—that's my opinion!—it gives the finest soil and the soundest crops to be got anywhere—you just manage it as Farmer Jocelyn managed it, with men's work, and you'll come to no harm! And, as I say, we'll all stick by you!"

Robin thanked him, and then moved slowly in and out among the other funeral guests, saying kindly things, and in his quiet, manly way creating a good impression among them, and making more friends than he himself was aware of. Presently Mr. Bayliss, a mild-looking man with round spectacles fixed very closely up against his eyes, approached him, beckoning him with one finger.

"When you're ready, Mr. Clifford," he said, "I should like to see you in the best parlour—and the young lady—I believe she is called Innocent?—yes, yes!—and the young lady also. Oh, there's no hurry— no hurry!—better wait till the guests have gone, as what I have to say concerns only yourself—and—er—yes—er, the young lady before mentioned. And also a—a"—here he pulled out a note-book from his pocket and studied it through his owl-like glasses—"yes!—er, yes!—a Miss Priscilla Priday—she must be present, if she can be found—I believe she is on the premises?"

"Priscilla is our housekeeper," said Robin—"and a faithful friend."

"Yes—I—er—thought so—a devoted friend," murmured Mr. Bayliss, meditatively—"and what a thing it is to have a devoted friend, Mr. Clifford! Your uncle was a careful man!—very careful!—he knew whom to trust—he thoroughly knew! Yes—WE don't all know— but HE did!"

Robin made no comment. The murmuring talk of the funeral party went on, buzzing in his ears like the noise of an enormous swarm of bees—he watched men eating and drinking the good things Priscilla had provided for the "honour of the farm"—and then, on a sudden impulse he slipped out of the hall and upstairs to Innocent's room, where he knocked softly at the door. She opened it at once, and stood before him—her face white as a snowdrop, and her eyes heavy and strained with the weight of unshed tears.

"Dear," he said, gently—"you will be wanted downstairs in a few minutes—Mr. Bayliss wishes you to be present when he reads Uncle Hugo's will."

She made a little gesture of pain and dissent.

"I do not want to hear it," she said—"but I will come."

He looked at her with anxiety and tenderness.

"You have eaten nothing since early morning; you look so pale and weak—let me get you something—a glass of wine."

"No, thank you," she answered—"I could not touch a morsel—not just yet. Oh, Robin, it hurts me to hear all those voices in the great hall!—men eating and drinking there, as if he were still alive!—and they have only just laid him down in the cold earth—so cold and dark!"

She shuddered violently.

"I do not think it is right," she went on—"to allow people to love each other at all if death must separate them for ever. It seems only a cruelty and wickedness. Now that I have seen what death can do, I will never love anyone again!"

"No—I suppose you will not," he said, somewhat bitterly—"yet, you have never known what love is—you do not understand it."

She sighed, deeply.

"Perhaps not!" she said—"And I'm not sure that I want to understand it—not now. What love I had in my heart is all buried—with Dad and the roses. I am not the same girl any more—I feel a different creature—grown quite old!"

"You cannot feel older than I do," he replied—"but you do not think of me at all,—why should you? I never used to think you selfish, Innocent!—you have always been so careful and considerate of the feelings of others—yet now!—well!—are you not so much absorbed in your own grief as to be forgetful of mine? For mine is a double grief—a double loss—I have lost my uncle and best friend—and I shall lose you because you will not love me, though I love you with all my heart and only want to make you happy!"

Her sad eyes met his with a direct, half-reproachful gaze.

"You think me selfish?"

"No!—no, Innocent!—but—"

"I see!" she said—"You think I ought to sacrifice myself to you, and to Dad's last wish. You would expect me to spoil your life by marrying you unwillingly and without love—"

"I tell you you know nothing about love!" he interrupted her, impatiently.

"So you imagine," she answered quietly—"but I do know one thing—and it is that no one who really loves a person wishes to see that person, unhappy. To love anybody means that above all things in the world you desire to see the beloved one well and prosperous and full of gladness. You cannot love me or you would not wish me to do a thing that would make me miserable. If I loved you, I would marry you and devote my life to yours—but I do not love you, and, therefore, I should only make you wretched if I became your wife. Do not let us talk of this any more—it tires me out!"

She passed her hand over her forehead with a weary gesture.

"It is wrong to talk of ourselves at all when Dad is only just buried," she continued. "You say Mr. Bayliss wants to see me—very well!—in a few minutes I will come."

She stepped back inside her little room and shut the door. Clifford walked away, resentful and despairing. There was something in her manner that struck him as new and foreign to her usual sweet and equable nature,—a grave composure, a kind of intellectual hardness that he had never before seen in her. And he wondered what such a change might portend.

Downstairs, the funeral party had broken up—many of the mourners had gone, and others were going. Some lingered to the last possible moment that their intimacy or friendship with the deceased would allow, curious to hear something of the will—what the amount of the net cash was that had been left, and how it had been disposed. But Mr. Bayliss, the lawyer, was a cautious man, and never gave himself away at any point. To all suggestive hints and speculative theories he maintained a dignified reserve—and it was not until the last of the guests had departed that he made his way to the vacant "best parlour," and sat there with his chair pulled well up to the table and one or two legal-looking documents in front of him. Robin Clifford joined him there, taking a seat opposite to him—and both men waited in more or less silence till the door opened softly to admit Innocent, who came in with Priscilla.

Mr. Bayliss rose.

"I'm sorry to have to disturb you, Miss—er—Miss Innocent," he said, with some awkwardness—"on this sad occasion—"

"It is no trouble," she answered, gently—"if I can be of any use—"

Mr. Bayliss waited till she sat down,—then again seated himself.

"Well, there is really no occasion to go over legal formalities," he said, opening one of the documents before him—"Your uncle, Mr. Clifford, was a business man, and made his will in a business-like way. Briefly, I may tell you that Briar Farm, its lands, buildings, and all its contents are left to you—who are identified thus—'to my nephew, Robin Clifford, only son of my only sister, the late Elizabeth Jocelyn, widow of John Clifford, wholesale trader in French wines, and formerly resident in the City of London, on condition that the said Robin Clifford shall keep and maintain the farm and house as they have always been kept and maintained. He shall not sell any part of the land for building purposes, nor shall he dispose of any of the furniture, pewter, plate, china, glass, or other effects belonging to Briar Farm House,—but shall carefully preserve the same and hand them down to his lawful heirs in succession on the same terms as heretofore'—etc., etc.,—yes!—well!—that is the gist of the business, and we need not go over the details. With the farm and lands aforesaid he leaves the sum of Twenty Thousand Pounds—"

"Twenty Thousand Pounds!" exclaimed Robin, amazed—"Surely my uncle was never so rich—!"

"He was a saving man and a careful one," said Mr. Bayliss, calmly,—"You may take it for granted, Mr. Clifford, that his money was made through the course of his long life, in a thoroughly honest and straightforward manner!"

"Oh—that, of course!—but—Twenty Thousand Pounds!"

"It is a nice little fortune," said Mr. Bayliss—"and you come into it at a time of life when you will be able to make good use of it. Especially if you should be inclined to marry—"

His eyes twinkled meaningly as they glanced from Clifford's face to that of Innocent—the young man's expression was absorbed and earnest, but the girl looked lost and far away in a dream of her own.

"I shall not marry," said Robin, slowly—"I shall use the money entirely for the good of the farm and the work-people—"

"Then, if you do not marry, you allow the tradition of heritage to lapse?" suggested Mr. Bayliss.

"It has lapsed already," he replied—"I am not a real descendant of the Jocelyns—"

"By the mother's side you are," said Mr. Bayliss—"and your mother being dead, it is open to you to take the name of Jocelyn by law, and continue the lineage. It would be entirely fair and reasonable."

Robin made no answer. Mr. Bayliss settled his glasses more firmly on his nose, and went on with his documents.

"Mr. Jocelyn speaks in his Last Will and Testament of the 'great love' he entertained for his adopted child, known as 'Innocent'—and he gives to her all that is contained in the small oak chest in the best parlour—this is the best parlour, I presume?"—looking round—"Can you point out the oak chest mentioned?"

Innocent rose, and moved to a corner, where she lifted out of a recess a small quaintly made oaken casket, brass-bound, with a heavy lock.

Mr. Bayliss looked at it with a certain amount of curiosity.

"The key?" he suggested—"I believe the late Mr. Jocelyn always wore it on his watch-chain."

Robin got up and went to the mantelpiece.

"Here is my uncle's watch and chain," he said, in a hushed voice— "The watch has stopped. I do not intend that it shall ever go again—I shall keep it put by with the precious treasures of the house."

Mr. Bayliss made no remark on this utterance, which to him was one of mere sentiment—and taking the watch and chain in his hand, detached therefrom a small key. With this he opened the oak casket— and looked carefully inside. Taking out a sealed packet, he handed it to Innocent.

"This is for you," he said—"and this also"—here he lifted from the bottom of the casket a flat jewel-case of antique leather embossed in gold.

"This," he continued, "Mr. Jocelyn explained to me, is a necklet of pearls—traditionally believed to have been given by the founder of the house, Amadis de Jocelin, to his wife on their wedding-day. It has been worn by every bride of the house since. I hope—yes—I very much hope—it will be worn by the young lady who now inherits it."

And he passed the jewel-case over the table to Innocent, who sat silent, with the sealed packet she had just received lying before her. She took it passively, and opened it—a beautiful row of pearls, not very large, but wonderfully perfect, lay within—clasped by a small, curiously designed diamond snap. She looked at them with half-wondering, half-indifferent eyes—then closed the case and gave it to Robin Clifford.

"They are for your wife when you marry," she said—"Please keep them."

Mr. Bayliss coughed—a cough of remonstrance.

"Pardon me, my dear young lady, but Mr. Jocelyn was particularly anxious the pearls should be yours—"

She looked at him, gravely.

"Yes—I am sure he was," she said—"He was always good—too good and generous—but if they are mine, I give them to Mr. Clifford. There is nothing more to be said about them."

Mr. Bayliss coughed again.

"Well—that is all that is contained in this casket, with the exception of a paper unsealed—shall I read it?"

She bent her head.

"The paper is written in Mr. Jocelyn's own hand, and is as follows," continued the lawyer: "I desire that my adopted child, known as 'Innocent,' shall receive into her own possession the Jocelyn pearls, valued by experts at L2,500, and that she shall wear the same on her marriage-morning. The sealed packet, placed in this casket with the pearls afore-said, contains a letter for her own personal and private perusal, and other matter which concerns herself alone."

Mr. Bayliss here looked up, and addressed her.

"From these words it is evident that the sealed packet you have there is an affair of confidence."

She laid her hand upon it.

"I quite understand!"

He adjusted his glasses, and turned over his documents once more.

"Then I think there is nothing more we need trouble you with—oh yes!—one thing—Miss—er—Miss Priday—?"

Priscilla, who during the whole conversation had sat bolt upright on a chair in the corner of the room, neither moving nor speaking, here rose and curtsied.

The lawyer looked at her attentively.

"Priday-Miss Priscilla Priday?"

"Yes, sir—that's me," said Priscilla, briefly.

"Mr. Jocelyn thought very highly of you, Miss Friday," he said—"he mentions you in the following paragraph of his will—'I give and bequeath to my faithful housekeeper and good friend, Priscilla Priday, the sum of Two Hundred Pounds for her own personal use, and I desire that she shall remain at Briar Farm for the rest of her life. And that, if she shall find it necessary to resign her duties in the farm house, she shall possess that cottage on my estate known as Rose Cottage, free of all charges, and be allowed to live there and be suitably and comfortably maintained till the end of her days. And,—er—pray don't distress yourself, Miss Priday!"

For Priscilla was crying, and making no effort to hide her emotion.

"Bless'is old'art!" she sobbed—"He thort of everybody,'e did! An' what shall I ever want o' Rose Cottage, as is the sweetest o' little places, when I've got the kitchen o' Briar Farm!—an' there I'll'ope to do my work plain an' true till I drops!—so there!—an' I'm much obliged to ye, Mr. Bayliss, an' mebbe ye'll tell me where to put the two'underd pounds so as I don't lose it, for I never'ad so much money in my life, an' if any one gets to'ear of it I'll 'ave all the 'alt an' lame an' blind round me in a jiffy. An' as for keepin' money, I never could—an' p'raps it 'ud be best for Mr. Robin to look arter it—" Here she stopped, out of breath with talk and tears.

"It will be all right," said Mr. Bayliss, soothingly, "quite all right, I assure you! Mr. Clifford will no doubt see to any little business matter for you with great pleasure—"

"Dear Priscilla!"—and Innocent went to her side and put an arm round her neck—"Don't cry!—you will be so happy, living always in this dear old place!—and Robin will be so glad to have you with him."

Priscilla took the little hand that caressed her, and kissed it.

"Ah, my lovey!" she half whispered—"I should be 'appy enough if I thought you was a-goin' to be 'appy too!—but you're flyin' in the face o' fortune, lovey!—that's what you're a-doin'!"

Innocent silenced her with a gesture, and stood beside her, patiently listening till Mr. Bayliss had concluded his business.

"I think, Mr. Clifford," he then said, at last—"there is no occasion to trouble you further. Everything is in perfect order—you are the inheritor of Briar Farm and all its contents, with all its adjoining lands—and the only condition attached to your inheritance is that you keep it maintained on the same working methods by which it has always been maintained. You will find no difficulty in doing this—and you have plenty of money to do it on. There are a few minor details respecting farm stock, etc., which we can go over together at any time. You are sole executor, of course—and—and—er—yes!—I think that is all."

"May I go now?" asked Innocent, lifting her serious blue-grey eyes to his face—"Do you want me any more?"

Mr. Bayliss surveyed her curiously.

"No—I—er—I think not," he replied—"Of course the pearls should be in your possession—"

"I have given them away," she said, quickly—"to Robin."

"But I have not accepted them," he answered—"I will keep them if you like—for You."

She gave a slight, scarcely perceptible movement of vexation, and then, taking up the sealed packet which was addressed to her personally, she left the room.

The lawyer looked after her in a little perplexity.

"I'm afraid she takes her loss rather badly," he said—"or—perhaps—is she a little absent-minded?"

Robin Clifford smiled, sadly.

"I think not," he answered. "Of course she feels the death of my uncle deeply—she adored him—and then-I-suppose you know—my uncle may have told you—"

"That he hoped and expected you to marry her?" said Mr. Bayliss, nodding his head, sagaciously—"Yes—I am aware that such was his dearest wish. In fact he led me to believe that the matter was as good as settled."

"She will not have me," said Clifford, gently—"and I cannot compel her to marry me against her will—indeed I would not if I could."

The lawyer was so surprised that he was obliged to take off his glasses and polish them.

"She will not have you!" he exclaimed. "Dear me! That is indeed most unexpected and distressing! There is—there is nothing against you, surely?—you are quite a personable young man—"

Robin shrugged his shoulders, disdainfully.

"Whatever I am does not matter to her," he said—"Let us talk no more about it."

Priscilla looked from one to the other.

"Eh well!" she said—"If any one knows 'er at all 'tis I as 'ave 'ad 'er with me night an' day when she was a baby—and 'as watched 'er grow into the little beauty she is,—an' 'er 'ed's just fair full o' strange fancies that she's got out o' the books she found in the old knight's chest years ago—we must give 'er time to think a bit an' settle. 'Tis an awful blow to 'er to lose 'er Dad, as she allus called Farmer Jocelyn—she's like a little bird fallen out o' the nest with no strength to use 'er wings an' not knowin' where to go. Let 'er settle a bit!—that's what I sez—an' you'll see I'm right. You leave 'er alone, Mister Robin, an' all'll come right, never fear! She's got the queerest notions about love—she picked 'em out o' they old books—an' she'll 'ave to find out they's more lies than truth. Love's a poor 'oldin' for most folks—it don't last long enough."

Mr. Bayliss permitted himself to smile, as he took his hat, and prepared to go.

"I'm sure you're quite right, Miss Priday!" he said—"you speak—er—most sensibly! I'm sure I hope, for the young lady's sake, that she will 'settle down'—if she does not—"

"Ay, if she does not!" echoed Clifford.

"Well! if she does not, life may be difficult for her"—and the lawyer shook his head forebodingly—"A girl alone in the world—with no relatives!—ah, dear, dear me! A sad look-out!—a very sad look-out! But we must trust to her good sense that she will be wise in time!"

X

Upstairs, shut in her own little room with the door locked, Innocent opened the sealed packet. She found within it a letter and some bank-notes. With a sensitive pain which thrilled every nerve in her body she unfolded the letter, written in Hugo Jocelyn's firm clear writing—a writing she knew so well, and which bore no trace of weakness or failing in the hand that guided the pen. How strange it was, she thought, that the written words should look so living and distinct when the writer was dead! Her head swam.—her eyes were dim—for a moment she could scarcely see—then the mist before her slowly dispersed and she read the first words, which made her heart swell and the tears rise in her aching throat.

My Little Wilding!

When you read this I shall be gone to that wonderful world which all the clergymen tell us about, but which none of them are in any great hurry to see for themselves. I hope—and I sometimes believe—such a world exists—and that perhaps it is a place where a man may sow seed and raise crops as well and as prosperously as on Briar Farm—however, I'm praying I may not be taken till I've seen you safely wed to Robin—and yet, something tells me this will not be; and that's the something that makes me write this letter and put it with the pearls that are, by my will, destined for you on your marriage-morning. I'm writing it, remember, on the same night I've told you all about yourself—the night of the day the doctor gave me my death-warrant. I may live a year,—I may live but a week,—it will be hard if I may not live to see you married!—but God's will must be done. The bank-notes folded in this letter make up four hundred pounds—and this money you can spend as you like—on your clothes for the bridal, or on anything you fancy—I place no restriction on you as to its use. When a maid weds there are many pretties she needs to buy, and the prettier they are for you the better shall I be pleased. Whether I live or whether I die, you need say nothing of this money to Robin, or to anyone. It is your own absolutely—to do as you like with.

I am thankful to feel that you will be safe in Robin's loving care—for the world is hard on a woman left alone as you would be, were it not for him. I give you my word that if I had any clue, however small, to your real parentage, I would write down here for you all I know—but I know nothing more than I have told you. I have loved you as my own child and you have been the joy of my old days. May God bless you and give you joy and peace in Briar Farm!—you and your children, and your children's children! Amen!

Your "Dad"

HUGO JOCELYN

She read this to the end, and then some tension in her brain seemed to relax, and she wept long and bitterly, her head bent down on the letter and her bright hair falling over it. Presently, checking her sobs, she rose, and looked about her in a kind of dream—the familiar little room seemed to have suddenly become strange to her, and she thought she saw standing in one corner a figure clad in armour,—its vizor was up, showing a sad pale face and melancholy eyes—the lips moved—and a sighing murmur floated past her ears—"Mon coeur me soutien!" A cold terror seized her, and she trembled from head to foot—then the vision or hallucination vanished as swiftly and mysteriously as it had appeared. Rallying her forces, she gradually mastered the overpowering fear which for a moment had possessed her,—and folding up Hugo Jocelyn's last letter, she kissed it, and placed it in her bosom. The banknotes were four in number—each for one hundred pounds;—these she put in an envelope, and shut them in the drawer containing her secret manuscript.

"Now the way is clear!" she said—"I can do what I like—I have my wings, and I can fly away! Oh Dad, dear Dad!—you would be so unhappy if you knew what I mean to do!—it would break your heart, Dad!—but you have no heart to break now, poor Dad!—it is cold as stone!—it will never beat any more! Mine is the heart that beats!—the heart that burns, and aches, and hurts me!—ah!—how it hurts! And no one can understand—no one will ever care to understand!"

She locked her manuscript-drawer—then went and bathed her eyes, which smarted with the tears she had shed. Looking at herself in the mirror she saw a pale plaintive little creature, without any freshness of beauty—all the vitality seemed gone out of her. Smoothing her ruffled hair, she twisted it up in a loose coil at the back of her head, and studied with melancholy dislike and pain the heavy effect of her dense black draperies against her delicate skin.

"I shall do for anything now," she said—"No one will look at me, and I shall pass quite unnoticed in a crowd. I'm glad I'm not a pretty girl—it might be more difficult to get on. And Robin called me 'lovely' the other day!—poor, foolish Robin!"

She went downstairs then to see if she could help Priscilla—but Priscilla would not allow her to do anything in the way of what she called "chores."

"No, lovey," she said—"you just keep quiet, an' by-an'-bye you an' me'll 'ave a quiet tea together, for Mister Robin he's gone off for the rest o' the day an' night with Mr. Bayliss, as there's lots o' things to see to, an' 'e left you this little note"—here Priscilla produced a small neatly folded paper from her apron pocke-t-"an' sez 'e—'Give this to Miss Innocent' 'e sez, 'an' she won't mind my bein' out o' the way—it'll be better for 'er to be quiet a bit with you'—an' so it will, lovey, for sometimes a man about the 'ouse is a worrit an' a burden, say what we will, an' good though 'e be."

Innocent took the note and read—

"I have made up my mind to go with Bayliss into the town and stay at his house for the night—there are many business matters we have to go into together, and it is important for me to thoroughly understand the position of my uncle's affairs. If I cannot manage to get back to-morrow, I will let you know. Robin."

She heaved a sigh of intense relief. For twenty-four hours at least she was free from love's importunity—she could be alone to think, and to plan. She turned to Priscilla with a gentle look and smile.

"I'll go into the garden," she said—"and when it's tea-time you'll come and fetch me, won't you? I shall be near the old stone knight, Sieur Amadis—"

"Oh, bother 'im," muttered Priscilla, irrelevantly—"You do think too much o' that there blessed old figure!—why, what's 'e got to do with you, my pretty?"

"Nothing!" and the colour came to her pale cheeks for a moment, and then fled back again—"He never had anything to do with me, really! But I seem to know him."

Priscilla gave a kind of melancholy snort—and the girl moved slowly away through the open door and beyond it, out among the radiant flowers. Her little figure in deep black was soon lost to sight, and after watching her for a minute, Priscilla turned to her home-work with tears blinding her eyes so thickly that she could scarcely see.

"If she winnot take Mister Robin, the Lord knows what'll become of 'er!" sighed the worthy woman—"For she's as lone i' the world as a thrush fallen out o' the nest before it's grown strong enough to fly! Eh, we thort we did a good deed, Mister Jocelyn an' I, when we kep' 'er as a baby, 'opin' agin 'ope as 'er parents 'ud turn up an' be sorry for the loss of 'er—but never a sign of a soul!—an' now she's grow'd up she's thorts in 'er 'ed which ain't easy to unnerstand—for since Mister Jocelyn told 'er the tale of 'erself she's not been the same like—she's got suddin old!"

The afternoon was very peaceful and beautiful—the sun shone warmly over the smooth meadows of Briar Farm, and reddened the apples in the orchard yet a little more tenderly, flashing in flecks of gold on the "Glory" roses, and touching the wings of fluttering doves with arrowy silver gleams. No one looking at the fine old house, with its picturesque gables and latticed windows, would have thought that its last master of lawful lineage was dead and buried, and that the funeral had taken place that morning. Briar Farm, though more than three centuries old, seemed full of youthful life and promise—a vital fact, destined to outlast many more human lives than those which in the passing of three hundred years had already left their mark upon it, and it was strange and incredible to realise that the long chain of lineally descended male ancestors had broken at last, and that no remaining link survived to carry on the old tradition. Sadly and slowly Innocent walked across the stretches of warm clover-scented grass to the ancient tomb of the "Sieur Amadis"—and sat down beside it, not far from the place where so lately she had sat with Robin—what a change had come over her life since then! She watched the sun sinking towards the horizon in a mellow mist of orange-coloured radiance,—the day was drawing to an end—the fateful, wretched day which had seen the best friend she had ever known, and whom for years she had adored and revered as her own "father," laid in the dust to perish among perishable things.

"I wish I had died instead of him," she said, half aloud—"or else that I had never been born! Oh, dear 'Sieur Amadis'!—you know how hard it is to live in the world unless some one wants you—unless some one loves you!—and no one wants me—no one loves me—except Robin!"

Solitary, and full of the heaviest sadness, she tried to think and to form plans—but her mind was tired, and she could come to no decisive resolution beyond the one all-convincing necessity—that of leaving Briar Farm. Of course she must go,—there was no other alternative. And now, thanks to Hugo Jocelyn's forethought in giving her money for her bridal "pretties," no financial difficulty stood in the way of her departure. She must go—but where? To begin with, she had no name. She would have to invent one for herself—"Yes!" she murmured—"I must invent a name—and make it famous!" Involuntarily she clenched her small hand as though she held some prize within its soft grasp. "Why not? Other people have done the same—I can but try! If I fail—!"

Her delicate fingers relaxed,—in her imagination she saw some coveted splendour slip from her hold, and her little face grew set and serious as though she had already suffered a whole life's disillusion.

"I can but try," she repeated—"something urges me on—something tells me I may succeed. And then—!"

Her eyes brightened slowly—a faint rose flushed her cheeks,—and with the sudden change of expression, she became almost beautiful. Herein lay her particular charm,—the rarest of all in women,—the passing of the lights and shadows of thought over features which responded swiftly and emotionally to the prompting and play of the mind.

"I should have to go," she went on—"even if Dad were still alive. I could not—I cannot marry Robin!—I do not want to marry anybody. It is the common lot of women—why they should envy or desire it, I cannot think! To give one's self up entirely to a man's humours—to be glad of his caresses, and miserable when he is angry or tired—to bear his children and see them grow up and leave you for their own 'betterment' as they would call it—oh!—what an old, old drudging life!—a life of monotony, sickness, pain, and fatigue!—and nothing higher done than what animals can do! There are plenty of women in the world who like to stay on this level, I suppose—but I should not like it,—I could not live in this beautiful, wonderful world with no higher ambition than a sheep or a cow!"

At that moment she suddenly saw Priscilla running from the house across the meadow, and beckoning to her in evident haste and excitement. She got up at once and ran to meet her, flying across the grass with light airy feet as swiftly as Atalanta.

"What is it?" she cried, seeing Priscilla's face, crimson with hurry and nervousness—"Is there some new trouble?"

Priscilla was breathless, and could scarcely speak.

MARIE CORELLI

"There's a lady"—she presently gasped—"a lady to see you—from London—in the best parlour—she asked for Farmer Jocelyn's adopted daughter named Innocent. And she gave me her card—here it is"— and Priscilla wiped her face and gasped again as Innocent took the card and read "Lady Maude Blythe,"—then gazed at Priscilla, wonderingly.

"Who can she be?—some one who knew Dad—?"

"Bless you, child, he never knew lord nor lady!" replied Priscilla, recovering her breath somewhat—"No—it's more likely one o' they grand folks what likes to buy old furniture, an' mebbe somebody's told 'er about Briar Farm things, an' 'ow they might p'raps be sold now the master's gone—"

"But that would be very silly and wicked talk," said Innocent. "Nothing will be sold—Robin would never allow it—"

"Well, come an' see the lady," and Priscilla hurried her along—"She said she wished to see you partikler. I told 'er the master was dead, an' onny buried this mornin', an' she smiled kind o' pleasant like, an' said she was sorry to have called on such an unfortunate day, but her business was important, an' if you could see 'er—"

"Is she young?"

"No, she's not young—but she isn't old," replied Priscilla—"She's wonderful good-looking an' dressed beautiful! I never see such clothes cut out o' blue serge! An' she's got a scent about her like our stillroom when we're makin' pot-purry bags for the linen."

By this time they had reached the house, and Innocent went straight into the best parlour. Her unexpected and unknown visitor stood there near the window, looking out on the beds of flowers, but turned round as she entered. For a moment they confronted each other in silence,— Innocent gazing in mute astonishment and enquiry at the tall, graceful, self-possessed woman, who, evidently of the world, worldly, gazed at her in turn with a curious, almost quizzical interest. Presently she spoke in a low, sweet, yet cold voice.

"So you are Innocent!" she said.

The girl's heart beat quickly,—something frightened her, though she knew not what.

"Yes," she answered, simply—"I am Innocent. You wished to see me—?"

"Yes—I wished to see you,"—and the lady quietly shut the window— "and I also wish to talk to you. In case anyone may be about listening, will you shut the door?"

With increasing nervousness and bewilderment, Innocent obeyed.

"You had my card, I think?" continued the lady, smiling ever so slightly—"I gave it to the servant—"

Innocent held it half crumpled in her hand.

"Yes," she said, trying to rally her self-possession—"Lady Maude Blythe—"

"Exactly!—you have quite a nice pronunciation! May I sit down?" and, without waiting for the required permission, Lady Blythe sank indolently into the old oaken arm-chair where Farmer Jocelyn had so long been accustomed to sit, and, taking out a cobweb of a handkerchief powerfully scented, passed it languorously across her lips and brow.

"You have had a very sad day of it, I fear!" she continued—"Deaths and funerals are such unpleasant affairs! But the farmer—Mr. Jocelyn—was not your father, was he?" The question was put with a repetition of the former slight, cold smile.

"No,"—and the girl looked at her wonderingly—"but he was better than my own father who deserted me!"

"Dear me! Your own father deserted you! How shocking of him!" and Lady Blythe turned a pair of brilliant dark eyes full on the pale little face confronting her—"And your mother?"

"She deserted me, too."

"What a reprehensible couple!" Here Lady Blythe extended a delicately gloved hand towards her. "Come here and let me look at you!"

But Innocent hesitated.

"Excuse me," she said, with a quaint and simple dignity—"I do not know you. I cannot understand why you have come to see me—if you would explain—"

While she thus spoke Lady Blythe had surveyed her scrutinisingly through a gold-mounted lorgnon.

"Quite a proud little person it is!" she remarked, and smiled—"Quite proud! I suppose I really must explain! Only I do hope you will not make a scene. Nothing is so unpleasant! And Such bad form! Please sit down!"

Innocent placed a chair close to the table so that she could lean her arm on that friendly board and steady her trembling little frame. When she was seated, Lady Blythe again looked at her critically through the lorgnon. Then she continued—

"Well, I must first tell you that I have always known your history—such a romance, isn't it! You were brought here as a baby by a man on horseback'—and he left you with the good old farmer who has taken care of you ever since. I am right? Yes!—I'm quite sure about it—because I knew the man—the curious sort of parental Lochinvar!—who got rid of you in such a curious way!"

Innocent drew a sharp breath.

"You knew him?"

Lady Blythe gave a delicate little cough.

"Yes—I knew him—rather well! I was quite a girl—and he was an artist—a rather famous one in his way—half French—and very good-looking. Yes, he certainly was remarkably good-looking! We ran away together—most absurd of us—but we did. Please don't look at me like that!—you remind me of Sara Bernhardt in 'La Tosca'!"

Innocent's eyes were indeed full of something like positive terror. Her heart beat violently—she felt a strange dread, and a foreboding that chilled her very blood.

"People often do that kind of thing—fall in love and run away," continued Lady Blythe, placidly—"when they are young and silly. It is quite a delightful sensation, of course, but it doesn't last. They don't know the world—and they never calculate results. However, we had quite a good time together. We went to Devon and Cornwall, and he painted pictures and made love to me—and it was all very nice and pretty. Then, of course, trouble came, and we had to get out of it as best we could—we were both tired of each other and quarrelled dreadfully, so we decided to give each other up. Only you were in the way!"

Innocent rose, steadying herself with one hand against the table.

"I!" she exclaimed, with a kind of sob in her throat.

"Yes—you! Dear me,—how you stare! Don't you understand? I suppose you've lived such a strange sort of hermit life down here that you know nothing. You were in the way—you, the baby!"

"Do you mean—?"

"Yes—I mean what you ought to have guessed at once—if you were not as stupid as an owl! I've told you I ran away with a man—I wouldn't marry him, though he asked me to—I should have been tied up for life, and I didn't want that—so we decided to separate. And he undertook to get rid of the baby—"

"Me!" cried Innocent, wildly—"oh, dear God! It was me!"

"Yes—it was you—but you needn't be tragic about it!" said Lady Blythe, calmly—"I think, on the whole, you were fortunately placed—and I was told where you were—"

"You were told?—oh, you were told!—and you never came! And you—you are—my MOTHER!"—and overpowered by the shock of emotion, the girl sank back on her chair, and burying her head in her hands, sobbed bitterly. Lady Blythe looked at her in meditative silence.

"What a tiresome creature!" she murmured, under her breath—"Quite undisciplined! No repose of manner—no style whatever! And apparently very little sense! I think it's a pity I came,—a mistaken sense of duty!"

Aloud she said—

"I hope you're not going to cry very long! Won't you get it over? I thought you would be glad to know me—and I've come out of pure kindness to you, simply because I heard your old farmer was dead. Why Pierce Armitage should have brought you to him I never could imagine—except that once he was painting a picture in the neighbourhood and was rather taken with the history of this place—Briar Farm isn't it called? You'll make your eyes quite sore if you go on crying like that! Yes—I am your mother—most unfortunately!—I hoped you would never know it!—but now—as you are left quite alone in the world, I have come to see what I can do for you."

Innocent checked her sobs, and lifting her head looked straight into the rather shallow bright eyes that regarded her with such cold and easy scrutiny.

"You can do nothing for me," she answered, in a low voice—"You never have done anything for me. If you are my mother, you are an unnatural one!" And moved by a sudden, swift emotion, she stood up with indignation and scorn lighting every feature of her face. "I was in your way at my birth—and you were glad to be rid of me. Why should you seek me now?"

Lady Blythe glanced her over amusedly.

"Really, you would do well on the stage!" she said—"If you were taller, you would make your fortune with that tragic manner! It is quite wasted on me, I assure you! I've told you a very simple commonplace truth—a thing that happens every day—a silly couple run away together, madly in love, and deluded by the idea that love will last—they get into trouble and have a child—naturally, as they are not married, the child is in the way, and they get rid of it—some people would have killed it, you know! Your father was quite a kind-hearted person—and his one idea was to place you where there were no other children, and where you would have a chance of being taken care of. So he brought you to

Briar Farm—and he told me where he had left you before he went away and died."

"Died!" echoed the girl—"My father is dead?"

"So I believe,"—and Lady Blythe stifled a slight yawn—"He was always a rather reckless person—went out to paint pictures in all weathers, or to 'study effects' as he called it—how I hated his 'art' talk!—and I heard he died in Paris of influenza or pneumonia or something or other. But as I was married then, it didn't matter."

Innocent's deep-set, sad eyes studied her "mother" with strange wistfulness.

"Did you not love him?" she asked, pitifully.

Lady Blythe laughed, lightly.

"You odd girl! Of course I was quite crazy about him!—he was so handsome—and very fascinating in his way—but he could be a terrible bore, and he had a very bad temper. I was thankful when we separated. But I have made my own private enquiries about you, from time to time—I always had rather a curiosity about you, as I have had no other children. Won't you come and kiss me?"

Innocent stood rigid.

"I cannot!" she said.

Lady Blythe flushed and bit her lips.

"As you like!" she said, airily—"I don't mind!"

The girl clasped her hands tightly together.

"How can you ask me!" she said, in low, thrilling tones—"You who have let me grow up without any knowledge of you!—you who had no shame in leaving me here to live on the charity of a stranger!—you who never cared at all for the child you brought into the world!—can you imagine that I could care—now?"

"Well, really," smiled Lady Blythe—"I'm not sure that I have asked you to care! I have simply come here to tell you that you are not entirely alone in the world, and that I, knowing myself to be your mother—(although it happened so long ago I can hardly believe I was ever such a fool!)—am willing to do something for you—especially as I have no children by my second marriage. I will, in fact, 'adopt' you!" and she laughed—a pretty, musical laugh like a chime of little silver bells. "Lord Blythe will be delighted—he's a kind old person!"

Innocent looked at her gravely and steadily.

"Do you mean to say that you will own me?—name me?—acknowledge me as your daughter—"

"Why, certainly not!" and Lady Blythe's eyes flashed over her in cold disdain—"What are you thinking of? You are not legitimate—and you really have no lawful name—besides, I'm not bound to do anything at all for you now you are old enough to earn your own living. But I'm quite a good-natured woman,—and as I have said already I have no other children—and I'm willing to 'adopt' you, bring you out in society, give you pretty clothes, and marry you well if I can. But to own that I ever made such an idiot of myself as to have you at all is a little too much to ask!—Lord Blythe would never forgive me!"

"So you would make me live a life of deception with you!" said Innocent—"You would make me pretend to be what I am not—just as you pretend to be what you are not!—and yet you say I am your child! Oh God, save me from such a mother! Madam"—and she spoke in cold, deliberate accents—"you have lived all these years without children, save me whom you have ignored—and I, though nameless and illegitimate, now ignore you! I have no mother! I would not own you any more than you would own me;—my shame in saying that such a woman is my mother would be greater than yours in saying that I am your child! For the stigma of my birth is not my fault, but yours!—I am, as my father called me—'innocent'!"

Her breath came and went quickly—a crimson flush was on her cheeks—she looked transfigured—beautiful. Lady Blythe stared at her in wide-eyed disdain.

"You are exceedingly rude and stupid," she said—"You talk like a badly-trained actress! And you are quite blind to your own interests. Now please remember that if you refuse the offer I make you, I shall never trouble about you again—you will have to sink or swim—and you can do nothing for yourself—without even a name—"

"Have you never heard," interrupted Innocent, suddenly, "that it is quite possible to MAKE a name?"

Her "mother" was for the moment startled—she looked so intellectually strong and inspired.

"Have you never thought," she went on—"even you, in your strange life of hypocrisy—"

"Hypocrisy!" exclaimed Lady Blythe—"How dare you say such a thing!"

"Of course it is hypocrisy," said the girl, resolutely—"You are married to a man who knows nothing of your past life—is not that hypocrisy? You are a great lady, no doubt—you have everything you want in this

MARIE CORELLI

world, except children—one child you had in me, and you let me be taken from you—yet you would pretend to 'adopt' me though you know I am your own! Is not that hypocrisy?"

Lady Blythe for a moment tightened her lips in a line of decided temper—then she smiled ironically.

"It is tact," she said—"and good manners. Society lives by certain conventions, and we must be careful not to outrage them. In your own interests you should be glad to learn how to live suitably without offence to others around you."

Innocent looked at her with straight and relentless scorn.

"I have done that," she answered—"so far. I shall continue to do it. I do not want any help from you! I would rather die than owe you anything! Please understand this! You say I am your daughter, and I suppose I must believe it—but the knowledge brings me sorrow and shame. And I must work my way out of this sorrow and shame,—somehow! I will do all I can to retrieve the damaged life you have given me. I never knew my mother was alive—and now—I wish to forget it! If my father lived, I would go to him—"

"Would you indeed!" and Lady Blythe rose, shaking her elegant skirts, and preening herself like a bird preparing for flight—"I'm afraid you would hardly receive a parental welcome! Fortunately for himself and for me, he is dead,—so you are quite untrammelled by any latent notions of filial duty. And you will never see me again after to-day!"

"No?"—and the interrogation was put with the slightest inflection of satire—so fine as to be scarcely perceptible—but Lady Blythe caught it, and flushed angrily.

"Of course not!" she said—"Do you think you, in your position of a mere farmer's girl, are likely to meet me in the greater world? You, without even a name—"

"Would you have given me a name?" interposed the girl, calmly.

"Of course! I should have invented one for you—

"I can do that for myself," said Innocent, quietly—"and so you are relieved from all trouble on my score. May I ask you to go now?"

Lady Blythe stared at her.

"Are you insolent, or only stupid?" she asked—"Do you realise what it is that I have told you—that I, Lady Blythe, wife of a peer, and moving in the highest ranks of society, am willing to take charge of you, feed you, clothe you, bring you out and marry you well? Do you understand, and still refuse?"

"I understand—and I still refuse," replied Innocent—"I would accept, if you owned me as your daughter to your husband and to all the world—but as your 'adopted' child—as a lie under your roof—I refuse absolutely and entirely! Are you astonished that I should wish to live truly instead of falsely?"

Lady Blythe gathered her priceless lace scarf round her elegant shoulders.

"I begin to think it must have been all a bad dream!" she said, and laughed softly—"My little affair with your father cannot have really happened, and you cannot really be my child! I must consider it in that light! I feel I have done my part in the matter by coming here to see you and talk to you and make what I consider a very kind and reasonable proposition—you have refused it—and there is no more to be said." She settled her dainty hat more piquantly on her rich dark hair, and smiled agreeably. "Will you show me the way out? I left my motor-car on the high-road—my chauffeur did not care to bring it down your rather muddy back lane."

Innocent said nothing—but merely opened the door and stood aside for her visitor to pass. A curious tightening at her heart oppressed her as she thought that this elegant, self-possessed, exquisitely attired creature was actually her "mother!"—and she could have cried out with the pain which was so hard to bear. Suddenly Lady Blythe came to an abrupt standstill.

"You will not kiss me?" she said—"Not even for your father's sake?"

With a quick sobbing catch in her breath, the girl looked up—her "mother" was a full head taller than she. She lifted her fair head—her eyes were full of tears. Her lips quivered—Lady Blythe stooped and kissed them lightly.

"There!—be a good girl!" she said. "You have the most extraordinary high-flown notions, and I think they will lead you into trouble! However, I'll give you one more chance—if at the end of this year you would like to come to me, my offer to you still holds good. After that—well!—as you yourself said, you will have no mother!"

"I have never had one!" answered Innocent, in low choked accents—"And—I shall never have one!"

Lady Blythe smiled—a cold, amused smile, and passed out through the hall into the garden.

"What delightful flowers!" she exclaimed, in a sweet, singing voice, for the benefit of anyone who might be listening—"A perfect paradise!

MARIE CORELLI

No wonder Briar Farm is so famous! It's perfectly charming! Is this the way? Thanks ever so much!" This, as Innocent opened the gate—"Let me see!—I go up the old by-road?—yes?—and the main road joins it at the summit?—No, pray don't trouble to come with me—I can find my car quite easily! Good-bye!"

And picking up her dainty skirt with one ungloved hand, on which two diamond rings shone like circlets of dew, she nodded, smiled, and went her way—Innocent standing at the gate and watching her go with a kind of numbed patience as though she saw a figure in a dream vanishing slowly with the dawn of day. In truth she could hardly grasp the full significance of what had happened—she did not feel, even remotely, the slightest attraction towards this suddenly declared "mother" of hers—she could hardly believe the story. Yet she knew it must be true,—no woman of title and position would thus acknowledge a stigma on her own life without any cause for the confession. She stood at the gate still watching, though there was nothing now to watch, save the bending trees, and the flowering wild plants that fringed each side of the old by-road. Priscilla's voice calling her in a clear, yet lowered tone, startled her at last—she slowly shut the gate and turned in answer.

"Yes, dear? What is it?"

Priscilla trotted out from under the porch, full of eager curiosity.

"Has the lady gone?"

"Yes."

"What did she want with ye, dearie?"

"Nothing very much!" and Innocent smiled—a strange, wistful smile—"Only just what you thought!—she wished to buy something from Briar Farm—and I told her it was not to be sold!"

XI

That night Innocent made an end of all her hesitation. Resolutely she put away every thought that could deter her from the step she was now resolved to take. Poor old Priscilla little imagined the underlying cause of the lingering tenderness with which the girl kissed her "good-night," looking back with more than her usual sweetness as she went along the corridor to her own little room. Once there, she locked and bolted the door fast, and then set to work gathering a few little things together and putting them in a large but light-weight satchel, such as she had often used to carry some of the choicest apples from the orchard when they were being gathered in. Her first care was for her manuscript,—the long-treasured scribble, kept so secretly and so often considered with hope and fear, and wonder and doubting— then she took one or two of the more cherished volumes which had formerly been the property of the "Sieur Amadis" and packed them with it. Choosing only the most necessary garments from her little store, she soon filled her extemporary travelling-bag, and then sat down to write a letter to Robin. It was brief and explicit.

"Dear Robin,"—it ran—"I have left this beloved home. It is impossible for me to stay. Dad left me some money in bank-notes in that sealed letter—so I want for nothing. Do not be anxious or unhappy—but marry soon and forget me. I know you will always be good to Priscilla—tell her I am not ungrateful to her for all her care of me. I love her dearly. But I am placed in the world unfortunately, and I must do something that will help me out of the shame of being a burden on others and an object of pity or contempt. If you will keep the old books Dad gave me, and still call them mine, you will be doing me a great kindness. And will you take care of Cupid?—he is quite a clever bird and knows his friends. He will come to you or Priscilla as easily as he comes to me. Good-bye, you dear, kind boy! I love you very much, but not as you want me to love you,—and I should only make you miserable if I stayed here and married you. God bless you!

Innocent

She put this in an envelope and addressed it,—then making sure that everything was ready, she took a few sovereigns from the little pile of housekeeping money which Priscilla always brought to her to count over every week and compare with the household expenses.

"I can return these when I change one of Dad's bank-notes," she said to herself—"but I must have something smaller to pay my way with just now than a hundred pounds."

Indeed the notes Hugo Jocelyn had left for her might have given her some little trouble and embarrassment, but she did not pause to consider difficulties. When a human creature resolves to dare and to do, no impediment, real or imaginary, is allowed to stand long in the way. An impulse pushes the soul forward, be it ever so reluctantly—the impulse is sometimes from heaven and sometimes from hell—but as long as it is active and peremptory, it is obeyed blindly and to the full.

This little ignorant and unworldly girl passed the rest of the night in tidying the beloved room where she had spent so many happy hours, and setting everything in order,—talking in whispers between whiles to the ghostly presence of the "Sieur Amadis" as to a friend who knew her difficult plight and guessed her intentions.

"You see," she said, softly, "there is no way out of it. It is not as if I were anybody—I am nobody! I was never wanted in the world at all. I have no name. I have never been baptised. And though I know now that I have a mother, I feel that she is nothing to me. I can hardly believe she is my mother. She is a lady of fashion with a secret—and *I* am the secret! I ought to be put away and buried and forgotten!—that would be safest for her, and perhaps best for me! But I should like to live long enough to make her wish she had been true to my father and had owned me as his child! Ah, such dreams! Will they ever come true!"

She paused, looking up by the dim candle-light at the arms of the "Sieur Amadis"—who "Here seekinge Forgetfulnesse did here fynde Peace"—and at the motto "Mon coeur me soutien."

"Poor 'Sieur Amadis!'" she murmured—"He sought forgetfulness!—shall I ever do the same? How strange it will be not to Wish to remember!—surely one must be very old, or sad, to find gladness in forgetting!"

A faint little thrill of dread ran through her slight frame—thoughts began to oppress her and shake her courage—she resolutely put them away and bent herself to the practical side of action. Re-attiring herself in the plain black dress and hat which Priscilla had got for her mourning garb, she waited patiently for the first peep of daylight—a daylight which was little more than darkness—and then, taking her satchel, she crept softly out of her room, never once looking back. There was nothing to stay her progress, for the great mastiff Hero, since Hugo Jocelyn's death, had taken to such dismal howling that it had been found necessary to keep him away from the house in, a far-off shed where his melancholy plaints could not be heard. Treading with light, soundless footsteps down the stairs, she reached the front-door,—unbarred and unlocked it without any noise, and as softly closed it behind her,—then she stood in the open, shivering slightly in the sweet coldness of the coming dawn, and inhaling the fragrance of awakening unseen flowers. She knew of a gap in the hedge by means of which she could leave the garden without opening the big farm-gate which moved on rather creaking hinges— and she took this way over a couple of rough stepping-stones. Once out on the old by-road she paused. Briar Farm looked like a house in a dream—there was not enough daylight yet to show its gables distinctly, and it was more like the shadowy suggestion of a building than any actual substance. Yet there was something solemn and impressive in its scarcely defined outline—to the girl's sensitive imagination it was like the darkened and disappearing vision of her youth and happiness,—a curtain falling, as it were, between the past and the future like a drop-scene in a play.

"Good-bye, Briar Farm!" she whispered, kissing her hand to the quaintly peaked roof just dimly perceptible—"Good-bye, dear, beloved home! I shall never forget you! I shall never see anything like you! Good-bye, peace and safety!—good-bye!"

The tears rushed to her eyes, and for the moment blinded her,—then, overcoming this weakness, she set herself to walk quickly and steadily away. Up the old by-road, through the darkness of the overhanging trees, here and there crossed by pale wandering gleams of fitful light from the nearing dawn, she moved swiftly, treading with noiseless footsteps as though she thought the unseen spirits of wood and field might hear and interrupt her progress—and in a few minutes she found herself upon the broad highway branching right and left and leading in either direction to the wider world. Briar Farm had disappeared behind the trees,—it was as though no such place existed, so deeply was it hidden.

She stopped, considering. She was not sure which was the way to the nearest railway-station some eight miles distant. She was prepared to walk it, but feared to take the wrong road, for she instinctively felt that if she had to endure any unexpected delay, some one from Briar Farm would be sent to trace her and find out where she went. While she thus hesitated, she heard the heavy rumbling of slow cart-wheels, and waited to see what sort of vehicle might be approaching. It was a large waggon drawn by two ponderous horses and driven by a man who, dimly perceived by the light of the lantern fastened in front of him, appeared to be asleep. Innocent hailed him—and after one or two efforts succeeded at last in rousing his attention.

"Which is the way to the railway-station?" she asked.

The man blinked drowsily at her.

"Railway-station, is it? I be a-goin' there now to fetch a load o' nitrates. Are ye wantin' to git?"

"Wantin' to git" was a country phrase to which Innocent was well accustomed. She answered, gently—

"Yes. I should be so glad if you'd give me a lift—I'll pay you for it. I have to catch the first train to London."

"Lunnon? Quiet, ye rascals!"—this to the sturdy horses who were dragging away at their shafts in stolid determination to move on— "Lunnon's a good way off! Ever bin there?"

"No."

"Nor I, nayther. Seekin' service?"

"Yes."

"Wal, ye can ride along wi' me, if so be ye likes it—we be goin' main slow, but we'll be there before first engine. Climb up!—that's right! 'Ere's a corner beside me—ye could sit in the waggon if ye liked, but it's 'ard as nails. 'Ere's a bit of 'oss-cloth for a cushion."

The girl sprang up as he bade her and was soon seated.

"Ye're a light 'un an' a little 'un, an' a young 'un," he said, with a chuckle—"an' what ye're doin' all alone i' the wake o' the marnin' is more than yer own mother knows, I bet!"

"I have no mother," she said.

"Eh, eh! That's bad—that's bad! Yet for all that there's bad mothers wot's worse than none. Git on wi' ye!"—this in a stentorian voice to the horses, accompanied by a sounding crack of the whip. "Git on!"

The big strong creatures tugged at the shafts and obeyed, their hoofs making a noisy clatter in the silence of the dawn. The daylight was beginning to declare itself more openly, and away to the east, just above a line of dark trees, the sky showed pale suggestions of amber and of rose. Innocent sat very silent; she was almost afraid of the coming light lest by chance the man beside her should ever have seen her before and recognise her. His sleep having been broken, he was disposed to be garrulous.

"Ever bin by train afore?" he asked.

"No."

"No! Eh, that's mighty cur'ous. A'most everyone goes somewhere by train nowadays—there's such a sight o' cheap 'scursions. I know a man wot got up i' the middle o' night, 'e did, an' more fool 'e!—an' off 'e goes by train down to seaside for the day—'e'd never seen the sea before an' it giv' 'im such a scare as 'e ain't got over it yet. 'E said there was such a sight o' wobblin' water that 'e thort it 'ud wobble off altogether an' wash away all the land and 'im with it. Ay, ay! 'e was main scared with 'is cheap 'scursion!"

"I've never seen the sea," said Innocent then, in a low clear tone— "but I've read about it—and I think I know what it is like. It is always changing,—it is full of beautiful colours, blue and green, and grey and violet—and it has great waves edged with white foam!—oh yes!—the poets write about it, and I have often seen it in my dreams."

The dawning light in the sky deepened—and the waggoner turned his head to look more closely at his girl-companion.

"Ye talks mighty strange!" he said—"a'most as if ye'd been eddicated up to it. I ain't been eddicated, an' I've no notions above my betters, but ye may be right about the sea—if ye've read about it, though the papers is mostly lies, if ye asks me, telling ye one thing one day an' another to-morrow—"

"I don't read the papers"—and Innocent smiled a little as in the widening light she began to see the stolid, stupid, but good-natured face of the man—"I don't understand them. I've read about the sea in books,—books of poetry."

He uttered a sound between a whistle and a grunt.

"Books of poetry! An' ye're goin' to seek service in Lunnon? Take my word for't, my gel, they won't want any folks there wi' sort o' gammon like that in their 'eds—they're all on the make there, an' they don't care for nothin' 'cept money an' 'ow to grab it. I ain't bin there, but I've heerd a good deal."

"You may have heard wrong," said Innocent, gathering more courage as she realised that the light was now quite clear enough for him to see her features distinctly and that it was evident he did not know her—"London is such a large place that there must be all sorts in it—good as well as bad—they can't all be greedy for money. There must be people who think beautiful things, and do beautiful work—"

"Oh, there's plenty o' work done there"—and the waggoner flicked his long whip against the sturdy flanks of his labouring horses—"I ain't denyin' that. An' You'll 'ave to work, my gel!—you bet! you'll 'ave to wash down steps an' sweep kitchens a good while afore you gits into the way of it! Why not take a service in the country?"

"I'm a little tired of the country," she answered—"I'd like a change."

"An' a change ye're likely to git!" he retorted, somewhat gruffly—"Lor' bless yer 'art! There ain't nothin' like the country! All the trees a-greenin' an' the flowers a-blowin' an' the birds a-singin'! 'Ave ye ever 'era tell of a place called Briar Farm?"

She controlled the nervous start of her body, and replied quietly—

"I think I have. A very old place."

"Ah! Old? I believe ye! 'Twas old in the time o' good Queen Bess—an' the same fam'ly 'as 'ad it these three 'undred years—a fam'ly o' the name o' Jocelyn. Ay, if ye could a' got service wi' Farmer Jocelyn ye'd a' bin in luck's way! But 'e's dead an' gone last week—more's the pity!—an' 'is nephew's got the place now, forbye 'e ain't a Jocelyn."

She was silent, affecting not to be interested. The waggoner went on—

"That's the sort o' place to seek service in! Safe an' clean an' 'onest as the sunshine—good work an' good pay—a deal better than a place in Lunnon. An' country air, my gel!—country air!—nuthin' like it!"

A sudden blaze of gold lit up the trees—the sun was rising—full day was disclosed, and the last filmy curtains of the night were withdrawn, showing a heavenly blue sky flecked lightly with wandering trails of white cloud like swansdown. He pointed eastward with his long whip.

"Look at that!" he said—"Fine, isn't it! No roofs and chimneys—just the woods and fields! Nuthin' like it anywhere!"

Innocent drew a long breath—the air was indeed sweet and keen—new life seemed given to the world with its exhilarating freshness. But she made no reply to the enthusiastic comments of her companion. Thoughts were in her brain too deep for speech. Not here, not here, in this quiet pastoral scene could she learn the way to wrest the golden circlet of fame from the hands of the silent gods!—it must be in the turmoil and rush of endeavour—the swift pursuit of the flying Apollo! And—as the slow waggon jogged along—she felt herself drawn, as it were, by a magnet—

on—on—on!—on towards a veiled mystery which waited for her—a mystery which she alone could solve.

Presently they came within sight of several rows of ugly wooden sheds with galvanised iron roofs and short black chimneys.

"A'most there now," said the waggoner—"'Ere's a bit o' Lunnon a'ready!—dirt an' muck and muddle! Where man do make a mess o' things 'e makes a mess all round! Spoils everything 'e can lay 'is 'ands on!"

The approaches to the railway were certainly not attractive—no railway approaches ever are. Perhaps they appear more than usually hideous when built amid a fair green country, where for miles and miles one sees nothing but flowering hedgerows and soft pastures shaded by the graceful foliage of sheltering trees. Then the shining, slippery iron of the railway running like a knife through the verdant bosom of the land almost hurts the eyes, and the accessories of station-sheds, coal-trucks, and the like, affront the taste like an ill-done foreground in an otherwise pleasing picture. A slight sense of depression and foreboding came like a cloud over the mind of poor little lonely Innocent, as she alighted at the station at last, and with uplifted wistful eyes tendered a sovereign to the waggoner.

"Please take as much of it as you think right," she said—"It was very kind of you to let me ride with you."

The man stared, whistled, and thought. Feeling in the depth of a capacious pocket he drew out a handful of silver and counted it over carefully.

"'Ere y'are!" he said, handing it all over with the exception of one half-crown—"Ye'll want all yer change in Lunnon an' more. I'm takin' two bob an' sixpence—if ye thinks it too much, say so!"

"Oh no, no!" and Innocent looked distressed—"Perhaps it's too little—I hope you are not wronging yourself?"

The waggoner laughed, kindly enough.

"Don't ye mind ME!" he said—"I'M all right! If I 'adn't two kids at 'ome I'd charge ye nothin'—but I'm goin' to get 'em a toy they wants, an' I'll take the 'arf-crown for the luck of it. Good-day t'ye! Hope you'll find an easy place!"

She smiled and thanked him,—then entered the station and, finding the ticket-office just open, paid a third-class fare to London. A sudden thrill of nervousness came over her. She spoke to the booking-clerk, peering wistfully at him through his little ticket-aperture.

"I have never been in a train before!" she said, in a small, anxious voice.

The clerk smiled, and yawned expansively. He was a young man who considered himself a "gentleman," and among his own particular set passed for being a wit.

"Really!" he drawled—"Quite a new experience for you! A little country mouse, is it?"

Innocent drew back, offended.

"I don't know what you mean," she said, coldly—and moved away.

The young clerk fingered his embryo moustache dubiously—conscious of a blunder in manners. This girl was a lady—not a mere country wench to joke with. He felt rather uncomfortable—and presently leaving his office, went out on the platform where she was walking up and down, and slightly lifted his cap.

"I beg your pardon!" he said, his face reddening a little—"If you are travelling alone you would like to get into a carriage with other people, wouldn't you?"

"Oh yes!" she answered, eagerly—"If you would be so kind—"

He made no answer, as just then, with a rush and crash and clatter, and deafening shriek of the engine-whistle, the train came thundering in. There was opening and shutting of doors, much banging and confusion, and before she very well knew where she was, Innocent found herself in a compartment with three other persons—one benevolent-looking old gentleman with white hair who was seated opposite to her, and a man and woman, evidently husband and wife. Another shriek and roar, and the train started—as it began to race along, Innocent closed her eyes with a sickening sensation of faintness and terror—then, opening them, saw hedges, fields, trees and ponds all flying past her like scud in the wind, and sat watching in stupefied wonderment—one little hand grasping the satchel that held all her worldly possessions—the other hanging limply at her side. Now and then she looked at her companions—the husband and wife sat opposite each other and spoke occasionally in monosyllables—the old gentleman on the seat facing herself was reading a paper which showed its title—"The Morning Post." Sometimes he looked at her over the top of the paper, but for the most part he appeared absorbed in the printed page. On, on, on, the train rushed at a pace which to her seemed maddening and full of danger—she felt sick and giddy—would it never stop, she thought?—and a deep sense of relief came over her when, with a scream from the engine-whistle loud enough to tear the drum of a sensitive ear, the whole shaking, rattling concern came to an abrupt standstill at a station. Then she mustered up courage to speak.

"Please, would you tell me—" she began, faintly.

The old gentleman laid down his "Morning Post" and surveyed her encouragingly.

"Yes? What is it?"

"Will it be long before we get to London?"

"About three hours."

"Three hours!"

She gave a deep and weary sigh. Three hours! Hardly till then had she realised how far she was from Briar Farm—or how entirely she had cut herself off from all the familiar surroundings of her childhood's home, her girlhood's life. She leaned back in her seat, and one or two tears escaped from under her drooping eyelids and trickled slowly down her cheeks. The train started off again, rushing at what she thought an awful speed,—she imagined herself as being torn away from the peaceful past and hurled into a stormy future. Yet it was her own doing—whatever chanced to her now she would have no one but herself to blame. The events of the past few days had crushed and beaten her so with blows,— the old adage "Misfortunes never come singly" had been fulfilled for her with cruel and unlooked-for plenitude. There is a turning-point in every human life—or rather several turning-points—and at each one are gathered certain threads of destiny which may either be involved in a tangle or woven distinctly as a clue—but which in any case lead to change in the formerly accepted order of things. We may thank the gods that this is so—otherwise in the jog-trot of a carefully treasured conservatism and sameness of daily existence we should become the easy prey of adventurers, who, discovering our desire for the changelessness of a convenient and comfortable routine, would mulct us of all individuality. Our very servants would become our masters, and would take advantage of our easy-going ways to domineer over us, as in the case of "lone ladies" who are often half afraid to claim obedience from the domestics they keep and pay. Ignorant of the ways of the world and full of such dreams as the world considers madness, Innocent had acted on a powerful inward impetus which pushed her spirit towards liberty and independence—but of any difficulties or dangers she might have to encounter she never thought. She had the blind confidence of a child that runs along heedless of falling, being instinctively sure that some hand will be stretched out to save it should it run into positive danger.

Mastering the weakness of tears, she furtively dried her eyes and endeavoured not to think at all—not to dwell on the memory of her "Dad" whom she had loved so tenderly, and all the sweet surroundings of Briar Farm which already seemed so far away. Robin would be sorry she had gone—indeed he would be very miserable for a time—she was certain of that!—and Priscilla! yes, Priscilla had loved her as her own child,—here her thoughts began running riot again, and she moved impatiently. Just then the old gentleman with the "Morning Post" folded it neatly and, bending forward, offered it to her.

"Would you like to see the paper?" he asked, politely.

The warm colour flushed her cheeks—she accepted it shyly.

"Thank you very much!" she murmured—and, gratefully shielding her tearful eyes behind the convenient news-sheet, she began glancing up and down the front page with all its numerous announcements, from the "Agony" column down to the latest new concert-singers and sailings of steamers.

Suddenly her attention was caught by the following advertisement—

"A Lady of good connection and position will be glad to take another lady as Paying Guest in her charming house in Kensington. Would suit anyone studying art or for a scholarship. Liberal table and refined surroundings. Please communicate with 'Lavinia' at—" Here followed an address.

Over and over again Innocent read this with a sort of fascination. Finally, taking from her pocket a little note-book and pencil, she copied it carefully.

"I might go there," she thought—"If she is a poor lady wanting money, she might be glad to have me as a 'paying guest,' Anyhow, it will do no harm to try. I must find some place to rest in, if only for a night."

Here she became aware that the old gentleman who had lent her the paper was eyeing her curiously yet kindly. She met his glance with a mixture of frankness and timidity which gave her expression a wonderful charm. He ventured to speak as he might have spoken to a little child.

"Are you going to London for the first time?" he asked.

"Yes, sir."

He smiled. He had a pleasant smile, distinctly humorous and good-natured.

"It's a great adventure!" he said—"Especially for a little girl, all alone."

She coloured.

"I'm not a little girl," she answered, with quaint dignity—"I'm eighteen."

"Really!"—and the old gentleman looked more humorous than ever—"Oh well!—of course you are quite old. But, you see, I am seventy, so to me you seem a little girl. I suppose your friends will meet you in London?"

She hesitated—then answered, simply—

"No. I have no friends. I am going to earn my living."

The old gentleman whistled. It was a short, low whistle at first, but it developed into a bar of "Sally in our Alley." Then he looked round—the other people in the compartment, the husband and wife, were asleep.

"Poor child!" he then said, very gently—"I'm afraid that will be hard work for you. You don't look very strong."

"Oh, but I am!" she replied, eagerly—"I can do anything in housework or dairy-farming—I've been brought up to be useful—"

"That's more than a great many girls can say!" he remarked, smiling—"Well, well! I hope you may succeed! I also was brought up to be useful—but I'm not sure that I have ever been of any use!"

She looked at him with quick interest.

"Are you a clever man?" she asked.

The simplicity of the question amused him, and he laughed.

"A few people have sometimes called me so," he answered—"but my 'cleverness,' or whatever it may be, is not of the successful order. And I'm getting old now, so that most of my activity is past. I have written a few books—"

"Books!"—she clasped her hands nervously, and her eyes grew brilliant—"Oh! If you can write books you must always be happy!"

"Do you think so?" And he bent his brows and scrutinised her more intently. "What do You know about it? Are you fond of reading?"

A deep blush suffused her fair skin.

"Yes—but I have only read very old books for the most part," she said—"In the farm-house where I was brought up there were a great many manuscripts on vellum, and curious things—I read those—and some books in old French—"

"Books in old French!" he echoed, wonderingly. "And you can read them? You are quite a French scholar, then?"

"Oh no, indeed!" she protested—"I have only taught myself a little. Of course it was difficult at first,—but I soon managed it,—just as I learned how to read old English—I mean the English of Queen

Elizabeth's time. I loved it all so much that it was a pleasure to puzzle it out. We had a few modern books—but I never cared for them."

He studied her face with increasing interest.

"And you are going to earn your own living in London!" he said—"Have you thought of a way to begin? In old French, or old English?"

She glanced at him quickly and saw that he was smiling kindly.

"Yes," she answered, gently—"I have thought of a way to begin! Will you tell me of some book you have written so that I may read it?"

He shook his head.

"Not I!" he declared—"I could not stand the criticism of a young lady who might compare me with the writers of the Elizabethan period—Shakespeare, for instance—"

"Ah no!" she said—"No one can ever be compared with Shakespeare—that is impossible!"

He was silent,—and as she resumed her reading of the "Morning Post" he had lent her, he leaned back in his seat and left her to herself. But he was keenly interested,—this young, small creature with her delicate, intelligent face and wistful blue-grey eyes was a new experience for him. He was a well-seasoned journalist and man of letters,—clever in his own line and not without touches of originality in his work—but hardly brilliant or forceful enough to command the attention of the public to a large or successful issue. He was, however, the right hand and chief power on the staff of one of the most influential of daily newspapers, whose proprietor would no more have thought of managing things without him than of going without a dinner, and from this post, which he had held for twenty years, he derived a sufficiently comfortable income. In his profession he had seen all classes of humanity—the wise and the ignorant,—the conceited and the timid,—men who considered themselves new Shakespeares in embryo,—women in whom the unbounded vanity of a little surface cleverness was sufficient to place them beyond the pale of common respect,—but he had never till now met a little country girl making her first journey to London who admitted reading "old French" and Elizabethan English as unconcernedly as she might have spoken of gathering apples or churning cream. He determined not to lose sight of her, and to improve the acquaintance if he got the chance. He heard her give a sudden sharp sigh as she read the "Morning Post,"—she had turned to the middle of the newspaper where the events of the day were chronicled, and where a column of fashionable intelligence announced the ephemeral doings of the so-called "great" of the world. Here one paragraph had caught and riveted her attention—it ran thus—"Lord and Lady Blythe have left town for Glen-Alpin, Inverness-shire, where they will entertain a large house-party to meet the Prime Minister."

Her mother!—It was difficult to believe that but a few hours ago this very Lady Blythe had offered to "adopt" her!—"adopt" her own child and act a lie in the face of all the "society" she frequented,—yet, strange and fantastic as it seemed, it was true! Possibly she—Innocent—had she chosen, could have been taken to "Glen-Alpin, Inverness-shire!"—she too might have met the Prime Minister! She almost laughed at the thought of it!—the paper shook in her hand. Her "mother"! Just then the old gentleman bent forward again and spoke to her.

"We are very near London now," he said—"Can I help you at the station to get your luggage? You might find it confusing at first—"

"Oh, thank you!" she murmured—"But I have no luggage—only this"—and she pointed to the satchel beside her—"I shall get on very well."

Here she folded up the "Morning Post" and returned it to him with a pretty air of courtesy. As he accepted it he smiled.

"You are a very independent little lady!" he said—"But—just in case you ever do want to read a book of mine,—I am going to give you my name and address." Here he took a card from his waistcoat pocket and gave it to her. "That will always find me," he continued—"Don't be afraid to write and ask me anything about London you may wish to know. It's a very large city—a cruel one!"—and he looked at her with compassionate kindness—"You mustn't lose yourself in it!"

She read the name on the card—"John Harrington"—and the address was the office of a famous daily journal. Looking up, she gave him a grateful little smile.

"You are very kind!" she said—"And I will not forget you. I don't think I shall lose myself—I'll try not to be so stupid! Yes—when I have read one of your books I will write to you!"

"Do!"—and there was almost a note of eagerness in his voice—"I should like to know what you think"—here a loud and persistent scream from the engine-whistle drowned all possibility of speech as the train rushed past a bewildering wilderness of houses packed close together under bristling black chimneys—then, as the deafening din ceased, he added, quietly, "Here is London."

She looked out of the window,—the sun was shining, but through a dull brown mist, and nothing but bricks and mortar, building upon building, met her view. After the sweet freshness of the country she had left behind, the scene was appallingly hideous, and her heart sank with a sense of fear and foreboding. Another few minutes and the train stopped.

"This is Paddington," said John Harrington; then, noting her troubled expression—"Let me get a taxi for you and tell the man where to drive."

She submitted in a kind of stunned bewilderment. The address she had found in the "Morning Post" was her rescue—she could go there, she thought, rapidly, even if she had to come away again. Almost before she could realise what had happened in all the noise and bustling to and fro, she found herself in a taxi-cab, and her kind fellow-traveller standing beside it, raising his hat to her courteously in farewell. She gave him the address of the house in Kensington which she had copied from the advertisement she had seen in the "Morning Post," and he repeated it to the taxi-driver with a sense of relief and pleasure. It was what is called "a respectable address"—and he was glad the child knew where she was going. In another moment the taxi was off,—a parting smile brightened the wistful expression of her young face, and she waved her little hand to him. And then she was whirled away among the seething crowd of vehicles and lost to sight. Old John Harrington stood for a moment on the railway-platform, lost in thought.

"A sweet little soul!" he mused—"I wonder what will become of her! I must see her again some day. She reminds me of—let me see!—who does she remind me of? By Jove, I have it! Pierce Armitage!—haven't seen him for twenty years at least—and this girl's face has a look of his—just the same eyes and intense expression. Poor old Armitage!— he promised to be a great artist once, but he's gone to the dogs by this time, I suppose. Curious, curious that I should remember him just now!"

And he went his way, thinking and wondering, while Innocent went hers, without any thought at all, in a blind and simple faith that God would take care of her.

XII

To be whirled along through the crowded streets of London in a taxi-cab for the first time in one's life must needs be a somewhat disconcerting, even alarming experience, and Innocent was the poor little prey of so many nervous fears during her journey to Kensington in this fashion, that she could think of nothing and realise nothing except that at any moment it seemed likely she would be killed. With wide-open, terrified eyes, she watched the huge motor-omnibuses almost bearing down upon the vehicle in which she sat, and shivered at the narrow margin of space the driver seemed to allow for any sort of escape from instant collision and utter disaster. She only began to breathe naturally again when, turning away out of the greater press of traffic, the cab began to run at a smoother and less noisy pace, till presently, in less time than she could have imagined possible, it drew up at a modestly retreating little door under an arched porch in a quiet little square, where there were some brave and pretty trees doing their best to be green, despite London soot and smoke. Innocent stepped out, and seeing a bell-handle pulled it timidly. The summons was answered by a very neat maid-servant, who looked at her in primly polite enquiry.

"Is Mrs.—or Miss 'Lavinia' at home?" she murmured. "I saw her advertisement in the 'Morning Post.'"

The servant's face changed from primness to propitiation.

"Oh yes, miss! Please step in! I'll tell Miss Leigh."

"Thank you. I'll pay the driver."

She thereupon paid for the cab and dismissed it, and then followed the maid into a very small but prettily arranged hall, and from thence into a charming little drawing-room, with French windows set open, showing a tiny garden beyond—a little green lawn, smooth as velvet, and a few miniature flower-beds gay with well-kept blossoms.

"Would you please take a seat, miss?" and the maid placed a chair. "Miss Leigh is upstairs, but she'll be down directly."

She left the room, closing the door softly behind her.

Innocent sat still, satchel in hand, looking wistfully about her. The room appealed to her taste in its extreme simplicity—and it instinctively suggested to her mind resigned poverty making the best of itself. There were one or two old miniatures on little velvet stands set on the mantelpiece—these were beautiful, and of value; some engravings of famous pictures adorned the walls, all well chosen; the quaint china bowl on the centre table was full of roses carefully arranged—and there was a very ancient harpsichord in one corner which apparently served only as a stand for the portrait of a man's strikingly handsome face, near which was placed a vase containing a stem of Madonna lilies. Innocent found herself looking at this portrait now and again—there was something familiar in its expression which had a curious fascination for her. But her thoughts revolved chiefly round a difficulty which had just presented itself—she had no real name. What name could she take to be known by for the moment? She would not call herself "Jocelyn"—she felt she had no right to do so. "Ena" might pass muster for an abbreviation of "Innocent"—she decided to make use of that as a Christian name—but a surname that would be appropriately fitted to her ultimate intentions she could not at once select. Then she suddenly thought of the man who had been her father and had brought her as a helpless babe to Briar Farm. Pierce Armitage was his name—and he was dead. Surely she might call herself Armitage? While she was still puzzling her mind over the question the door opened and a little old lady entered—a soft-eyed, pale, pretty old lady, as dainty and delicate as the fairy-godmother of a child's dream, with white hair bunched on either side of her face, and a wistful, rather plaintive expression of mingled hope and enquiry.

"I'm sorry to keep you waiting," she began—then paused in a kind of embarrassment. The two looked at each other. Innocent spoke, a little shyly:

"I saw your advertisement in the 'Morning Post,'" she said, "and I thought perhaps—I thought that I might come to you as a paying guest. I have to live in London, and I shall be very busy studying all day, so I should not give you much trouble."

"Pray do not mention it!" said the old lady, with a quaint air of old-fashioned courtesy. "Trouble would not be considered! But you are a much younger person than I expected or wished to accommodate."

"You said in the advertisement that it would be suitable for a person studying art, or for a scholarship," put in Innocent, quickly. "And I am studying for literature."

"Are you indeed?" and the old lady waved a little hand in courteous deprecation of all unnecessary explanation—a hand which Innocent noticed had a delicate lace mitten on it and one or two sparkling rings. "Well, let us sit down together and talk it over. I have two spare rooms—a bedroom and a sitting-room—they are small but very comfortable, and for these I have been told I should ask three guineas a week, including board. I feel it a little difficult"—and the old lady heaved a sigh—"I have never done this kind of thing before—I don't know what my poor father, Major Leigh, would have said—he was a very proud man—very proud—!"

While she thus talked, Innocent had been making a rapid calculation in her own mind. Three guineas a week! It was more than she had meant to pay, but she was instinctively wise enough to realise the advantage of safety and shelter in this charming little home of one who was evidently a lady, gentle, kindly, and well-mannered. She had plenty of money to go on with—and in the future she hoped to make more. So she spoke out bravely.

"I will pay the three guineas a week gladly," she said. "May I see the rooms?"

The old lady meanwhile had been studying her with great intentness, and now asked abruptly—

"Are you an English girl?"

Innocent flushed a sudden rosy red.

"Yes. I was brought up in the country, but all my people are dead now. I have no friends, but I have a little money left to me—and for the rest—I must earn my own living."

"Well, my dear, that won't hurt you!" and an encouraging smile brightened Miss Leigh's pleasantly wrinkled face. "You shall see the rooms. But you have not told me your name yet."

Again Innocent blushed.

"My name is Armitage," she said, in a low, hesitating tone—"Ena Armitage."

"Armitage!"—Miss Leigh repeated the name with a kind of wondering accent—"Armitage? Are you any relative of the painter, Pierce Armitage?"

The girl's heart beat quickly—for a moment the little drawing-room seemed to whirl round her—then she collected her forces with a strong effort and answered—"No!"

The old lady's wistful blue eyes, dimmed with age, yet retaining a beautiful tenderness of expression, rested upon her anxiously.

"You are quite sure?"

Repressing the feeling that prompted her to cry out—"He was my father!" she replied—

"I am quite sure!"

Lavinia Leigh raised her little mittened hand and pointed to the portrait standing on the harpsichord:

"That was Pierce Armitage!" she said. "He was a dear friend of mine"—her voice trembled a little—"and I should have been glad if you had been in any way connected with him."

As she spoke Innocent turned and looked steadily at the portrait, and it seemed to her excited fancy that its eyes gave her glance for glance. She could hardly breathe—the threatening tears half choked her. What strange fate was it, she thought, that had led her to a house where she looked upon her own father's likeness for the first time!

"He was a very fine man," continued Miss Leigh in the same half-tremulous voice—"very gifted—very clever! He would have been a great artist, I think—"

"Is he dead?" the girl asked, quietly.

"Yes—I—I think so—he died abroad—so they say, but I have never quite believed it—I don't know why! Come, let me show you the rooms. I am glad your name is Armitage."

She led the way, walking slowly,—Innocent followed like one in a dream. They ascended a small staircase, softly carpeted, to a square landing, and here Miss Leigh opened a door.

"This is the sitting-room," she said. "You see, it has a nice bow-window with a view of the garden. The bedroom is just beyond it—both lead into one another."

Innocent looked in and could not resist giving a little exclamation of pleasure. Everything was so clean and dainty and well kept—it seemed to her a perfect haven of rest and shelter. She turned to Miss Leigh in eager impulsiveness.

"Oh, please let me stay!" she said. "Now, at once! I have only just arrived in London and this is the first place I have seen. It seems so—so fortunate that you should have had a friend named Armitage! Perhaps—perhaps I may be a friend too!"

A curious tremor seemed to pass over the old lady as though she shivered in a cold wind. She laid one hand gently on the girl's arm.

"You may, indeed!" she said. "One never can tell what may happen in this strange world! But we have to be practical—and I am very poor and pressed for money. I do not know you—and of course I should expect references from some respectable person who can tell me who you are and all about you."

Innocent grew pale. She gave a little expressive gesture of utter hopelessness.

"I cannot give you any references," she said—"I am quite alone in the world—my people are dead—you see I am in mourning. The last friend I had died a little while ago and left me four hundred pounds in bank-notes. I have them here"—and she touched her breast—"and if you like I will give you one of them in advance payment for the rooms and board at once."

The old lady heaved a quick sharp sigh. One hundred pounds! It would relieve her of a weight of pressing difficulty—and yet—! She paused, considering.

"No, my child!" she said, quietly. "I would not on any account take so much money from you. If you wish to stay, and if I must omit references and take you on trust—which I am quite willing to do!"—and she smiled, gravely—"I will accept two months' rent in advance if you think you can spare this—can you?"

"Yes—oh, yes!" the girl exclaimed, impulsively. "If only I may stay—now!"

"You may certainly stay now," and Miss Leigh rang a bell to summon the neat maid-servant. "Rachel, the rooms are let to this young lady, Miss Armitage. Will you prepare the bedroom and help her unpack her things?" Then, turning round to Innocent, she said kindly,—"You will of course take your meals with me at my table—I keep very regular hours, and if for any cause you have to be absent, I should wish to know beforehand."

Innocent said nothing;—her eyes were full of tears, but she took the old lady's little hand and kissed it. They went down together again to the drawing-room, Innocent just pausing to tell the maid Rachel that she would prefer to unpack and arrange the contents of her satchel—all her luggage,—herself; and in a very few minutes the whole business was settled. Eager to prove her good faith to the gentle lady who had so readily trusted her, she drew from her bosom the envelope containing the bank-notes left to her by Hugo Jocelyn, and, unfolding all four, she spread them out on the table.

"You see," she said, "this is my little fortune! Please change one of them and take the two months' rent and anything more you want—please do!"

A faint colour flushed Miss Leigh's pale cheeks.

"No, my dear, no!" she answered. "You must not tempt me! I will take exactly the two months' rent and no more; but I think you ought not to carry this money about with you—you should put it in a bank. We'll talk of this afterwards—but go and lock it up somewhere now—there's a little desk in your room you could use—but a bank would be safest. After dinner this evening I'll tell you what I think you ought to do—you are so very young!"—and she smiled—"such a young little thing! I shall have to look after you and play chaperone!"

Innocent looked up with a sweet confidence in her eyes.

"That will be kind of you!" she said, and leaving the one bank-note of a hundred pounds on the table, she folded up the other three in their original envelope and returned them to their secret place of safety. "In a little while I will tell you a great deal about myself—and I do hope I shall please you! I will not give any trouble, and I'll try to be useful in the house if you'll let me. I can cook and sew and do all sorts of things!"

"Can you, indeed!" and Miss Leigh laughed good-naturedly. "And what about studying for literature?"

"Ah!—that of course comes first!" she said. "But I shall do all my writing in the mornings—in the afternoons I can help you as much as you like."

"My dear, your time must be your own," said Miss Leigh, decisively. "You have paid for your accommodation, and you must have perfect liberty to do as you like, as long as you keep to my regular hours for meals and bed-time. I think we shall get on well together,—and I hope we shall be good friends!"

As she spoke she bent forward and on a sudden impulse drew the girl to her and kissed her. Poor lonely Innocent thrilled through all her being to the touch of instinctive tenderness, and her heart beat quickly as she saw the portrait on the harpsichord—her father's pictured face—apparently looking at her with a smile.

"Oh, you are very good to me!" she murmured, with a little sob in her breath, as she returned the gentle old lady's kiss. "I feel as if I had known you for years! Did you know him"—and she pointed to the portrait—"very long?"

Miss Leigh's eyes grew bright and tender.

"Yes!" she answered. "We were boy and girl together—and once—once we were very fond of each other. Perhaps I will tell you the story some day! Now go up to your rooms and arrange everything as you like, and rest a little. Would you like some tea? Anything to eat?"

Poor Innocent, who had left Briar Farm at dawn without any thought of food, and had travelled to London almost unconscious of either hunger or fatigue, was beginning to feel the lack of nourishment, and she gratefully accepted the suggestion.

"I lunch at two o'clock," continued Miss Leigh. "But it's only a little past twelve now, and if you have come a long way from the country you must be tired. I'll send Rachel up to you with some tea."

She went to give the order, and Innocent, left to herself for a moment, moved softly up to her father's picture and gazed upon it with all her soul in her eyes. It was a wonderful face—a face expressive of the highest thought and intelligence—the face of a thinker or a poet, though the finely moulded mouth and chin had nothing of the weakness which sometimes marks a mere dreamer of dreams. Timidly glancing about her to make sure she was not observed, she kissed the portrait, the cold glass which covered it meeting her warm caressing lips with a repelling chill. He was dead—this father whom she could never claim!—dead as Hugo Jocelyn, who had taken that father's place in her life. She might love the ghost of him if her fancy led her that way, as she loved the ghost of the "Sieur Amadis"—but there was nothing else to love! She was alone in the world, with neither father nor "knight of old" to protect or defend her, and on herself alone depended her future. She turned away and left the room, looking a fragile, sad, unobtrusive little creature, with nothing about her to suggest either beauty or power. Yet the mind in that delicate body had a strength of which she was unconscious, and she was already bending it instinctively and intellectually like a bow ready for the first shot—with an arrow which was destined to go straight to its mark.

Meanwhile on Briar Farm there had fallen a cloud of utter desolation. The day was fair and brilliant with summer sunshine, the birds sang, the roses bloomed, the doves flew to and fro on the gabled roof, and Innocent's pet "Cupid" waited in vain on the corner of her window-sill for the usual summons that called it to her hand,—but a strange darkness and silence like a whelming wave submerged the very light from the eyes of those who suddenly found themselves deprived of a beloved presence—a personality unobtrusively sweet, which had bestowed on the old house a charm and grace far greater than had been fully recognised. The "base-born" Innocent, nameless, and unbaptised, and therefore shadowed by the stupid scandal of commonplace convention, had given the "home" its homelike quality— her pretty idealistic fancies about the old sixteenth-century knight "Sieur Amadis" had invested the place with a touch of romance and poetry which it would hardly have possessed with-out her—her gentle ways, her care of the flowers and the animals, and the never-wearying delight she had taken in the household affairs—all her part in the daily life of the farm had been as necessary to happiness as the mastership of Hugo Jocelyn himself—and without her nothing seemed the same. Poor Priscilla went about her work, crying silently, and Robin Clifford paced restlessly up and down the smooth grass in front of the old house with Innocent's farewell letter in his hand, reading it again and again. He had returned early from the market town where he had stayed the night, eager to explain to her all the details of the business he had gone through with the lawyer to whom his Uncle Hugo had entrusted his affairs, and to tell her how admirably everything had been arranged for the prosperous continuance of Briar Farm on the old traditional methods of labour by which it had always been worked to advantage. Hugo Jocelyn had indeed shown plenty of sound wisdom and foresight in all his plans save one—and that one was his fixed idea of Innocent's marriage with his nephew. It had evidently never occurred to him that a girl could have a will of her own in such a momentous affair—much less that she could or would be so unwise as to refuse a good husband and a settled home when both were at hand for her acceptance. Robin himself, despite her rejection of him, had still hoped and believed that when the first shock of his uncle's death had lessened, he might by patience and unwearying tenderness move her heart to softer yielding, and he had meant to plead his cause with her for the sake of the famous old house itself, so that she might become its mistress and help him to prove a worthy descendant of its long line of owners. But now! All hope was at an end—she had taken the law into her own hands and gone—no one knew whither. Priscilla was the last who had seen her—Priscilla could only explain, with many tears, that when she had gone to call her to breakfast she had found her room vacant, her bed unslept in, and the letter for Robin on the table—and that letter disclosed little or nothing of her intentions.

"Oh, the poor child!" Priscilla said, sobbingly. "All alone in a hard world, with her strange little fancies, and no one to take care of her! Oh, Mr. Robin, whatever are we to do!"

"Nothing!" and Robin's handsome face was pale and set. "We can only wait to hear from her—she will not keep us long in anxiety—she has too much heart for that. After all, it is My fault, Priscilla! I tried to persuade her to marry me against her will—I should have let her alone."

Sudden boyish tears sprang to his eyes—he dashed them away in self-contempt.

"I'm a regular coward, you see," he said. "I could cry like a baby—not for myself so much, but to think of her running away from Briar Farm out into the wide world all alone! Little Innocent! She was safe here—and if she had wished it, *I* would have gone away—I would have made HER the owner of the farm, and left her in peace to enjoy it and to marry any other man she fancied. But she wouldn't listen to any plan for her own happiness since she knew she was not my uncle's daughter—that is what has changed her! I wish she had never known!"

"Ay, so do I!" agreed Priscilla, dolefully. "But she's got the fancifullest notions! All about that old stone knight in the garden—an' what wi' the things he's left carved all over the wall of the room where she read them queer old books, she's fair 'mazed with ideas that don't belong to the ways o' the world at all. I can't think what'll become o' the child. Won't there be any means of findin' out where she's gone?"

"I'm afraid not!" answered Robin, sadly. "We muse trust to her remembrance of us, Priscilla, and her thoughts of the old home where she was loved and cared for." His voice shook. "It will be a dreary place without her! We shall miss her every minute, every hour of the day! I cannot fancy what the garden will look like without her little white figure flitting over the grass, and her sweet fair face smiling among the roses! Hang it all, Priscilla, if it were not for the last wishes of my Uncle Hugo I'd throw the whole thing up and go abroad!"

"Don't do that, Mister Robin!"—and Priscilla laid her rough work-worn hand on his arm—"Don't do it! It's turning your back on duty to give up the work entrusted to you by a dead man. You know it is! An' the child may come back any day! I shouldn't wonder if she got frightened at being alone and ran home again to-morrow! Think of it, Mister Robin! Suppose she came an' you weren't here? Why, you'd never forgive yourself! I can't think she's gone far or that she'll stay away long. Her heart's in Briar Farm all the while—I'd swear to that! Why, only yesterday when a fine lady came to see if she couldn't buy something out o' the house, you should just a' seen her toss her pretty little head when she told me how she'd said it wasn't to be sold."

"Lady? What lady?" and Robin looked, as he felt, bewildered by Priscilla's vague statement. "Did someone come here to see the house?"

"Not exactly—I don't know what it was all about," replied Priscilla. "But quite a grand lady called an' gave me her card. I saw the name

　　　　　　　　　MARIE CORELLI

on it—'Lady Maude Blythe'—and she asked to see 'Miss Jocelyn' on business. I asked if it was anything I could do, and she said no. So I called the child in from the garden, and she and the lady had quite a long talk together in the best parlour. Then when the lady went away, Innocent told me that she had wished to buy something from Briar Farm—but that it was not to be sold."

Robin listened attentively. "Curious!" he murmured—"very curious! What was the lady's name?"

"Lady Maude Blythe," repeated Priscilla, slowly.

He took out a note-book and pencil, and wrote it down.

"You don't think she came to engage Innocent for some service?" he asked. "Or that Innocent herself had perhaps written to an agency asking for a place, and that this lady had come to see her in consequence?"

Such an idea had never occurred to Priscilla's mind, but now it was suggested to her it seemed more than likely.

"It might be so," she answered, slowly. "But I can't bear to think the child was playin' a part an' tellin' me things that weren't true just to get away from us. No! Mister Robin! I don't believe that lady had anything to do with her going."

"Well, I shall keep the name by me," he said. "And I shall find out where the lady lives, who she is and all about her. For if I don't hear from Innocent, if she doesn't write to us, I'll search the whole world and never rest till I find her!"

Priscilla looked at him, pityingly, tears springing again to her eyes.

"Aye, you've lost the love o' your heart, my lad! I know that well enough!" she said. "An' it's mighty hard on you! But you must be a man an' turn to work as though nowt had happened. There's the farm—"

"Yes, there's the farm," he repeated, absently. "But what do I care for the farm without her! Priscilla, You will stay with me?"

"Stay with you? Surely I will, Mister Robin! Where should an old woman like me go to at this time o' day!" and Priscilla took his hand and clasped it affectionately. "Don't you fear! My place is in Briar Farm till the Lord makes an end of me! And if the child comes back at any hour of the day or night, she'll find old Priscilla ready to welcome her,—ready an' glad an' thankful to see her pretty face again."

Here, unable to control her sobs, she turned away and made a hasty retreat into the kitchen.

He did not follow her, but acting on the sudden impulse of his mind he entered the house and went up to Innocent's deserted room.

He opened the door hesitatingly,—the little study, in its severe simplicity and neatness, looked desolate—like an empty shrine from which the worshipped figure had been taken. He trod softly across the floor, hushing his footsteps, as though some one slept whom he feared to wake, and his eyes wandered from one familiar object to another till they rested on the shelves where the old vellum-bound books, which Innocent had loved and studied so much, were ranged in orderly rows. Taking one or two of them out he glanced at their title-pages;—he knew that most of them were rare and curious, though his Oxford training had not impressed him with as great a love of things literary as it might or should have done. But he realised that these strange black-letter and manuscript volumes were of unique value, and that their contents, so difficult to decipher, were responsible for the formation of Innocent's guileless and romantic spirit, colouring her outlook on life with a glamour of rainbow brilliancy which, though beautiful, was unreal. One quaint little book he opened had for its title—"Ye Whole Art of Love, Setting Forth ye Noble Manner of Noble Knights who woulde serve their Ladies Faithfullie in Death as in Lyfe"—this bore the date of 1590. He sighed as he put it back in its place.

"Ah, well," he said, half aloud, "these books are hers, and I'll keep them for her—but I believe they've done her a lot of mischief, and I don't love them! They've made her see the world as it is not—and life as it never will be! And she has got strange fancies into her head—fancies which she will run after like a child chasing pretty butterflies—and when the butterflies are caught, they die, much to the child's surprise and sorrow! My poor little Innocent! She has gone out alone into the world, and the world will break her heart! Oh dearest little love, come back to me!"

He sat down in her vacant chair and covered his face with his hands, giving himself up to the relief of unwitnessed tears. Above his head shone the worn glitter of the old armoured device of the "Sieur Amadis" with its motto—"Mon coeur me soutien"—and only a psychist could have thought or imagined it possible that the spirit of the old French knight of Tudor times might still be working through clouds of circumstance and weaving the web of the future from the torn threads of the past. And when Robin had regained his self-possession and had left the room, there was yet a Presence in its very emptiness,—the silent assertion of an influence which if it had been given voice and speech might have said—"Do what you consider is your own will and intention, but *I* am still your Master!—and all your thoughts and wishes are but the reflex of MY desire!"

It was soon known in the village that Innocent had left Briar Farm—"run away," the gossips said, eager to learn more. But they could get no information out of Robin Clifford or Priscilla Priday, and the labourers on the farm knew nothing. The farm work was going on as usual—that was all they cared about. Mr. Clifford was very silent—Miss Priday very busy. However, all anxiety and suspense came to an end very speedily so far as Innocent's safety was concerned, for in a few days letters arrived from her—both for Robin and Priscilla—kind, sweetly-expressed letters full of the tenderest affection.

"Do not be at all sorry or worried about me, dear good Priscilla!" she wrote. "I know I am doing right to be away from Briar Farm for a time—and I am quite well and happy. I have been very fortunate in finding rooms with a lady who is very kind to me, and as soon as I feel I can do so I will let you know my address. But I don't want anyone from home to come and see me—not yet!—not for a very long time! It would only make me sad—and it would make you sad too! But be quite sure it will not be long before you see me again."

Her letter to Robin was longer and full of restrained feeling:

"I know you are very unhappy, you kind, loving boy," it ran. "You have lost me altogether—yes, that is true—but do not mind, it is better so, and you will love some other girl much more than me some day. I should have been a mistake in your life had I stayed with you. You will see me again—and you will then understand why I left Briar Farm. I could not wrong the memory of the Sieur Amadis, and if I married you I should be doing a wicked thing to bring myself, who am base-born, into his lineage. Surely you do understand how I feel? I am quite safe—in a good home, with a lady who takes care of me—and as soon as I can I will let you know exactly where I am—then if you ever come to London I will see you. But your work is on Briar Farm—that dear and beloved home!—and you will keep up its old tradition and make everybody happy around you. Will you not? Yes! I am sure you will! You MUST, if ever you loved me.

INNOCENT

With this letter his last hope died within him. She would never be his—never, never! Some dim future beckoned her in which he had no part—and he confronted the fact as a brave soldier fronts the guns, with grim endurance, aware, yet not afraid of death.

"If ever I loved her!" he thought. "If ever I cease to love her then I shall be as stone-cold a man as her fetish of a French knight, the Sieur Amadis! Ah, my little Innocent, in time to come you may understand what love is—perhaps to your sorrow!—you may need a strong defender—and I shall be ready! Sooner or later—now or years hence—if you call me, I shall answer. I would find strength to rise from my death-bed and go to you if you wanted me! For I love you, my little love! I love you, and nothing can change me. Only once in a life-time can a man love any woman as I love you!"

And with a deep vow of fidelity sworn to his secret soul he sat alone, watching the shadows of evening steal over the landscape—falling, falling slowly, like a gradually descending curtain upon all visible things, till Briar Farm stood spectral in the gloom like the ghost of its own departed days, and lights twinkled in the lattice windows like little eyes glittering in the dark. Then silently bidding farewell to all his former dreams of happiness, he set himself to face "the burden and heat of the day"—that long, long day of life so difficult to live, when deprived of love!

BOOK II

HIS FACT

I

In London, the greatest metropolis of the world, the smallest affairs are often discussed with more keenness than things of national importance,—and it is by no means uncommon to find society more interested in the doings of some particular man or woman than in the latest and most money-milking scheme of Government finance. In this way it happened that about a year after Innocent had, like a small boat in a storm, broken loose from her moorings and drifted out to the wide sea, everybody who was anybody became suddenly thrilled with curiosity concerning the unknown personality of an Author. There are so many Authors nowadays that it is difficult to get up even a show of interest in one of them,—everybody "writes"—from Miladi in Belgravia, who considers the story of her social experiences, expressed in questionable grammar, quite equal to the finest literature, down to the stable-boy who essays a "prize" shocker for a penny dreadful. But this latest aspirant to literary fame had two magnetic qualities which seldom fail to arouse the jaded spirit of the reading public,—novelty and mystery, united to that scarce and seldom recognised power called genius. He or she had produced a Book. Not an ephemeral piece of fiction,—not a "Wells" effort of imagination under hydraulic pressure— not an hysterical outburst of sensual desire and disappointment such as moves the souls of demimondaines and dressmakers,—not even a "detective" sensation—but just a Book—a real Book, likely to live as long as literature itself. It was something in the nature of a marvel, said those who knew what they were talking about, that such a book should have been written at all in these modern days. The "style" of it was exquisite and scholarly—quaint, expressive, and all-sufficing in its artistic simplicity,—thoughts true for all time were presented afresh with an admirable point and delicacy that made them seem new and singularly imperative,—and the story which, like a silken thread, held all the choice jewels of language together in even and brilliant order, was pure and idyllic,—warm with a penetrating romance, yet most sincerely human. When this extraordinary piece of work was published, it slipped from the press in quite a modest way without much preliminary announcement, and for two or three weeks after its appearance nobody knew anything about it. The publishers themselves were evidently in doubt as to its reception, and signified their caution by economy in the way of advertisement—it was not placarded in the newspaper columns as "A Book of the Century" or "A New Literary Event." It simply glided into the crowd of books without noise or the notice of reviewers—just one of a pushing, scrambling, shouting multitude,—and quite suddenly found itself the centre of the throng with all eyes upon it, and all tongues questioning the how, when and where of its author. No one could say how it first began to be thus busily talked about,—the critics had bestowed upon it nothing of either their praise or blame,—yet somehow the ball had been set rolling, and it gathered size and force as it rolled, till at last the publishers woke up to the fact that they had, by merest chance, hit upon a "paying concern." They at once assisted in the general chorus of delight and admiration, taking wider space in the advertisement columns of the press for the "work of genius" which had inadvertently fallen into their hands—but when it came to answering the questions put to them respecting its writer they had very little to say, being themselves more or less in the dark.

"The manuscript was sent to us in the usual way," the head of the firm explained to John Harrington, one of the soundest and most influential of journalists, "just on chance,—it was neither introduced nor recommended. One of our readers was immensely taken with it and advised us to accept it. The author gave no name, and merely requested all communications to be made through his secretary, a Miss Armitage, as he wished for the time being to remain anonymous. We drew up an Agreement on these lines which was signed for the author by Miss Armitage,—she also corrected and passed the proofs—"

"Perhaps she also wrote the book," interrupted Harrington, with an amused twinkle in his eyes—"I suppose such a solution of the mystery has not occurred to you?"

The publisher smiled. "Under different circumstances it might have done so," he replied, "but we have seen Miss Armitage several times—she is quite a young girl, not at all of the 'literary' type, though she is very careful and accurate in her secretarial work—I mean as regards business letters and attention to detail. But at her age she could not have had the scholarship to produce such a book. The author shows a close familiarity with sixteenth-century literature such as could only be gained by a student of the style of that period,—Miss Armitage has nothing of the 'book-worm' about her—she is quite a simple young person—more like a bright school-girl than anything else—"

"Where does she live?" asked Harrington, abruptly.

The publisher looked up the address and gave it.

"There it is," he said; "if you want to write to the author she will forward any letters to him."

Harrington stared at the pencilled direction for a moment in silence. He remembered it—of course he remembered it!—it was the very address given to the driver of the taxi-cab in which the girl with whom he had travelled to London more than a year ago had gone, as it seemed, out of his sight. Every little incident connected with her came freshly back to his mind—how she had spoken of the books she loved in "old French" and "Elizabethan English"—and how she had said she knew the way to earn her own living. If this was the way—if she was indeed the author of the book which had stirred and wakened the drowsing soul of the age, then she had not ventured in vain!

Aloud he said:

"It seems to be another case of the 'Author of Waverley' and the 'Great Unknown'! I suppose you'll take anything else you can get by the same hand?"

"Rather!" And the publisher nodded emphatically—"We have already secured a second work."

"Through Miss Armitage?"

"Yes. Through Miss Armitage."

Harrington laughed.

"I believe you're all blinder than bats!" he said—"Why on earth you should think that because a woman looks like a school-girl she cannot write a clever book if gifted that way, is a condition of non-intelligence I fail to fathom! You speak of this author as a 'he.' Do you think only a male creature can produce a work of genius? Look at the twaddle men turn out every day in the form of novels alone! Many of them are worse than the worst weak fiction by women. I tell you I've lived long enough to know that a woman's brain can beat a man's if she cares to test it, so long as she does not fall in love. When once that disaster happens it's all over with her! It's the one drawback to a woman's career; if she would only keep clear of love and self-sacrifice she'd do wonders! Men never allow love to interfere with so much as their own smoke—very few among them would sacrifice a good cigar for a woman! As for this girl, Miss Armitage, I'll pluck out the heart of her mystery for you! I suppose you won't pay any less for good work if it turns out to be by a 'she' instead of a 'he'?"

The publisher was amused.

"Certainly not!" he answered. "We have already paid over a thousand pounds in royalties on the present book, and we have agreed to give two thousand in advance on the next. The author has expressed himself as perfectly satisfied—"

"Through Miss Armitage?" put in Harrington.

"Yes. Through Miss Armitage."

"Well!" And Harrington turned to go—"I hope Miss Armitage will also express herself as perfectly satisfied after I have seen her! I shall write and ask permission to call—"

"Surely"—and the publisher looked distressed—"surely you do not intend to trouble this poor girl by questions concerning her employer? It's hardly fair to her!—and of course it's only your way of joking, but your idea that she wrote the book we're all talking about is simply absurd! She couldn't do it! When you see her, you'll understand."

"I daresay I shall!" And Harrington smiled-"Don't you worry! I'm too old a hand to get myself or anybody else into trouble! But I'll wager you anything that your simple school-girl is the author!"

He went back then and there to the office of his big newspaper and wrote a guarded little note as follows:—

Dear Miss Armitage,

I wonder if you remember a grumpy old fellow who travelled with you on your first journey to London rather more than a year ago? You never told me your name, but I kept a note of the address you gave through me to your taxi-driver, and through that address I have just by chance heard that you and the Miss Armitage who corrected the proofs of a wonderful book recently published are one and the same person. May I call and see you?

Yours sincerely,
John Harrington

He waited impatiently for the answer, but none came for several days. At last he received a simple and courteous "put off," thus expressed:—

Dear Mr. Harrington,

I remember you very well—you were most kind, and I am grateful for your thought of me. But I hope you will not think me rude if I ask you not to call. I am living as a paying guest with an old lady whose health is not very strong and who does not like me to receive visitors, and you can understand that I try not to inconvenience her in any way. I do hope you are well and successful.

Yours sincerely,
ENA ARMITAGE

He folded up the note and put it in his pocket.

"That finishes me very decisively!" he said, with a laugh at himself for his own temerity. "Who is it says a woman cannot keep a secret? She can, and will, and does!—when it suits her to do so! Never mind, Miss Armitage! I shall find you out when, you least expect it—never fear!"

Meanwhile Miss Leigh's little house in Kensington was the scene of mingled confusion and triumph. The "paying guest"—the little unobtrusive girl, with all her wardrobe in a satchel and her legacy of four hundred pounds in bank-notes tucked into her bosom—had achieved a success beyond her wildest dreams, and now had only to declare her identity to become a "celebrity." Miss Lavinia had been for some days in a state of nervous excitement, knowing that it was Innocent's first literary effort which had created such a sensation. By this time she had learned all the girl's history—Innocent had told her everything, save and except the one fact of her parentage,—and this she held back, not out of shame for herself, but consideration for the memory of the handsome man whose portrait stood on the silent harpsichord. For she in her turn had discovered Miss Lavinia's secret,—how the dear lady's heart had been devoted to Pierce Armitage all her life, and how when she knew he had been drawn away from her and captivated by another woman her happiness had been struck down and withered like a flowering rose in a hard gale of wind. For this romance, and the disillusion she had suffered, Innocent loved her. The two had become fast friends, almost like devoted mother and daughter. Miss Leigh was, as she had stated in her "Morning Post" advertisement, well-connected, and she did much for the girl who had by chance brought a new and thrilling interest into her life—more than Innocent could possibly have done for herself. The history of the child,—as much as she was told of it,—who had been left so casually at a country farm on the mere chance of its being kept and taken care of, affected her profoundly, and when Innocent confided to her the fact that she had never been baptised, the gentle old lady was moved to tears. No time was lost in lifting this spiritual ban from the young life concerned, and the sacred rite was performed quietly one morning in the church which Miss Leigh had attended for many years, Miss Leigh having herself explained beforehand some of the circumstances to the Vicar, and standing as god-mother to the newly-received little Christian. And though there had arisen some question as to the name by which she should be baptised, Miss Leigh held tenaciously to the idea that she should retain the name her "unknown" father had given her—"Innocent."

"Suppose he should not be dead," she said, "then if he were to meet you some day, that name might waken his memory and lead him to identify you. And I like it—it is pretty and original—quite Christian, too,—there were several Popes named Innocent."

The girl smiled. She thought of Robin Clifford, and how he had aired his knowledge to her on the same subject.

"But it is a man's name, isn't it?" she asked.

"Not more so than a woman's, surely!" declared Miss Leigh. "You can always call yourself 'Ena' for short if you like—but 'Innocent' is the prettier name."

And so "Innocent" it was,—and by the sprinkling of water and the blessing of the Church the name was finally bestowed and sanctified. Innocent herself was peacefully glad of her newly-attained spiritual dignity and called Miss Lavinia her "fairy god-mother."

"Do you mind?" she asked, coaxingly. "It makes me so happy to feel that you are one of those kind people in a fairy-tale, bringing good fortune and blessing. I'm sure you ARE like that!"

Miss Lavinia protested against the sweet flattery, but all the same she was pleased. She began to take the girl out with her to the houses of various "great" personages—friends whom she knew well and who made an intimate little social circle of their own—"old-fashioned" people certainly, but happily free from the sort of suppressed rowdyism which distinguishes the "nouveaux riches" of the present day,—people who adhered rigidly to almost obsolete notions of honour and dignity, who lived simply and well within their means, who spoke reverently of things religious and believed in the old adage—"Manners makyth the man." So by degrees, Innocent found herself among a small choice "set" chiefly made up of the fragments of the real "old" aristocracy, to which Miss Leigh herself belonged,—and, with her own quick intuition and inborn natural grace, she soon became a favourite with them all. But no one knew the secret of her literary aspirations save Miss Leigh, and when her book was published anonymously and the reading world began to talk of it as something unusual and wonderful, she was more terrified than pleased. Its success was greater than she had ever dreamed of, and her one idea was to keep up the mystery of its authorship as long as possible, but every day made this more difficult. And when John Harrington wrote to her, she felt that disclosure was imminent. She had always kept the visiting-card he had given her when they had travelled to London together, and she knew he belonged to the staff of a great and leading newspaper,—he was a man not likely to be baffled in any sort of enquiry he might choose to make. She thought about this as she sat in her quiet little room, working at the last few chapters of her second book which the publishers were eagerly waiting for. What a magical change had been wrought in her life since she left Briar Farm more than a year, aye,—nearly eighteen months ago! For one thing, all fears of financial difficulty were at an end. Her first book had brought her more money than she had ever had in her life, and the publisher's offer for her second outweighed her most ambitious desires. She was independent—she could earn sufficient, and more than sufficient to keep herself in positive luxury if she chose,—but for this she had no taste. Her little rooms in Miss Leigh's house satisfied all her ideas of rest and comfort, and she stayed on with the kind old lady by choice and affection, helping her in many ways, and submitting to her guidance in every little social matter with the charming humility of a docile and obedient spirit all too rare in these days when youth is more full of effrontery than modesty. She had managed her "literary" business so far well and carefully, representing herself as the private secretary of an author who wished to remain anonymous, and who had gone abroad, entrusting her with his manuscript to "place" with any suitable firm that would make a suitable offer. The ruse would hardly have succeeded in the case of any ordinary piece of work, but the book itself was of too exceptional a quality to be passed over, and the firm to which it was first offered recognised this and accepted it without parley, astute enough to see its possibilities and to risk its chances of success. And now she realised that her little plot might be discovered any day, and that she would have to declare herself as the writer of a strange and brilliant book which was the talk of the moment.

"I wonder what they will say when they know it at Briar Farm!" she thought, with a smile and a half sigh.

Briar Farm seemed a long way off in these days. She had written occasionally both to Priscilla and Robin Clifford; giving her address and briefly stating that she had taken the name of Armitage, feeling that she had no right to that of Jocelyn. But Priscilla could not write, and contented herself with sending her "dear love and duty and do come back soon," through Robin, who answered for both in letters that were carefully cold and restrained. Now that he knew where she was he made no attempt to visit her,—he was too grieved and disappointed at her continued absence, and deeply hurt at what he considered her "quixotic" conduct in adopting a different name,—an "alias" as he called it.

"You have separated yourself from your old home by your own choice in more ways than one," he wrote, "and I see I have no right to criticise your actions. You are in a strange place and you have taken a strange name,—I cannot feel that you are Innocent,—the Innocent of our bygone happy years! It is better I should not go and see you—not unless you send for me, when, of course, I will come."

She was both glad and sorry for this,—she would have liked to see him again, and yet!—well!—she knew instinctively that if they met, it would only cause him fresh unhappiness. Her new life had bestowed new grace on her personality—all the interior intellectual phases of her mind had developed in her a beauty of face and form which was rare, subtle and elusive, and though she was not conscious of it herself, she had that compelling attraction about her which few can resist,—a fascination far greater than mere physical perfection. No one could have called her actually beautiful,—hardly could it have been said she was even "pretty"—but in her slight figure and intelligent face with its large blue-grey eyes half veiled under dreamy, drooping lids and long lashes, there was a magnetic charm which was both sweet and powerful. Moreover, she dressed well,—in quiet taste, with a careful avoidance of anything foolish or eccentric in fashion, and wherever she went she made her effect as a graceful young presence expressive of repose and harmony. She spoke delightfully,—in a delicious voice, attuned to the most melodious inflections, and her constant study of the finer literature of the past gave her certain ways of expressing herself in a manner so far removed from the abrupt slanginess commonly used to-day by young people of both sexes that she was called "quaint" by some and "weird" by others of her own sex, though by men young and old she was declared "charming." Guarded and chaperoned by good old Miss Lavinia Leigh, she had no cause to be otherwise than satisfied with her apparently reckless and unguided plunge into the mighty vortex of London,— some beneficent spirit had led her into a haven of safety and brought her straight to the goal of her ambition without difficulty.

"Of course I owe it all to Dad," she thought. "If it had not been for the four hundred pounds he left me to 'buy pretties' with I could not have done anything. I have bought my 'pretties!'—not bridal ones—but things so much better!"

As the memory of her "Dad" came over her, tears sprang to her eyes. In her mind she saw the smooth green pastures round Briar Farm—the beautiful old gabled house,—the solemn trees waving their branches in the wind over the tomb of the "Sieur Amadis,"—the doves wheeling round and round in the clear air, and her own "Cupid" falling like a snowflake from the roof to her caressing hand. All the old life of country sights and sounds passed before her like a fair mirage, giving place to dark days of sorrow, disillusion and loss,—the fleeting glimpse of her self-confessed "mother," Lady Maude Blythe,—and the knowledge she had so unexpectedly gained as to the actual identity of her father—he, whose portrait was in the very house to which she had come through no more romantic means than a chance advertisement in the "Morning Post!" And Miss Lavinia—her "fairy godmother"—could she have found a better friend, even in any elf stepping out of a magic pumpkin?

"If she ever knows the truth—if I am ever able to tell her that I am His daughter," she said to herself, "I wonder if she will care for me less or more? But I must not tell her!—She says he was so good and noble! It would break her heart to think he had done anything wrong—or that he had deserted his child."

And so she held her peace on this point, though she was often tempted to break silence whenever Miss Leigh reverted to the story of her being left in such a casual, yet romantic way at Briar Farm.

"I wonder who the handsome man was, my dear?" she would query— "Perhaps he'll go back to the place and enquire for you. He may be some very great personage!"

And Innocent would smile and shake her head.

"I fear not, my godmother!" she would reply. "You must not have any fairy dreams about me! I was just a deserted baby—not wanted in the world—but the world may have to take me all the same!"

And her eyes would flash, and her sensitive mouth would quiver as the vision of fame like a mystical rainbow circled the heaven of her youthful imagination—while Miss Leigh would sigh, and listen and wonder,—she, whose simple hope and faith had been centred in a love which had proved false and vain,—praying that the girl might realise her ambition without the wreckage and disillusion of her life.

One evening—an evening destined to mark a turning-point in Innocent's destiny—they went together to an "At Home" held at a beautiful studio in the house of an artist deservedly famous. Miss Leigh had a great taste for pictures, no doubt fostered since the early days of her romantic attachment to a man who had painted them,—and she knew most of the artists whose names were more or less celebrated in the modern world. Her host on this special occasion was what is called a "fashionable" portrait painter,—from the Queen downwards he had painted the "counterfeit presentments" of ladies of wealth and title, flattering them as delicately as his really clever brush would allow, and thereby securing golden opinions as well as golden guineas. He was a genial, breezy sort of man,—quite without vanity or any sort of "art" ostentation, and he had been a friend of Miss Leigh's for many years. Innocent loved going to his studio whenever her "godmother" would take her, and he, in his turn, found interest and amusement in talking to a girl who showed such a fresh, simple and unworldly nature, united to intelligence and perception far beyond her years. On the particular evening in question the studio was full of notable people,— not uncomfortably crowded, but sufficiently so as to compose a brilliant effect of colour and movement—beautiful women in wonderful attire fluttered to and fro like gaily-plumaged birds among the conventionally dark-clothed men who stood about in that aimless fashion they so often affect when disinclined to talk or to make themselves agreeable,—and there was a pleasantly subdued murmur of voices,—cultured voices, well-attuned, and incapable of breaking into the sheep-like snigger or asinine bray. Innocent, keeping close beside her "god-mother," watched the animated scene with happy interest, unconscious that many of those present watched her in turn with a good deal of scarcely restrained curiosity. For, somehow or other, rumour had whispered a flying word or two that it was possible she—even she—that young, childlike-looking creature—might be, and probably was the actual author of the clever book everybody was talking about, and though no one had the hardihood to ask her point-blank if the report was true, people glanced at her inquisitively and murmured their "asides" of suggestion or incredulity, finding it difficult to believe that a woman could at any time or by any means, alone and unaided, snatch one flower from the coronal of fame. She looked very fair and sweet and Non-literary, clad in a simple white gown made of some softly clinging diaphanous material, wholly unadorned save by a small posy of natural roses at her bosom,—and as she stood a little apart from the throng, several artists noticed the grace of her personality—one especially, a rather handsome man of middle age, who gazed at her observantly and critically with a frank openness which, though bold, was scarcely rude. She caught the straight light of his keen blue eyes—and a thrill ran through her whole being, as though she had been suddenly influenced by a magnetic current—then she flushed deeply as she fancied she saw him smile. For the first time in her life she found pleasure in the fact that a man had looked at her with plainly evinced admiration in his fleeting glance,—and she watched him talking to several people who all seemed delighted and flattered by his notice—then he disappeared. Later on in the evening she asked her host who he was. The famous R.A. considered for a moment.

"Do you mean a man with rough dark hair and a youngish face?—rather good-looking in an eccentric sort of way?"

Innocent nodded eagerly.

"Yes! And he had blue eyes."

"Had he, really!" And the great artist smiled. "Well, I'm sure he would be flattered at your close observation of him! I think I know him,—that is, I know him as much as he will let anybody know him—he is a curious fellow, but a magnificent painter—a real genius! He's half French by descent, and his name is Jocelyn,—Amadis de Jocelyn."

For a moment the room went round in a giddy whirl of colour before her eyes,—she could not credit her own hearing. Amadis de Jocelyn!—the name of her old stone Knight of France, on his tomb at Briar Farm, with his motto—"Mon coeur me soutien!"

"Amadis de Jocelyn!" she repeated, falteringly. . . "Are you sure? . . . I mean. . . is that his name really? . . . it's so unusual. . . so curious. . ."

"Yes—it Is curious"—agreed her host—"but it's quite a good old French name, belonging to a good old French family. The Jocelyns bore arms for the Duc d'Anjou in the reign of Queen Elizabeth—and this man is a sort of last descendant, very proud of his ancestry. I'll bring him along and introduce him to you if you'll allow me."

Innocent murmured something—she scarcely knew what,—and in a few minutes found herself giving the conventional bow in response to the formal words—"Miss Armitage, Mr. de Jocelyn"—and looking straight up at the blue eyes that a short while since had flashed an almost compelling glance into her own. A strange sense of familiarity and recognition moved her; something of the expression of her "Dad" was in the face of this other Jocelyn of whom she knew nothing,—and her heart beat so quickly that she could scarcely speak in answer when he addressed her, as he did in a somewhat abrupt manner.

"Are you an art student?"

She smiled a little.

"Oh no! I am—nothing! . . . I love pictures of course—"

"There is no 'of course' in it," he said, a humorous curve lifting the corners of his moustache—"You're not bound to love pictures at all! Most people hate them, and scarcely anybody understands them!"

She listened, charmed by the mellow and deep vibration of his voice.

"Everybody comes to see our friend here," he continued, with a slight gesture of his hand towards their host, who had moved away,—"because he is the fashion. If he were Not the fashion he might paint like Velasquez or Titian and no one would care a button!"

He seemed entertained by his own talk, and she did not interrupt him.

"You look like a stranger here," he went on, in milder accents—"a sort of elf who has lost her way out of fairyland! Is anyone with you?"

"Yes," she answered, quickly—"Miss Leigh—"

"Miss Leigh? Who is she? Your aunt or your chaperone?"

She was more at her ease now, and laughed at his quick, brusque manner of speech.

"Miss Leigh is my godmother," she said—"I call her my fairy godmother because she is always so good and kind. There she is, standing by that big easel."

He looked in the direction indicated.

"Oh yes!—I see! A charming old lady! I love old ladies when they don't pretend to be young. That white hair of hers is very picturesque! So she is your godmother!—and she takes care of you! Well! She might do worse!"

He ruffled his thick crop of hair and looked at her more or less quizzically.

"You have an air of suppressed enquiry," he said—"There is something on your mind! You want to ask me a question—what is it?"

A soft colour flew over her cheeks—she was confused to find him reading her thoughts.

"It is really nothing!" she answered, quickly—"I was only wondering a little about your name—because it is one I have known all my life."

His eyebrows went up in surprise.

"Indeed? This is very interesting! I thought I was the only wearer of such a very medieval appellation! Is there another so endowed?"

"There Was another—long, long ago"—and, unconsciously to herself her delicate features softened into a dreamy and rapt expression as she spoke,—while her voice fell into its sweetest and most persuasive tone. "He was a noble knight of France, and he came over to England with the Due d' Anjou when the great Elizabeth was Queen. He fell in love with a very beautiful Court lady, who would not care for him at all,—so, as he was unhappy and broken-hearted, he went away from London and hid himself from everybody in the far country. There he bought an old manor-house and called it Briar Farm—and he married a farmer's daughter and settled in England for good—and he had six sons and daughters. And when he died he was buried on his own land—and his effigy is on his tomb—it was sculptured by himself. I used to put flowers on it, just where his motto was carved—'Mon coeur me soutien.' For I—I was brought up at Briar Farm. . . and I was quite fond of the Sieur Amadis!"

She looked up with a serious, sweet luminance in her eyes—and he was suddenly thrilled by her glance, and moved by a desire to turn her romantic idyll into something of reality. This feeling was merely the physical one of an amorously minded man,—he knew, or thought he knew, women well enough to hold them at no higher estimate than that of sex-attraction,—yet, with all the cynicism he had attained through long experience of the world and its ways, he recognised a charm in this fair little creature that was strange and new and singularly fascinating, while the exquisite modulations of her voice as she told the story of the old French knight, so simply yet so eloquently, gave her words the tenderness of a soft song well sung.

"A pity you should waste fondness on a man of stone!" he said, lightly, bending his keen steel-blue eyes on hers. "But what you tell me is most curious, for your 'Sieur Amadis' must be the missing branch of my own ancestral tree. May I explain?—or will it bore you?"

She gave him a swift, eager glance.

"Bore me?" she echoed—"How could it? Oh, do please let me know everything—quickly!"

He smiled at her enthusiasm.

"We'll sit down here out of the crowd," he said,—and, taking her arm gently, he guided her to a retired corner of the studio which was curtained off to make a cosy and softly cushioned recess. "You have told me half a romance! Perhaps I can supply the other half." He paused, looking at her, whimsically pleased to see the warm young blood flushing her cheeks as he spoke, and her eyes drooping under his penetrating gaze. "Long, long ago—as you put it—in the days of good Queen Bess, there lived a certain Hugo de Jocelin, a nobleman of France, famed for fierce deeds of arms, and for making himself generally disagreeable to his neighbours with whom he was for ever at cross-purposes. This contentious personage had two sons,—Jeffrey and Amadis,—also knights-at-arms, inheriting the somewhat excitable nature of their father; and the younger of these, Amadis, whose name I bear, was selected by the Duc d'Anjou to accompany him with his train of nobles and gentles, when that 'petit grenouille' as he called himself, went to England to seek Queen Elizabeth's hand in marriage. The Duke failed in his ambitious quest, as we all know, and many of his attendants got scattered and dispersed,—among them Amadis, who was entirely lost sight of, and never returned again to the home of his fathers. He was therefore supposed to be dead—"

"My Amadis!" murmured Innocent, her eyes shining like stars as she listened.

"Your Amadis!—yes!" And his voice softened. "Of course he must have been Your Amadis!—your 'Knight of old and warrior bold!' Well! None of his own people ever heard of him again—and in the family tree he is marked as missing. But Jeffrey stayed at home in France,—and in due course inherited his father's grim old castle and lands. He married, and had a large family,—much larger than the six olive-branches allotted to your friend of Briar Farm,"—and he smiled. "He, Jeffrey, is my ancestor, and I can trace myself back to him in direct lineage, so you see I have quite the right to my curious name!"

She clasped and unclasped her little hands nervously—she was shy of raising her eyes to his face.

"It is wonderful!" she murmured—"I can hardly believe it possible that I should meet here in London a real Jocelyn!—one of the family of the Sieur Amadis!"

"Does it seem strange?" He laughed. "Oh no! Nothing is strange in this queer little world! But I don't quite know what the exact connection is between me and your knight—it's too difficult for me to grasp! I suppose I'm a sort of great-great-great-grand-nephew! However, nothing can alter the fact that I am also an Amadis de Jocelyn!"

She glanced up at him quickly.

"You are, indeed!" she said. "It is you who ought to be the master of Briar Farm!"

"Ought I?" He was amused at her earnestness. "Why?"

"Because there is no direct heir now to the Sieur Amadis!" she answered, almost sadly. "His last descendant is dead. His name was Hugo—Hugo Jocelyn—and he was a farmer, and he left all he had to his nephew, the only child of his sister who died before him. The nephew is very good, and clever, too,—he was educated at Oxford,—but he is not an actually lineal descendant."

He laughed again, this time quite heartily, at the serious expression of her face.

"That's very terrible!" he said. "I don't know when I've heard anything so lamentable! And I'm afraid I can't put matters right! I should never do for a farmer—I'm a painter. I had better go down and see this famous old place, and the tomb of my ever so great-great-grand-uncle! I could make a picture of it—I ought to do that, as it belonged to the family of my ancestors. Will you take me?"

She gave him a little fleeting, reluctant smile.

"You are making fun of it all," she said. "That is not wise of you! You should not laugh at grave and noble things."

He was charmed with her quaintness.

"Was he grave and noble?—Amadis, I mean?" he asked, his blue eyes sparkling with a kind of mirthful ardour. "You are sure? Well, all honour to him! And to You—for believing in him! I hope you'll consider me kindly for his sake! Will you?"

A quick blush suffused her cheeks.

"Of course!—I must do so!" she answered, simply. "I owe him so much—" then, fearful of betraying her secret of literary authorship, she hesitated—"I mean—he taught me all I know. I studied all his old books. . ."

Just then their cheery host came up.

"Well! Have you made friends? Ah!—I see you have! Mutual intelligence, mutual comprehension! Jocelyn, will you bring Miss Innocent in to supper?—I leave her in your charge."

"Miss Innocent?" repeated Jocelyn, doubtful as to whether this was said by way of a joke or not.

"Yes—some people call her Ena—but her real name is Innocent. Isn't it, little lady?"

She smiled and coloured. Jocelyn looked at her with a curious intentness.

"Really? Your name is Innocent?" he asked.

"Yes," she answered him—"I'm afraid it's a very unusual name—"

"It is indeed!" he said with emphasis. "Innocent by name and by nature! Will you come?"

She rose at once, and they moved away together.

II

C hance and coincidence play curious pranks with human affairs, and one of the most obvious facts of daily experience is that the merest trifle, occurring in the most haphazard way, will often suffice to change the whole intention and career of a life for good or for evil. It is as though a musician in the composition of a symphony should suddenly bethink himself of a new and strange melody, and, pleasing his fancy with the innovation, should wilfully introduce it at the last moment, thereby creating more or less of a surprise for the audience. Something of this kind happened to Innocent after her meeting with the painter who bore the name of her long idealised knight of France, Amadis de Jocelin. She soon learned that he was a somewhat famous personage,—famous for his genius, his scorn of accepted rules, and his contempt for all "puffery," push and patronage, as well as for his brusquerie in society and carelessness of conventions. She also heard that his works had been rejected twice by the Royal Academy Council, a reason he deemed all-sufficient for never appealing to that exclusive school of favouritism again,—while everything he chose to send was eagerly accepted by the French Salon, and purchased as soon as exhibited. His name had begun to stand very high—and his original character and personality made him somewhat of a curiosity among men—one more feared than favoured. He took a certain pleasure in analysing his own disposition for the benefit of any of his acquaintances who chose to listen,—and the harsh judgment he passed on himself was not altogether without justice or truth.

"I am an essentially selfish man," he would say—"I have met selfishness everywhere among my fellow men and women, and have imbibed it as a sponge imbibes water. I've had a fairly hard time, and I've experienced the rough side of human nature, getting more kicks than halfpence. Now that the kicks have ceased I'm in no mood for soft soap. I know the humbug of so-called 'friendship'—the rarity of sincerity— and as for love!—there's no such thing permanently in man, woman or child. What is called 'love' is merely a comfortable consciousness that one particular person is agreeable and useful to you for a time— but it's only for a time—and marriage which seeks to bind two people together till death is the heaviest curse ever imposed on manhood or womanhood! Devotion and self-sacrifice are merest folly—the people you sacrifice yourself for are never worth it, and devotion is generally, if not always, misplaced. The only thing to do in this life is to look after yourself,—serve yourself—please yourself! No one will do anything for you unless they can get something out of it for their own advantage,—you're bound to follow the general example!"

Notwithstanding this candid confession of cynical egotism, the man had greatness in him, and those who knew his works readily recognised his power. The impression he had made on Innocent's guileless and romantic nature was beyond analysis,—she did not try to understand it herself. His name and the connection he had with the old French knight of her childhood's dreams and fancies had moved and roused her to a new interest in life—and just as she had hitherto been unwilling to betray the secret of her literary authorship, she was now eager to have it declared—for one reason only,—that he might perhaps think well of her. Whereby it will be seen that the poor child, endowed with a singular genius as she was, knew nothing of men and their never-failing contempt for the achievements of gifted women. Delicate of taste and sensitive in temperament she was the very last sort of creature to realise the ugly truth that men, taken en masse, consider women in one only way—that of sex,—as the lower half of man, necessary to man's continuance, but always the mere vessel of his pleasure. To her, Amadis de Jocelyn was the wonderful realisation of an ideal,—but she was very silent concerning him,—reserved and almost cold. This rather surprised good Miss Lavinia Leigh, whose romantic tendencies had been greatly stirred by the story of the knight of Briar Farm and the discovery of a descendant of the same family in one of the most admired artists of the day. They visited Jocelyn's studio together—a vast, bare place, wholly unadorned by the tawdry paraphernalia which is sometimes affected by third-rate men to create an "art" impression on the minds of the uninstructed—and they had stood lost in wonder and admiration before a great picture he was painting on commission, entitled "Wild Weather." It was what is called by dealers an "important work," and represented night closing in over a sea lashed into fury by the sweep of a stormy wind. So faithfully was the scene of terror and elemental confusion rendered that it was like nature itself, and the imaginative eye almost looked for the rising waves to tumble liquidly from the painted canvas and break on the floor in stretches of creamy foam. Gentle Miss Leigh was conscious of a sudden beating of the heart as she looked at this masterpiece of form and colour,—it reminded her of the work of Pierce Armitage. She ventured to say so, with a little hesitation, and Jocelyn caught at the name.

"Armitage?—Yes—he was beginning to be rather famous some five-and-twenty years ago—I wonder what became of him? He promised great things. By the way"—and he turned to Innocent—"YOUR name is Armitage! Any relation to him?"

The colour rushed to her cheeks and fled again, leaving her very pale.

"No," she answered.

He looked at her inquisitively.

"Well, Armitage is not as outlandish a name as Amadis de Jocelyn," he said—"You will hardly find two of ME!—and I expect I shall hardly find two of You!" and he smiled—"especially if what I have heard is anything more than rumour!"

Her eyes filled with an eager light.

"What do you mean?"

He laughed,—yet in himself was conscious of a certain embarrassment.

"Well!—that a certain 'Innocent' young lady is a great author!" he said—"There! You have it! I'm loth to believe it, and hope the report isn't true, for I'm afraid of clever women! Indeed I avoid them whenever I can!"

A sudden sense of hopelessness and loss fell over her like a cloud—her lips quivered.

"Why should you do so?" she asked—"We do not avoid clever men!"

He smiled.

"Ah! That is different!"

She was silent. Miss Leigh looked a little distressed.

He went on lightly.

"My dear Miss Armitage, don't be angry with me!" he said—"You are so delightfully ignorant of the ways of our sex, and I for one heartily wish you might always remain so! But we men are proverbially selfish-and we like to consider cleverness, or 'genius' if you will, as our own exclusive property. We hate the feminine poacher on our particular preserves! We consider that women were made to charm and to amuse us—not to equal us. Do you see? When a woman is clever—perhaps cleverer than we are—she ceases to be amusing—and we must be amused! We cannot have our fun spoiled by the blue-stocking element,—though you—You do not look in the least 'blue!'"

She turned from him in a mute vexation. She thought his talk trifling and unmanly. Miss Leigh came to the rescue.

"No—Innocent is certainly not 'blue,'" she said, sweetly—"If by that term you mean 'advanced' or in any way unwomanly. But she has been singularly gifted by nature—yes, dear child, I must be allowed to speak!"—this, as Innocent made an appealing gesture,—"and if people say she is the author of the book that is just now being so much talked of, they are only saying the truth. The secret cannot be kept much longer."

He heard—then went quickly up to the girl where she stood in a somewhat dejected attitude near his easel.

"Then it Is true!" he said—"I heard it yesterday from an old journalist friend of mine, John Harrington—but I couldn't quite believe it. Let me congratulate you on your brilliant success—"

"You do not care!" she said, almost in a whisper.

"Oh, do I not?" He was amused, and taking her hand kissed it lightly. "If all literary women were like You—"

He left the sentence unfinished, but his eyes conveyed a wordless language which made her heart beat foolishly and her nerves thrill. She forgot the easy mockery which had distinguished his manner since when speaking of the "blue-stocking element"-and once more "Amadis de Jocelyn" sat firmly on her throne of the ideal!

That very afternoon, on her return from Jocelyn's studio to Miss Leigh's little house in Kensington which she now called her "home"—she found a reply-paid telegram from her publishers, running thus:

"Eminent journalist John Harrington reviews book favourably in evening paper suggesting that you are the actual author. May we deny or confirm?"

She thought for some minutes before deciding—and went to Miss Leigh with the telegram in her hand.

"Godmother mine!" she said, kneeling down beside her—"Tell me, what shall I do? Is it any use continuing to wear the veil of mystery? Shall I take up my burden and bear it like a man?"

Miss Lavinia smiled, and drew the girl's fair head to her bosom.

"Poor little one!" she said, tenderly—"I know just what you feel about it! You would rather remain quietly in your own dreamland than face the criticism of the world, or be pointed out as a 'celebrity'—yes, I quite understand! But I think you must, in justice to yourself and others, 'take up the burden'—as you put it—yes, child! You must wear your laurels, though for you I should prefer the rose!"

MARIE CORELLI

Innocent shivered, as with sudden cold.

"A rose has thorns!" she said, as she got up from her kneeling attitude and moved away—"It's beautiful to look at—but it soon fades!"

She sent off her reply wire to the publishers without further delay.

"Statement quite true. You can confirm it publicly."

And so the news was soon all over London, and for that matter all over the world. From one end of the globe to the other the fact was made known that a girl in her twentieth year had produced a literary masterpiece, admirable both in design and execution, worthy to rank with the highest work of the most brilliant and renowned authors. She was speedily overwhelmed by letters of admiration, and invitations from every possible quarter where "lion-hunting" is practised as a stimulant to jaded and over-wrought society, but amid all the attractions and gaieties offered to her she held fast by her sheet-anchor of safety, Miss Leigh, who redoubled her loving care and vigilance, keeping her as much as she could in the harbour of that small and exclusive "set" of well-bred and finely-educated people for whom noise and fuss and show meant all that was worst in taste and manners. And remaining more or less in seclusion, despite the growing hubbub around her name, she finished her second book, and took it herself to the great publishing house which was rapidly coining good hard cash out of the delicate dream of her woman's brain. The head of the firm received her with eager and respectful cordiality.

"You kept your secret very well!" he said—"I assure you I had no idea you could be the author of such a book!—you are so young—"

She smiled, a little sadly.

"One may be young in years and old in thought," she answered—"I passed all my childhood in reading and studying—I had no playmates and no games—and I was nearly always alone. I had only old books to read—mostly of the sixteenth century—I suppose I formed a 'style' unconsciously on these."

"It is a very beautiful and expressive style," said the publisher—"I told Mr. Harrington, when he first suggested that you might be the author, that it was altogether too scholarly for a girl."

She gave a slight deprecatory gesture.

"Pray do not let us discuss it," she said—"I am not at all pleased to be known as the author."

"No?" And he looked surprised—"Surely you must be happy to become so suddenly famous?"

"Are famous persons happy?" she asked—"I don't think they are! To be stared at and whispered about and criticised—that's not happiness! And men never like you!"

The publisher laughed.

"You can do without their liking, Miss Armitage," he said—"You've beaten all the literary fellows on their own ground! You ought to be satisfied. WE are very proud!"

"Thank you!" she said, simply, as she rose to go—"I am grateful for your good opinion."

When she had left him, the publisher eagerly turned over the pages of her new manuscript. At a glance he saw that there was no "falling-off"—he recognised the same lucidity of expression, the same point and delicacy of phraseology which had distinguished her first effort, and the wonderful charm with which a thought was pressed firmly yet tenderly home to its mark.

"It will be a greater triumph for her and for us than the previous book!" he said—"She's a wonder!—and the most wonderful thing about her is that she has no conceit, and is unconscious of her own power!"

Two or three days after the announcement of her authorship, came a letter from Robin Clifford.

> DEAR INNOCENT, it ran, "I see that your name, or rather the name you have taken for yourself, is made famous as that of the author of a book which is creating a great sensation—and I venture to write a word of congratulation, hoping it may be acceptable to you from your playmate and friend of bygone days. I can hardly believe that the dear little 'Innocent' of Briar Farm has become such a celebrated and much-talked-of personage, for after all it is not yet two years since you left us. I have told Priscilla, and she sends her love and duty, and hopes God will allow her to see you once again before she dies. The work of the farm goes on as usual, and everything prospers—all is as Uncle Hugo would have wished—all except one thing which I know will never be! But you must not think I grumble at my fate. I might feel lonely if I had not plenty of work to do and people dependent on me—but under such circumstances I manage to live a life that is at least useful to others and I want for nothing. In the evenings when the darkness closes in, and we light the tall candles in

the old pewter sconces, I often wish I could see a little fair head shining like a cameo against the dark oak panelling—a vision of grace and hope and comfort!—but as this cannot be, I read old books—even some of those belonging to your favourite French Knight Amadis!—and try to add to the little learning I gained at Oxford. I am sending for your book!—when it comes I shall read every word of it with an interest too deep to be expressed to you in my poor language. 'Cupid' is well—he flies to my hand, surprised, I think, to find it of so rough a texture as compared with the little rose-velvet palm to which he was accustomed. Will you ever come to Briar Farm again? God bless you!

ROBIN

She shed some tears over this letter—then, moved by a sudden impulse, sat down and answered it at once, giving a full account of her meeting and acquaintance with another Amadis de Jocelyn—"the real last descendant," she wrote, "of the real old family of the very Amadis of Briar Farm!" She described his appearance and manners,—descanted on his genius as a painter, and all unconsciously poured out her ardent, enthusiastic soul on this wonderful discovery of the Real in the Ideal. She said nothing of her own work or success, save that she was glad to be able to earn her living. And when Robin read the simple outflow of her thoughts his heart grew cold within him. He, with the keen instinct of a lover, guessed at once all that might happen,—saw the hidden fire smouldering, and became conscious of an inexplicable dread, as though a note of alarm had sounded mystically in his brain. What would happen to Innocent, if she, with her romantic, old-world fancies, should allow a possible traitor to intrude within the crystal-pure sphere where her sweet soul dwelt unsullied and serene? He told Priscilla the strange story—and she in her shrewd, motherly way felt something of the same fear.

"Eh, the poor lamb!" she sighed—"That old French knight was ever a fly in her brain and a stumbling-block in the way of us all!—and now to come across a man o' the same name an' family, turning up all unexpected like,—why, it's like a ghost's sudden risin' from the tomb! An' what does it mean, Mister Robin? Are you the master o' Briar Farm now?—or is he the rightful one?"

Clifford laughed, a trifle bitterly.

"I am the master," he said, "according to my uncle's will. This man is a painter—famous and admired,—he'll scarcely go in for farming! If he did—if he'd buy the farm from me—I should be glad enough to sell it and leave the country."

"Mister Robin!" cried Priscilla, reproachfully.

He patted her hand gently.

"Not yet—not yet anyhow, Priscilla!" he said—"I may be yet of some use—to Innocent." He paused, then added, slowly—"I think we shall hear more of this second Amadis de Jocelyn!"

But months went on, and he heard nothing, save of Innocent's growing fame which, by leaps and bounds, was spreading abroad like fire blown into brightness by the wind. He got her first book and read it with astonishment and admiration, utterly confounded by its brilliancy and power. When her second work appeared with her adopted name appended to it as the author, all the reading world "rushed" at it, and equally "rushed" at HER, lifting her, as it were, on their shoulders and bearing her aloft, against her own desire, above the seething tide of fashion and frivolity as though she were a queen of many kingdoms, crowned with victory. And again the old journalist, John Harrington, sought an audience of her, and this time was not refused. She received him in Miss Leigh's little drawing-room, holding out both her hands to him in cordial welcome, with a smile frank and sincere enough to show him at a glance that her "celebrity" had left her unscathed. She was still the same simple child-like soul, wearing the mystical halo of spiritual dreams rather than the brazen baldric of material prosperity—and he, bitterly seasoned in the hardest ways of humanity, felt a thrill of compassion as he looked at her, wondering how her frail argosy, freighted with fine thought and rich imagination, would weather a storm should storms arise. He sat talking for a long time with her and Miss Leigh—reminding her pleasantly of their journey up to London together,—while she, in her turn, amused and astonished him by avowing the fact that it was his loan of the "Morning Post" that had led her, through an advertisement, to the house where she was now living.

"So I've had something of a hand in it all!" he said, cheerily—"I'm glad of that! It was chance or luck, or whatever you call it!—but I never thought that the little girl with the frightened eyes, carrying a satchel for all her luggage, was a future great author, to whom I, as a poor old journalist, would have to bow!" He laughed kindly as he spoke—"And you are still a little girl!—or you look one! I feel disposed to play literary grandfather to you! But you want nobody's help—you have made yourself!"

"She has, indeed!" said Miss Leigh, with pride sparkling in her tender eyes—"When she came here, and suddenly decided to stay with me, I had no idea of her plans, or what she was studying. She used to shut herself up all the morning and write—she told me she was finishing off some work—in fact it was her first book,—a manuscript she brought with her from the country in that famous satchel! I knew nothing at all about it till she confided to me one day that she had written a book, and that it had been accepted by a publisher. I was amazed!"

"And the result must have amazed you still more," said Harrington,— "but I'm a very astute person!—and I guessed at once, when I was told the address of the 'Private Secretary of the author,' that the Secretary was the author herself!"

Innocent blushed.

"Perhaps it was wrong to say what was not true," she said, "but really I Was and Am the secretary of the author!—I write all the manuscript with my own hand!"

They laughed at this, and then Harrington went on to say—

"I believe you know the painter Amadis Jocelyn, don't you? Yes? Well, I was with him the other day, and I said you were the author of the wonderful book. He told me I was talking nonsense—that you couldn't be,—he had met you at an artist's evening party and that you had told him a story about some ancestor of his own family. 'She's a nice little thing with baby eyes,' he said, 'but she couldn't write a clever book! She may have got some man to write it for her!'"

Innocent gave a little cry of pain.

"Oh!—did he say that?"

"Of course he did! All men say that sort of thing! They can't bear a woman to do more than marry and have children. Simple girl with the satchel, don't you know that? You mustn't mind it—it's their way. Of course I rounded on Jocelyn and told him he was a fool, with a swelled head on the subject of his own sex—he Is a fool in many ways,—he's a great painter, but he might be much greater if he'd get up early in the morning and stick to his work. He ought to have been in the front rank long ago."

"But surely he Is in the front rank?" queried Miss Leigh, mildly— "He is a wonderful artist!"

"Wonderful—yes!—with a lot of wonderful things in him which haven't come out!" declared Harrington, "and which never will come out, I fear! He turns night into day too often. Oh, he's clever!—I grant you all that—but he hasn't a resolute will or a great mind, like Watts or Burne-Jones or any of the fellows who served their art nobly—he's a selfish sort of chap!"

Innocent heard, and longed to utter a protest—she wanted to say-"No, no!—you wrong him! He is good and noble—he must be!—he is Amadis de Jocelyn!"

But she repressed her thought and sat very quiet,—then, when Harrington paused, she told him in a sweet, even voice the story of the "Knight of France" who founded Briar Farm. He was enthralled—not so much by the tale as by her way of telling it.

"And so Jocelyn the painter is the lineal descendant of the BROTHER of your Jocelin!—the knight who disappeared and took to farming in the days of Elizabeth!" he said—"Upon my word, it's a quaint bit of history and coincidence—almost too romantic for such days as these!"

Innocent smiled.

"Is romance at an end now?" she asked.

Harrington looked at her kindly.

"Almost! It's gasping its last gasp in company with poetry. Realism is our only wear—Realism and Prose—very prosy Prose. You are a romantic child!—I can see that!—but don't over-do it! And if you ever made an ideal out of your sixteenth-century man, don't make another out of the twentieth-century one! He couldn't stand it!—he'd crumble at a touch!"

She answered nothing, but avoided his glance. He prepared to take his leave—and on rising from his chair suddenly caught sight of the portrait on the harpsichord.

"I know that face!" he said, quickly,—"Who is he?"

"He WAS also a painter—as great as the one we have just been speaking of," answered Miss Leigh—"His name was Pierce Armitage."

"That's it!" exclaimed Harrington, with some excitement. "Of course! Pierce Armitage! I knew him! One of the handsomest fellows I ever saw! THERE was an artist, if you like!—he might have been anything! What became of him?—do you know?"

"He died abroad, so it is said"—and Miss Leigh's gentle voice trembled a little—"but nothing is quite certainly known—"

Harrington turned swiftly to stare eagerly at Innocent.

"YOUR name is Armitage!" he said—"and do you know you are rather like him! Your face reminds me—Are you any relative?"

She gave the usual answer—

"No."

"Strange!" He bent his eyes scrutinisingly upon her. "I remember I thought the same thing when I first met you—and His features are not easily forgotten! You have his eyes—and mouth,—you might almost be his daughter!"

Her breath quickened—

"I wish I were!" she said.

He still looked puzzled.

"No—don't wish for what would perhaps be a misfortune!" he said—"You've done very well for yourself!—but don't be romantic! Keep that old 'French knight' of yours in the pages of an old French chronicle!—shut the volume,—lock it up,—and—lose the key!"

III

Some weeks later on, when the London season was at its height, and Fashion, that frilled and furbelowed goddess, sat enthroned in state, controlling the moods of the Elect and Select which she chooses to call "society," Innocent was invited to the house of a well-known Duchess, renowned for a handsome personality, and also for an unassailable position, notwithstanding certain sinister rumours. People said—people are always saying something!—that her morals were easy-going, but everyone agreed that her taste was unimpeachable. She—this great lady whose rank permitted her to entertain the King and Queen—heard of "Ena Armitage" as the brilliant author whose books were the talk of the town, and forthwith made up her mind that she must be seen at her house as the "sensation" of at least one evening. To this end she glided in her noiseless, satin-cushioned motor brougham up to the door of Miss Leigh's modest little dwelling and left the necessary slips of pasteboard bearing her titled name, with similar slips on behalf of her husband the Duke, for Miss Armitage and Miss Leigh. The slips were followed in due course by a more imposing and formal card of invitation to a "Reception and Small Dance. R.S.V.P." On receiving this, good old Miss Lavinia was a little fluttered and excited, and turning it over and over in her hand, looked at Innocent with a kind of nervous anxiety.

"I think we ought to go, my dear," she said—"or rather—I don't know about myself—but You ought to go certainly. It's a great house—a great family—and she is a very great lady—a little—well!—a little 'modern' perhaps—"

Innocent lifted her eyebrows with a slight, almost weary smile. A scarcely perceptible change had come over her of late—a change too subtle to be noticed by anyone who was not as keenly observant as Miss Lavinia—but it was sufficient to give the old lady who loved her cause for a suspicion of trouble.

"What is it to be modern?" she asked—"In your sense, I mean? I know what is called 'modern' generally—bad art, bad literature, bad manners and bad taste! But what do You call modern?"

Miss Leigh considered—looking at the girl with steadfast, kindly eyes.

"You speak a trifle bitterly—for You, dear child!" she said—"These things you name as 'modern' truly are so, but they are ancient as well!

The world has altered very little, I think. What we call 'bad' has always existed as badness—it is only presented to us in different forms—"

Innocent laughed—a soft little laugh of tenderness.

"Wise godmother!" she said, playfully—"You talk like a book!"

Miss Lavinia laughed too, and a pretty pink colour came into her wan cheeks.

"Naughty child, you are making fun of me!" she said—"What I meant about the Duchess—"

Innocent stretched out her hand for the card of invitation and looked at it.

"Well!" she said, slowly—"What about the Duchess?"

Miss Leigh hesitated.

"I hardly know how to put it," she answered, at last—"She's a kind-hearted woman—very generous—and most helpful in works of charity. I never knew such energy as she shows in organising charity bails and bazaars!—perfectly wonderful!—but she likes to live her life—"

"Who would not!" murmured the girl, scarcely audibly.

"And she lives it—very much so!—rather to the dregs!" continued the old lady, with emphasis. "She has no real aim beyond the satisfaction of her own vanity and social power—and you, with your beautiful thoughts and ideals, might not like the kind of people she surrounds herself with—people, who only want amusement and 'sensation'—particularly sensation—"

Innocent said nothing for a minute or two—then she looked up, brightly.

"To go or not to go, godmother mine! Which is it to be? The decision rests with you! Yes, or no?"

"I think it must be 'yes'"—and Miss Leigh emphasised the word with a little nod of her head. "It would be unwise to refuse—especially just now when everyone is talking of you and wishing to see you. And you are quite worth seeing!"

The girl gave a slight gesture of indifference and moved away slowly and listlessly, as though fatigued by the mere effort of speech. Miss Leigh noted this with some concern, watching her as she went, and admiring the supple grace of her small figure, the well-shaped little head so proudly poised on the slim throat, and the burnished sheen of her bright hair.

"She grows prettier every day," she thought—"But not happier, I fear!—not happier, poor child!"

Innocent meanwhile, upstairs in her own little study, was reading and re-reading a brief letter which had come for her by the same post that had delivered the Duchess's invitation.

"I hear you are among the guests invited to the Duchess of Deanshire's party," it ran—"I hope you will go—for the purely selfish reason that I want to meet you there. Hers is a great house with plenty of room, and a fine garden—for London. People crowd to her 'crushes', but one can always escape the mob. I have seen so little of you lately, and you are now so famous that I shall think myself lucky if I may touch the hem of your garment. Will you encourage me thus far? Like Hamlet, 'I lack advancement!' When will you take me to Briar Farm? I should like to see the tomb of my very ancestral uncle—could we not arrange a day's outing in the country while the weather is fine? I throw myself on your consideration and clemency for this—and for many other unwritten things!

Yours,
AMADIS DE JOCELYN

There was nothing in this easily worded scrawl to make an ordinarily normal heart beat faster, yet the heart of this simple child of the gods, gifted with genius and deprived of worldly wisdom as all such divine children are, throbbed uneasily, and her eyes were wet. More than this, she touched the signature,—the long-familiar name—with her soft lips,—and as though afraid of what she had done, hurriedly folded the letter and locked it away.

Then she sat down and thought. Nearly two years had elapsed since she had left Briar Farm, and in that short time she had made the name she had adopted famous. She could not call it her own name; born out of wedlock, she had no right, by the stupid law, to the name of her father. She could, legally, have worn the maiden name of her mother had she known it—but she did not know it. And what she was thinking of now, was this: Should she tell her lately discovered second "Amadis de Jocelyn" the true story of her birth and parentage at this, the outset of their friendship, before—well, before it went any further? She could not consult Miss Leigh on the point, without smirching the reputation of Pierce Armitage, the man whose memory was enshrined in that dear lady's heart as a thing of unsullied honour. She puzzled herself over the question for a long time, and then decided to keep her own counsel.

"After all, why should I tell him?" she asked herself. "It might make trouble—he is so proud of his lineage, and I too am proud of it for him! . . . why should I let him know that I inherit nothing but my mother's shame!"

Her heart grew heavy as her position was thus forced back upon her by her own thoughts. Up to the present no one had asked who she was, or where she came from—she was understood to be an orphan, left alone in the world, who by her own genius and unaided effort had lifted herself into the front rank among the "shining lights" of the day. This, so far, had been sufficient information for all with whom she had come in contact—but as time went on, would not people ask more about her?—who were her father and mother?—where she was born?— how she had been educated? These inquisitorial demands were surely among the penalties of fame! And, if she told the truth, would she not, despite the renown she had won, be lightly, even scornfully esteemed by conventional society as a "bastard" and interloper, though the manner of her birth was no fault of her own, and she was unjustly punishable for the sins of her parents, such being the wicked law!

The night of the Duchess's reception was one of those close sultry nights of June in London when the atmosphere is well-nigh as suffocating as that of some foetid prison where criminals have been pacing their dreary round all day. Royal Ascot was just over, and space and opportunity were given for several social entertainments to be conveniently checked off before Henley. Outside the Duke's great house there was a constant stream of motor-cars and taxi-cabs; a passing stranger might have imagined all the world and his wife were going to the Duchess's "At Home." It was difficult to effect an entrance, but once inside, the scene was one of veritable enchantment. The lovely hues and odours of flowers, the softened glitter of thousands of electric lamps shaded with rose-colour, the bewildering brilliancy of women's clothes and jewels, the exquisite music pouring like a rippling stream through the magnificent reception-rooms, all combined to create a magical effect of sensuous beauty and luxury; and as Innocent, accompanied by the sweet-faced old-fashioned lady who played the part of chaperone with such gentle dignity, approached her hostess, she was a little dazzled and nervous. Her timidity made her look all the more charming—she had the air of a wondering child called up to receive an unexpected prize at school. She shrank visibly when her name was shouted out in a stentorian voice by the gorgeously liveried major-domo in attendance, quite unaware that it created a thrill throughout the fashionable assemblage, and that all eyes were instantly upon her. The Duchess, diamond-crowned and glorious in gold-embroidered tissue, kept back by a slight gesture the pressing crowd of guests, and extended her hand with marked graciousness and a delightful smile.

"Such a pleasure and honour!" she said, sweetly—"So good of you to come! You will give me a few words with you later on? Yes? Everybody will want to speak to you!—but you must let me have a chance too!"

Innocent murmured something gently deprecatory as a palliative to this sort of society "gush" which always troubled her—and moved on. Everybody gazed, whispered and wondered, astonished at the youth and evident unworldliness of the "author of those marvellous books!"—so the commentary ran;—the women criticised her gown, which was one of pale blue silken stuff caught at the waist and shoulders by quaint clasps of dull gold—a gown with nothing remarkable about it save its cut and fit—melting itself, as it were, around her in harmonious folds of fine azure which suggested without emphasising the graceful lines of her form. The men looked, and said nothing much except "A pity she's a writing woman! Mucking about Fleet Street!"—mere senseless talk which they knew to be senseless, inasmuch as "mucking" about Fleet Street is no part of any writer's business save that of the professional journalist. Happily ignorant of comment, the girl made her way quietly and unobtrusively through the splendid throng, till she was presently addressed by a stoutish, pleasant-featured man, with small twinkling eyes and an agreeable surface manner.

"I missed you just now when my wife received you," he said—"May I present myself? I am your host—proud of the privilege!"

Innocent smiled as she bowed and held out her hand; she was amused, and taken a little by surprise. This was the Duke of Deanshire—this quite insignificant-looking personage—he was the owner of the great house and the husband of the great lady,—and yet he had the appearance of a very ordinary nobody. But that he was a "somebody" of paramount importance there was no doubt; and when he said, "May I give you my arm and take you through the rooms? There are one or two pictures you may like to see," she was a little startled. She looked round for Miss Leigh, but that tactful lady, seeing the position, had disappeared. So she laid her little cream-gloved hand on the Duke's arm and went with him, shyly at first, yet with a pretty stateliness which was all her own, and moving slowly among the crowd of guests, gradually recovered her ease and self-possession, and began to talk to him with a delightful naturalness and candour which fairly captivated His Grace, in fact, "bowled him over," as he afterwards declared. She was blissfully unaware that his manner of escorting her on his arm through the long vista of the magnificent rooms had been commanded and arranged by the Duchess, in order that she should be well looked at and criticised by all assembled as the "show" person of the evening. She was so unconscious of the ordeal to which she was being subjected that she bore it with the perfect indifference which such unconsciousness gives. All at once the Duke came to a standstill.

"Here is a great friend of mine—one of the best I have in the world," he said—"I want to introduce him to you,"—this, as a tall old man paused near them with a smile and enquiring glance, "Lord Blythe—Miss Armitage."

Innocent's heart gave a wild bound; for a moment she felt a struggling sensation in her throat moving her to cry out, and it was only with a violent effort that she repressed herself.

"You've heard of Miss Armitage—Ena Armitage,—haven't you, Blythe?" went on the Duke, garrulously. "Of course! all the world has heard of her!"

"Indeed it has!" and Lord Blythe bowed ceremoniously. "May I congratulate you on winning your laurels while you are young enough to enjoy them! One moment!—my wife is most anxious to meet you—"

He turned to look for her, while Innocent, trembling violently, wondered desperately whether it would be possible for her to run away!—anywhere—anywhere, rather than endure what she knew must come! The Duke noticed her sudden pallor with concern.

"Are you cold?" he asked—"I hope there is no draught—"

"Oh no—no!" she murmured—"It is nothing—"

Then she braced herself up in every nerve—drawing her little body erect, as though a lily should lift itself to the sun—she saw Lord Blythe approaching with a handsome woman dressed in silvery grey and wearing a coronet of emeralds—and in one more moment looked full in the face—of her mother!

"Lady Blythe—Miss Armitage."

Lady Blythe turned white to the lips. Her dark eyes opened widely in amazement and fear—she put out a hand as though to steady herself. Her husband caught it, alarmed.

"Maude! Are you ill?"

"Not at all!" and she forced a laugh. "I am perfectly—perfectly well!—a little faint perhaps! The heat, I think! Yes—of course! Miss Armitage—the famous author! I am—I am very proud to meet you!"

"Most kind of you!" said Innocent, quietly.

And they still looked at each other, very strangely.

The men beside them were a little embarrassed, the Duke twirled his short white moustache, and Lord Blythe glanced at his wife with some wonder and curiosity. Both imagined, with the usual short-sightedness of the male sex, that the women had taken a sudden fantastic dislike to one another.

"By jove, she's jealous!" thought the Duke, fully aware that Lady Blythe was occasionally "moved that way."

"The girl seems frightened of her," was Lord Blythe's inward comment, knowing that his wife did not always create a sympathetic atmosphere.

But her ladyship was soon herself again and laughed quite merrily at her husband's anxious expression.

"I'm all right—really!" she said, with a quick, almost defiant turn of her head towards him, the emeralds in her dark hair flashing with a sinister gleam like lightning on still water. "You must remember it's rather overwhelming to be introduced to a famous author and think of just the right thing to say at the right moment! Isn't it, Miss Armitage?"

"It is as you feel," replied Innocent, coldly.

Lady Blythe rattled on gaily.

"Do come and talk to me for a few moments!—it will be so good of you! The garden's lovely!—shall we go there? Now, my dear Duke, don't look so cross, I'll bring her back to you directly!" and she nodded pleasantly. "You want her, of course!—everybody wants her!—such a celebrity!" then, turning again to Innocent, "Will you come?"

As one in a dream the girl obeyed her inviting gesture, and they passed out of the room together through a large open French window to a terraced garden, dimly illumined in the distance by the glitter of fairy lamps, but for the most part left to the tempered brilliancy of a misty red moon. Once away from the crowd, Lady Blythe walked quickly and impatiently, scarcely looking at the youthful figure that accompanied her own, like a fair ghost gliding step for step beside her. At last she stopped; they were well away from the house in a quaint bit of garden shaded with formal fir-trees and clipped yews, where a fountain dashed up a slender spiral thread of white spray. A strange sense of fury in her broke loose; with pale face and cruel, glittering eyes she turned upon her daughter.

"How dare you!" she half whispered, through her set teeth—"How dare you!"

Innocent drew back a step, and looked at her steadfastly.

"I do not understand you," she said.

"You do understand!—you understand only too well!" and Lady Blythe put her hand to the pearls at her throat as though she felt them choking her. "Oh, I could strike you for your insolence! I wish I had never sought you out or told you how you were born! Is this your revenge for the manner of your birth, that you come to shame me among my own class—my own people—"

Innocent's eyes flashed with a fire seldom seen in their soft depths.

"Shame you?" she echoed. "I? What shame have I brought you? What shame shall I bring? Had you owned me as your child I would have made you proud of me! I would have given you honour,—you abandoned me to strangers, and I have made honour for myself! Shame is Yours and yours only!—it would be mine if I had to acknowledge You as my mother!—you who never had the courage to be true!" Her young voice thrilled with passion.—"I have won my own way! I am something beyond and above you!—'your own class—your own people,' as you call them, are at My feet,—and you—you who played with my father's heart and spoilt his career—you have lived to know that I, his deserted child, have made his name famous!"

Lady Blythe stared at her like some enraged cat ready to spring.

"His name—his name!" she muttered, fiercely. "Yes, and how dare you take it? You have no right to it in law!"

"Wise law, just law!" said the girl, passionately. "Would you rather I had taken yours? I might have done so had I known it—though I think not, as I should have been ashamed of any 'maiden' name you had dishonoured! When you came to Briar Farm to find me—to see me—so late, so late!—after long years of desertion—I told you it was possible to make a name;—one cannot go nameless through the world! I have made mine!—independently and honestly—in fact"—and she smiled, a sad cold smile—"it is an honour for you, my mother, to know me, your daughter!"

Lady Blythe's face grew ghastly pale in the uncertain light of the half-veiled moon. She moved a step and caught the girl's arm with some violence.

"What do you mean to do?" she asked, in an angry whisper, "I must know! What are your plans of vengeance?—your campaign of notoriety?—your scheme of self-advertisement? What claim will you make?"

"None!" and Innocent looked at her fully, with calm and fearless dignity. "I have no claim upon you, thank God! I am less to you than a dropped lamb, lost in a thicket of thorns, is to the sheep that bore it! That's a rough country simile,—I was brought up on a farm, you know!—but it will serve your case. Think nothing of me, as I think nothing of you! What I am, or what I may be to the world, is my own affair!"

There was a pause. Presently Lady Blythe gave a kind of shrill hysterical laugh.

"Then, when we meet in society, as we have met to-night, it will be as comparative strangers?"

"Why, of course!—we have always been strangers," the girl replied, quietly. "No strangers were ever more strange to each other than we!"

"You mean to keep My secret?—and your own?"

"Certainly. Do you suppose I would give my father's name to slander?"

"Your father!—you talk of your father as if HE was worth consideration!—he was chiefly to blame for your position—"

"Was he? I am not quite sure of that," said Innocent, slowly—"I do not know all the circumstances. But I have heard that he was a great artist; and that some woman he loved ruined his life. And I believe you are that woman!"

Lady Blythe laughed—a hard mirthless laugh.

"Believe what you like!" she said—"You are an imaginative little fool! When you know more of the world you will find out that men ruin women's lives as casually as cracking nuts, but they take jolly good care of their own skins! Pierce Armitage was too selfish a man to sacrifice his own pleasure and comfort for anyone—he was glad to get rid of me—and of You! And now—now!" She threw up her hands with an expressive, half-tragic gesture. "Now you are famous!— actually famous! Good heavens!—why, I thought you would stay in that old farmhouse all your life, scrubbing the floors and looking after the poultry, and perhaps marrying some good-natured country yokel! Famous!—you!—with social London dancing attendance on you! What a ghastly comedy!" She laughed again. "Come!—we must go back to the house."

They walked side by side—the dark full-figured woman and the fair slight girl—the one a mere ephemeral unit in an exclusively aristocratic and fashionable "set,"—the other, the possessor of a sudden brilliant fame which was spreading a new light across the two hemispheres. Not another word was exchanged between them, and as they re-entered the ducal reception-rooms, now more crowded than ever, Lord Blythe met them.

"I was just going to look for you," he said to his wife—"There are dozens of people waiting to be presented to Miss Armitage; the Duchess has asked for her several times."

Lady Blythe turned to Innocent with a dazzling smile.

"How guilty I feel!" she exclaimed. "Everybody wanting to see you, and I selfishly detaining you in the garden! It was so good of you to give me a few minutes!—you, the guest of the evening too! Good-night!—in case I don't find you again in this crowd!"

She moved away then, leaving Innocent fairly bewildered by her entire coolness and self-possession. She herself, poor child, moved to the very soul by the interview she had just gone through, was trembling with extreme nervousness, and could hardly conceal her agitation.

"I'm afraid you've caught cold!" said Lord Blythe, kindly—"That will never do! I promised I would take you to the Duchess as soon as I found you—she has some friends with her who wish to meet you. Will you come?"

She smiled assent, looking up at him gratefully and thinking what a handsome old man he was, with his tall, well-formed figure and fine intellectual face on which the constant progress of good thoughts had marked many a pleasant line. Her mother's husband!—and she wondered how it happened that such a woman had been chosen for a wife by such a man!

"They're going to dance in the ball-room directly," he continued, as he guided her through the pressing throng of people. "You will not be without partners! Are you fond of dancing?"

Her face lighted up with the lovely youthful look that gave her such fascination and sweetness of expression.

"Yes, I like it very much, though before I came to London I only knew country dances such as they dance at harvest-homes; but of course here, you all dance so differently!—it is only just going round and round! But it's quite pleasant and rather amusing."

"You were brought up in the country then?" he said.

"Yes, entirely. I came to London about two years ago."

"But—I hope you don't think me too inquisitive!—where did you study literature?"

She laughed a little.

"I don't think I studied it at all," she answered, "I just loved it! There was a small library of very old books in the farmhouse where I lived, and I read and re-read these. Then, when I was about sixteen, it suddenly came into my head that I would try to write a story myself—and I did. Little by little it grew into a book, and I brought it to London and finished it here. You know the rest!"

"Like Byron, you awoke one morning to find yourself famous!" said Lord Blythe, smiling. "You have no parents living?"

Her cheeks burned with a hot blush as she replied.

"No."

"A pity! They would have been very proud of you. Here is the Duchess!"

And in another moment she was drawn into the vortex of a brilliant circle surrounding her hostess—men and women of notable standing in politics, art and letters, to whom the Duchess presented her with the half kindly, half patronising air of one who feels that any genius in man or woman is a kind of disease, and that the person affected by it must be soothingly considered as a sort of "freak" or nondescript creature, like a white crow or a red starling.

"These abnormal people are so interesting!" she was wont to say. "These prodigies and things! I love them! They're often quite ugly and have rude manners—Beethoven used to eat with his fingers I believe; wasn't it wonderful of him! Such a relief from the conventional way! When I was quite a girl I used to adore a man in Paris who played the 'cello divinely—a perfect marvel!—but he wouldn't comb his hair or blow his nose properly—and it wasn't very nice!—not that it mattered much, he was such a wonderful artist! Oh yes, I know! it wouldn't have lessened his genius to have wiped his nose with a handkerchief instead of—! well!—perhaps we'd better not mention it!" And she would laugh charmingly and again murmur, "These deaf abnormal people!"

With Innocent, however, she was somewhat put off her usual line of conduct; the girl was too graceful and easy-mannered to be called "abnormal" or eccentric; she was perfectly modest, simple and unaffected, and the Duchess was a trifle disappointed that she was not ill-dressed, frowsy, frumpish and blue-spectacled.

"She's so young too!" thought her Grace, half crossly—"Almost a child!—and not in the least 'bookish.' It seems quite absurd that such a baby-looking creature should be actually a genius, and famous at twenty! Simply amazing!"

And she watched the little "lion" or lioness of the evening with keen interest and curiosity, whimsically vexed that it did not roar, snort, or make itself as noticeable as certain other animals of the literary habitat whom she had occasionally entertained. Just then a mirthful, mellow voice spoke close beside her.

"Where is the new Corinne? The Sappho of the Leucadian rock of London? Has she met her Phaon?"

"How late you are, Amadis!" and the Duchess smiled captivatingly as she extended her hand to Jocelyn, who gallantly stooped and kissed the perfectly fitting glove which covered it. "If you mean Miss Armitage, she is just over there talking to two old fogies. I think they're Cabinet ministers—they look it! She's quite the success of the evening,—and pretty, don't you think?"

Jocelyn looked, and saw the small fair head rising like a golden flower from sea-blue draperies; he smiled enigmatically.

"Not exactly," he answered, "But spirituelle—she has what some painters might call an imaginative head—she could pose very well for St. Dorothy. I can quite realise her preferring the executioner's axe to the embraces of Theophilus."

The Duchess gave him a swift glance and touched his arm with the edge of her fan.

"Are you going to make love to her?" she asked. "You make love to every woman—but most women understand your sort of love-making—"

"Do they?" and his blue eyes flashed amusement. "And what do they think of it?"

"They laugh at it!" she answered, calmly. "But that clever child would not laugh—she would take it au grand serieux."

He passed his hand carelessly through the rough dark hair which gave his ruggedly handsome features a singular softness and charm.

"Would she? My dear Duchess, nobody takes anything 'au grand serieux' nowadays. We grin through every scene of life, and we don't know and don't care whether it's comedy or tragedy we're grinning at! It doesn't do to be serious. I never am. 'Life is real, life is earnest' was the line of conduct practised by my French ancestors; they cut up all their enemies with long swords, and then sat down to wild boar roasted whole for dinner. That was real life, earnest life! We in our day don't cut up our enemies with long swords—we cut them up in the daily press. It's so much easier!"

"How you love to hear yourself talk!" commented the Duchess. "I let you do it—but I know you don't mean half you say!"

"You think not? Well, I'm going to join the court of Corinne—she's not the usual type of Corinne—I fancy she has a heart—"

"And you want to steal it if you can, of course!" and the Duchess laughed. "Men always long for what they haven't got, and tire of what they have!"

"True, O Queen! We are made so! Blame, not us, but the Creator of the poor world-mannikins!"

He moved away and was soon beside Innocent, who blushed into a pretty rose at sight of him.

"I thought you were never coming!" she said, shyly. "I'm so glad you are here!"

He looked at her with an admiring softness in his eyes.

"May I have the first dance?" he said. "I timed myself to gain the privilege."

She gave him her dance programme where no name was yet inscribed. He took it and scribbled his name down several times, then handed it back to her. Several of the younger men in the group which had gathered about her laughed and remonstrated.

"Give somebody else a chance, Miss Armitage!"

She looked round upon them, smiling.

"But of course! Mr. Amadis de Jocelyn has not taken all?"

They laughed again.

"His name dominates your programme, anyhow!"

Her eyes shone softly.

"It is a beautiful name!" she said.

"Granted! But show a little mercy to the unbeautiful names!" said one man near her. "My name, for instance, is Smith—can you tolerate it?"

　　　　　　　　　　　　　　　　　　MARIE CORELLI

She gave a light gesture of protest.

"You play with me!" she said—"Of course! You will find a dance, Mr. Smith!—and I will dance it with you!"

They were all now ready for fun, and taking her programme handed it round amongst themselves and soon filled it. When it came back to her she looked at it, amazed.

"But I shall never dance all these!" she exclaimed.

"No, you will sit out some of them," said Jocelyn, coolly—"With me!"

The ball-room doors were just then thrown invitingly open and entrancing strains of rhythmical music came swinging and ringing in sweet cadence on the ears. He passed his arm round her waist.

"We'll begin the revelry!" he said, and in another moment she felt herself floating deliciously, as it were, in his arms—her little feet flying over the polished floor, his hand warmly clasping her slim soft body—and her heart fluttered wildly like the beating wings of a snared bird as she fell into the mystic web woven by the strange and pitiless loom of destiny. The threads were already tangling about her—but she made no effort to escape. She was happy in her dream; she imagined that her Ideal had been found in the Real.

IV

The first waltz over, Jocelyn led his partner out of the ball-room.

"Come into the garden," he said. "It's quite a real garden for London—and I know every inch of it. We'll find a quiet corner and sit down and rest."

She answered nothing—she was flushed, and breathing quickly from the excitement of the dance, and he paused on his way to pick up a light wrap he found on one of the sofas, and put it round her shoulders.

"You mustn't catch a chill," he went on. "But it's not a cold night—in fact it's very close and sultry—almost like thunder. A little air will be good for us."

They went together, pacing along slowly—she meanwhile thinking of her previous walk in that same garden!—what would he, Amadis de Jocelyn, say of it and of her "mother" if he knew! He looked at her sideways now and then, curiously moved by mingled pity, admiration and desire,—the cruelty latent in every man made him long to awaken the first spark of passion in that maidenly soul,—and with the full consciousness of a powerful personality, he was perfectly aware that he could do so if he chose. But he waited, playing with the fire of his own inclinations, and talking lightly and charmingly of things which he knew would interest her sufficiently to make her, in her turn, talk to him naturally and candidly, thereby displaying more or less of her disposition and temperament. With every word she spoke he found her more and more fascinating—she had a quaint directness of speech which was extremely refreshing after the half-veiled subtleties conveyed in the often dubious conversation of the women he was accustomed to meet in society—while there was no doubt she was endowed with extraordinary intellectual grasp and capacity. Her knowledge of things artistic and literary might, perhaps, have been termed archaic, but it was based upon the principles which are good and true for all time—and as she told him quite simply and unaffectedly of her studies by herself among the old books which had belonged to the "Sieur Amadis" of Briar Farm, he was both touched and interested.

"So you made quite a friend of the Sieur Amadis!" he said. "He was your teacher and guide! I'm jealous of him!"

She laughed softly. "He was a spirit," she said—"You are a man."

"Well, his spirit has had a good innings with you!" and, taking her hand, he drew it within his arm—"I bear his name, and it's time I came in somewhere!"

She laughed again, a trifle nervously.

"You think so? But you do come in! You are here with me now!"

He bent his eyes upon her with an ardour he did not attempt to conceal, and her heart leaped within her—a warmth like fire ran swiftly through her veins. He heard her sigh,—he saw her tremble beneath his gaze. There was an elf-like fascination about her child-like face and figure as she moved glidingly beside him—a "belle dame sans merci" charm which roused the strongly amorous side of his nature. He quickened his steps a little as he led her down a sloping path, shut in on either side by tall trees, where there was a seat placed invitingly in the deepest shadow and where the dim uplifted moon cast but the faintest glimmer, just sufficiently to make the darkness visible.

"Shall we stay here a little while?" he said, in a low tone.

She made no reply. Something vaguely sweet and irresistible overpowered her,—she was barely conscious of herself, or of anything, save that "Amadis de Jocelyn" was beside her. She had lived so long in her dream of the old French knight, whose written thoughts and confessions had influenced her imagination and swayed her mind since childhood, that she could not detach herself from the idealistic conception she had formed of his character,—and to her the sixteenth-century "Amadis" had become embodied in this modern man of brilliant but erratic genius, who, if the truth were told, had nothing idealistic about him but his art, which in itself was more the outcome of emotionalism than conviction. He drew her gently down beside him, feeling her quiver like a leaf touched by the wind, and his own heart began to beat with a pleasurable thrill. The silence around them seemed waiting for speech, but none came. It was one of those tense moments on which sometimes hangs the happiness or the misery of a lifetime—a stray thread from the web of Chance, which may be woven into a smooth pattern or knotted into a cruel tangle,—a freakish circumstance in which the human beings most concerned are helplessly involved without any conscious premonition of impending fate. Suddenly, yielding to a passionate impulse, he caught her close in his arms and kissed her.

"Forgive me!" he whispered—"I could not help it!"

She put him gently back from her with two little hands that caressed rather than repulsed him, and gazed at him with startled, tender eyes in which a new and wonderful radiance shone,—while he in self-confident audacity still held her in his embrace.

"You are not angry?" he went on, in quick, soft accents. "No! Why should you be? Why should not love come to you as to other women! Don't analyse!—don't speak! There is nothing to be said—we know all!"

Silently she clung to him, yielding more and more to the sensation of exquisite joy that poured through her whole being like sunlight—her heart beat with new and keener life,—the warm kindling blood burned her cheeks like the breath of a hot wind—and her whole soul rose to meet and greet what she in her poor credulousness welcomed as the crown and glory of existence—love! Love was hers, she thought—at last!—she knew the great secret,—the long delight that death itself could not destroy,—her ideal of romance was realised, and Amadis de Jocelyn, the brave, the true, the chivalrous, the strong, was her very own! Enchanted with the ease of his conquest, he played with her pretty hair as with a bird's wing, and held her against his heart, sensuously gratified to feel her soft breast heaving with its pent-up emotion, and to hear her murmured words of love confessed.

"How I have wished and prayed that you might love me!" she said, raising her dewy eyes to his in the darkness. "Is it good when God grants one's prayers? I am almost afraid! My Amadis! It is a dream come true!"

He was amused at her fidelity to the romance which surrounded his name.

"Dear child, I am not a 'knight of old'—don't think it!" he said. "You mustn't run away with that idea and make me a kind of sixteenth-century sentimentalist. I couldn't live up to it!"

"You are more than a knight of old," she answered, proudly—"You are a great genius!"

He was embarrassed by her simple praise.

"No," he answered—"Not even that—sweet soul as you are!—not even that! You think I am—but you do not know. You are a clever, imaginative little girl—and I love to hear you praise me—but—"

Her lips touched his shyly and sweetly.

"No 'buts!'" she said,—"I shall always stop your mouth if you put a 'but' against any work you do!"

"In that way?" he asked, smiling.

"Yes! In that way."

"Then I shall put a 'but' to everything!" he declared.

They laughed together like children.

"Where is Miss Leigh all this while?" he queried.

She started, awaking suddenly to conventions and commonplaces.

"Poor little godmother! She must be wondering where I am! But I did not leave her,—she left me when the Duke took charge of me—I lost sight of her then."

"Well, we must go and find her now"—and Jocelyn again folded his arms closely round the dainty, elf-like figure in its moonlight-blue draperies. "Innocent, look at me!"

She lifted her eyes, and as she met his, glowing with the fervent fire of a new passion, her cheeks grew hot and she was thankful for the darkness. His lips closed on hers in a long kiss.

"This is our secret!" he said—"You must not speak of it to anyone."

"How could I speak of it?" she asked, wonderingly.

He let her go from his embrace, and taking her hand began to walk slowly with her towards the house.

"You might do so," he continued—"And it would not be wise!— neither for you in your career, nor for me in mine. You are famous,— your name is being talked of everywhere—you must be very careful. No one must know we are lovers."

She thrilled at the word "lovers," and her hand trembled in his.

"No one shall know," she said.

"Not even Miss Leigh," he insisted.

"If I say 'no one' of course I mean 'no one,'" she answered, gently— "not even Miss Leigh."

He raised her hand to his lips and kissed it, relieved by this assurance. He wanted his little "amour" to go on without suspicion or interference, and he felt instinctively that if this girl made any sort of a promise she would fulfil it.

"You can keep a secret then?" he said, playfully—"Unlike most women!"

She looked up at him, smiling.

"Do men keep secrets better?" she asked. "I think not! Will you, for instance, keep mine?"

"Yours?" And for a moment he was puzzled, being a man who thought chiefly of himself and his own pleasure for the moment. "What is your secret?"

She laughed. "Oh, 'Sieur Amadis'! You pretend not to know! Is it not the same as yours? You must not tell anybody that I—I—"

He understood-and pressed hard the little hand he held.

"That you—well? Go on! I must not tell anybody—what?"

"That I love you!" she said, in a tone so grave and sweet and angelically tender, that for a second he was smitten with a sudden sense of shame.

Was it right to steal all this unspoilt treasure of love from a heart so warm and susceptible? Was it fair to enter such an ivory castle of dreams and break open all the "magic casements opening on the foam, Of perilous seas in fairy lands forlorn"? He was silent, having no response to give to the simple ardour of her utterance. What he felt for her was what all men feel for each woman who in turn attracts their wandering fancies— the desire of conquest and possession. He was moved to this desire by the irritating fact that this girl had startled an apathetic public on both sides of the Atlantic by the display of her genius in the short space of two years—whereas he had been more than fifteen years intermittently at work without securing any such fame. To throw the lasso of Love round the flying Pegasus on which she rode so lightly and securely, would be an excitement and amusement which he was not inclined to forgo—a triumph worth attaining. But love such as she imagined love to be, was not in his nature—he conceived of it merely as a powerful physical attraction which exerted its influence between two persons of opposite sexes and lasted for a certain time—then waned and wore off—and he recognised marriage as a legal device to safeguard a woman when the inevitable indifference and coldness of her mate set in, making him no longer a lover, but a household companion of habit and circumstance, lawfully bound to pay for the education of children and the necessary expenses of living. In his inmost consciousness he knew very well that Innocent was not of the ordinary feminine mould—she had visions of the high and unattainable, and her ideals of life were of that pure and transcendental quality which belongs to finer elements unseen. The carnal mind can never comprehend spirituality,—nevertheless, Jocelyn was a man cultured and clever enough to feel that though he himself could not enter, and did not even care to enter the uplifted spheres of thought, this strange child with a gift of the gods in her brain, already dwelt in them, serenely unconscious of any lower plane. And she loved him!—and he would, on that ground of love, teach her many things she had never known—he would widen her outlook,—warm her senses— increase her perceptions—train her like a wild rose on the iron trellis of his experience—while thus to instruct an unworldly soul in worldliness would be for him an interesting and pleasurable pastime.

"And I can make her happy"—was his additional thought—"in the only way a woman is ever happy—for a little while!"

All this ran through his mind as he held her hand a moment longer, till the convincing music of the band and the brilliant lights of the house warned them to break away from each other.

"We had better go straight to the ball-room and dance in," he said. "No one will have missed us long. We've only been absent about a quarter of an hour."

"So much in such a little time!" she said, softly.

He smiled, answering the adoring look of her eyes with his own amorous glance, and in another few seconds they were part of the brilliant whirl of dancers now crowding the ball-room and swinging round in a blaze of colour and beauty to the somewhat hackneyed strains of the "Fruhlings Reigen." And as they floated and flew, the delight of their attractiveness to each other drew them closer together till the sense of separateness seemed lost and whelmed in a magnetic force of mutual comprehension.

When this waltz was finished she was claimed by many more partners, and danced till she was weary,—then, between two "extras," she went in search of Miss Leigh, whom she found sitting patiently in one of the great drawing-rooms, looking somewhat pale and tired.

"Oh, my godmother!" she exclaimed, running up to her. "I had forgotten how late it is getting!"

Miss Lavinia smiled cheerfully.

"Never mind, child!" she said. "You are young and ought to enjoy yourself. I am old, and hardly fit for these late assemblies—and how very late they are too! When I was a girl we never stayed beyond midnight—"

"And is it midnight now?" asked Innocent, amazed, turning to her partner, a young scion of the aristocracy, who looked as if he had not been to bed for a week.

He smiled simperingly, and glanced at his watch.

"It's nearly two o'clock," he said. "In fact it's tomorrow morning!"

Just then Jocelyn came up.

"Are you going?" he inquired. "Well, perhaps it's time! May I see you to your carriage?"

Miss Leigh gratefully accepted this suggestion—and Innocent, smiling her "good-night" to partners whom she had disappointed, walked with her through the long vista of rooms, Jocelyn leading the way. They soon ran the gauntlet of the ladies' cloak-room and the waiting mob of footmen and chauffeurs that lined the long passage leading to the entrance-hall, and Jocelyn, going out into the street succeeded in finding their modest little hired motor-brougham and assisting them into it.

"Good-night, Miss Leigh!" he said, leaning on the door of the vehicle and smiling at them through the open window—"Good-night, Miss Armitage! I hope you are not very tired?"

"I am not tired at all!" she answered, with a thrill of joy in her voice like the note of a sweet bird. "I have been so very happy!"

He smiled. His face was pale and looked unusually handsome,—she stretched one little hand out to him.

"Good-night, 'Sieur Amadis!'"

He bent down and kissed it.

"Good-night!"

The motor began to move—another moment, and they were off. Innocent sank back in the brougham with a sigh.

"You are tired, child!—you must be!" said Miss Leigh.

"No, godmother mine! That sigh was one of pleasure. It has been a most wonderful evening!—wonderful!"

"It was certainly very brilliant," agreed Miss Leigh. "And I'm glad you were made so much of, my dear! That was as it ought to be. Lord Blythe told me he had seldom met so charming a girl!"

Innocent sat up suddenly. "Lord Blythe? Do you know him?"

"No, I cannot say I really know him," replied Miss Leigh. "I've met him several times—and his wife too—there was some scandal about her years and years ago before she was married—nobody ever knew exactly what it was, and her people hushed it up. I daresay it wasn't very much. Anyhow Lord Blythe married her—and he's a very fine man with a great position. I thought I saw you talking to Lady Blythe?"

"Yes"—Innocent spoke almost mechanically—"I had a few minutes' conversation with her."

"She's very handsome," went on Miss Leigh. "She used to be quite beautiful. A pity she has no children."

Innocent was silent. The motor-brougham glided along.

"You and Mr. Jocelyn seem to get on very well together," observed the old lady, presently. "He is a very 'taking' man—but I wonder if he is quite sincere?"

Innocent's colour rose,—fortunately the interior of the brougham was too dark for her face to be seen.

"Why should he not be?" she asked—"Surely with his great art, he would be more sincere than most men?"

"Well, I hope so!" and Miss Leigh's voice was a little tremulous; "But artists are very impressionable, and live so much in a world of their own that I sometimes doubt whether they have much understanding or sympathy with the world of other people! Even Pierce Armitage—who was very dear to me—ran away with impressions like a child with toys. He would adore a person one day—and hate him, or her, the next!"— and she laughed softly and compassionately—"He would indeed, poor fellow! He was rather like Shelley in his likes and dislikes—you've read all about your Shelley of course?"

"Indeed I have!" the girl answered,—"A glorious poet!—but he must have been difficult to live with!"

"Difficult, if not impossible!"—and the gentle old lady took her hand and held it in a kind, motherly clasp—"You are a genius yourself—but you are a human little creature, not above the sweet and simple ways of life,—some of the poets and artists were and are in-human! Now Mr. Jocelyn—"

"He is human!" said Innocent, quickly—"I'm sure of that!"

"You are sure? Well, dear, you like him very much and you have made a friend of him,—which is quite natural considering the long association you have had with his name—such a curious and romantic coincidence!—but I hope he won't disappoint you."

Innocent laughed, happily.

"Don't be afraid, you dear little godmother!" she said—"I don't expect anything of him, so no disappointment is possible! Here we are!"

The brougham stopped and they alighted. Opening the house-door with a latch-key they entered, and pausing one moment in the drawing-room, where the lights had been left burning for their return, Miss Leigh took Innocent tenderly by the arm and pointed to the portrait on the harpsichord.

"There was a true genius!" she said—"He might have been the greatest artist in England to-day if he had not let his impressions and prejudices overmaster his judgment. You know—for I have told you my story—that he loved me, or thought he did—and I loved him and knew I did! There was the difference between us! He tired of me—all artists tire of the one face—they want dozens!—and he lost his head over some woman whose name I never knew. The result must have been fatal to his career, for it stopped short just when he was succeeding;—

for me, it only left me resolved to be true to his memory till the end. But, my child, it's a hard lot to be alone all one's days, with only the remembrance of a past love to keep one's heart from growing cold!"

There was a little sob in her voice,—Innocent, touched to the quick, kissed her tenderly.

"Why do you talk like this so sadly to-night?" she asked—"Has something reminded you of—of HIM?" And she glanced half nervously towards the portrait.

"Yes," answered the old lady, simply—"Something has reminded me—very much—of him! Good-night, dear little child! Keep your beautiful dreams and ideals as long as you can! Sleep well!"

She turned off the lights, and they went upstairs together to their several rooms.

Once alone, Innocent flung off her dainty ball attire,—released her bright hair from the pins that held it bound in rippling waves about her shapely head, and slipping on a loose white wrapper sat down to think. She had to realise the unpleasing fact that against her own wish and will she had become involved in mysteries,—secrets which she dared not, for the sake of others, betray. Her parentage could not be divulged, because her father was Pierce Armitage, the worshipped memory of Miss Leigh's heart,—while her mother, Lady Blythe, occupied a high social position which must not be assailed. And now—now, Amadis de Jocelyn was her lover!—yet no one must know, because he did not wish it. For some cause or other which she could not determine, he insisted on secrecy. So she was meshed in nets of others' weaving, and could not take a step to disentangle herself and stand clear. Of her own accord she would have been frank and open as the daylight,—but from the first, a forward fate appeared to have taken delight in surrounding her with deceptions enforced by the sins of others. Her face burned as she thought of Jocelyn's passionate kisses—she must hide all that joy!—it had already become almost a guilty secret. He was the first man that had ever kissed her since her "Dad" died,—the first that had ever kissed her as a lover. Her mind flew suddenly and capriciously back to Briar Farm—to Robin Clifford who had longed to kiss her, and yet had refused to do so unless she could have loved him. She had never loved him—no!— and yet the thought of him just now gave her a thrill of remorseful tenderness. She knew in herself at last what love could mean,—and with that knowledge she realised what Robin must have suffered.

MARIE CORELLI

"To love without return—without hope!" she mused—"Oh, it would be torture!—to me, death! Poor Robin!"

Poor Robin, indeed! He would not have dared to caress her with the wild and tender audacity of Amadis de Jocelyn!

"My love!" she whispered to the silence.—"My love!" she repeated, as she knelt down to say her prayers, sending the adored and idealised name up on vibrations of light to the throne of the Most High,—and "My love!" were the last words she murmured as she nestled into her little bed, her fair head on its white pillow looking like the head of one of Botticelli's angels. Her own success,—her celebrity as a genius in literature,—her dreams of fame—these now were all as naught!—less than the clouds of a night or the mists of a morning—there was nothing for her in earth or heaven save "My love!"

V

L ord Blythe was sitting alone in his library. He was accustomed to sit alone, and rather liked it. It was the evening after that of the Duchess of Deanshire's reception; his wife had gone to another similar "crush," but had graciously excused his attendance, for which he was honestly grateful. He was old enough, at sixty-eight, to appreciate the luxury of peace and quietness,—he had put on an old lounge coat and an easy pair of slippers, and was thoroughly enjoying himself in a comfortable arm-chair with a book and a cigar. The book was by "Ena Armitage"—the cigar, one of a choice brand known chiefly to fastidious connoisseurs of tobacco. The book, however, was a powerful rival to the charm of the fragrant Havana—for every now and again he allowed the cigar to die out and had to re-light it, owing to his fascinated absorption in the volume he held. He was an exceedingly clever man— deeply versed in literature and languages, and in his younger days had been a great student,—he had read nearly every book of note, and was as familiar with the greatest authors as with his greatest friends, so that he was well fitted to judge without prejudice the merits of any new aspirant to literary fame. But he was wholly unprepared for the power and the daring genius which stamped itself on every page of the new writer's work,—he almost forgot, while reading, whether it was man or woman who had given such a production to the world, so impressed was he by the masterly treatment of a simple subject made beautiful by a scholarly and incisive style. It was literature of the highest kind,— and realising this with every sentence he perused, it was with a shock of surprise that he remembered the personality of the author—the unobtrusive girl who had been the "show animal" at Her Grace of Deanshire's reception and dance.

"Positively, I can scarcely believe it!" he exclaimed sotto-voce—"That child I met last night actually wrote this amazing piece of work! It's almost incredible! A nice child too,—simple and perfectly natural,— nothing of the blue-stocking about her. Well, well! What a career she'll make!—what a name!—that is, if she takes care of herself and doesn't fall in love, which she's sure to do! That's the worst of women—God occasionally gives them brains, but they've scarcely begun to use them when heart and sentiment step in and overthrow all reason. Now, we men—"

He paused,—thinking. There had been a time in his life—long ago, when he was very young—when heart and sentiment had very nearly overthrown reason in his own case—and sometimes he was inclined to regret that such overthrow had been averted.

"For the moment it is perhaps worth everything else!" he mused—"But—for the moment only! The ecstasy does not last."

His cigar had gone out again, and he re-lit it. The clock on the mantelpiece struck twelve with a silvery clang, and almost at the same instant he heard the rustle of a silk gown and a light footstep,—the door opened, and his wife appeared.

"Are you busy?" she enquired—"May I come in?"

He rose, with the stately old-fashioned courtesy habitual to him.

"By all means come in!" he said—"You have returned early?"

"Yes." She loosened her rich evening cloak, lined with ermine, and let it fall on the back of the chair in which she seated herself—"It was a boresome affair,—there were recitations and music which I hate—so I came away. You are reading?"

"Not now"—and he closed the volume on the table beside him—"But I Have been reading—that amazing book by the young girl we met at the Deanshires' last night—Ena Armitage. It's really a fine piece of work."

She was silent.

"You didn't take to her, I'm afraid?" he went on—"Yet she seemed a charming, modest little person. Perhaps she was not quite what you expected?"

Lady Blythe gave a sudden harsh laugh.

"You are right! She certainly was not what I expected! Is the door well shut?"

Surprised at her look and manner, he went to see.

"The door is quite closed," he said, rather stiffly. "One would think we were talking secrets—and we never do!"

"No!" she rejoined, looking at him curiously—"We never do. We are model husband and wife, having nothing to conceal!"

He took up his cigar which he had laid down for a minute, and with careful minuteness flicked off the ash.

"You have something to tell me," he remarked, quietly—"Pray go on, and don't let me interrupt you. Do you object to my smoking?"

"Not in the least."

He stood with his back to the fireplace, a tall, stately figure of a man, and looked at her expectantly,—she meanwhile reclined in a cushioned chair with the folds of her ermine falling about her, like a queen of languorous luxury.

"I suppose," she began—"hardly anything in the social life of our day would very much surprise or shock you—?"

"Very little, certainly!" he answered, smiling coldly—"I have lived a long time, and am not easily surprised!"

"Not even if it concerned some one you know?"

His fine open brow knitted itself in a momentary line of puzzled consideration.

"Some one I know?" he repeated—"Well, I should certainly be very sorry to hear anything of a scandalous nature connected with the girl we saw last night—she looked too young and too innocent—"

"Innocent—oh yes!" and Lady Blythe again laughed that harsh laugh of suppressed hysterical excitement—"She is innocent enough!"

"Pardon! I thought you were about to speak of her, as you said she was not what you expected—"

He paused,—startled by the haggard and desperate expression of her face.

"Richard," she said—"You are a good man, and you hold very strong opinions about truth and honour and all that sort of thing. I don't believe you could ever understand badness—real, downright badness—could you?"

"Badness? . . . in that child?" he exclaimed.

She gave an impatient, angry gesture.

"Dear me, you are perfectly obsessed by 'that child,' as you call her!" she answered—"You had better know the truth then at once,—'that child' is my daughter!"

"Your daughter?—your—your—"

The words died on his lips—he staggered slightly as though under a sudden physical blow, and gripped the mantelpiece behind him with one hand.

"Good God!" he half whispered—"What do you mean?—you have had no children—"

"Not by you,—no!" she said, with a flash of scorn—"Not in marriage, that church-and-law form of union!—but by love and passion—yes! Stop!—do not look at me like that! I have not been false to you—I have not betrayed you! Your honour has been safe with me! It was before I met you that this thing happened."

He stood rigid and very pale.

"Before you met me?"

"Yes. I was a silly, romantic, headstrong girl,—my parents were compelled to go abroad, and I was left in the charge of one of my mother's society friends—a thoroughly worldly, unprincipled woman whose life was made up of intrigue and gambling. And I ran away with a man—Pierce Armitage—"

"Pierce Armitage!"

The name broke from him like a cry of agony.

"Yes—Pierce Armitage. Did you know him?"

He looked at her with eyes in which there was a strange horror.

"Know him? He was my best friend!"

She shrugged her shoulders, and a slight weary smile parted her lips.

"Well, you never told me,—I have never heard you mention his name. But the world is a small place!—and when I was a girl he was beginning to be known by a good many people. Anyhow, he threw up everything in the way of his art and work, and ran away with me. I went quite willingly—I took a maid whom we bribed,—we pretended we were married, and we had a charming time together—a time of real romance, till he began to get tired and want change—all men are like that! Then he became a bore with a bad temper. He certainly behaved very well when he knew the child was coming, and offered to marry me in real earnest—but I refused."

"You refused!" Lord Blythe echoed the words in a kind of stupefied wonderment.

"Of course I did. He was quite poor—and I should have been miserable running about the world with a man who depended on art for a living. Besides he was ceasing to be a lover—and as a husband he would have been insupportable. We managed everything very well—my own people were all in India—and my mother's friend, if she guessed my affair, said nothing about it,—wisely enough for her own sake!—so that when my time came I was able to go away on an easy pretext and get it all over secretly. Pierce came and stayed in a hotel close at hand— he was rather in a fright lest I should die!—it would have been such an awkward business for him!—however, all went well, and when I had quite recovered he took the child away from me, and left it at an old farmhouse he had once made a drawing of, saying he would call back for it—as if it were a parcel!" She laughed lightly. "He wrote and told me what he had done and gave me the address of the farm—then he went abroad, and I never heard of him again—"

"He died," interposed Lord Blythe, slowly—"He died—alone and very poor—"

"So I was told," she rejoined, indifferently—"Oh yes! I see you look at me as if you thought I had no heart! Perhaps I have not,—I used to have something like one,—your friend Armitage killed it in me. Anyhow, I knew the child had been adopted by the farm people as their own, and I took no further trouble. My parents came home from India to inherit an unexpected fortune, and they took me about with them a great deal—they were never told of my romantic escapade!—then I met you—and you married me."

A sigh broke from him, but he said nothing.

"You are sorry you did, I suppose!" she went on in a quick, reckless way—"Anyhow, I tried to do my duty. When I heard by chance that the old farmer who had taken care of the child was dead, I made up my mind to go and see what she was like. I found her, and offered to adopt her—but she wouldn't hear of it—so I let her be."

Lord Blythe moved a little from his statuesque attitude of attention.

"You told her you were her mother?"

"I did."

"And offered to 'adopt' your own child?" She gave an airy gesture.

"It was the only thing to do! One cannot make a social scandal."

"And she refused?"

"She refused."

"I admire her for it," said Lord Blythe, calmly.

She shot an angry glance at him. He went on in cold, deliberate accents.

"You were unprepared for the strange compensation you have received?—the sudden fame of your deserted daughter?"

Her hands clasped and unclasped themselves nervously.

"I knew nothing of it! Armitage is not an uncommon name, and I did not connect it with her. She has no right to wear it."

"If her father were alive he would be proud that she wears it!—moreover he would give her the right to wear it, and would make it legal," said Lord Blythe sternly—"Out of old memory I can say that for him! You recognised each other at once, I suppose, when I presented her to you at the Duchess's reception?"

"Of course we did!" retorted his wife—"You yourself saw that I was rather taken aback,—it was difficult to conceal our mutual astonishment—"

"It must have been!" and a thin ironic smile hovered on his lips—"And you carried it off well! But—the poor child!—what an ordeal for her! You can hardly have felt it so keenly, being seasoned to hypocrisy for so many years!" Her eyes flashed up at him indignantly. He raised his hand with a warning gesture.

"Permit me to speak, Maude! You can scarcely wonder that I am—well!—a little shaken and bewildered by the confession you have made,—the secret you have—after years of marriage—suddenly divulged. You suggested—at the beginning of this interview—that perhaps there was nothing in the social life of our day that would very much shock or surprise me—and I answered you that I was not easily surprised—but—I was thinking of others.—it did not occur to me that—that my own wife—" he paused, steadying his voice,—then continued—"that my own wife's honour was involved in the matter—" he paused again. "Sentiment is of course out of place—nobody is supposed to feel anything nowadays—or to suffer—or to break one's heart, as the phrase goes,—that would be considered abnormal, or bad form,—but I had the idea—a foolish one, no doubt!—that though you may not have married me for love on your own part, you did so because you recognised the love,—the truth—the admiration and respect—on mine. I was at any rate happy in believing you did!—I never dreamed you married me for the sake of convenience!—to kill the memory of a scandal, and establish a safe position—"

She moved restlessly and gathered her ermine cloak about her as though to rise and go.

"One moment!" he went on—"After what you have told me I hope you see clearly that it is impossible we can live together under the same roof again. If You could endure it, *I* could not!"

She sprang up, pale and excited.

"What? You mean to make trouble? I, who have kept my own counsel all these years, am to be disgraced because I have at last confided in you? You will scandalise society—you will separate from me—"

She stopped, half choked by a rising paroxysm of rage.

He looked at her as he might have looked at some small angry animal.

"I shall make no trouble," he answered, quietly—"and I shall not scandalise society. But I cannot live with you. I will go away at once on some convenient excuse—abroad—anywhere—and you can say whatever you please of my prolonged absence. If I could be of any use or protection to the girl I saw last night—the daughter of my friend Pierce Armitage—I would stay, but circumstances render any such service from me impossible. Besides, she needs no one to assist her—she has made a position for herself—a position more enviable than yours or mine. You have that to think about by way of—consolation?—or reproach?"

She stood drawn up to her full height, looking at him.

"You cannot forgive me, then?" she said.

He shuddered.

"Forgive you! Is there a man who could forgive twenty years of deliberate deception from the wife he thought the soul of honour? Maude, Maude! We live in lax times truly, when men and women laugh at principle and good faith, and deal with each other less honestly than the beasts of the field,—but for me there is a limit!—a limit you have passed! I think I could pardon your wrong to me more readily than I can pardon your callous desertion of the child you brought into the world—your lack of womanliness—motherliness!—your deliberate refusal to give Pierce Armitage the chance of righting the wrong he had committed in a headstrong, heart-strong rush of thoughtless passion!— he WOULD have righted it, I know, and been a loyal husband to you, and a good father to his child. For whatever his faults were he was neither callous nor brutal. You prevented him from doing this,—you were tired of him—your so-called 'love' for him was a mere selfish caprice of the moment—and you preferred deceit and a rich marriage to the simple duty of a woman! Well!—you may find excuses for yourself,—I cannot find them for you! I could not remain by your side as a husband and run the risk of coming constantly in contact, as we did last night, with that innocent girl, placed as she is, in a situation of so much difficulty, by the sins of her parents—her mother, my wife!—her father, my dead friend! The position is, and would be untenable!"

Still she stood, looking at him.

"Have you done?" she asked.

He met her fixed gaze, coldly.

"I have. I have said all I wish to say. So far as I am concerned the incident is closed. I will only bid you good-night—and farewell!"

"Good-night—and farewell!" she repeated, with a mocking drawl,— then she suddenly burst into a fit of shrill laughter. "Oh dear, oh dear!" she cried, between little screams of hysterical mirth—"You are so very funny, you know! Like—what's-his-name?—Marius in the ruins of Carthage!—or one of those antique classical bores with their household gods broken around them! You—you ought to have lived in their days!—you are so terribly behind the times!" She laughed recklessly again. "We don't do the Marius and Carthage business now—life's too full and too short! Really, Richard, I'm afraid you're getting very old!—poor dear!—past sixty I know!—and you're quite prehistoric in some of your fancies!—'Good-night!'—er—'and farewell!' Sounds so stagey, doesn't it!" She wiped the spasmodic tears of mirth from her eyes, and still shaking with laughter gathered up her rich ermine wrap on one white, jewelled arm. "Womanliness—motherliness!—good Lord, deliver us!—I never thought you likely to preach at me—if I had I wouldn't have told you anything! I took you for a sensible man of the world—but you are only a stupid old-fashioned thing after all! Good-night!—and farewell!"

She performed the taunting travesty of an elaborate Court curtsey and passed him—a handsome, gleaming vision of satins, laces and glittering jewels—and opening the door with some noise and emphasis, she turned her head gracefully over her shoulder. Unkind laughter still lit up her face and hard, brilliant eyes.

"Good-night!—farewell!" she said again, and was gone.

For a moment he stood inert where she left him—then sinking into a chair he covered his face with his hands. So he remained for some time—silently wrestling with himself and his own emotions. He had to realise that at an age when he might naturally have looked for a tranquil home life—a life tended and soothed into its natural decline by the care and devotion of the wife he had undemonstratively but most tenderly loved, he was suddenly cast adrift like the hulk of an old battleship broken from its moorings, with nothing but solitude and darkness closing in upon his latter days. Then he thought of the girl,—his wife's child—the child too of his college chum and dearest friend,—he saw, impressed like a picture on the cells of his brain, her fair young face, pathetic eyes and sweet intelligence of expression,—he remembered how modestly she wore her sudden fame, as a child might wear a wild flower,—and, placed by her parentage in a difficulty for which she was not responsible, she must have suffered considerable pain and sorrow.

"I will go and see her to-morrow," he said to himself—"It will be better for her to know that I have heard all her sad little history—then— if she ever wants a friend she can come to me without fear. Ah!—if only she were MY daughter!"

He sighed,—his handsome old head drooped,—he had longed for children and the boon had been denied.

"If she were my daughter," he repeated, slowly—"I should be a proud man instead of a sorrowful one!"

He turned off the lights in the library and went upstairs to his bedroom. Outside his wife's door he paused a moment, thinking he heard a sound,—but all was silent. Imagining that he probably would not sleep he placed a book near his bedside—but nature was kind to his age and temperament, and after about an hour of wakefulness and sad perplexity, all ruffling care was gradually smoothed away from his mind, and he fell into a deep and dreamless slumber.

Meanwhile Lady Blythe had been disrobed by a drowsy maid whom she sharply reproached for being sleepy when she ought to have been wide awake, though it was long past midnight,—and dismissing the girl at last, she sat alone before her mirror, thinking with some pettishness of the interview she had just had with her husband.

"Old fool!" she soliloquised—"He ought to know better than to play the tragic-sentimental with me at his time of life! I thought he would accept the situation reasonably and help me to tackle it. Of course it will be simply abominable if I am to meet that girl at every big society function—I don't know what I shall do about it! Why didn't she stay in her old farm-house!—who could ever have imagined her becoming famous! I shall go abroad, I think—that will be the best thing to do. If Blythe leaves me as he threatens, I shall certainly not stay here by myself to face the music! Besides, who knows?—the girl herself may 'round' on me when her head gets a little more swelled with success. Such a horrid bore!—I wish I had never seen Pierce Armitage!"

Even as she thought of him the vision came back to her of the handsome face and passionate eyes of her former lover,—again she saw the romantic little village by the sea where they had dwelt together as in another Eden,—she remembered how he would hurry up from the shore bringing with him the sketch he had been working at, eager for her eyes to look at it, thrilling at her praise, and pouring out upon her such tender words and caresses such as she had never known since those wild and ardent days! A slight shiver ran through her—something like a pang of remorse stung her hardened spirit.

"And the child," she murmured—"The child—it clung to me and I kissed it!—it was a dear little thing!"

She glanced about her nervously—the room seemed full of wandering shadows.

"I must sleep!" she thought—"I am worried and out of sorts—I must sleep and forget—"

She took out of a drawer in her dressing-table a case of medicinal cachets marked "Veronal."

"One or two more or less will not hurt me," she said, with a pale, forced smile at herself in the mirror—"I am accustomed to it—and I must have a good long sleep!"

SHE HAD HER WAY. MORNING came,—and she was still sleeping. Noon—and nothing could waken her. Doctors, hastily summoned, did their best to rouse her to that life which with all its pains and possibilities still throbbed in the world around her—but their efforts were vain.

"Suicide?" whispered one.

"Oh no! Mere accident!—an overdose of veronal—some carelessness—quite a common occurrence. Nothing to be done!"

No!—nothing to be done! Her slumber had deepened into that strange stillness which we call death,—and her husband, a statuesque and rigid figure, gazed on her quiet body with tearless eyes.

"Good-night!" he whispered to the heavy silence—"Good-night! Farewell!"

VI

One of the advantages or disadvantages of the way in which we live in these modern days is that we are ceasing to feel. That is to say we do not permit ourselves to be affected by either death or misfortune, provided these natural calamities leave our own persons unscathed. We are beginning not to understand emotion except as a phase of bad manners, and we cultivate an apathetic, soulless indifference to events of great moment whether triumphant or tragic, whenever they do not involve our own well-being and creature comforts. Whole boatloads of fishermen may go forth to their doom in the teeth of a gale without moving us to pity so long as we have our well-fried sole or grilled cod for breakfast,—and even such appalling disasters as the wicked assassination of hapless monarchs, or the wrecks of palatial ocean-liners with more than a thousand human beings all whelmed at once in the pitiless depths of the sea, leave us cold, save for the uplifting of our eyes and shoulders during an hour or so,—an expression of slight shock, followed by forgetfulness. Air-men, recklessly braving the spaces of the sky, fall headlong, and are smashed to mutilated atoms every month or so, without rousing us to more than a passing comment, and a chorus of "How dreadful!" from simpering women,—and the greatest and best man alive cannot hope for long remembrance by the world at large when he dies. Shakespeare recognised this tendency in callous human nature when he made his Hamlet say—

"O heavens! Die two months ago and not forgotten yet? Then there's hope a great man's memory may outlive his life half a year, but by 'r lady, he must build churches then, or else shall he suffer not thinking on."

Wives recover the loss of their husbands with amazing rapidity,—husbands "get over" the demise of their wives with the galloping ease of trained hunters leaping an accustomed fence—families forget their dead as resolutely as some debtors forget their bills,—and to express sorrow, pity, tenderness, affection, or any sort of "sentiment" whatever is to expose one's self to derision and contempt from the "normal" modernist who cultivates cynicism as a fine art. Many of us elect to live, each one, in a little back-yard garden of selfish interests—walled round carefully, and guarded against possible intrusion by uplifted spikes of conventionalism,—the door is kept jealously closed—and only now and then does some impulsive spirit bolder than the rest, venture to put up a ladder and peep over the wall. Shut in with various favourite forms of hypocrisy and cowardice, each little unit passes its short life in mistrusting its neighbour unit, and death finds none of them wiser, better or nearer the utmost good than when they were first uselessly born.

Among such vain and unprofitable atoms of life Lady Maude Blythe had been one of the vainest and most unprofitable,—though of such "social" importance as to be held in respectful awe by tuft-hunters and parasites, who feed on the rich as the green-fly feeds on the rose. The news of her sudden death briefly chronicled by the fashionable intelligence columns of the press with the usual—"We deeply regret"— created no very sorrowful sensation—a few vapid people idly remarked to one another—"Then her great ball won't come off!"—somewhat as if she had retired into the grave to avoid the trouble and expense of the function. Cards inscribed—"Sympathy and kind enquiries"—were left for Lord Blythe in the care of his dignified butler, who received them with the impassiveness of a Buddhist idol and deposited them all on the orthodox salver in the hall—and a few messages of "Deeply shocked and grieved. Condolences"—by wires, not exceeding sixpence each, were despatched to the lonely widower,—but beyond these purely formal observances, the handsome brilliant society woman dropped out of thought and remembrance as swiftly as a dead leaf drops from a tree. She had never been loved, save by her two deluded dupes—Pierce Armitage and her husband,—no one in the whole wide range of her social acquaintance would have ever thought of feeling the slightest affection for her. The first announcement of her death appeared in an evening paper, stating the cause to be an accidental overdose of veronal taken to procure sleep, and Miss Leigh, seeing the paragraph by merest chance, gave a shocked exclamation—

"Innocent! My dear!—how dreadful! That poor Lady Blythe we saw the other night is dead!"

The girl was standing by the tea-table just pouring out a cup of tea for Miss Leigh—she started so nervously that the cup almost fell from her hand.

"Dead!" she repeated, in a low, stifled voice. "Lady Blythe? Dead?"

"Yes!—it is awful! That horrid veronal! Such a dangerous drug! It appears she was accustomed to take it for sleep—and unfortunately she took an over-dose. How terrible for Lord Blythe!"

Innocent sat down, trembling. Her gaze involuntarily wandered to the portrait of Pierce Armitage—the lover of the dead woman, and her father! The handsome face with its dreamy yet proud eyes appeared conscious of her intense regard—she looked and looked, and longed to speak—to tell Miss Leigh all—but something held her silent. She had her own secret now—and it restrained her from disclosing the secrets of others. Nor could she realise that it was her mother—actually her own mother—who had been taken so suddenly and tragically from the world. The news barely affected her—nor was this surprising, seeing that she had never entirely grasped the fact of her mother's personality or existence at all. She had felt no emotion concerning her, save of repulsion and dislike. Her unexpected figure had appeared on the scene like a strange vision, and now had vanished from it as strangely. Innocent was in very truth "motherless"—but so she had always been—for a mother who deserts her child is worse than a mother dead. Yet it was some few minutes before she could control herself sufficiently to speak or look calmly—and her eyes were downcast as Miss Leigh came up to the tea-table, newspaper in hand, to discuss the tragic incident.

"She was a very brilliant woman in society," said the gentle old lady, then—"You did not know her, of course, and you could not judge of her by seeing her just one evening. But I remember the time when she was much talked of as 'the beautiful Maude Osborne'—she was a very lively, wilful girl, and she had been rather neglected by her parents, who left her in England in charge of some friends while they were in India. I think she ran rather wild at that time. There was some talk of her having gone off secretly somewhere with a lover—but I never believed the story. It was a silly scandal—and of course it stopped directly she married Lord Blythe. He gave her a splendid position,—and he was devoted to her—poor man!"

"Yes?" murmured Innocent, mechanically. She did not know what to say.

"If she had been blessed with children—or even one child," went on Miss Leigh—"I think it would have been better for her. I am sure she would have been happier! He would, I feel certain!"

"No doubt!" the girl answered in the same quiet tone.

"My dear, you look very pale!" said Miss Leigh, with some anxiety— "Have you been working too hard?"

She smiled.

"That would be impossible!" she answered. "I could not work too hard—it is such happiness to work—one forgets!—yes—one forgets all that one does not wish to remember!"

The anxious expression still remained on Miss Lavinia's face,—but, true to the instincts of an old-fashioned gentlewoman, she did not press enquiries where she saw they might be embarrassing or unwelcome. And though she now loved Innocent as much as if she had been her own child, she never failed to remember that after all, the girl had earned her own almost wealthy independence, and was free to do as she liked without anybody's control or interference, and that though she was so young she was bound to be in all respects untrammelled in her life and actions. She went where she pleased—she had her own little hired motor-brougham—she also had many friends who invited her out without including Miss Leigh in the invitations, and she was still the "paying guest" at the little Kensington house,—a guest who was never tired of doing kindly and helpful deeds for the benefit of the sweet old woman who was her hostess. Once or twice Miss Leigh had made a faint half-hearted protest against her constant and lavish generosity.

"My dear," she had said—"With all the money you earn now you could live in a much larger house—you could indeed have a house of your own, with many more luxuries—why do you stay here, showering advantages on me, who am nothing but a prosy old body?—you could do much better!"

"Could I really?" And Innocent had laughed and kissed her. "Well!—I don't want to do any better—I'm quite happy as I am. One thing is— (and you seem to forget it!)—that I'm very fond of you!—and when I'm very fond of a person it's difficult to shake me off!"

So she stayed on—and lived her life with a nun-like simplicity and economy—spending her money on others rather than herself, and helping those in need,—and never even in her dress, which was always exquisite, running into vagaries of extravagance and follies of fashion. She had discovered a little French dressmaker, whose husband had deserted her, leaving her with two small children to feed and educate, and to this humble, un-famous plier of the needle she entrusted her wardrobe with entirely successful results. Worth, Paquin, Doucet and other loudly advertised personages were all quoted as "creators" of her gowns, whereat she was amused.

"A little personal taste and thought go so much further in dress than money," she was wont to say to some of her rather envious women friends. "I would rather copy the clothes in an old picture than the clothes in a fashion book."

Odd fancies about her dead mother came to her when she was alone in her own room—particularly at night when she said her prayers. Some mysterious force seemed compelling her to offer up a petition for the peace of her mother's soul,—she knew from the old books written by the "Sieur Amadis" that to do this was a custom of his creed. She missed it out of the Church of England Prayer-book, though she dutifully followed the tenets of the faith in which Miss Leigh had had her baptised and confirmed—but in her heart of hearts she thought it good and right to pray for the peace of departed souls—

"For who can tell"—she would say to herself—"what strange confusion and sorrow they may be suffering!—away from all that they once knew and cared for! Even if prayers cannot help them it is kind to pray!"

And for her mother's soul she felt a dim and far-off sense of pity—almost a fear, lest that unsatisfied spirit might be lost and wandering in a chaos of dark experience without any clue to guide or any light to shine upon its dreadful solitude. So may the dead come nearer to the living than when they also lived!

Some three or four weeks after Lady Blythe's sudden exit from a world too callous to care whether she stayed in it or went from it, Lord Blythe called at Miss Leigh's house and asked to see her. He was admitted at once, and the pretty old lady came down in a great flutter to the drawing-room to receive him. She found him standing in front of the harpsichord, looking at the portrait upon it. He turned quickly round as she entered and spoke with some abruptness.

"I must apologise for calling rather late in the afternoon," he said—"But I could not wait another day. I have something important to tell you—" He paused—then went on—"It's rather startling to me to find that portrait here!—I knew the man. Surely it is Pierce Armitage, the painter?"

"Yes"—and Miss Leigh's eyes opened in a little surprise and bewilderment—"He was a great friend of mine—and of yours?" "He was my college chum"—and he walked closer to the picture and looked at it steadfastly—"That must have been taken when he was quite a young man—before—" He paused again,—then said with a forced smile—"Talking of Armitage—is Miss Armitage in?"

"No, she is not"—and the old lady looked regretful—"She has gone out to tea—I'm sorry—"

"It's just as well"—and Lord Blythe took one or two restless paces up and down the little room—"I would rather talk to you alone first. Yes!—that portrait of Pierce must have been taken in early days—just about the time he ran away with Maude Osborne—"

Miss Leigh gazed at him enquiringly.

"With Maude Osborne?"

"Yes—with Maude Osborne, who afterwards became my wife."

Miss Leigh trembled and drew back, looking about her in a dazed way as though seeking for some place to hide in. Lord Blythe saw her agitation.

"I'm afraid I'm worrying you!" he said, kindly. "Sit down, please,"—and he placed a chair for her. "We are both elderly folk and shocks are not good for us. There!"—and he took her hand and patted it gently—"As I was saying, that portrait must have been taken about then—did he give it to you?"

"Yes," she answered, faintly—"He did. We were engaged—"

"Engaged! Good God! You?—to Pierce?—My dear lady, forgive me!—I'm very sorry!—I had no idea—"

But Miss Leigh composed herself very quickly.

"Please do not mind me!" she said—"It all happened so very long ago! Yes—Pierce Armitage and I were engaged—but he suddenly went away—and I was told he had gone with some very beautiful girl he had fallen head over ears in love with—and I never saw him again. But I never reproached him—I—I loved him too well!"

Silently Lord Blythe took the worn little hand and raised it to his lips.

"Pierce was more cruel than I thought was possible to him"—he said, at last, very gently—"But—you have the best of him with you in—his daughter!"

"His daughter!"

She sprang up, white and scared.

He gripped her arm and held it fast to support her.

"Yes," he said—"His daughter! That is what I have come to tell you! The girl who lives with you—the famous author whose name is just now ringing through the world is his child!—and her mother was my wife!"

There was a little stifled cry—she dropped back in her chair and covered her face with her hands to hide the tears that rushed to her eyes.

"Innocent!" she murmured, sobbingly—"His child!—Innocent!"

He was silent, watching her, his own heart deeply moved. He thought of her life of unbroken fidelity—wasted in its youth—solitary in its age—all for the sake of one man. Presently, mastering her quiet weeping, she looked up.

"Does she—the dear girl!—does she know this?" she asked, in a half whisper.

"She has known it all the time," he answered—"She knew who her mother was before she came to London—but she kept her own counsel—I think to save the honour of all concerned. And she has made her name famous to escape the reproach of birth which others fastened upon her. A brave child!—it must have been strange to her to find her father's portrait here—did you ever speak of him to her?"

"Often!" replied Miss Leigh. "She knows all my story!"

He smiled, very kindly

"No wonder she was silent!" he said.

Just then they heard the sound of a latch-key turning in the lock of the hall door—there was a light step in the passage—they looked at one another half in wonder, half in doubt. A moment more and Innocent entered, radiant and smiling. She stopped on the threshold, amazed at the sight of Lord Blythe.

"Why, godmother"—she began. Then, glancing from one to the other, her cheeks grew pale—she hesitated, instinctively guessing at the truth. Lord Blythe advanced and took her gently by both hands.

"Dear child, your secret is ours!" he said, quietly. "Miss Leigh knows, and *I* know that you are the daughter of Pierce Armitage, and that your mother was my late wife. No one can be dearer to us both than you are—for your father's sake!"

VII

S tartled and completely taken aback, she let her hands remain passively in his for a moment,—then quietly withdrew them. A hot colour rushed swiftly into her cheeks and as swiftly receded, leaving her very pale.

"How can you know?" she faltered—"Who has told you?"

"Your mother herself told me on the night she died," he answered—"She gave me all the truth of herself,—at last—after long years!"

She was silent—standing inert as though she had received a numbing blow. Miss Leigh rose and came tremblingly towards her.

"My dear, my dear!" she exclaimed—"I wish I had known it all before!—I might have done more—I might have tried to be kinder—"

The girl sprang to her side and impulsively embraced her.

"You would have tried in vain!" she said, fondly, "No one on earth could have been kinder than my beloved little godmother! You have been the dearest and best of friends!"

Then she turned towards Lord Blythe.

"It is very good of you to come here and say what you have said"—and she spoke in soft, almost pathetic accents—"But I am sorry that anyone knows my story—it is no use to know it, really! I should have always kept it a secret—for it chiefly concerns me, after all,—and why should my existence cast a shadow on the memory of my father? Perhaps you may have known him—"

"I knew him and loved him!" said Lord Blythe, quickly.

She looked at him with wistful, tear-wet eyes.

"Well then, how hard it must be for you to think that he ever did anything unworthy of himself!" she said—"And for this dear lady it is cruel!—for she loved him too. And what am I that I should cause all this trouble! I am a nameless creature—I took his name because I wanted to kindle a little light of my own round it—I have done that! And then I wanted to guard his memory from any whisper of scandal—will you help me in this? The secret must still be kept—and no one must ever know I am his daughter. For though your wife is dead her name must not be shamed for the long ago sin of her youth—nor must I be branded as what I am—base-born."

Profoundly touched by the simple straightforward eloquence of her appeal, Lord Blythe went up to her where she stood with one arm round Miss Leigh.

"My dear child," he said, earnestly—"believe me, I shall never speak of your parentage or give the slightest hint to anyone of the true facts of your history—still less would I allow you to be lightly esteemed for what is no fault of your own. You have made a brilliant name and fame for yourself—you have the right to that name and fame. I came here to-day for two reasons—one to tell you that I was fully acquainted with all you had endured and suffered—the other to ask if you will let me be your guardian—your other father—and give me some right to shelter you from the rough ways of the world. I may perhaps in this way make some amends to you for the loss of mother-love and father-love—I would do my best—"

He stopped—a little troubled by unusual emotion. Innocent, drawing her embracing arm away from Miss Leigh, looked at him with wondering, grateful eyes.

"How good you are!" she said, softly—"You would take care of me—you with your proud name and place!—and I—the poor, unfortunately born child of your dead friend! Ah, you kind, gentle heart!—I thank you!—but no!—I must not accept such a sacrifice on your part—"

"It would be no sacrifice"—he interrupted her, eagerly—"No, child!—it would be pure selfishness!—for I'm getting old and am lonely—and—and I want someone to look after me!" He laughed a little awkwardly. "Why not come to me and be my daughter?"

She smiled—caught his hand and kissed it.

"I will be a daughter to you in affection and respect," she said—"But I will not take any benefits from you—no, none! Oh, I know well all you could and would do for me!—you would place me in the highest ranks of that society where you are a leader, and you would surround me with so many advantages and powerful friends that I should forget my duty, which is to work for myself, and owe nothing to any man! Dear, kind Lord Blythe!—do not think me ungrateful! But I have made my own little place in the world, and I must keep it—independently! Am I not right, my godmother?"

Miss Leigh looked at her anxiously, and sighed.

"My dear, you must think well about it," she said—"Lord Blythe would care for you as his own child, I am sure—and his home would be a safe and splendid one for you—but there!—do not ask Me!" and the old lady wiped away one or two trickling tears from her eyes—"I am selfish!—and now I know you are Pierce's daughter I want to keep you for myself!—to have you near me!—to look at you and love you!—"

Her voice broke—her gaze instinctively wandered to the portrait of the man whose memory she had cherished so long and so fondly.

"What did you think—what must you have thought the first day you came here when I asked you if you were any relation to Pierce Armitage, and told you that was his portrait!" she said, wistfully.

"I thought that God had guided me to you," the girl answered, in soft, grave accents—"And that my father's spirit had not forsaken me!"

There was a moment's silence. Then she spoke more lightly—

"Dear Lord Blythe," she said—"Now that you know so much may I tell you my own story? It will not take long! Come and sit here—yes!"—and she placed a comfortable arm-chair for him, while she drew Miss Leigh gently down on the sofa and sat next to her—"It is nothing of a story!—my little life is not at all like the lives lived by all the girls of my age that I have ever met or seen—it's all in the past, as it were,—the old, very old past!—as far back as the days of Elizabeth!"

She laughed, but there were tears in her eyes—she brushed them away and holding Miss Leigh's hand in her own, she told with simple truth and directness the narrative of her childhood's days—her life on Briar Farm—how she had been trained by Priscilla to bake, and brew, and wash and sew,—and how she had found her chief joy and relaxation from household duties in the reading of the old books she had found stowed away in the dower-chests belonging to the "Sieur Amadis de Jocelin."

As she pronounced the name with an unconsciously tender accentuation Lord Blythe interrupted her.

"Why, that's a curious thing! I know a rather clever painter named Amadis de Jocelyn—and surely you were dancing with him on the evening I first met you?"

A wave of rosy colour swept over her cheeks.

"Yes!—that is what I was just going to tell you!" she said. "He is another Amadis de Jocelyn!—and he is actually connected with a branch of the same family! His ancestor was the brother of that very Amadis who lies buried at Briar Farm! Is it not strange that I should have met him!—and he is going to paint my portrait!"

"Is he indeed!" and Lord Blythe did not look impressed—"I thought he was a landscape man."

"So he is," she explained, with eagerness—"But he can do portraits—and he wishes to make a picture of me, because I have been a student of the books written by one of his ancient line. Those books taught me all I know of literature. You see, it is curious, isn't it?"

"It is," he agreed, rather hesitatingly—"But I've never quite liked Jocelyn—he's clever—yet he has always struck me as being intensely selfish,—a callous sort of man—many artists are."

Her eyes drooped, and her breath came and went quickly.

"I suppose all clever men get self-absorbed sometimes!" she said, with a quaint little air of wisdom—"But I don't think he is really callous—" She broke off, and laughed brightly—"Anyhow we needn't discuss him—need we? I just wanted to tell you what an odd experience it has been for me to meet and to know someone descended from the family of the old French knight whose spirit was my instructor in beautiful things! The little books of his own poems were full of loveliness—and I used to read them over and over again. They were all about love and faith and honour—"

"Very old-fashioned subjects!" said Lord Blythe, with a slight smile—"And not very much in favour nowadays!"

Miss Leigh looked at him questioningly.

"You think not?" she said.

He gave a quick sigh.

"It is difficult to know what to think," he answered—"But I have lived a long life—long enough to have seen the dispersal of many illusions! I fear selfishness is the keynote of the greater part of humanity. Those who do the kindest deeds are invariably the worst rewarded—and love in its highest form is so little known that it may be almost termed non-existent. You"— and he looked at Innocent—"you write in a very powerful and convincing way about things of which you can have had no real experience—and therein lies your charm! You restore the lost youth of manhood by idealisation, and you compel your readers to 'idealise' with you—but 'to idealise' is rather a dangerous verb!—and its conjugation generally means trouble and disaster. Ideals—unless they are of the spiritual kind unattainable on this planet—are apt to be very disappointing."

Innocent smiled.

"But love is an ideal which cannot disappoint, because it is everlasting!" she said, almost joyously. "The story of the old French knight is, in its way, a proof of that. He loved his ideal all his life, even though he could not win her."

"Very wonderful if true!" he answered—"But I cannot quite believe it! I am too familiar with the ways of my own sex! Anyhow, dear child, I should advise you not to make too many ideals apart from the characters in the books you write. Fortunately your special talent brings you an occupation which will save you from that kind of thing. You have ambition as an incentive, and fame for a goal."

She was silent for a moment. In relating the story of her life at Briar Farm she had not spoken of Robin Clifford,—some instinct told her that the sympathies of her hearers might be enlisted in his favour, and she did not want this.

"Well, now you know what my 'literary education' has been," she went on—"Since I came to London I have tried to improve myself as much as I can—and I have read a great many modern books—but to me they seem to lack the real feeling of the old-time literature. For instance, if you read the account of the battle of the Armada by a modern historian it sounds tame and cold,—but if you read the same account in Camden's 'Elizabeth'—the whole scene rises before you,— you can almost see every ship riding the waves!"

Her cheeks glowed and her eyes shone,—Lord Blythe smiled approvingly.

"I see you are an enthusiast!" he said—"And you could not have better teachers than the Elizabethans. They lived in a great age and they were great men. Our times, though crowded with the splendid discoveries of science, seem small and poor compared to theirs. If you ever come to me, I can give you the run of a library where you will find many friends."

She thanked him by a look, and he went on—

"You will come and see me often, will you not?—you and Miss Leigh—by-and-by, when the conventional time of mourning for my poor wife is over. Make my house your second home, both of you!—and when I return from Italy—"

"Oh!" the girl exclaimed, impulsively—"Are you going to Italy?"

"For a few weeks—yes!—will you come with me—you and your godmother?"

His old heart beat,—a sudden joy lighted his eyes. It would have been like the dawn of a new day to him had she consented, but she shook her fair little head decisively.

"I must not!" she said-"-I am bound to finish some work that I have promised. But some day—ah, yes!—some day I should love to see Italy!"

The light went slowly from his face.

"Some day!—well!—I hope I may live to be with you on that 'some day.' I ought not to leave London just now—but the house is very lonely—and I think I am best away for a time—"

"Much best!" said Miss Leigh, sympathetically—"And if there is anything we can do—"

"Yes—there is one thing that will please me very much," said Lord Blythe, drawing from his pocket a small velvet case—"I want my friend Pierce's daughter to wear this—it was my first gift to her mother." Here he opened the case and showed an exquisite pendant, in the shape of a dove, finely wrought in superb brilliants, and supported on a thin gold chain. "I gave it as an emblem of innocence"—a quick sigh escaped him—"I little knew!—but you, dear girl, are the one to wear it now! Let me fasten it round your neck."

She stooped forward, and he took a lingering pleasure in putting the chain on and watching the diamonds flash against her fair skin. She was too much moved to express any worded thanks—it was not the value or the beauty of the gift that touched her, but its association and the way it was given. And then, after a little more desultory conversation, he rose to go.

"Remember!" he said, taking her tenderly by both hands—"Whenever you want a home and a father, both are ready and waiting for you!" And he kissed her lightly on the forehead. "You are famous and independent, but the world is not always kind to a clever woman even when she is visibly known to be earning her own living. There are always spiteful tongues wagging in the secret corners and byways, ready to assert that her work is not her own and that some man is in the background, helping to keep her!"

He then shook hands warmly with Miss Leigh.

"If she ever comes to me"—he went on—"you are free to come with her—and be assured of my utmost friendship and respect. I shall feel I am in some way doing what I know my old friend Pierce Armitage would, in his best moments, approve, if I can be of the least service to you. You will not forget?"

Miss Leigh was too overcome by the quiet sweetness and dignity of his manner to murmur more than a few scarcely audible words of gratitude in reply—and when at last he took his leave, she relieved her heart by throwing her arms round Innocent and having what she called "a good cry."

"And you Pierce's child!" she half laughed, half sobbed—"Oh, how could he leave you at that farm!—poor little thing!—and yet it might have been much worse—"

"Indeed I should think so!" and Innocent soothed her fondly with the tenderest caresses—"Very much worse! Why, if I had not been left at Briar Farm, I should never have known Dad!—and he was one of the best of men—and I should never have learned how to think, and write my thoughts, from the teaching of the Sieur Amadis de Jocelin!"

There was a little thrill of triumph in her voice—and Miss Leigh, wiping away her tears, looked at her timidly and curiously.

"How you dwell on the memory of that French knight!" she said. "When are you going to have your portrait painted by the modern Amadis?"

Innocent smiled.

"Very soon!" she answered—"We are to begin our sittings next week. I am to wear a white frock—and I told him about my dove Cupid, and how it used to fly from the gables of the house to my hand—and he is going to paint the bird as well as me!"

She laughed with the joy of a child.

"Fancy! Cupid will be there!"

"Cupid?" echoed Miss Leigh, wonderingly.

"Yes—Cupid!—usually known as the little god of love,—but only a dove this time!—so much more harmless than the god!"

Miss Leigh touched the diamond pendant at the girl's neck.

"You have a dove there now," she said—"All in jewels! And in your heart, dear child, I pray there is a spiritual dove of holy purity to guard you from all evil and keep your sweet soul safe and clean!"

A startled look came into the girl's soft grey-blue eyes,—a deep flush of rose flew over her cheeks and brow.

"A blessing or a warning, godmother mine?" she said.

Miss Leigh drew her close in her arms and kissed her.

"Both!" she answered, simply.

There was a moment's silence.

Then Innocent, her face still warm with colour, walked close up to the harpsichord where her father's picture stood.

"Let us talk of HIM!" she said—"Now that you know I am his daughter, tell me all you remember of him!—how he spoke, how he looked!—what sort of pictures he painted—and what he used to say to you! He loved you once, and I love you now!—so you must tell me everything!"

VIII

Fame, or notoriety, whichever that special noise may be called when the world like a hound "gives tongue" and announces that the quarry in some form of genius is at bay, is apt to increase its clamour in proportion to the aloofness of the pursued animal,—and Innocent, who saw nothing remarkable in remaining somewhat secluded and apart from the ordinary routine of social life so feverishly followed by more than half her sex, was very soon classified as "proud"—"eccentric"— "difficult" and "vain," by idle and ignorant persons who knew nothing about her, and only judged her by their own limited conceptions of what a successful author might or could possibly be like. Some of these, more foolish than the rest, expressed themselves as afraid or unwilling to meet her—"lest she should put them into her books"—this being a common form of conceit with many individuals too utterly dull and uninteresting to "make copy" for so much as the humblest paragraphist. It was quite true that she showed herself sadly deficient in the appreciation of society functions and society people,—to her they seemed stupid and boresome, involving much waste of precious time,—but notwithstanding this, she was invited everywhere, and the accumulation of "R.S.V.P." cards on her table and desk made such a formidable heap that it was quite a business to clear them, as she did once a week, with the assistance of the useful waste-paper basket. As a writer her popularity was unquestionable, and so great and insistent was the public demand for anything from her pen that she could command her own terms from any publishing quarter. Her good fortune made very little effect upon her,—sometimes it seemed as if she hardly realised or cared to realise it. She had odd, almost child-like ways of spending some of her money in dainty "surprise" gifts to her friends—that is to say, such friends as had shown her kindness,—beautiful flowers and fruit for invalids—choice wines for those who needed yet could not afford them,—a new drawing-room carpet for Miss Leigh, which was, in the old lady's opinion, a most important and amazing affair!—costly furs, also for Miss Leigh,—and devices and adornments of all sorts for the pleasure, beauty or comfort of the house—but on herself personally she spent nothing save what was necessary for such dress and appearance as best accorded with her now acknowledged position. Dearly as she would have loved to shower gifts and benefits on the inhabitants of never-forgotten Briar Farm, she knew that if she did anything of the kind poor lonely old Priscilla Friday and patiently enduring Robin Clifford were more likely to be hurt than gratified. For a silence had fallen between that past life, which had been like a wild rose blossoming in a country lane, and the present one, which resembled a wonderful orchid flower, flaming in heat under glass,—and though she wrote to Robin now and again, and he replied, his letters were restrained and formal—almost cold. He knew too well how far she was removed from him by more than distance, and bravely contented himself with merely giving her such news of the farm and her former home surroundings as might awaken her momentary interest without recalling too many old memories to her mind.

She seemed, and to a very great extent she was, unconscious of the interest and curiosity both her work and her personality excited—the more so now as the glamour and delight of her creative imagination had been obscured by what she considered a far greater and more lasting glory—that of love!—the golden mirage of a fancied sun, which for a time had quenched the steadier shining of eternal stars. Since that ever memorable night when he had suddenly stormed the fortress of her soul, and by the mastery of a lover's kiss had taken full possession, Amadis de Jocelyn had pursued his "amour" with admirable tact, cleverness and secrecy. He found a new and stimulating charm in making love to a tender-hearted, credulous little creature who seemed truly "of such stuff as dreams are made of"—and to a man of his particular type and temperament there was an irresistible provocation to his vanity in the possibility of being able to lure her gradually and insidiously down from the high ground of intellectual ambition and power to the low level of that pitiful sex-submission which is responsible for so much more misery than happiness in this world. Little by little, under his apparently brusque and playful, but really studied training, she began to think less and less of her work,—the books she had loved to read and refer to, insensibly lost their charm,—she went reluctantly to her desk, and as reluctantly took up her pen,—what she had written already, appeared to her utterly worthless,—and what she attempted to write now was to her mind poor and unsatisfying. She was not moved by the knowledge, constantly pressed upon her, that she was steadily rising, despite herself, to the zenith of her career in such an incredibly swift and brilliant way as to be the envy of all her contemporaries,— she was hardly as grateful for her honours as weary of them and a little contemptuous. What did it all matter to her when half of her once busy working mornings were now often passed in the studio of Amadis de Jocelyn! He was painting a full-length portrait of her—a mere excuse to give her facilities for visiting him, and ensure his own privacy and convenience in receiving her—and every day she went to him, sometimes late in the afternoons as well as the mornings, slipping in and out familiarly and quite unnoticed, for he had given her a key to the private door of his studio, which was reached through a small, deeply shaded garden, abutting on an old-fashioned street near Holland Park. She could enter at any time, and thought it was the customary privilege accorded by an artist to his sitter, while it saved the time and trouble of the rheumatic "odd man" or servant whose failing limbs were slow to respond to a summons at the orthodox front entrance. She would come in, dressed in her simple navy blue serge walking costume, and then in a little room just off the studio would change and put on the white dress which her lover had chosen as the most suitable for his purpose, and which he called the "portrait gown." It was simple, and severely Greek, made of the softest and filmiest material which fell gracefully away in enchanting folds from her childishly rounded neck and arms,—it gave her the appearance of a Psyche or an Ariadne,—and at the first sitting, when he had posed her in several attitudes before attempting to draw a line, she had so much sweet attractiveness about her that he was hardly to be blamed for throwing aside all work and devoting himself to such ardent delight in woman's fairness as may sometimes fall to the lot of man. While moving from one position to another as he suggested or commanded, she had playfully broken off one flower from a large plant of "marguerite" daisies growing in a quaint Japanese pot, close at hand, and had begun pulling off the petals according to the old fanciful charm—"Il m'aime!—un peu!—beaucoup!—passionement!—pas du tout!" He stopped her at the word "passionement," and caught her in his arms.

"Not another petal must be plucked!" he whispered, kissing her soft warm neck—"I will not have you say 'Pas du tout!'"

She laughed delightedly, nestling against him.

"Very well!" she said—"But suppose—"

"Suppose what?"

"Suppose it ever came to that?"—and she sighed as she spoke—"Then the last petal must fall!"

"Do you think it ever will or can come to that?" he asked, pressing a kiss on the sweet upturned lips—"Does it seem like it?"

She was too happy to answer him, and he was too amorous just then to think of anything but her soft eyes, dewy with tenderness— her white, ivory-smooth skin—her small caressing hands, and the fine bright tendrils of her waving hair—all these were his to play with as a child plays with beautiful toys unconscious of or indifferent to their value.

Many such passages of love occupied their time—though he managed to make a good show of progressive work after the first rough outline drawing of the picture was completed. He was undeniably a genius in his way, uncertain and erratic of impulse, but his art was strong because its effects were broad and simple. He had begun Innocent's portrait out of the mere desire to have her with him constantly,—but as day after day went on and the subject developed under his skilled hand and brush he realised that it would probably be "the" picture of the Salon in the following year. As this conviction dawned upon him, he took greater pains, and worked more carefully and conscientiously with the happiest results, feeling a thrill of true artistic satisfaction as the picture began to live and smile in response to his masterly touch and treatment. Its composition was simple—he had drawn the girl as though she were slowly advancing towards the spectator, giving her figure all the aerial grace habitual to it by nature,—one little daintily shaped hand held a dove lightly against her breast, as though the bird had just flown there for protection from its own alarm,—her face was slightly uplifted,—the lips smiled, and the eyes looked straight out at the world with a beautiful, clear candour which was all their own. Yet despite the charm and sweetness of the likeness there was a strange pathos about it,—a sadness which Jocelyn had never set there by his own will or intention.

"You are a puzzling subject," he said to her one day—"I wanted to give you a happy expression—and yet your portrait is actually growing sad!—almost reproachful! . . . do you look at me like that?"

She opened her pretty eyes wonderingly.

"Amadis! Surely not! I could not look sad when I am with you!—that is impossible!"

He paused, palette in hand.

"Nor reproachful?"

"How? When I have nothing to reproach you for?" she answered.

He put his palette aside and came and sat at her feet on the step of the dais where he had posed her.

"You may rest," he said, smiling up at her—"And so may I." She sat down beside him and he folded her in his arms. "How often we rest in this way, don't we!" he murmured—"And so you think you have nothing to reproach me for! Well,—I'm not so sure of that—Innocent!"

She looked at him questioningly.

"Are you talking nonsense, my 'Sieur Amadis'?—or are you serious?" she asked.

"I am quite serious—much more serious than is common with me," he replied, taking one of her hands and studying it as the perfect model it was—"I believe I am involving you in all sorts of trouble—and you, you absurd little child, don't see it! Suppose Miss Leigh were to find out that we make the maddest love to each other in here—you all alone with me—what would she say?"

"What Could she say?" Innocent demanded, simply—"There is no harm!—and I should not mind telling her we are lovers."

"I should, though!" was his quick thought, while he marvelled at her unworldliness.

"Besides"—she continued—"she has no right over me."

"Who Has any right over you?" he asked, curiously.

She laughed, softly.

"No one!—except you!"

"Oh, hang me!" he exclaimed, impatiently—"Leave me out of the question. Have you no father or mother?"

She was a little hurt at his sudden irritability.

"No," she answered, quietly—"I have often told you I have no one. I am alone in the world—I can do as I like." Then a smile brightened her face. "Lord Blythe would have me as a daughter if I would go to him."

He started and loosened her from his embrace.

"Lord Blythe! That wealthy old peer! What does he want with you?"

"Nothing, I suppose, but the pleasure of my company!" and she laughed—"Doesn't that seem strange?"

He rose and went back to work at his easel.

"Rather!" he said, slowly—"Are you going to accept his offer?"

Her eyes opened widely.

"I? My Amadis, how can you think it? I would not accept it for all the world! He would load me with benefits—he would surround me with luxuries—but I do not want these. I like to work for myself and be independent." He laid a brush lightly in colour and began to use it with delicate care.

"You are not very wise," he then said—"It's a great thing for a young girl like you who are all alone in the world, to be taken in hand by such a man as Blythe. He's a statesman,—very useful to his country,—he's very rich and has a splendid position. His wife's sudden death has left him very lonely as he has no children,—you could be a daughter to him, and it would be a great leap upwards for you, socially speaking. You would be much better off under his care than scribbling books."

She drew a sharp breath of pain,—all the pretty colour fled from her cheeks.

"You do not care for me to scribble books!" she said, in low, stifled accents.

He laughed.

"Oh, I don't mind!—I never read them,—and in a way it amuses me! You are such an armful of sweetness—such a warm, nestling little bird of love in my arms!—and to think that you actually write books that the world talks about!—the thing is so incongruous—so 'out of drawing' that it makes me laugh! I don't like writing women as a rule—they give themselves too many airs to please me—but you—"

He paused.

"Well, go on," she said, coldly.

He looked at her, smiling.

"You are cross? Don't be cross,—you lose your enchanting expression! Well—you don't give yourself any airs, and you seem to play at literature like a child playing at a game: of course you make money by it,—but— you know better than I do that the greatest writers"—he emphasized the word "greatest" slightly—"never make money and are never popular."

"Does failure constitute greatness?" she asked, with a faintly satirical inflection in her sweet voice which he had never heard before.

"Sometimes—in fact pretty often," he replied, dabbing his brush busily on his canvas—"You should read about great authors—"

"I HAVE read about them," she said—"Walter Scott was popular and made money,—Charles Dickens was popular and made money— Thackeray was popular and made money—Shakespeare himself seemed to have had the one principal aim of making sufficient money enough to live comfortably in his native town, and he was 'popular' in his day—indeed he 'played to the gallery.' But he was not a 'failure'— and the whole world acknowledges his greatness now, though in his life-time he was unconscious of it."

Surprised at her quick eloquence, he paused in his work.

"Very well spoken!" he remarked, condescendingly—"I see you take a high view of your art! But like all women, you wander from the point. We were talking of Lord Blythe—and I say it would be far better for you to be—well!—his heiress!—for he might leave you all his fortune—than go on writing books."

Her lips quivered: despite her efforts, tears started to her eyes. He saw, and throwing down his brush came and knelt beside her, passing his arm round her waist.

"What have I said?" he murmured, coaxingly—"Innocent—sweet little love! Forgive me if I have—what?"—and he laughed softly—"rubbed you up the wrong way!"

She forced a smile, and her delicate white hands wandered caressingly through his hair as he laid his head against her bosom.

"I am sorry!" she said, at last—"I thought—I hoped—you might be proud of my work, Amadis! I was planning it all for that! You see"—she hesitated—"I learned so much from the Sieur Amadis de Jocelin—the brother of your ancestor!—that I have been thinking all the time how I could best show you that I was worthy of his teaching. The world—or the public—you know the things they say of me—but I do not want their praise. I believe I could do something really great if You cared!—for now it is only to please you that I live."

A sense of shame stung him at this simple avowal.

"Nonsense!" he said, almost brusquely—"You have a thousand other things to live for—you must not think of pleasing me only. Besides I'm not very—keen on literature,—I'm a painter."

"Surely painting owes something to literature?" she queried—"We should not have had all the wonderful Madonnas and Christs of the old masters if there had been no Bible!"

"True!—but perhaps we could have done without them!" he said, lightly—"I'm not at all sure that painting would not have got on just as well without literature at all. There is always nature to study—sky, sea, landscape and the faces of lovely women and children,—quite enough for any man. Where is Lord Blythe now?"

"In Italy," she replied—"He will be away some months."

She spoke with constraint. Her heart was heavy—the hopes and ambitions she had cherished of adding lustre to her fame for the joy and pride of her lover, seemed all crushed at one blow. She was too young and inexperienced to realise the fact that few men are proud of any woman's success, especially in the arts. Their attitude is one of amused tolerance when it is not of actual sex-jealousy or contempt. Least of all can any man endure that the woman for whom he has a short spell of passionate fancy should be considered notable, or in an intellectual sense superior to himself. He likes her to be dependent on him alone for her happiness,—for such poor crumbs of comfort he is pleased to give her when the heat of his first passion has cooled,—but he is not altogether pleased when she has sufficient intelligent perception to see through his web of subterfuge and break away clear of the entangling threads, standing free as a goddess on the height of her own independent attainment. Innocent's idea of love was the angelic dream of truth and everlastingness set forth by poets, whose sweet singing deludes themselves and others,—she was ready to devote all the unique powers of her mind and brain to the perfecting of herself for her lover's delight. She wished to be beautiful, brilliant, renowned and admired, simply that he might take joy in knowing that this beautiful, brilliant, renowned and admired creature was HIS, body and soul—existing solely for him and content to live only so long as he lived, to work only so long as he worked,—to be nothing apart from his love, but to be everything he could desire or command while his love environed her. She thought of the eternal union of souls,—while he had no belief in the soul at all, his half French materialism persuading him that there was nothing eternal. And like all men of his type he estimated her tenderness for him, her clinging arms, and the lingering passion of her caresses, to be chiefly the outflow of pleased vanity—the kittenish satisfaction of being stroked and fondled—the sense of her own sex-attractiveness,—but of anything deep and closely rooted in the centre of a more than usually sensitive nature he had not the faintest conception, taking it for granted that all women, even clever ones, were more or less alike, easily consoled by new millinery when lovers failed.

Sometimes, during the progress of their secret amour, a thrill of uneasiness and fear ran coldly through her veins—a wondering doubt which she repelled with indignation whenever it suggested itself. Amadis de Jocelyn was and must be the very embodiment of loyalty and honour to the woman he loved!—it could not be otherwise. His tenderness was ardent,—his passion fiery and eager,—yet she wondered—timidly and with deep humiliation in herself for daring to think so far—why, if he loved her so much as he declared, did he not ask her to be his wife? She supposed he would do so,—though she had heard him depreciate marriage as a necessary evil. Evidently he had his own good reasons for deferring the fateful question. Meanwhile she made a little picture-gallery of ideal joys in her brain,—and one of her fancies was that when she married her Amadis she would ask Robin Clifford to let her buy Briar Farm.

"He could paint well there!" she thought, happily, already seeing in her mind's eye the "Great Hall" transformed into an artist's studio—"and I almost think *I* could carry on the farm—Priscilla would help me,—and we know just how Dad liked things to be done—if—if Robin went away. And the master of the house would again be a true Jocelyn!"

The whole plan seemed perfectly natural and feasible. Only one obstacle presented itself like a dark shadow on the brightness of her dream—and that was her own "base" birth. The brand of illegitimacy was upon her,—and whereas once she alone had known what she judged to be a shameful secret, now two others shared it with her—Miss Leigh and Lord Blythe. They would never betray it—no!—but they could not alter what unkind fate had done for her. This was one reason why she was glad that Amadis de Jocelyn had not as yet spoken of their marriage.

"For I should have to tell him!" she thought, woefully—"I should have to say that I am the illegitimate daughter of Pierce Armitage—and then—perhaps he would not marry me—he might change—ah no!—he could not!—he would not!—he loves me too dearly! He would never let me go—he wants me always! We are all the world to each other!—nothing could part us now!"

And so the time drifted on—and with its drifting her work drifted too, and only one all-absorbing passion possessed her life with its close and consuming fire. Amadis de Jocelyn was an expert in the seduction of a soul—little by little he taught her to judge all men as worthless save himself, and all opinions unwarrantable and ill-founded unless he confirmed them. And, leading her away from the contemplation of high visions, he made her the blind worshipper of a very inadequate idol. She was happy in her faith, and yet not altogether sure of happiness. For there are two kinds of love—one with strong wings which lift the soul to a dazzling perfection of immortal destiny,—the other with gross and heavy chains which fetter every hope and aspiration and drag the finest intelligence down to dark waste and nothingness.

I n affairs of love a woman is perhaps most easily ensnared by a man
who can combine passion with pleasantry and hot pursuit with social
tact and diplomacy. Amadis de Jocelyn was an adept at this kind of
thing—he was, if it may be so expressed, a refined libertine, loving
women from a purely physical sense of attraction and pleasure conveyed
to himself, and obtusely ignorant of the needs or demands of their
higher natures. From a mental or intellectual standpoint all women to
him were alike, made to be "managed" alike, used alike, and alike set
aside when their use was done with. The leaven of the Jew or the Turk
was in the temperament of this descendant of a long line of French
nobles, who had gained their chief honours by killing men, ravishing
women and plundering their neighbours' lands—though occasional
flashes of bravery and chivalry had glanced over their annals in history
like the light from a wandering will o' the wisp flickering over a morass.
Gifted in his art, but wholly undisciplined in his nature, he had lived
a life of selfish aims to selfish ends, and in the course of it had made
love to many women,—one especially, on whose devoted affections
he had preyed like an insect that ungratefully poisons the flower from
which it has sucked the honey. This woman, driven to bay at last by
his neglect and effrontery, had roused the scattered forces of her pride
and had given him his conge—and he had been looking about for a
fresh victim when he met Innocent. She was a complete novelty to him,
and stimulated his more or less jaded emotions,—he found her quaint
and charming as a poet's dream of some nymph of the woodlands,—
her manner of looking at life and the things of life was so deliciously
simple—almost mediaeval,—for she believed that a man should die
rather than break his word or imperil his honour, which to Jocelyn was
such a primitive state of things as to seem prehistoric. Then there was
her fixed and absurd "fancy" about the noble qualities and manifold
virtues of the French knight who had served the Duc d'Anjou,—and
who had been to her from childhood a kind of lover in the spirit,—a
being whom she had instinctively tried to serve and to please; and he
had sufficient imagination to understand and take advantage of the
feeling aroused in her when she had met one of the same descent, and
bearing the same name, in himself. He had run through the gamut of
many emotions and sentiments,—he had joined one or two of the new

schools of atheism and modernism started by certain self-opinionated young University men, and in the earlier stages of his career had in the cock-sure impulse of youth designed schemes for the regeneration of the world, till the usual difficulties presented themselves as opposed to such vast business,—he had associated himself with men who followed what is called the "fleshly school" of poetry and art generally, and had evolved from his own mentality a comfortable faith of which the chief tenet was "Self for Self"—a religion which lifts the mind no higher than the purely animal plane;—and in its environment of physical consciousness and agreeable physical sensations, he was content to live.

With such a temperament and disposition as he possessed, which swayed him hither and thither on the caprice or impulse of the moment, his intentions toward Innocent were not very clear even to himself. When he had begun his "amour" with her he had meant it to go just as far as should satisfy his own whim and desire,—but as he came to know her better, he put a check on himself and hesitated as one may hesitate before pulling up a rose-bush from its happy growing place and flinging it out on the dust-heap to die. She was so utterly unsuspicious and unaware of evil, and she had placed him on so high a pedestal of honour, trusting him with such perfect and unquestioning faith, that for very manhood's sake he could not bring himself to tear the veil from her eyes. Moreover he really loved her in a curious, haphazard way of love,—more than he had ever loved any one of her sex,—and, when in her presence and under her influence, he gained a glimmering of consciousness of what love might mean in its best and purest sense.

He laughed at himself however for this very thought. He had always pooh-pooh'd the idea of love as having anything divine or uplifting in its action,—nevertheless in his more sincere moments he was bound to confess that since he had known Innocent his very art had gained a certain breadth and subtlety which it had lacked before. It was a pleasure to him to see her eyes shine with pride in his work, to hear her voice murmur dulcet praises of his skill, and for a time he took infinite pains with all his subjects, putting the very best of himself into his drawing and colouring with results that were brilliant and convincing enough to ensure success for all his efforts. Sometimes—lost in a sudden fit of musing—he wondered how his life would shape itself if he married her? He had avoided marriage as a man might avoid hanging,— considering it, not without reason, the possible ruin of an artist's greater career. Among many men he had known, men of undoubted promise, it had proved the fatal step downward from the high to the low. One particular "chum" of his own, a gifted painter, had married a plump rosy young woman with "a bit o' money," as the country folks say,—and from that day had been steadily dragged down to the domestic level of sad and sordid commonplace. Instead of studying form and colour, he was called upon to examine drains and superintend the plumber, mark house linen and take care of the children—his wife believing in "making a husband useful." Of regard for his art or possible fame she had none,—while his children were taught to regard his work in that line as less important than if he had been a bricklayer at so much pence the hour.

"Children!" thought Jocelyn—"Do I want them? . . . No—I think not! They're all very well when they're young—really young!—two to five years old is the enchanting age,—but, most unfortunately, they grow! Yes!—they grow,—often into hideous men and women—a sort of human vultures sitting on their fathers' pockets and screaming 'Give! Give!' The prospect does not attract me! And she?—Innocent? I don't think I could bear to watch that little flower-like face gradually enlarging into matronly lines and spreading into a double chin! Those pretty eyes peering into the larder and considering the appearance of uncooked bacon! Perish the thought! One might as well think of Shakespeare's Juliet paying the butcher's bill, or worse still, selecting the butcher's meat! Forbid it, O ye heavens! Of course if ideals could be realised, which they never are, I can see myself wedded for pure love, without a care, painting my pictures at ease, with a sweet woman worshipping me, ever at my beck and call, and shielding me from trouble with all the tender force of her passionate little soul!—but commonplace life will net fit itself into these sort of beatific visions! Babies, and the necessary provision of food and clothes and servants—this is what marriage means—love having sobered down to a matter-of-fact conclusion. No—no! I will not marry her! It would be like catching a fairy in the woods, cutting off its sunbeam wings and setting it to scrub the kitchen floor!"

It was curious that while he pleased himself with this fanciful soliloquy it did not occur to him that he had already caught the "fairy in the woods," and ever since the capture had been engaged in cutting off its "sunbeam wings" with all a vivisector's scientific satisfaction. And in his imaginary pictures of what might have been if "ideals" were realised, he did not for a moment conceive HIMSELF as "worshipping" the woman who was to worship HIM, or as being at HER "beck and call," or as shielding HER from trouble—oh no! He merely considered himself, and how she would care for HIM,—never once did he consider how he would care for HER.

Meanwhile things went on in an outwardly even and uneventful course. Innocent worked steadily to fulfil certain contracts into which she had entered with the publishers who were eager to obtain as much of her work as she could give them,—but she had lost heart, and her once soaring ambition was like a poor bird that had been clumsily shot at, and had fallen to the ground with a broken wing. What she had dreamed of as greatness, now seemed vain and futile. The "Amadis de Jocelin" of the sixteenth century had taught her to love literature—to believe in it as the refiner of thought and expression, and to use it as a charm to inspire the mind and uplift the soul,—but the Amadis de Jocelyn of the twentieth had no such lessons to teach. Utterly lacking in reverence for great thinkers, he dismissed the finest passages of poetry or prose from his consideration with light scorn as "purple patches," borrowing that hackneyed phrase from the lower walks of the press,—the most inspired writers, both of ancient and modern times, came equally under the careless lash of his derision,—so that Innocent, utterly bewildered by his sweeping denunciation of many brilliant and famous authors, shrank into her wounded self with pain, humiliation and keen disappointment, feeling that there was certainly no chance for her to appeal to him in any way through the thoughts she cherished and expressed with truth and fervour to a listening world. That world listened—but HE did not!—therefore the world seemed worthless and its praise mere mockery. She had no vanity to support her,—she was not "strong-minded" enough to oppose her own individuality to that of the man she loved. And so she began to droop a little,—her bright and ardent spirit sank like a sinking flame,—much to the concern of Miss Leigh, who watched her with a jealous tenderness of love beyond all expression. The child of Pierce Armitage, lawfully or unlawfully begotten, was now to her the one joy of existence,—the link that fastened her more closely to life,—and she worried herself secretly over the evident listlessness, fatigue and depression of the girl who had so lately been the very embodiment of happiness. But she did not like to ask questions,—she knew that Innocent had a very resolute mind of her own, and that if she elected to remain silent on any subject whatsoever, nothing, not even the most affectionate appeal, would induce her to speak.

"You will not let her come to any harm, Pierce!" murmured the old lady prayerfully one day, standing before the portrait of her former and faithless lover—"You will step in if danger threatens her!—yes, I am sure you will! You will guide and help her again as you have guided and helped her before. For I believe you brought her to me, Pierce!—yes, I am sure you did! In that other world where you are, you have learned how much I loved you long ago!—how much I love you now!—and how I love your child for your sake as well as for her own! All wrongs and mistakes are forgiven and forgotten, Pierce! and when we meet again we shall understand!"

And with her little trembling worn hands she set a rose, just opening its deep red heart-bud into flower, in a crystal vase beside the portrait as a kind of votive offering, with something of the same superstitious feeling that induces a devout Roman Catholic to burn a candle before a favourite saint, in the belief that the spirit of the dead man heard her words and would respond to them.

Just at this time, Innocent went about a good deal among the few friends who had learned to know her well and to love her accordingly. Lord Blythe was still away, having prolonged his tour in order to enjoy the beauty of the Italian lakes in autumn. Summer in England was practically over, but the weather was fine and warm still, and country-house parties, especially in Scotland, were the order of the day. The "social swim" was subsiding, and what are called "notable" people were beginning to leave town. Once or twice, infected by the general exodus, Innocent thought of going down to Briar Farm just for a few days as a surprise to Priscilla— but a feeling for Robin held her back. It would be needless unkindness to again vex his mind with the pain of a hopeless passion. So she paid a few casual visits here and there, chiefly at houses where Amadis de Jocelyn was also one of the invited guests. She was made the centre of a considerable amount of adulation, which did not move her to any sort of self-satisfaction, because in the background of her thoughts there was always the light jest and smile of her lover, who laughed at praise, except, be it here said, when it was awarded to himself. Then he did not laugh— he assumed a playful humility which, being admirably acted, almost passed for modesty. But if by chance he had to listen to any praise of "Ena Armitage" as author or woman, he changed the subject as soon as he could conveniently do so without brusquerie. And very gradually it dawned upon her that he took no pride in her work or in the position she had won, and that he was more reluctant than glad to hear her praised.

He seemed to prefer she should be unnoticed, save by himself, and more or less submissive to his will. Had she been worldly-wise, she would by every action have moved a silent protest against this, his particular form of sex-dominance, but she was of too loving a nature to dispute any right of command he chose to assume. Other men, younger and far higher in place and position than Jocelyn, admired her, and made such advances as they dared, finding her very coldness attractive, united as it was to such sweetness of manner as few could resist, but they had no chance with her. Once or twice some of her women friends had sounded her on the subject of love and lovers, and she had put aside all their questions with a smile. "Love is not to be talked about," she had said—"It is like God, served best in silence."

But by scarcely perceptible degrees, busy rumour got hold of a thread or two of the clue leading to the labyrinth of her mystery,—people nodded mysteriously at each other and began to whisper suggestions—suggestions which certainly did not go very far, but just floated in the air like bits of thistledown.

"She is having her portrait painted, isn't she?"

"Yes—by that man with the queer name—Amadis de Jocelyn."

"Has she given him the commission?"

"Oh no! I believe not. He's painting it for the French Salon."

"Oh!"

Then there would follow a silence, with an exchange of smiles all round. And presently the talk would begin again.

"Will it be a 'case,' do you think?"

"A 'case'? You mean a marriage? Oh dear no! Jocelyn isn't a marrying man."

"Isn't she a little—er—well!—a little taken with him?"

"Perhaps! Very likely! Clever women are always fools on one point—if not on several!"

"And he? Isn't he very attentive?"

"Not more so than he has been and is to dozens of other women. He's too clever to show her any special attention—it might compromise him. He's a man that takes care of Number One!"

So the gossip ran,—and only Jocelyn himself caught wind of it sufficiently to set him thinking. His "affaire de coeur" had gone far enough,—and he realised that the time had come for him to beat a retreat. But how to do it? The position was delicate and difficult. If Innocent had been an ordinary type of woman, vain and selfish, fond of frivolities and delighting in new conquests, his task would have been easy,—but with a girl who believed in love as the ultimatum of all good, and who trusted her lover with implicit faith as next in order of worship to God, what was to be done?

"We talk a vast amount of sentimental rubbish about women being pure and faithful!" he soliloquised—"But when they ARE pure and faithful we are more bored with them than if they were the worst women in town!"

He had however one subject of congratulation for which he metaphorically patted himself on the back as being "a good boy"—he had not gone to such extremes in his love-affair as could result in what is usually called "trouble" for the girl. He had left her unscathed, save in a moral and spiritual sense. The sweet body, with its delicate wavering tints of white and rose was as the unspoilt sheath of a lily-bud,—no one could guess that within the sheath the lily itself was blighted and slowly withering. One may question whether it is not a more cruel thing to seduce the soul than the body,—to crush all the fine faiths and happy illusions of a fair mind and leave them scorched by a devastating fire whose traces shall never be obliterated. Amadis de Jocelyn would have laughed his gayest and most ironical laugh at the bare possibility of such havoc being wrought by the passion of love alone.

"What's the use of loving or remembering anything?" he would exclaim—"One loves—one tires of love!—and by-and-by one forgets that love ever existed. I look forward to the time when my memory shall dwell chiefly on the agreeable entremets of life—a good dinner—a choice cigar! These things never bother you afterwards,—unless you eat too much or smoke too much,—then you have headache and indigestion—distinctly your own fault! But if you love a woman for a time and tire of her afterwards she always bothers you!—reminding you of the days when you 'once' loved her with persistent and dreadful monotony! I believe in forgetting,—and 'letting go.'"

With these sentiments, which were the true outcome of his real self, it was not and never would be possible for him to conceive that with certain high and ultra-sensitive natures love is a greater necessity than life itself, and that if they are deprived of the glory they have been led to imagine they possessed, nothing can make compensation for what to them is eternal loss, coupled with eternal sorrow.

Meanwhile Innocent's portrait on which he had worked for a considerable time was nearly completed. It was one of the best things he had ever done, and he contemplated it with a pleasant thrill of artistic triumph, forgetting the "woman" entirely in satisfied consideration of the "subject." As a portrait he realised that it would be the crown of the next year's Salon, bearing comparison with any work of the greater modern masters. He was however a trifle perplexed, and not altogether pleased at the expression, which, entirely away from his will and intention, had insensibly thrown a shadow of sadness on the face,—it had come there apparently of itself, unbidden. He had been particularly proud of his success in the drawing of the girl's extremely sensitive mouth, for he had, as he thought, caught the fleeting sweetness of the smile which was one of her greatest charms,—but now, despite his pains, that smile seemed to lose itself in the sorrow and pathos of an unspoken reproach, which, though enthralling and appealing to the beholder as the look of the famous "Mona Lisa," had fastened itself as it were on the canvas without the painter's act or consent. He was annoyed at this, yet dared not touch it in any attempt to alter what asserted itself as convincingly finished,—for the picture was a fine work of art and he realised that it would add to his renown.

"I shall not name it as the portrait of a living woman," he said to himself—"I shall call it simply—'Innocent.'"

As he thought this, the subject of the painting herself entered the studio. He turned at the sound of the door opening, and caught a strange new impression of her,—an impression that moved him to a touch of something like fear. Was she going to be tiresome, he wondered?—would she make him a "scene"—or do something odd as women generally did when their feelings escaped control? Her face was very pale—her eyes startlingly bright,—and the graceful white summer frock she wore, with soft old lace falling about it, a costume completed in perfection by a picturesque Leghorn hat bound with black velvet and adorned with a cluster of pale roses, made her a study worthy the brush of many a greater artist than Amadis de Jocelyn. His quick eye noted every detail of her dainty dress and fair looks as he went to meet her and took her in his arms. She clung to him for a moment—and he felt her tremble.

"What's the matter?" he asked, with unconscious sharpness—"Is anything wrong?"

She put him away from her tenderly and looked up smiling—but there was a sparkling dew in her eyes.

"No, my Amadis! Nothing wrong!"

He heaved a quick sigh of relief.

"Thank heaven! You looked at me as if you had a grievance—all women have grievances—but they should keep them to themselves."

She gave the slightest little shrug of her shoulders; then went and sat on the highest step of the familiar dais where she had posed for her picture, and waited a moment. He did not at once come to sit beside her as he had so often done—he stood opposite his easel, looking at her portrait but not at her.

"I have no grievance," she said then, making an effort to steady her voice, which trembled despite herself—"And if I had I should not vex you with it. But—when you can quite spare the time I should like a quiet little talk with you."

He looked round at her with a kind smile.

"Just what I want to have with you! 'Les beaux esprits se rencontrent'— and we both want exactly the same thing! Dear little girl, how sensible you are! Of course we must talk—about the future."

A lovely radiance lit up her face.

"That is what I thought you would wish," she said—"Now that the portrait is finished."

"Well,—all but a touch or two," he rejoined—"I shall ask a few people to come here and see it before it leaves London. Then it must be property packed in readiness for Paris before—before I go—"

Her eyes opened in sudden terrified wonderment.

"Before you go—where?"

He laughed a little awkwardly.

"Oh—only a short journey—on business—I will explain when we have our talk out—not now—in a day or two—"

He left the easel, and coming to where she sat, lifted her in his arms and folded her close to his breast.

"You sweet soul!" he murmured—"You little Innocent! You are so pretty to-day!—you madden me—"

He unfastened her hat and put it aside,—then drawing her closer, showered quick eager kisses on her lips, eyes and warm soft neck. He felt her heart beating wildly and her whole body trembling under his gust of passion.

"You love me—you truly love me?" she questioned, between little sighs of pleasure—"Tell me!—are you sure?"

"Am I not proving it?" he answered—"Does a man behave like this if he does not love?"

"Ah, yes!" And she looked up with a wild piteousness in her sweet eyes—"A man will behave like this to any woman!"

He loosened his clasp of her, astonished—then laughed.

"Where did you learn that?" he asked—"Who told you men were so volatile?"

"No one!"—and her caressing arms fell away from him—"My Amadis, you find it pleasant to kiss and to embrace me for the moment—but perhaps not always will you care! Love—real love is different—"

"What do You mean by love?" he asked still smiling.

She sighed.

"I can hardly tell you," she said—"But one thing I Do know—love would never hurt or wrong the thing it loved! Words, kisses, embraces—they are just the sweet outflow of a great deep!—but love is above and beyond all these, like an angel living with God!"

He was silent.

She came up to him and laid her little hand timidly on his arm.

"It is time we were quite sure of that angel, my Amadis!" she said—"We Are sure—but—"

He looked her full and quietly in the eyes.

"Yes, child!" he answered—"It is time! But I cannot talk about angels or anything else just now—it is growing late in the afternoon and you must not stay here too long. Come to-morrow or next day, and we'll consult together as to what is best to be done for your happiness—"

"For yours!" she interposed, gently.

He smiled, curiously.

"Very well! As you will! For mine!"

X

L ord Blythe stood at the open window of his sitting-room in the Grand Hotel at Bellaggio—a window opening out to a broad balcony and commanding one of the most enchanting views of the lake and mountains ever created by Divine Beneficence for the delight of man. The heavenly scene, warm with rich tints of morning in Italy, glowed like a jewel in the sun: picturesque boats with little red and blue awnings rocked at the edge of the calm lake, in charge of their bronzed and red-capped boatmen, waiting for hire,—the air was full of fragrance, and every visible thing appealed to beauty-loving eyes with exquisite and irresistible charm. His attention, however, had wandered far from the enjoyable prospect,—he was reading and re-reading a letter he had just received from Miss Leigh, in which certain passages occurred which caused him some uneasiness. On leaving England he had asked her to write regularly, giving him all the news of Innocent, and she had readily undertaken what to her was a pleasing duty. His thoughts were constantly with the little house in Kensington, where the young daughter of his dead friend worked so patiently to bring forth the fruits of her genius and live independently by their results, and his intense sympathy for the difficult position in which she had been placed through no fault of her own and the courage with which she had surmounted it, was fast deepening into affection. He rather encouraged this sentiment in himself with the latent hope that possibly when he returned to England she might still be persuaded to accept the position he was so ready to offer her—that of daughter to him and heiress,—and just now he was troubled by an evident anxiety which betrayed itself in Miss Leigh's letter—anxiety which she plainly did her best to conceal, but which nevertheless made itself apparent.

"The dear child works incessantly," she wrote, "but she is very quiet and seems easily tired. She is not as bright as she used to be, and looks very pale, so that I fear she is doing too much, though she says she is perfectly well and happy. We had a call from Mr. John Harrington the other afternoon—I think you know him—and he seemed quite to think with me that she is over-working herself. He suggested that I should persuade her to go for a change somewhere, either with me or with other friends. I wonder if you would care for us to join you at the Italian Lakes? If you would I might be able to manage it. I have not mentioned the idea to her yet, as I know she is finishing some work—but she tells me it will all be done in a few days, and that then she will take a rest. I hope she will, for I'm sure she needs it."

Another part of the letter ran as follows:—

"I rather hesitate to mention it, but I think so many prolonged sittings for her portrait to that painter with the strange name, Amadis de Jocelyn, have rather tired her out. The picture is finished now, and I and a few friends went to see it the other day. It is a most beautiful portrait, but very sad!—and it is wonderful how the likeness of her father as he was in his young days comes out in her face! She and Mr. de Jocelyn are very intimate friends—and some people say he is in love with her! Perhaps he may be!—but I do hope she is not in love with Him!"

Lord Blythe took off his spectacles, folded up the letter and put it in his pocket. Then he looked out towards the lake and the charming picture it presented. How delightful it would be to see Innocent in one of those dainty boats scattered about near the water's edge, revelling with all the keenness of a bright, imaginative temperament in the natural loveliness around her! Young, and with the promise of a brilliant career opening out before her, happiness seemed ready and waiting to bless and to adorn the life of the little deserted girl who, left alone in the world, had nevertheless managed to win the world's hearing through the name she had made for herself—yet now—yes!—now there was the cruel suggestion of a shadow—an ugly darkness like a black cloud, blotting the fairness of a blue sky,—and Blythe felt an uncomfortable sense of premonition and wrong as the thought of Amadis de Jocelyn came into his head and stayed there. What was he that he should creep into the unspoiled sphere of a woman's opening life? A painter, something of a genius in his line, but erratic and unstable in his character,—known more or less for several "affairs of gallantry" which had slipped off his easy conscience like water off a duck's back,—not a highly cultured man by any means, because ignorant of many of the finer things in art and letters, and without any positively assured position. Yet, undoubtedly a man of strong physical magnetism and charm—fascinating in his manner, especially on first acquaintance, and capable of overthrowing many a stronger citadel than the tender heart of a sensitive girl like Innocent, who by a most curious mischance had been associated all her life with the romance of his medieval name and lineage.

"Yes—of course she must come out here," Blythe decided, after a few minutes' cogitation. "I'll send a wire to Miss Leigh this morning and follow it up by a letter to the child herself, urging her to join me. The change and distraction will perhaps save her from too much association with Jocelyn,—I do not trust that man—never have trusted him! Poor little girl! She shall not have her spirit broken if I can help it."

He stayed yet another few minutes at the open window, and taking out a cigar from his case began to light it. While doing this his eye was suddenly caught by the picturesque, well-knit figure of a man sitting easily on a step near the clustering boats gathered close to the hotel's special landing place. He was apparently one of the many road-side artists one meets everywhere about the Italian Lakes, ready to paint a sunset or moonlight on Como or Maggiore on commission at short notice for a few francs. He was not young—his white hair and grizzled moustache marked the unpleasing passage of resistless time,—yet there was something lissom and graceful about him that suggested a kind of youth in age. His attire consisted of much worn brown trousers and a loose white shirt kept in place by a red belt,—his shirt sleeves were rolled up to the elbow, displaying thin brown muscular arms, expressive of energy, and he wore a battered brown hat which might once have been of the so-called "Homburg" shape, but which now resembled nothing ever seen in the way of ordinary head-gear. He was busily engaged in sketching a view of the lake and the opposite mountains, evidently to the order of some fashionably dressed women who stood near him watching the rapid and sure movements of his brush—he had his box of water-colours beside him, and smiled and talked as he worked. Lord Blythe watched him with lively interest, while enjoying the first whiffs of his lately lit cigar.

"A clever chap, evidently!" he thought. "These Italians are all artists and poets at heart. When those women have finished with him I'll get him to do a sketch for me to send to Innocent—just to show her the loveliness of the place. She'll be delighted! and it may tempt her to come here."

He waited a few minutes longer, till he saw the artist hand over the completed drawing to his lady patrons, one of whom paid him with a handful of silver coin. Something in the bearing and attitude of the man as he rose from the step where he had been seated and lifted his shapeless brown hat to his customers in courteous acknowledgment of their favours as they left him, struck Blythe with an odd sense of familiarity.

"I must have seen him somewhere before," he thought. "In Venice, perhaps—or Florence—these fellows are like gipsies, they wander about everywhere."

He sauntered out of the Hotel into the garden and from the garden down to the landing-place, where he slowly approached the artist, who was standing with his back towards him, slipping his lately earned francs into his trouser pocket. Several sample drawings were set up in view beside him,—lovely little studies of lake and mountain which would have done honour to many a Royal Academician, and Blythe paused, looking at these with wonder and admiration before speaking, unaware that the artist had taken a backward glance at him of swift and more or less startled recognition.

"You are an admirable painter, my friend!" he said, at last—speaking in Italian of which he was a master. "Your drawings are worth much more than you are asking for them. Will you do one specially for me?"

"I've done a good many for you in my time, Blythe!" was the half-laughing answer, given in perfect English. "But I don't mind doing another."

And he turned round, pushing his cap off his brows, and showing a wonderfully handsome face, worn with years and privation, but fine and noble-featured and full of the unquenchable light which is given by an indomitable and enduring spirit.

Lord Blythe staggered back and caught at the handrail of the landing steps to save himself from falling.

"My God!" he gasped. "You! You, of all men in the world! You!—you, Pierce Armitage!"

And he stared wildly, his brain swimming,—his pulses beating hammer-strokes—was it—could it be possible? The artist in brown trousers and white shirt straightened himself, and instinctively sought to assume a less tramp-like appearance, looking at his former friend meanwhile with a half-glad, half-doubtful air.

"Well, well, Dick!" he said, after a moment's pause—"Don't take it badly that you find me pursuing my profession in this peripatetic style! It's a nice life—better than being a pavement artist in Pimlico! You mustn't be afraid! I'm not going to claim acquaintance with you before the public eye—you, a peer of the realm, Dick! No, no! I won't shame you. . ."

"Shame me!" Blythe sprang forward and caught his hand in a close warm grip. "Never say that, Pierce! You know me better! Thank God you are here—alive!—thank God I have met you!—"

He stopped, too overcome to say another word, and wrung the hand he held with unconscious fervour, tears springing to his eyes. The two looked full at each other, and Armitage smiled a little confusedly.

"Why, Dick!" he began,—then turning his head quickly he glanced up at the clear blue sky to hide and to master his own emotion—"I believe we feel like a couple of sentimental undergrads still, Dick in spite of age and infirmities!"

He laughed forcedly, while Blythe, at last releasing his hand, took him by the arm, regardless of the curious observation of some of the hotel guests who were strolling about the garden and terraces.

"Come with me, Pierce," he said, in hurried nervous accents—"I have news for you—such news as you cannot guess or imagine. Put away all those drawings and come inside the hotel—to my room—"

"What? In this guise?" and Armitage shook his head—"My dear fellow, your enthusiasm is running away with you! Besides—there is some one else to consider—"

"Some one else? Whom do you mean?" demanded Blythe with visible impatience.

Armitage hesitated.

"Your wife," he said, at last.

Blythe looked him steadily in the eyes.

"My wife is dead."

"Dead!" Armitage loosened his arm from the other's hold, and stood inert as though he had received a numbing blow. "Dead! When did she die?"

In a few words Blythe told him.

Armitage heard in silence. Mechanically he began to collect his drawings and put them in a portfolio. His face was pale under its sun-browned tint,—his expression almost tragic. Lord Blythe watched him for a moment, moved by strong heart-beats of affection and compassion.

"Pierce," he then said, in a low tone—"I know everything!"

Armitage turned on him sharply.

"You—you know?—What?—How?—"

"She—Maude—told me all," said Blythe, gently—"And I think—your wrong to her—was not so blameworthy as her wrong to you! But I have something to tell you of one whose wrong is greater than hers or yours—one who is Innocent!"

He emphasised the name, and Armitage started as though struck with a whip.

"Innocent!" he muttered—"The child—yes!—but I couldn't make enough to send money for it after a while—I paid as long as I could—"

He trembled,—his fine eyes had a strained look of anguish in them.

"Not dead too?" he said—"Surely not—the people at the farm had a good name—they would not be cruel to a child—"

Blythe gripped him by the arm.

"Come," he said—"We cannot talk here—there are too many people about—I must have you to myself. Never mind your appearance—many an R. A. cuts a worse figure than you do for the sake of 'pose'! You are entirely picturesque"—and he relieved his pent-up feelings by a laugh—"And there's nothing strange in your coming to my room to see the particular view I want from my windows."

Thus persuaded, Armitage gathered his drawings and painting materials together, and followed his friend, who quickly led the way into the Hotel. The gorgeously liveried hall-porter nodded familiarly to the artist, whom he had seen for several seasons selling his work on the landing, and made a good-natured comment on his "luck" in having secured the patronage of a rich English "Milor," but otherwise little notice was taken of the incongruous couple as they passed up the stairs to "Milor's" private rooms on the first floor, where, as soon as they entered, Blythe shut and locked the door.

"Now, Pierce, I have you!" he said, affectionately taking him by the shoulders and pushing him towards a chair. "Why, in heaven's name, did you never let me know you were alive? Everyone thought you were dead years and years ago!"

Armitage sat down, and taking off his cap, passed his hand through his thick crop of silvery hair.

"I spread that report myself," he said. "I wanted to get out of it all—to give up!—to forget that such a place as London existed. I was sick to death of it!—of its conventions, and vile hypocrisies—its 'bounders' in art as in everything else!—besides, I should have been in the way—Maude was tired of me—"

He broke off, with an abstracted look.

"You know all about it, you say?" he went on after a pause—"She told you—"

"She told me the night she died," answered Blythe quietly—"After a silence of nearly twenty years!"

Armitage gave a short, sharp sigh. "Women are strange creatures!" he said. "I don't think they know when they are loved. I loved her—

much more than she knew,—she seemed to me the most beautiful thing on earth!—and when she asked me to run away with her—"

"She asked you?"

"Yes—of course! Do you think I would have taken her against her own wish and will? She suggested and planned the whole thing—and I was mad for her at the time—even now those weeks we passed together seem to me the only real living of my life! I thought she loved me as I loved her—and if she had married me, as I begged her to do, I believe I should have done something as a painter,—something great, I mean. But she got tired of my 'art-jargon,' as she called it—and she couldn't bear the idea of having to rough it a bit before I could hope to make any large amount of money. Then I was disappointed—and I told her so—and SHE was disappointed, and she told ME so—and we quarrelled—but when I heard a child was to be born, I urged her again to marry me—"

"And she refused?" interposed Blythe.

"She refused. She said she intended to make a rich marriage and live in luxury. And she declared that if I ever loved her at all, the only way to prove it was to get rid of the child. I don't think she would have cared if I had been brute enough to kill it."

Blythe gave a gesture of horror.

"Don't say that, man! Don't think it!"

Armitage sighed.

"Well, I can't help it, Blythe! Some women go callous when they've had their fling. Maude was like that. She didn't care for me any more,— she saw nothing in front of her but embarrassment and trouble if her affair with me was found out—and as it was all in my hands I did the best I could think of,—took the child away and placed it with kind country folks—and removed myself from England and out of Maude's way altogether. The year after I came abroad I heard she had married you,—rather an unkind turn of fate, you being my oldest friend! and this was what made me resolve to 'die'—that is, to be reported dead, so that she might have no misgivings about me or my turning up unexpectedly to cause you any annoyance. I determined to lose myself and my name too—no one knows me here as Pierce Armitage,—I'm Pietro Corri for all the English amateur art-lovers in Italy!"

He laughed rather bitterly.

"I think I lost a good deal more than myself and my name!" he went on. "I believe if I had stayed in England I should have won something of a reputation. But—you see, I really loved Maude—in a stupid man's way of love,—I didn't want to worry her or remind her of her phase of youthful madness with me—or cause scandal to her in any way—"

"But did you ever think of the child?" interrupted Blythe, suddenly.

Armitage looked up.

"Think of it? Of course I did! The place where I left it was called Briar Farm,—a wonderful old sixteenth-century house—I made a drawing of it once when the apple-blossom was out—and the owner of it, known as Farmer Jocelyn, had a wonderful reputation in the neighbourhood for integrity and kindness. I left the child with him—one stormy night in autumn—saying I would come back for it—of course I never did—but for twelve years I sent money for it from different places in Europe—and before I left England I told Maude where it was, in case she ever wanted to see it—not that such an idea would ever occur to her! I thought the probabilities were that the farmer, having no children of his own, would be likely to adopt the one left on his hands, and that she would grow up a happy, healthy country lass, without a care, and marry some good, sound, simple rustic fellow. But you know everything, I suppose!—or so your looks imply. Is the child alive?"

Lord Blythe held up his hand.

"Now, Pierce, it is my turn," he said—"Your share in the story I already knew in part—but one thing you have not told me—one wrong you have not confessed."

"Oh, there are a thousand wrongs I have committed," said Armitage, with a slight, weary gesture. "Life and love have both disappointed me—and I suppose when that sort of thing happens a man goes more or less to the dogs—"

"Life and love have disappointed a good many folks," said Blythe—"Women perhaps more than men. And one woman especially, who hardly merited disappointment—one who loved you very truly, Pierce!—have you any idea who it is I mean?"

Armitage moved restlessly,—a slight flush coloured his face.

"You mean Lavinia Leigh?" he said—"Yes—I behaved like a cad. I know it! But—I could not help myself. Maude drew me on with her lovely eyes and smile! And to think she is dead!—all that beauty in the grave!—cold and mouldering!" He covered his eyes with one hand, and a visible tremor shook him. "Somehow I have always fancied her as young as ever and endowed with a sort of earthly immortality! She was so bright, so imperious, so queen-like! You ask me why I did not let you know I was living? Blythe, I would have died in very truth by my own hand rather than trouble her peace in her married life with you!" He paused—then glanced up at his friend, with the wan flicker of a smile—"And—do you know Lavinia Leigh?"

"I do," answered Blythe—"I know and honour her! And—your daughter is with her now!"

Armitage sprang up.

"My daughter! With Lavinia! No!—impossible—incredible!—"

"Sit down again, Pierce," and Lord Blythe himself drew up a chair close to Armitage—"Sit down and be patient! You know the lines— 'There's a divinity that shapes our ends, rough-hew them how we will'? Divinity has worked in strange ways with you, Pierce!—and still more strangely with your child. Will you listen while I tell you all?"

Armitage sank into his chair,—his hands trembled—he was greatly agitated,—and his eyes were fixed on his friend's face in an eager passion of appeal.

"I will listen as if you were an angel speaking, Dick!" he said. "Let me know the worst!—or the best—of everything!"

And Blythe, in a low quiet voice, thrilled in its every accent by the affection and sympathy of his honest spirit, told him the whole story of Innocent—of her sweetness and prettiness—of her grace and genius—of the sudden and brilliant fame she had won as "Ena Armitage"—of the brief and bitter knowledge she had been given of her mother—of her strange chance in going straight to the house of Miss Leigh when she travelled alone and unguided from the country to London—and lastly of his own admiration for her courage and independence, and his desire to adopt her as a daughter in order to leave her his fortune.

"But now you have turned up, Pierce, I resign my hopes in that direction!" he concluded, with a smile. "You are her father!—and you may well be proud of such a daughter! And there is a duty staring you in the face—a duty towards her which, when once performed, will release her from a good deal of pain and perplexity—you know what it is?"

"Rather!" and Armitage rose and began pacing to and fro—"To acknowledge and legalise her as my child! I can do this now—and I will! I can declare she was born in wedlock, now Maude is dead—for no one will ever know. The real identity of her mother"—he paused and came up to Blythe, resting his hands on his shoulders—"the real identity of her mother is and shall ever be OUR secret!"

There was a pause. Then Armitage's mellow musical voice again broke the silence.

"I can never thank you, Blythe!" he said—"You blessed old man as you are! You seem to me like a god disguised in a tweed suit! You have changed life for me altogether! I must cease to be a wandering scamp on the face of the earth!—I must try to be worthy of my fair and famous daughter! How strange it seems! Little Innocent!—the poor baby I left to the mercies of a farm-yard training!—for her I must become respectable! I think I'll even try to paint a great picture, so that she isn't ashamed of her Dad! What do you say? Will you help me?"

He laughed,—but there were great tears in his eyes. They clasped hands silently.

Then Lord Blythe spoke in a light tone.

"I'll wire to Miss Leigh this morning," he said. "I'll ask her to come out here with Innocent as soon as possible. I won't break the news of You to them yet—it would quite overpower Miss Leigh—it might almost kill her—"

"Why, how?" asked Armitage.

"With joy!" answered Blythe. "Hers is a faithful soul!"

He waited a moment—then went on:

"I'll prepare the way cautiously in a letter—it would never do to blurt the whole thing out at once. I'll tell Innocent I have a very great and delightful surprise awaiting her—"

"Oh, very great and delightful indeed!" echoed Armitage with a sad little laugh. "The discovery of a tramp father with only a couple of shirts to his back and a handful of francs in his pocket!"

"My dear chap, what does that matter?" and Blythe gave him a light friendly blow on the shoulder. "We can put all these exterior matters right in no time. Trust me!—Are we not old friends? You have come back from death, as it seems, just when your child may need you—she Does need you—every young girl needs some protector in this world, especially when her name has become famous, and a matter of public talk and curiosity. Ah! I can already see her joy when she throws her arms around your neck and says 'My father!' I would gladly change places with you for that one exquisite moment!"

They stayed together all that day and night. Lord Blythe sent his wire to Miss Leigh, and wrote his letter,—then both men settled down, as it were, to wait. Armitage went off for two days to Milan, and returned transformed in dress, looking the very beau-ideal of an handsome

Englishman,—and the people at Bellaggio who had known him as the wandering landscape painter "Pietro Corri" failed to recognise him now in his true self.

"Yes," said Blythe again, with the fine unselfishness which was part of his nature, when at the end of one of their many conversations concerning Innocent, he had gone over every detail he could think of which related to her life and literary success—"When she comes she will give you all her heart, Pierce! She will be proud and glad,—she will think of no one but her beloved father! She is like that! She is full of an unspent love—you will possess it all!"

And in his honest joy for the joy of others, he never once thought of Amadis de Jocelyn.

XI

It was a gusty September afternoon in London, and autumn had given some unpleasing signs of its early presence in the yellow leaves that flew whirling over the grass in Kensington Gardens and other open spaces where trees spread their kind boughs to the rough and chilly wind. A pretty little elm in Miss Leigh's tiny garden was clothed in gold instead of green, and shook its glittering foliage down with every breath of air like fairy coins minted from the sky. Innocent, leaning from her study window, watched the falling brightness with an unwilling sense of pain and foreboding.

"Summer is over, I'm afraid!" she sighed—"Such a wonderful summer it has been for me!—the summer of my life—the summer of my love! Oh, dear summer, stay just a little longer!"

And the verse of a song, sung so often as to have become hackneyed, rang in her ears—

"Falling leaf and fading tree, Lines of white in a sullen sea, Shadows rising on you and me—The swallows are making them ready to fly, Wheeling out on a windy sky: Good-bye, Summer! Good-bye, good-bye!"

She shivered, and closed the window. She was dressed for going out, and her little motor-brougham waited for her below. Miss Leigh had gone to lunch and to spend the afternoon with some old friends residing out of town,—an unusual and wonderful thing for her to do, as she seldom accepted invitations now where Innocent was not concerned,—but the people who had asked her were venerable folk who could not by the laws of nature be expected to live very much longer, and as they had known Lavinia Leigh from girlhood she considered it somewhat of a duty to go and see them when, as in this instance, they earnestly desired it. Moreover she knew Innocent had her own numerous engagements and was never concerned at being left alone—especially on this particular afternoon when she had an appointment with her publishers,—and another appointment afterwards, of which she said nothing, even to herself. She had taken more than usual pains with her attire, and looked her sweetest in a soft dove-coloured silk gown gathered about her slight figure in cunning folds of exquisite line and drapery, while the tender gold of her hair shone like ripening corn from under the curved brim of a graceful "picture" hat of black velvet, adorned with one drooping pale grey plume. A small knot of roses nestled among the delicate lace on her bodice, and the diamond dove-pendant Lord Blythe had given her sparkled like a frozen sunbeam against the ivory whiteness of her throat. She glanced at herself in the mirror with a smile,—wondering if "he" would be pleased with her appearance,—"he" had been what is called "difficult" of late, finding fault with some of the very points of her special way of dress which he had once eagerly admired. But she attributed his capricious humour to fatigue and irritability from "over-strain"—that convenient ailment which is now-a-days brought in as a disguise for mere want of control and bad temper. "He has been working so hard to finish his portrait of me!" she thought, tenderly—"Poor fellow!—he must have got quite tired of looking at my face!"

She glanced round her study to see that everything was in order—and then took up a neatly tied parcel of manuscript—her third book—completed. She had a fancy—one of many, equally harmless,—that she would like to deliver it herself to the publishers rather than send it by post, on this day of all days, when plans for the future were to be discussed with her lover and everything settled for their mutual happiness. Her heart grew light with joyous anticipation as she ran downstairs and nodded smilingly at the maid Rachel, who stood ready at the door to open it for her passing.

"If Miss Leigh comes home before I do, tell her I will not be long," she said, as she stepped into her brougham and was whirled away. At the office of her publishers she was expected and received with eager homage. The head of the firm took the precious packet of manuscript from her hand with a smile of entire satisfaction.

"You are up to your promised time, Miss Armitage!" he said, kindly—"And you must have worked very hard. I hope you'll give yourself a good long rest now?"

She laughed, lightly.

"Oh, well!—perhaps!" she answered—"If I feel I can afford it! I want to work while I'm young—not to rest. But I think Miss Leigh would like a change—and if she does I'll take her wherever she wishes to go. She is so kind to me!—I can never do enough for her!"

The publisher looked at her sweet, thoughtful face curiously.

"Do you never think of yourself?" he asked—"Must you always plan some pleasure for others?"

She glanced at him in quick surprise.

"Why, of course!" she replied—"Pleasure for others is the only pleasure possible to me. I assure you I'm quite selfish!—I'm greedy for the happiness of those I love—and if they can't or won't be happy I'm perfectly miserable!"

He smiled,—and when she left, escorted her himself out of his office to her brougham with a kind friendliness that touched her.

"You won't let me call you a brilliant author," he said, as he shook hands with her—"Perhaps it will please you better if I say you are a true woman!"

Her eyes flashed up a bright gratitude,—she waved her hand in parting—as the brougham glided off. And never to his dying day did that publisher and man of hard business detail forget the radiance of the face that smiled at him that afternoon,—a face of light and youth and loveliness, as full of hope and faith as the face of a pictured angel kneeling at the feet of the Madonna with heaven's own glory encircling it in gold.

The quick little motor-brougham seemed unusually slow-going that afternoon. Innocent, with her full happy heart and young pulsing blood, grew impatient with its tardy progress, yet, as a matter of fact, it travelled along at its most rapid speed. The well-known by-street near Holland Park was reached at last, and while the brougham went off to an accustomed retired corner chosen by the chauffeur to await her pleasure, she pushed open the gate of the small garden leading to the back entrance of Jocelyn's studio—a garden now looking rather damp and dreary, strewn as it was with wet masses of fallen leaves. It was beginning to rain—and she ran swiftly along the path to the familiar door which she opened with her private key. Jocelyn was working at his easel—he heard the turn of the lock and looked round. She entered, smiling—but he did not at once go and meet her. He was finishing off some special touch of colour over which he bent with assiduous care,— and she was far too unselfishly interested in his work to disturb him at what seemed to be an anxious moment. So she waited.

Presently he spoke, with a certain irritability in his tone.

"Are you there? I wish you would come forward where I can see you!"

She laughed—a pretty rippling laugh of kindly amusement.

"Amadis! If you are a true Knight, it is you who should turn round and look at me for yourself!"

"But I am busy," he said, with the same sharpness of voice—"Surely you see that?"

She made no answer, but moved quietly to a position where she stood facing him at about an arm's length. Never had she made a prettier picture than in that attitude of charming hesitation, with a tender little smile on her pretty mouth and a wistful light in her eyes. He laid down his palette and brushes.

"I must give up work for to-day," he said—and going to her he took her in his arms—"You are too great an attraction for me to resist!" He kissed her lightly, as he would have kissed a child. "You are very fascinating this afternoon! Are you bent on some new conquest?"

She gave him a sweet look.

"Why will you talk nonsense, my Amadis!" she said—"You know I never wish for 'conquests' as you call them,—I only want you! Nothing but you!"

With his arm about her he drew her to a corner of the studio, half curtained, where there was a double settee or couch, comfortably cushioned, and here he sat down still holding her in his embrace.

"You only want me!—Nothing but me!" he repeated, softly—"Dear little Innocent!—Ah!—But I fear I am just what you cannot have!"

She smiled, not understanding.

"What do you mean?" she asked—"You always play with me! Are you not all mine as I am all yours?"

He was silent. Then he slowly withdrew his arm from her waist.

"Now, child," he said—"listen to me and be good and sensible! You know this cannot go on."

She lifted her eyes trustfully to his face.

"What cannot go on?" she queried, as softly as though the question were a caress.

He moved restlessly.

"Why—this—this love-making, of ours! We mustn't give ourselves over to sentiment—we must be normal and practical. We must look the thing squarely in the face and settle on some course that will be best and wisest for us both—"

She trembled a little. Something cold and terrifying began to creep through her blood.

"Yes—I know," she faltered, nervously—"You said—you said we would arrange everything together to-day."

"True! So I did! Well, I will!" He drew closer to her and took her little hand in his own. "You see, dear, we can't live on the heights of ecstasy for ever" and he smiled,—a forced, ugly smile—"We've had a very happy time together, haven't we?"—and he was conscious of a certain nervousness as he felt her soft little body press against him in answer—"But the time has come for us to think of other things—other interests—your career,—my future—"

She looked up at him in sudden alarm.

"Amadis!" she said—"What is it? You frighten me!—you speak so strangely! What do you mean?"

"Now if you are unreasonable I shall go away!" he said, with sudden harshness, dropping her hand—"I shall leave you here by yourself without another word!"

She turned deathly pale—then flushed a faint crimson—a sense of giddy faintness overcame her,—she put up her hands to her head tremblingly, and loosening her hat took it off as though its weight oppressed her.

"I—I am not unreasonable, Amadis," she faltered—"only—I don't understand—"

"Well, you ought to understand," he answered, heatedly—"A clever little woman like you who writes books should not want any explanation. You ought to be able to grasp the whole position at a glance!"

Her breath came and went quickly—she tried to smile.

"I'm afraid I'm very stupid then," she answered, gently—"For I can only see that you seem angry with me for nothing."

He took her hand again.

"Dear little goose, I am not angry," he said—"If you were to make me a 'scene' I SHOULD be angry—very angry! But you won't do that, will you? It would upset my nerves. And you are such a wise, independent little person that I feel quite safe with you. Well, now let us talk sensibly,—I've a great deal to tell you. In the first place, I'm going to Algiers."

Her lips were dry and stiff, but she managed to ask—

"When?"

"Oh, any time!—to-morrow. . . next day—before the week is over, certainly. There are some fine subjects out there that I want to paint—and I feel I could do good work—"

Her hand in his contracted a little,—she instinctively withdrew it. . . then she heard herself speaking as though it were someone else a long way off.

"When are you coming back?"

"Ah!—That's my own affair!" he answered carelessly—"In the spring perhaps,—perhaps not for a year or two—"

"Amadis!"

The name sprang from her lips like the cry of an animal wounded to death. She rose suddenly from his side and stood facing him, swaying slightly like a reed in a cruel wind.

"Well!" he rejoined—"You say 'Amadis' as though it hurt you! What now?"

"Do you mean," she said, faintly—"by—what—you—say,—do you mean—that we are—to part?"

The strained agony in her eyes compelled him to turn his own away. He got up from the settee and left her where she stood.

"We must part sooner or later," he answered, lightly—"surely you know that?"

"Surely I know that!" she repeated, with a bewildered look,—then running to him, she caught his arm—"Amadis! Amadis! You don't mean it!—say you don't mean it!—You can't mean it, if you love me! . . . Oh, my dearest!—if you love me! . . ."

She stopped, half choked by a throbbing ache in her throat,—and tottered against him as though about to fall. Alarmed at this he caught her round the waist to support her.

"Of course I love you!" he said, hurriedly—"When you are good and reasonable!—not when you behave like this! If I DON'T love you, it will be quite your own fault—"

"My own fault?" she murmured, sobbingly—"My own fault? Amadis! What have I done?"

"What have you done? It's what you are doing that matters! Giving way to temper and making me uncomfortable! Do you call that 'love'?"

She dropped her hand from his arm and drew herself away from him. She was trembling from head to foot.

"Please—please don't misunderstand me!" she stammered, like a frightened child—"I—I have no temper! I—I—feel nothing—I only want to please you—to know what you wish—"

She broke off—her eyes, lifted to his, had a strange, wild stare, but he was too absorbed in his own particular and personal difficulty to notice this. He went on, speaking rapidly—

"If you want to please me you will first of all be perfectly normal," he said—"Make up your mind to be calm and good-natured. I cannot stand an emotional woman all tantrums and tears. I like good sense and good manners. You ought to have both, with all the books you have read—"

She gave a sudden low laugh, empty of mirth.

"Books!" she echoed—and raising her arms above her head she let them drop again at her sides with a gesture of utter abandonment. "Ah yes! Books! Books by the Sieur Amadis de Jocelin!"

Her hair was ruffled and fell about her face,—her cheeks had flamed into a feverish red. The tragic beauty of her expression annoyed him.

"Your hair is coming down," he said, with a coldly critical smile— "You look like a Bacchante!"

She paid no attention to this remark. She was apparently talking to herself.

"Books!" she said again—"Such sweet love-letters and poems by the Sieur Amadis de Jocelin!"

He grew impatient.

"You're a silly child!" he said—"Are you going to listen to me or not?"

She gazed at him with an almost awful directness.

"I am listening!" she answered.

"Well, don't be melodramatic while you listen!" he retorted—"Be normal!"

She was silent, still gazing fixedly at him.

He turned his eyes away, and taking up one of his brushes, dipped it in colour and made a great pretence of working in a bit of sky on his canvas.

"You see, dear child," he resumed, with an unctuous air of patient kindness—"your ideas of love and mine are totally different. You want to live in a paradise of romance and tenderness—I want nothing of the sort. Of course, with a sweet caressable creature like you it's very pleasant to indulge in a little folly for a time,—and we've had quite four months of the 'divine rapture' as the poets call it,—four months is a long time for any rapture to last! You have—yes!—you have amused me!—and I've made you happy—given you something to think about besides scribbling and publishing—yes—I'm sure I have made you happy—and,—what is much more to my credit—I have taken care of you and left you unharmed. Think of that! Day after day I have had you here entirely in my power!—and yet—and yet"—here he turned his cold blue eyes upon her with an under-gleam of mockery in their steely light—"you are still—Innocent!"

She did not move—she scarcely seemed to breathe.

"That is why I told you it would be a good thing for you if you accepted Lord Blythe's offer,—in his great position he would be able to marry you well to some rich fellow with a title"—he went on, easily. "Now I am not a marrying man. Domestic bliss would not suit me. I have sometimes thought it would hardly suit You!"

She stirred slightly, as though some invisible creature had touched her, and held up one little trembling hand.

"Stop!" she said, and her voice though faint was clear and steady—"Do you think—can you imagine that I am of so low and common a nature as to marry any man, after—" She paused, struggling with herself.

"After what?" he queried, smilingly.

She shuddered, as with keenest cold.

"After your kisses!" she answered—"After your embraces which have held me away from everything save you!—After your caresses— oh God!—after all this,—do you think I would shame my body and perjure my soul by giving myself to another man?"

He almost laughed at her saintly idea of a lover's chastity.

"Every woman would!" he declared—"And I'm sure every woman does!"

She looked straight before her into vacancy.

"I am not 'every woman,'" she said, slowly—"I am only one unhappy girl!"

He was still dabbing colour on his canvas, but now threw down his brush and came to her.

"Dear child, why be tragic?" he said—"Life is such a pleasant thing and holds so much for both of us! I shall always love you—if you're good!" and he laughed, pleasantly—"and you can always love ME—if you like! But I cannot marry you—I have never thought of such a thing! Marriage would not suit me at all. I know, of course, what You would like. You would like a grand wedding with lots of millinery and presents, and then a honeymoon at your old Briar Farm—in fact, I daresay you'd like to buy Briar Farm and imprison me there for life, along with the dust and ashes of my ancestor's long-lost brother—but I shouldn't like it! No, child!—not even you, attractive as you are, could turn me into a Farmer Jocelyn!"

He tried to take her in his arms, but she drew herself back from him.

"You speak truly," she said, in a measured, lifeless tone—"Nothing could turn you into a Farmer Jocelyn. For he was an honest man!"

He winced as though a whip had struck him, and an ugly frown darkened his features.

"He would not have hurt a dog that trusted him," she went on in the same monotonous way—"He would not have betrayed a soul that loved him!"

All at once the unnatural rigidity of her face broke up into piteous, terrible weeping, and she flung herself at his feet.

"Amadis, Amadis!" she cried. "It is not—it cannot be you who are so cruel!—no, no!—it is some devil that speaks to me—not you, not you, my love, my heart! Oh, say it isn't true!—say it isn't true! Have mercy—mercy! I love you, I love you! You are all my life!—I cannot live without you! Amadis!"

Vexed and frightened for himself at her sudden wild abandonment of grief, he stooped, and gripping her by the arm tried to draw her up from the floor.

"Be quiet!" he said, roughly—"I will not have a scandal here in my studio! You'll bring my man-servant up in a moment with your stupid noise! I'm ashamed of you!—screaming and crying like a virago! If you make this row I shall go away!"

"Oh, no, no, no!—do not go away!" she moaned, sobbingly—"Have some little pity! Do not leave me, Amadis! Is everything forgotten so soon? Think for a moment what you have said to me!—what you have been to me! I thought you loved me, dear!—yes, I thought you loved me!—you told me so!" And she held up her little hands to him folded as in prayer, the tears raining down her cheeks—"But if for some fault of mine you do not love me any more, kill me now—here—just where I am!—kill me, Amadis!—or tell me to go away and kill myself—I will obey you!—but don't—don't send me into the empty darkness of life again all alone! Oh, no, no! Let me die rather than that!—you would not think unkindly of me if I were dead!"

He took her uplifted hands in his own—he began to be "artistically" interested,—with the same sort of interest Nero might have felt while watching the effects of some new poison on a tortured slave,—and a slight, very slight sense of regret and remorse tugged at his tough heart-strings.

"I should think of you exactly as I do now," he said, resolutely—"If you were to kill yourself I should not pity you in the least! I should say that though you were a bit of a clever woman, you were much more of a fool! So you would gain nothing that way! You see, I'm sane and sensible—you are not. You are excited and hysterical—and don't know what you are talking about. Yes, child!—that's the fact!" He patted the hands he held consolingly, and then let them go. "I wish you'd get up from the floor and be reasonable! The position is quite simple and clear. We've had an ideal time of it together—but isn't it Shakespeare who says 'These violent delights have violent ends'? My work calls me to Algiers—yours keeps you in London—therefore we must part—but we shall meet again—some day—I hope. . ."

She slowly rose to her feet,—her sobbing ceased.

"Then—you never loved me?" she said—"It was all a lie?"

"I never lie," he answered, coldly—"I loved you—for the time being. You amused me."

"And for your 'amusement' you have ruined me?"

"Ruined you?" He turned upon her in indignant protest—"You must be mad! You have been as safe with me as in the arms of your mother—"

At this she laughed,—a shrill little laugh with tears submerging it.

"You may laugh, but it is true!" he went on, in a righteously aggrieved tone—"I have done you no harm,—on the contrary, you have to thank me for a great deal of happiness—"

She gave a tragic gesture of eloquent despair.

"Oh, yes, I have to thank you!" she said, and her voice now vibrated with intense and passionate sorrow—"I have to thank you for so much— for so very much indeed! You have been so kind and good! Yes! And you have never thought of yourself or your own pleasure at all—but only of me! And I have been as safe with you as in my mother's arms, . . . yes!—you have been quite as careful of me as she was!" And a wan smile flitted over her agonised face—"All this I have to thank you for!—but you have ruined me just the same—not my body, but my soul!"

He looked at her,—she returned his gaze unflinchingly with eyes that glowed like burning stars—and he thought she was, as he put it to himself, "calming down." He laughed, a little uneasily.

"Soul is an unknown quantity," he said—"It doesn't count."

She seemed not to hear him.

"You have ruined my soul!" she repeated steadily—"You have stolen it from God—you have made it all your own—for your 'amusement'! What remainder of life have you left to me? Nothing! I have no hope, no faith, no power to work—no ambition to fulfil—no dreams to realise! You gave me love—as I thought!—and I lived; you take love from me, and I die!"

He bent his eyes upon her with a kind, almost condescending gentleness,—his personal vanity was immense, and the utter humiliation of her love for him flattered the deep sense he had of his own value.

"Dear little goose, you will not die!" he said—"For heaven's sake have done with all this sentimental talk!—I am not a man who can tolerate it. You are such a pleasant creature when you are cheerful and self-possessed,—so bright and clever and companionable—and there is no reason why we shouldn't make love to each other again as often as we like,—but change and novelty are good for both of us. Come!—kiss me!—be a good child—and let us part friends!"

He approached her,—there was a smile on his lips—a smile in which lurked a suspicion of mockery as well as victorious self-satisfaction. She saw it—and swiftly there came swooping over her brain the horrible realisation of the truth—that it was all over!—that never, never again would she be able to dwell on the amorous looks and words and love-phrases of Her "Amadis de Jocelyn!"—that no happy future was in store for her with him—that he had no interest whatever in her cherished memories of Briar Farm, and that he would never care to accept the right of dwelling there even if she secured it for him,—moreover, that he viewed her very work with indifference, and had no concern as to her name or fame—so that everything—every pretty fancy, every radiant hope, every happy possibility was at an end. Life stretched before her dreary as the dreariest desert—for her, whose nature was to love but once, there was no gleam of light in all the world's cruel darkness! A red mist swam before her eyes—black clouds seemed descending upon her and whirling round about her—she looked wildly from right to left, as though seeking to escape from some invisible pursuer. Startled at her expression Jocelyn tried to hold her—but she shook him off. She made a few unsteady steps along the floor.

"What is it?" he said—"Innocent—don't stare like that!"

She smiled strangely and nodded at him—she was fingering the plant of marguerite daisies that stood in its accustomed place between the easel and the wall. She plucked a flower and began hurriedly stripping off its petals.

"'Il m'aime—un peu!—beaucoup—passionement—pas du tout!' Pas du tout!" she cried—"Amadis! Amadis de Jocelyn! You hear what it says? Pas du tout! You promised it should never come to that!—but it has come!"

She threw away the stripped flower, . . . there was a quick hot throbbing behind her temples—she put up her hands—then all suddenly a sharp involuntary scream broke from her lips. He sprang towards her to seize and silence her—she stuffed her handkerchief into her mouth.

MARIE CORELLI

"I'm sorry!" she panted—"Forgive!—I couldn't help it!—Amadis—Amadis!—"

And she flung herself against his breast. Her eyes, large and feverishly brilliant, searched his face for any sign of tenderness, and searched in vain.

"Say it isn't true!" she whispered—"Amadis—oh my love, say it isn't true!" Her little hands caressed him—she drew his head down towards her and her pleading kiss touched his lips. "Say that you didn't really mean it!—that you love me still—Amadis!—you could not be cruel!—you will not break my heart!—"

But he was too angry to be pitiful. Her scream had infuriated him—he thought it would alarm the street, bring up the servant, and give rise to all sorts of scandal in which he might be implicated, and he roughly loosened her clinging arms from his neck and pushed her from him.

"Break your heart!" he exclaimed, bitterly—"I wish I could break your temper! You behave like a madwoman; I shall go away to my room! When I come back I expect to find you calm, and reasonable—or else, gone! Remember!"

She stood gazing at him as though petrified. He swung past her rapidly, and opening the principal door of the studio passed through it and disappeared. She ran to it—tried to open it—it was locked on the other side. She was alone.

She looked about her bewildered, like a child that has lost its way. She saw her pretty little velvet hat on the settee where she had left it, and in a trembling hurry she put it on—then paused. Going on tip-toe to the easel, she looked vaguely at her own portrait and smiled.

"You must be good and reasonable!" she said, waving her hand to it—"When you have lost every thing in the world, you must be calm! You mustn't think of love any more!—that's only a fancy!—you mustn't—no, you mustn't have any fancies or your dove will fly away! You are holding it to your heart just now—and it seems quite safe—but it will fly away presently—yes!—it will fly away!"

She lifted the painter's palette and looked curiously at it,—then took up the brush, moist with colour, which Jocelyn had lately used. Softly she kissed its handle and laid it down again. Then she waited, with a puzzled air, and listened. There was no sound. Another moment, and she moved noiselessly, almost creepingly to the little private door by which she had always entered the studio, and unlocking it, slipped out leaving the key in the lock. It was raining heavily, but she was not conscious of this,—she had no very clear idea what she was doing. There was a curious calm upon her,—a kind of cold assertiveness, like that of a dying person who has strength enough to ask for some dear friend's presence before departing from life. She walked steadily to the place where her motor-brougham waited for her, and entered it. The chauffeur looked at her for orders.

"To Paddington Station," she said—"I am going out of town. Stop at the first telegraph office on your way."

The man touched his hat. He thought she seemed very ill, but it was his place to obey instructions, not to proffer sympathy. At the telegraph office she got out, moving like one in a dream and sent a wire to Miss Leigh.

"Am staying with friends out of town. Don't wait up for me."

Back to the brougham she went, still in a dream-like apathy, and at Paddington dismissed the chauffeur.

"If I want you in the morning, I will let you know," she said, with matter-of-fact composure, and turning, was lost at once in the crowd of passengers pouring into the station.

The man was for a moment puzzled by the paleness of her face and the wildness of her eyes, but like most of his class, made little effort to think beyond the likelihood of everything being "all right to-morrow," and went his way.

Meanwhile Miss Leigh had returned to her house to find it bereft of its living sunshine. There were two telegrams awaiting her,—one from Lord Blythe, urging her to start at once with Innocent for Italy— the other from Innocent herself, which alarmed her by its unusual purport. In all the time she had lived with her "god-mother" the girl had never stayed away a night, and that she was doing so now worried and perplexed the old lady to an acute degree of nervous anxiety. John Harrington happened to call that evening, and on hearing what had occurred, became equally anxious with herself, and, moved by some curious instinct, went, on his way home, to Jocelyn's studio to ascertain if Innocent had been there that afternoon. But he knocked and rang at the door in vain,—all was dark and silent. Amadis de Jocelyn was a wise man in his generation. When he had returned to confront Innocent again and find her, as he had suggested, either recovered from her "temper" and "calm and reasonable"—or else "gone"—he had rejoiced to see that she had accepted the latter alternative. There was no trace of her save the unlocked private door of the studio, which he now locked, putting the key in his pocket. He gave a long breath of relief—a sort of "Thank God that's over!"—and arranged his affairs of both art and business with such dispatch as to leave for Paris in peace and comfort by the night boat-train.

XII

That evening the fitful and gusty wind increased to a gale which swept the land with devastating force, breaking down or uprooting great trees that had withstood the storms of centuries, and torrential rain fell, laying whole tracts of country under water. All round the coast the sea was lashed into a tossing tumult, the waves rolling in like great green walls of water streaked with angry white as though flashed with lightning, and the weather reports made the usual matter-of-fact statement that "Cross-Channel steamers made rough passages." Winds and waves, however, had no disturbing effect on the mental or physical balance of Amadis de Jocelyn, who, wrapped in a comfortable fur-lined overcoat, sat in a sheltered corner on the deck of the Calais boat, smoking a good cigar and congratulating himself on the ease with which he had slipped out of what threatened to have been a very unpleasant and embarrassing entanglement.

"If she were an ordinary sort of girl it wouldn't matter so much," he thought—"She would be practical, with sufficient vanity not to care,—she would see more comedy than tragedy in the whole thing. But with her romantic ideas about love, and her name in everybody's mouth, I might have got into the devil's own mess! I wonder where she went to when she left the studio? Straight home, I suppose, to Miss Leigh,—will she tell Miss Leigh? No—I think not!—she's not likely to tell anybody. She'll keep it all to herself. She's a silly little fool!—but she's—she's loyal!"

Yes, she was loyal! Of that there could be no manner of doubt. Callous and easy-going man of the world as he had ever been and ever would be, the steadfast truth and tender devotion of the poor child moved him to a faint sense of shamed admiration. On the inky blackness of the night he saw her face, floating like a vision,—her little uplifted, praying hands,—he heard her voice, piteously sweet, crying "Amadis! Amadis! Say you didn't mean it!—say it isn't true!—I thought you loved me, dear!—you told me so!"

The waves hissed round the rolling steamer, and every now and again white tongues of foam darted at him from the crests of the heaving waters, yet amid all the shattering roar and turbulence of the storm, he could not get the sound of that pleading voice out of his ears.

"Silly little fool!" he repeated over and over again with inward vexation—"Nothing could be more absurd than her way of looking at life as though it was only made for love! Yet—she suited her name!—she was really the most 'innocent' creature I have ever known! And—and—she loved me!"

The sea and the wind shrieked at him as the vessel plunged heavily on her difficult way—his nerves, cool as they were, seemed to himself on edge: and at certain moments during that Channel passage he felt a pang of remorse and pity for the young life on which he had cast an ineffaceable shadow,—a life instinct with truth, beauty, and brightness, just opening out as it were into the bloom of fulfilled promise. He had not "betrayed" her in the world's vulgar sense of betrayal,—he had not wronged her body—but he had done far worse,—he had robbed her of her peace of mind. Little by little he had stolen from the flower of her life its honey of sweet content,—he had checked the active impulses of her ambition, and as they soared upwards like bright birds to the sun, had brought them down, to the ground, slain with a mere word of light mockery,—he had led her to judge all things of no value save himself,—and when he had attained to this end he had destroyed her last dream of happiness by voluntarily proving his own insincerity and worthlessness.

"It has all been her own fault," he mused, trying to excuse and to console himself—"She fell into my arms as easily as a ripe peach falls at a touch—that childish fancy about 'Amadis de Jocelin' did the trick! Curious!—very curious that a sixteenth-century member of my own family tree should be mixed up in my affair with this girl! Of course she'll say nothing,—there's nothing to say! We've kept our secret very well, and except for a few playful suggestions and hints dropped here and there, nobody knows we were in love with each other. Then—she's got her work to do,—it isn't as if she were an idle woman without an occupation,—and she'll think it down and live it down. Of course she will! I'm worrying myself quite needlessly! It will be all right. And as she doesn't go to her Briar Farm now, I daresay she'll even forget her fetish of a knight, the 'Sieur Amadis de Jocelin'!"

He laughed idly, amused as he always had been at the romantic ideal she had made of the old French knight who had so strangely turned out to be the brother of his own far-away ancestor,—and then, on landing at Calais, was soon absorbed in numerous other thoughts and interests, and gradually dismissed the whole subject from his mind. After all, for him it was only one "little affair" out of at least a dozen or more, which from time to time had served to entertain him and provide a certain stimulus for his artistic emotions.

The storm had it all its own way in the fair English country,—sweeping in from the sea it tore over hill and dale with haste and fury, working terrible havoc among the luxuriant autumnal foliage and bringing down whirling wet showers of gold and crimson leaves. Round Briar Farm it raged all day long, tearing away from the walls one giant branch of the old "Glory" rose and snapping it off at its stem. Robin Clifford, coming home from the fields in the late afternoon, saw the fallen bough covered with a scented splendour of late roses, and lifting it tenderly carried it into the house, thinking somewhat sadly that in the old days Innocent would have been grieved had she seen such havoc made. Setting it in a big brown jar full of water, he put it in the entrance hall where its shoots reached nearly to the ceiling, and Priscilla Priday exclaimed at the sight of it—

"Eh, eh, is the old rose-tree broken, Mister Robin! That's never happened before in all the time I've been 'ere! I don't like the looks of it!—no, Mister Robin, I don't!"

"It's only one of the bigger branches," answered Robin soothingly. "The rose-tree itself is all right—I don't think any storm can hurt that—it's too deeply rooted. This was certainly a very fine branch, but it must have got loosened by the wind."

Even as he spoke a fierce gust swept over the old house with a sound like a scream of wrath and agony, and a furious torrent of rain emptied itself as though from a cloud-burst, half drowning the flower-beds and for the moment making a pool of the court-yard. Priscilla hurried to see that all the windows were shut and the doors well barred, and when evening closed in the picturesque gables of the roof were but a black blur in the almost incessant whirl of rain.

As the night deepened the storm grew worse, and the howling of the wind through the cracks and crannies of the ancient building was like the noise of wild animals clamouring for food. Priscilla and Robin Clifford sat together in the kitchen,—the most comfortable apartment to be in on such an unkind night of elemental uproar. It had become more or less their living-room since Innocent's departure, for Robin could not bear to sit in the "best parlour," as it was called, now that there was no one to share its old-world charm and comfort with him,—and when Priscilla's work was done, and everything was cleared and the other servants gone to their beds, he preferred to bring his book and pipe into the kitchen, and sit in an old cushioned arm-chair on one side of the fire-place, while Priscilla sat on the other, mending the house-linen, both of them talking at intervals of the past, and of the happy and unthinking days when Farmer Jocelyn had been alive and well, and when Innocent was like a fairy child flitting over the meadows with her light and joyous movements, her brown-gold hair flying loose like a trail of sunbeams on the wind, her face blossoming into rose-and-white loveliness as a flower blossoms on its slender stem,—her voice carrying sweet cadences through the air and making music wherever it rang. Latterly, however, they had not spoken so much of her,—the fame of her genius and the sudden leap she had made into a position of public note and brilliancy had somewhat scared the simple soul of Priscilla, who felt that the child she had reared from infancy had been taken by some strange and not to be contested fate away, far out of her reach,—while Robin—whose experiences at Oxford had taught him that persons of his own sex attaining to even a mild literary celebrity were apt to become somewhat "touch-me-not" characters—almost persuaded himself that perhaps Innocent, sweet and ideally simple of nature as he had ever known her to be, might, under the influence of her rapid success and prosperity, change a little (and such change, he thought, would be surely natural!)—if only just as much as would lessen by ever so slight a degree her former romantic passion for the home of her childhood. And,—lurking sometimes at the back of all his thoughts there crept the suggestive shadow of "Amadis de Jocelyn,"—not the French Knight of old, but the French painter, of whom she had told him and of whose very existence he had a strange and secret distrust.

On this turbulent night the old kitchen looked very peaceful and home-like,—the open fire burned brightly, flashing its flame-light against the ceiling's huge oak beams—everything was swept clean and polished to the utmost point of perfection,—and the table on which Robin rested the book he was reading was covered with a tapestried cloth, embroidered in many colours, dark and bright contrasted cunningly, with an effect that was soothing and restful to the eyes. In the centre there was placed a quaintly shaped jar of old brown lustre which held a full tall bunch of golden-rod and deep wine-coloured dahlias,—a posy expressing autumn with a greater sense of gain than loss. Robin was reading with exemplary patience and considerable difficulty one of the old French poetry books belonging to the "Sieur Amadis de Jocelin," and Priscilla's small glittering needle flew in and out the open-work stitchery of a linen pillow-slip she was mending as deftly as any embroideress of Tudor times. Over the old, crabbed yet delicately fine writing of the "Sieur" whose influence on Innocent's young mind had been so pronounced and absolute, and in Robin's opinion so malign, he pored studiously, slowly mastering the meaning of the verses, though written in a language he had never cared to study. He was conscious of a certain suave sweetness and melancholy in the swing of the lines, though they did not appeal to him very forcibly.

"En un cruel orage
On me laisse perir;
En courant au naufrage
Je vois chacun me plaindre et mil me secourir,
Felicite passee
Qui ne peux revenir
Tourment de ma pensee
Que n'ai-je en te perdant perdu le souvenir!
Le sort, plein d'injustice
M'ayant enfin rendu
Ce reste un pur supplice,
Je serais plus heureux si j'avais tout perdu!"

A sudden swoop of the wind shook the very rafters of the house as though some great bird had grasped it with beak and talons, and Priscilla stopped her swift needle, drawing it out to its full length of linen thread and holding it there. A strange puzzled look was on her face—she seemed to be listening intently. Presently, taking off her spectacles, she laid them down, and spoke in a half whisper:

"Mister Robin! Robin, my dear!"

He looked up, surprised at the grave wistfulness and wonder of her old eyes.

"Yes, Priscilla?"

"I'm thinkin' my time is drawin' short, dear lad!" she said, slowly— "I've got a call, an' I'll not be much longer here! That's a warnin' for me—"

"A warning? Priscilla, what do you mean?"

Drawing in her needle and thread, she pricked it through the linen she held and looked full at him.

"Didn't ye hear it?" she asked.

A sudden chill crept through the young man's blood,—there was something so wan and mournful in her expression.

"Dear Priscilla, you are dreaming! Hear what?"

She lifted one brown wrinkled hand with a gesture of attention.

"The crying of the child!" she answered—"Crying, crying, crying! Crying for me!"

Robin held his breath and listened. The wind had for the moment lessened in violence, and its booming roar had dropped to a moaning sigh. Now and again there was a pause that was almost silence, and during one of these intervals he fancied—but surely it was only fancy!—that he actually did hear a faint human cry. He looked at Priscilla questioningly and in doubt,—she met his eyes with a fixed and solemn resignation in her own.

"It's as I tell you," she said—"My time has come! It's for me the child is calling—just as she used to call whenever she wanted anything."

Robin rose slowly and moved a step or two towards the door. The storm was gathering fresh force, and heavy rain pattered against the windows making a continuous steely sound like the clashing of swords. Straining his ears to close attention, he waited,—and all at once as he stood in suspense and something of fear, a plaintive sobbing wail crept thinly above the noise of the wind.

"Priscilla! . . . Priscilla!" There was no mistaking the human voice this time—and Priscilla got up from where she sat, though trembling so much that she had to lean one hand on the table to steady herself.

"Ye heard THAT, surely!" she said.

Robin answered her by a look. His heart beat thickly,—an awful fear beset him, paralysing his energies. Was Innocent dead? Was that pitiful wail the voice of her departed spirit crying at the door of her childhood's home?

"Priscilla! . . . Oh, Priscilla!"

The old woman straightened her bent figure and lifted her head.

"Mister Robin, I must answer that call!" she said—"Storm or rain, we've no right to sit here with the child's voice crying and the old house shut and barred against her! We must open the door!"

He could not speak—but he obeyed her gesture, and went quickly out of the kitchen into the adjacent hall,—there he unbarred and unlocked the massive old entrance door and threw it open. A sheet of rain flung itself in his face, and the wind was so furious that for a moment he could scarcely stand. Then, recovering himself, he peered into the darkness and could see nothing,—till all at once he became vaguely aware of a small dark object crouching in one corner of the deep porch like a frightened animal or a lost child. He stooped and touched it—it was wet and clammy—he grasped it more firmly, and it moved under his hand shudderingly and lifted itself, turning a white face up to the light that streamed out from the hall—a face wan and death-like, but still the face he had ever thought the sweetest in the world—the face of Innocent! With a loud cry of mingled terror and rapture, he caught her up and held her to his heart.

"Innocent!—My little love!—Innocent!"

She made no answer—no sort of resistance. Her little body hung heavily in his arms—her head drooped helplessly against his shoulder.

"Priscilla!" he called—"Priscilla!"

Priscilla was already beside him—she had hurried into the hall directly she heard his exclamation of fear and amazement, and now as she saw him carrying the forlorn little burden tenderly along she threw up her hands with a piteous, almost despairing gesture.

"God save us all!—It's the child herself!" she exclaimed—"Mercy on the poor lamb!—what can have happened to her?—she's half drowned with rain!"

As quickly as Robin's strong arms could bear her, she was carried gently into the kitchen and laid in Robin's own deep arm-chair by the fire. Roused to immediate practical service and with all her superstitious terrors at an end, old Priscilla took off a soaked little velvet hat and began to unfasten a wet mass of soft silk that clung round the fragile little figure.

"Go and bar the door fast, Mister Robin, my dear!" she said, looking up at the young man's pale, agonised face,—"We don't want any one comin' in here to see the child in trouble!—besides, the wind's enough to scare a body to death! Poor lamb, poor lamb!— where she can have come from the good Lord only knows! It's for all the world like the night when she was left here, long ago! Lock and bar the door, dearie, and get me some of that precious old wine out of the cupboard in the best parlour." Here her active fingers came upon the glittering diamond pendant in the shape of a dove that hung by its slender gold chain round Innocent's neck. She unclasped it, looking at it wonderingly—then she handed it to Robin who regarded it with sombre, grudging eyes. Was it a love-gift?—and from whom?

"And while you're about helping me," went on Priscilla—"you might go to the child's room and fetch me that old white woolly gown she used to wear—it's warm and soft, and we'll put it on her and wrap her in a blanket when she comes to herself. She'll be all right presently."

Like a man in a moving dream he obeyed, and while he went on his errands Priscilla managed to get off some of the dripping garments which clung to the girl's slight form as closely as the wrappings of a shroud. Chafing the small icy hands, she smoothed the drenched fair hair, loosening its pins and combs, and spreading it out to dry, murmuring fond words of motherly pity and tenderness while the tears trickled slowly down her furrowed cheeks.

"My poor baby!—my pretty child!" she murmured—"What has broken her like this?—The world's been too rough for her—I misdoubt me if her fancies about love an' the like o' that nonsense aren't in the mischief,—but praise the Lord that's brought her home again, an' if so be it pleases Him we'll keep her home!"

As she thought this, Innocent suddenly opened her eyes. Beautiful, wild eyes that stared at her wonderingly without recognition.

"Amadis!" The voice was thin and faint, but exquisitely tender. "Amadis! How kind you are! Ah, yes!—at last!—I was sure you did not mean to be cruel—I knew you would come back and be good to me again! My Amadis!—You ARE good!—you could not be anything else but good and true!" She laughed weakly and went on more rapidly— "It is raining—yes! Oh, yes—raining very much!—such a cold, sharp rain! I've walked quite a long way—but I felt I must come back to you, Amadis!—just to ask you once more to say a kind word-to kiss me. . ."

She closed her eyes again and her head fell back on the pillow of the chair in which she lay. Priscilla's heart sank.

"She doesn't know what she's talking about, poor lamb!" she thought,—"Just wandering and off her head!—and fancying things about that old French knight again!"

Here Robin entered, and stood a moment, lost in a maze of enchanted misery at the sight of the pitiful little half-disrobed figure in the chair, till Priscilla took the white garment he had been sent to fetch out of his passive hand.

"There, dear lad, don't look like that!" she said. "Go, and come back in a few minutes with the wine—we'll be ready for you then. Cheer up!—she's opened her pretty eyes once—she'll open them again directly and smile at you!"

He moved away slowly with an aching heart, and a tightness in his throat that impelled him to cry like a woman. Innocent!—little

Innocent!—she who had once been all brightness and gaiety,—was this desolate, half-dying, stricken creature the same girl? Ah, no! Not the same! Never the same any more! Some numbing blow had smitten her,—some withering fire had swept over her, and she was no longer what she once had been. This he felt by a lover's intuition,—intuition keener and surer than all positive knowledge; and not the faintest hope stirred within him that she would ever shake off the trance of that death-in-life into which she had been plunged by some as yet unknown disaster—unknown to him, yet dimly guessed. Meanwhile Priscilla's loving task was soon done, and Innocent was clothed, warm and dry, in one of the old hand-woven woollen gowns she had been accustomed to wear in former days, and a thick blanket was wrapped cosily round her. She was still more or less unconscious, but the reviving heat gradually penetrated her body, and she began to sigh and move restlessly. She opened her eyes again and fixed them on the bright fire. Robin came in with the glass of wine, and Priscilla held it to her lips, forcing her to swallow a few drops.

The strong cordial started a little pulse of warmth in her failing blood, and she made an effort to sit up. She looked vaguely round her,—then her wandering gaze fixed itself on Priscilla's anxious old face, and a faint smile, more pitiful than tears, trembled on her lips.

"Priscilla!" she said—"I believe it is Priscilla I Oh, dear Priscilla! I called you but you would not hear or answer me!"

"Oh, my lamb, I heard ye right enough!"—and Priscilla fondled and warmed the girl's passive hands—"But I couldn't think it was yourself—I thought I was dreaming—"

"So did I!" she answered feebly—"I thought I was dreaming. . . yes!—I have been dreaming such a long, long time! All dreams! I have walked through the rain—it was very dark and the wind was cold and cruel—but I walked on and on—I don't know how I came—but I wanted to get home to Briar Farm—do you know Briar Farm?"

Stricken to the soul by the look of the wistful eyes expressing a mind in chaos, Priscilla answered gently—"You're in Briar Farm now, dearie!—Surely you know you are! This is your own old home—don't you know it?—don't you remember the old kitchen?—of course you do! There, there!—look up and see!"

She lifted her head and gazed about her in a lost way.

"No!" she murmured—"I wish I could believe it, but I cannot. I believe nothing now. It is all strange to me—I have lost the way home, and I shall never find it—never—never!" Here she suddenly pointed to Robin standing aloof in utter misery.

"Who is that?" she asked.

Irresistibly impelled by love, fear, and pity, he came and knelt beside her.

"It's Robin!" he said—"Dear Innocent, don't you know me?"

She touched his hair with one little hand, smiling like a pleased child.

"Robin?" she queried—"Oh, no!—you cannot be Robin—he is ever so many miles away!" She looked at him curiously,—then laughed, a cold, mirthless little laugh. "I thought for a moment you might be Amadis—his hair is like yours, thick and soft—you know him, of course—he is the great painter, Amadis de Jocelyn—all the world has heard of him! He went out just now and shut the door and locked it—but he will come back—yes!—he will come back!"

Robin heard and understood—the whole explanation of her misery suddenly flashed on his mind, and inwardly he cursed the man who had wreaked such havoc on her trusting soul. All at once she sprang up with a wild cry.

"He will come back—he must come back! Amadis!—Amadis!—you will not leave me all alone?—No, no, you cannot be so cruel!" She stretched out her arms as though to embrace some invisible treasure in the air—"Priscilla! . . . Priscilla!" Then as Priscilla took her gently round the waist and tried to calm her she began to laugh again. "The old motto!—you remember it?—the motto of the Sieur Amadis de Jocelin!—'Mon coeur me soutien!' You know what it means—'My heart sustains me.' Yes—and you know why his heart is so strong? Because it is made of stone! A stone heart can sustain anything!—it is hard and firm and cold—no rain, no tears can soften it!—no flowers ever grow on it—it does not beat—it feels nothing—nothing!"—and her hands dropped wearily at her sides. "It is not like MY heart! my heart burns and aches—it is a foolish heart, and my brain is a foolish brain—I cannot think with it—it is all dark and confused! And I have no one to help me—I am all alone in the world!"

"Innocent!" cried Robin passionately—"Oh, my love, my darling!—try to recall your dear wandering mind! You are here in the old home you used to love so well—you are not alone—you never shall be alone any more. I am with you to love you and take care of you—I have loved you always—I shall love you till I die!"

She looked at him with a sudden smile.

"Robin!—It is Robin!—you poor boy! You always talked like that!—but you must not love me,—I have no love to give you—I would make you happy if I could, but I cannot!"

A violent shudder as of icy cold shook her limbs—she stretched out her hands pitifully.

"Would you take me somewhere to sleep?" she murmured—"I am very tired! And when he comes you will wake me—I will not keep him a moment waiting! Tell him I am quite well—and that I knew he did not mean to be unkind—"

Her voice broke—she tottered and nearly fell. Robin caught her in his arms and laid her gently back in the chair, where she seemed to lapse into unconsciousness. He turned a white, desperate face on Priscilla.

"What is to be done?" he asked,—"Shall I go for the doctor?"

Priscilla shook her head.

"The doctor would be no use," she answered—"She's just fairly worn out and wants rest. Her little room is ready,—I've kept it aired, and the bed made warm and cosy ever since she went away—lest she should ever come back sudden like. . . could you carry her up, d'ye think? She'll be better in her bed—and she would come to herself quicker."

Gently and with infinite tenderness he lifted the girl as though she were a baby and carried her lightly up the broad oak staircase, Priscilla leading the way—and soon they brought her into her own room, unchanged since she had occupied it, and kept by Priscilla's loving and half superstitious care ready for her return at any moment. Laying her down on her little bed, Robin left her, though hardly able to tear himself away, and going downstairs again he flung himself into a chair and wept like a child for the ruin and wreck of the fair young life which might have been the joy and sunshine of his days!

"Amadis de Jocelyn!" he muttered—"A curse on him! Why should the founder of this house bring evil on us?—Rising up like a ghost to overshadow us and spoil our happiness?—Let the house perish and all its traditions if it must be so, rather than that she should suffer!—for she is innocent!"

Yes—she was quite innocent,—the little "base-born" intruder on the unbroken line and history of the Jocelyns!—and yet—it was with a kind of horror that the memory of that unbroken line and history recurred to him. Was there—could there be anything real in the long prevalent idea that if the direct line of the Jocelyns were broken, the peace and prosperity so long attendant on the old farm would be at an end? He put the thought away with a sense of anger.

"No, no! She could only bring joy wherever she went—no matter who her parents were, or how she was born, my poor little one!—she has suffered for no fault at all of her own!"

He listened to the dying clamour of the storm—the wind still careered round the house, making a noise like the beating wings of a great bird, but the rain was ceasing and there was a deeper sense of quiet. An approaching step startled him—he looked up and saw Priscilla. She smiled encouragingly.

"Cheer up, Mister Robin!" she said. . . "She is much better—she knows where she is now, bless her heart!—and she's glad to be at home. Let her alone—and if she 'as a good sleep she'll be a'most herself again in the morning. I'll leave my bedroom door open all night—an' I'll be lookin' in at 'er when she doesn't know it, watchin' her lovin' like for all I'm worth! . . . so don't ye worry, my lad!—there's a good God in Heaven an' it'll all come right!"

Robin took her rough work-worn hands and clasped them in his own.

"Bless you, you dear woman!" he said, huskily. "Do you really think so? Will she be herself again?—our own dear little Innocent?"

"Of course she will!" and Priscilla blinked away the tears in her eyes— "An' you'll mebbe win 'er yet!—The Lord's ways are ever wonderful an' past findin' out—"

A clear voice calling from the staircase interrupted them.

"Priscilla! Robin!"

Running to answer the summons, they saw Innocent at the top of the stairs, a little vision of pale, smiling sweetness, in her white wool wrapper—her hair falling loose over her shoulders. She kissed her hands to them.

"Only to say good-night!" she said,—"I know just where I am now!— it was so foolish of me to forget! I am at home—and this is Briar Farm— and I feel almost well and—happy! Robin!"

He sprang up the stairs and, kneeling, took one of her hands and kissed it.

"That's my true knight!" she said. "Dear Robin! You deserve everything good—and if it will give you joy I will marry you!"

"Marry me!" he cried, scarcely believing his ears—"Innocent! You will?—Dearest little love, you will?"

She looked down upon him where he knelt, like some small compassionate angel.

"Yes—I will!—To please you and Dad!—Tomorrow if you like! But you must say good-night now and let me sleep!"

He kissed her hand again.

"Good-night, sweet!"

She started—and drew her hand away.

"He said that once,—and once—in a letter—he wrote it. It seemed to me beautiful!—'Good-night, sweet!'" She waited as if to think a moment, then—

"Good-night!" again she said—"Do not be anxious about me—I shall sleep well! Good-night!"

She waved her hand once more, and disappeared like a little white phantom in the dark corridor.

"Does she mean it, do you think?" asked Robin, turning eagerly to Priscilla—"Will she marry me, after all?"

"I shouldn't wonder!" and the old woman nodded sagaciously—"Let her sleep on it, lad!—an' you sleep on it, too!—The storm's nigh over— an' mebbe our dark cloud 'as a silver lining!"

Half-an-hour later on she went to her own bed—and on the way thought she would peep into Innocent's room and see how she fared— but the door was locked. Vexed at her own lack of foresight in not possessing herself of the key before the girl had been carried to her room, she left her own door open that she might be ready in case of any call—and for a long time she lay awake watchfully, thinking and wondering what the next day would bring forth—till at last anxiety and bewilderment of mind were overcome by sheer fatigue and she slept. Not so Robin Clifford. Excited and full of new hope which he hardly dared breathe to himself, he made no attempt to rest—but paced his room up and down, up and down, like a restless animal in a cage, waiting with hardly endurable impatience for the dawn. Thoughts chased each other in his brain too quickly to evolve any practical order out of them,—he tried to plan out what he would do with the coming day—how he would let the farm people know that Innocent had returned—how he would send a telegram to her friend Miss Leigh in London to say she was safe in her old home—and then the recollection of her literary success swept over his mind like a sort of cloud—her fame!—the celebrity she had won in that wider world outside Briar Farm—was it fair or honest to her that he should take advantage of her weak and half-distraught condition and allow her to become his wife?—she, whose genius was already acknowledged by a wide and discerning public, and who might be considered as only at the beginning of a brilliant and prosperous career?

"For, after all, I am only a farmer," he said—"And with the friends she has made for herself she might marry any one! The best way for me will be to give her time—time to recover from this—this terrible trouble she seems to have on her mind—this curse of that fancy for Amadis de Jocelyn!—by Heaven, I'd kill him without a minute's grace if I had him in my power!"

Still pacing to and fro and thinking, he wore the slow hours away, and at last the grey peep of a misty, silvery dawn peered through his window. He threw the lattice open and leaned out—the scent of the wet fields and trees after the night's storm was sweet and refreshing, and copied his heated blood. He reviewed the whole situation with greater calmness,—and decided that he must not be selfish enough to grasp at the proffered joy of marriage with the only woman he had ever loved unless he could be made sure that it would be for her own happiness.

"Just now she hardly knows what she is saying or doing," he mused, sadly—"Some great disappointment has broken her spirit and she is wounded and in pain,—but when she is quite herself and has mastered her grief, she will see things in a different light—she will realise the fame she has won,—the brilliant name she has made—yes!—she must think of all this—she must not wrong herself or injure her position by marrying me!"

The silver-grey dawn brightened steadily, and in the eastern sky long folds of silky mist began to shred away in thin strips of delicate vapour showing peeps of pale amber between,—fitful touches of faint rose-colour flitted here and there against the gold,—and with a sense of relief that the day was at last breaking and that the sky showed promise of the sun, he left his room, and stepping noiselessly into the outside corridor, listened. Priscilla's door was wide open—and as he passed he looked in,—she was fast asleep. He could not hear a sound,—and though he walked on cautious tip-toe along the little passage which led to the room where Innocent slept and waited there a minute or two, straining his ears for any little sigh, or sob, or whisper, none came;—all was silent. Quietly he went downstairs, and, opening the hall door, stepped out into the garden. Every shrub and plant was dripping with wet—many were beaten down and broken by the fury of the night's storm, and there was more desolation than beauty in the usually well-ordered and carefully-tended garden. The confusion of fallen flowers and trailing stems made a melancholy impression on his mind,—at another time he would scarcely have heeded what was, after all, only the natural havoc wrought by high winds and heavy rains,—but this morning there seemed to be more than the usual ruin. He walked slowly round to the front of the house—and there looked up at the projecting lattice window of Innocent's room. It was wide open. Surprised, he stopped underneath it and looked up, half expecting to see her,—but only a filmy white curtain moved gently with the first stirrings of the morning air. He stood a moment or two irresolute, recalling the night when he had climbed up by the natural ladder of the old wistaria and had heard her tell the plaintive little story of her "base-born" condition, with tears in her eyes, and the pale moonshine lighting up her face like the face of an angel in a dream.

"And she had written her first book already then!" he thought—"She had all that genius in her and I never knew!"

A deeper brightness in the sky began to glow, and a light spread itself over the land—the sun was rising. He looked towards the low hills in the east, and saw the golden rim lifting itself like the edge of a cup above the horizon,—and as it ascended higher and higher, some fleecy white clouds rolled softly away from its glittering splendour, showing glimpses of tenderest ethereal blue. A still and solemn beauty invested all the visible scene,—a sacred peace—the peace of an obedient and law-abiding nature wherein man alone creates strange discord. Robin looked long and lovingly at the fair prospect,-the wide meadows, the stately trees warmly tinted with autumnal glory, and thought—

"Could she be happier than here?—safe in the arms of love?—safe and sheltered from all trouble in the home she once idolised?"

He would not answer his own inward query—and suddenly the fancy seized him to call her by name, as he had called her on that moonlit night long ago, and persuade her to look out on the familiar fields shining in the sunlight of the morning.

"Innocent!"

There was no answer.

He called a little louder—

"Innocent!"

Still silence. A robin hopped out from the cover of wet leaves and peered at him questioningly with its bold bright eye. Acting on an irresistible impulse he set his foot on the gnarled root of the old wistaria and started to climb to the window-sill. Three minutes sufficed him to reach it—he looked into the little room,—the room which had formerly been the study of the "Sieur Amadis de Jocelin"—and there seated at the old oak table with her head bowed down upon her hands and her hair covering her as with a veil, was Innocent. The sunlight flashed brightly in upon her—and immediately above her the golden beams traced out as with a pencil of light the arms of the old French knight with the faded rose and blue of his shield and motto illumining with curiously marked distinctness the words he himself had carved beneath his own heraldic emblems:

"Who here seekynge Forgetfulness Did here fynde Peace!"

She was very strangely still,—and a cold fear suddenly caught at Robin's heart and half choked his breath.

"Innocent!" he cried. Then, leaping into the room like a man in sudden frenzy, he rushed towards that motionless little figure—threw his arms about it—lifted it—caressed it. . .

"Innocent! Look at me! Speak to me!"

The fair head fell passively back against his shoulder with all its wealth of rippling hair—the fragile form he clasped was helpless, lifeless, breathless!—and with a great shuddering sob of agony, he realised the full measure of his life's despair. Innocent was dead!—and for her, as for the "Sieur Amadis," the quaint words shining above her in the morning sunlight were aptly fitted—

"Who here seekynge Forgetfulness Did here fynde Peace!"

MANY THINGS IN LIFE COME too late to be of rescue or service, and justice is always tardy in arrival. Too late was Pierce Armitage, after long years of absence, to give his innocent child the simple heritage of a father's acknowledgment; he could but look upon her dead face and lay flowers on her in her little coffin. The world heard of the sudden death of the young and brilliant writer with a faintly curious concern—but soon forgot that she had ever existed. No one knew, no one guessed the story of her love for the French painter, Amadis de Jocelyn—he was abroad at the time of her death, and only three persons secretly connected him with the sorrow of her end—and these were Lord Blythe, Miss Leigh and Robin Clifford. Yet even these said nothing, restrained by the thought of casting the smallest scandal on the sweet lustre of her name. And Amadis de Jocelyn himself?—had he no regret?—no pity?

If the truth must be told, he was more relieved than pained,—more flattered than sorry! The girl had died for him,—well!—that was more or less a pleasing result of his power! She was a silly child—obsessed by a "fancy"—it was not his fault if he could not live up to that "fancy"—he liked "facts." His picture of her was the success of the Salon that year, and he was admired and congratulated,—this was enough for him.

"One of your victims, Amadis?" asked a vivacious society woman he knew, critically studying the portrait on the first day of its exhibition.

He nodded, smilingly.

"Really? And yet—Innocent?"

He nodded again.

"Very much so! She is dead!"

SORROW AND JOY, STRANGELY INTERMINGLED, divided the last years of life for good Miss Leigh. The shock of the loss and death of the girl to whom she had become profoundly attached, followed by the startling discovery that her old lover Pierce Armitage was alive, proved almost too much for her frail nerves—but her gratitude to God for the joy of seeing the beloved face once again, and hearing the beloved voice, was so touching and sincere that Armitage, smitten to the heart by the story of her long fidelity and her tenderness for his forsaken daughter, offered to marry her, earnestly praying her to let him share life with her to the end. This she gently refused,—but for the rest of her days she—with him and Lord Blythe—made a trio of friends,—a compact of affection and true devotion such as is seldom known in this work-a-day world. They were nearly always together,—and the memory of Innocent, with her young life's little struggle against fate ending so soon in disaster, was a link never to be broken save by death, which breaks all.

MARIE CORELLI

L'Envoi

A few evenings since, I who have written this true story of a young girl's romantic fancy, passed by Briar Farm. The air was very still, and a red sun was sinking in a wintry sky. The old Tudor farmhouse looked beautiful in the clear half-frosty light—but the trees in the old bye road were leafless, and though the courtyard gate stood open there were no flowers to be seen beyond, and no doves flying to and fro among the picturesque gables. I knew, as I walked slowly along, that just a mile distant, in the small churchyard of the village, Innocent, the "base-born" child of sorrow, lay asleep by her "Dad," the last of the Jocelyns,—I knew also that not far off from their graves, the mortal remains of the faithful Priscilla were also resting in peace—and I felt, with a heavy sadness at my heart, that the fame of the old house was wearing out and that presently its tradition, like many legendary and romantic things, would soon be forgotten. But just at the turn of a path, where a low stile gives access to the road, I saw a man standing, his arms folded and leaning on the topmost bar of the stile—a man neither old nor young, with a strong quiet face, and almost snow-white hair—a man quite alone, whose attitude and bearing expressed the very spirit of solitude. I knew him for the master of the farm—a man greatly honoured throughout the neighbourhood for justice and kindness to all whom he employed, but also a man stricken by a great sorrow for which there can be no remedy.

"Will he never marry?" I thought,—but as I put the question to myself I dismissed it almost as a blasphemy. For Robin Clifford is one of those rarest souls among men who loves but once, and when love is lost finds it not again. Except,—perhaps?—in a purer world than ours, where our "fancies" may prove to have had a surer foundation than our "facts."

THE END

A Note About the Author

Marie Corelli (1855–1924) was an English novelist. Born Mary Mackay in London, she was sent to a Parisian convent to be educated in 1866. Returning to England in 1870, Corelli worked as a pianist and began her literary career with the novel *A Romance of Two Worlds* (1886). A favorite writer of Winston Churchill and the British Royal Family, Corelli was the most popular author of her generation. Known for her interest in mysticism and the occult, she earned a reputation through works of fantasy, Gothic, and science fiction. From 1901 to 1924, she lived in Stratford-upon-Avon, where she continued to write novels, short story collections, and works of non-fiction. Corelli, whose works have been regularly adapted for film and the theater, was largely rejected by the male-dominated literary establishment of her time. Despite this, she is remembered today as a pioneering author who wrote for the public, not for the critics who sought to deny her talent.

A Note from the Publisher

Spanning many genres, from non-fiction essays to literature classics to children's books and lyric poetry, Mint Edition books showcase the master works of our time in a modern new package. The text is freshly typeset, is clean and easy to read, and features a new note about the author in each volume. Many books also include exclusive new introductory material. Every book boasts a striking new cover, which makes it as appropriate for collecting as it is for gift giving. Mint Edition books are only printed when a reader orders them, so natural resources are not wasted. We're proud that our books are never manufactured in excess and exist only in the exact quantity they need to be read and enjoyed.

Discover more of your favorite classics with Bookfinity™.

- Track your reading with custom book lists.
- Get great book recommendations for your personalized Reader Type.
- Add reviews for your favorite books.
- AND MUCH MORE!

Visit **bookfinity.com** and take the fun Reader Type quiz to get started.

Enjoy our classic and modern companion pairings!